BOND STREET STORY

Books by Norman Collins

Novels

BOND STREET STORY

CHILDREN OF THE ARCHBISHOP

DULCIMER STREET

THE QUIET LADY

GOLD FOR MY BRIDE

LOVE IN OUR TIME

FLAMES COMING OUT OF THE TOP

TRINITY TOWN

THE THREE FRIENDS

PENANG APPOINTMENT

THE BAT THAT FLITS (A THRILLER)

For Children

BLACK IVORY

Criticism

THE FACTS OF FICTION

BOND STREET STORY

by

NORMAN COLLINS

Harper & Brothers Publishers
New York

For
MARY & ERIC

Library of Congress catalog card number: 59-10612

AUTHOR'S NOTE

Bond Street is Bond Street all right. You can find it in any street directory. But the big store, by the name of Rammell's, is entirely imaginary. So is everybody connected with it. The directors, the management, the models, the assistants, the buyers, the shop-walkers, the secretaries, have no living counterparts. Nor have the manufacturers, the wholesalers and the travellers. All wives are imaginary, too. In short, this is a work of fiction. And nothing but fiction. Only Bond Street itself is real.

CONTENTS

Introduction in the Rush Hour

You CAN tell the time of the day simply by looking at them. Not accurately enough to re-set your watch, of course. No split-second chronometer precision. But near enough. Take one glance at the faces around you, and you'd be right somewhere within ordinary sun-dial limits.

Up to 8.15 or thereabouts, they're a pretty mixed lot—workmen, office-cleaners, early-shift postal clerks, messengers, doorkeepers, that kind of thing. But by about 8.20 the Underground system has begun to get its clients sorted out. From then on until a quarter-to-nine, youth has it. It is shopgirl and typist time, cashier and junior secretary hour.

And with them a new sense of speed and alertness comes over the place, as though the whole world were celebrating its eighteenth birthday. The original spring freshness is still on everything. It's all brisk. And snappy. And staccato. There's the chink and rattle as the change is delivered into the little metal cup at the booking office. The quick snatch as it is scooped up again. And then the sprinter's dash down the escalator and the panic fight to get on to the train. From the way everyone behaves, all the alarm clocks in London might have been set five minutes too late. But that's always the way with the younger generation. Slapdash. Last minute. No proper planning. They're living on borrowed time every one of them.

Then as nine o'clock comes round, there's a second revolution. Sex and age go abruptly into reverse. Maleness takes over. Umbrellas and brief cases everywhere. Seasons as well as singles. Pipes as well as cigarettes. Indeed, the subtle, distinctive odour of Underground travel has changed entirely during the last ten minutes. And there's one ingredient that has faded out completely. That's the hot-house mixture of all the proprietary cosmetics, mingled regardless of their makers' reputations, and blown about by the gale of ozone that the London Transport engineers industriously keep pumping along the platforms.

It's the Older Woman who shares this predominantly male company. Confidential personal secretaries who are practically running the whole show. And the nearer it gets to nine-thirty, the more settled and unperfumed these responsible females become. Simply good straight-forward toilet soap and plenty of cold water, and the glint of no nonsense staring out from behind their spectacles. By five-and-twenty to ten, in fact, there is hardly a woman of under forty left in the whole Underground System. A sailor straight home from the South Pole could go all the way from Colindale to Kennington, and never have any reason to glance up except to check what station he'd got to.

For, by then, London has settled down to work. Only the old guard, the heavy stuff, are still travelling. It is chairmans' and directors' session. Take a look down any carriage and it might be simply the London editions of *The Times* and the *Telegraph*—merely open newspapers, with a black hat on top and a pair of neatly creased trousers underneath—that you are travelling with. Not a face, or even a waistcoat, anywhere. Just foreign news and home affairs and the financial columns all being borne along at thirty-five miles an hour underneath the streets and the houses, the sewers and the subways, the water mains and the telephone cables. It is a world exclusively of paper people. The nylon stockings and the toeless shoes, the *Daily Mirror* and little handbags—they've all vanished, along with the rest of the under-forties. It's the same carriage. Same advertisement of the same girl with the same permanent wave. Same rattle and roar in the tunnels. Same stopping places. But it might be the inhabitants of another planet who are travelling.

That's because it's in the tail-end of Mr. Marx's Class-Society that we're living. And five minutes either way mean that you have changed Classes.

BOOK ONE

Reluctance of a Female Apprentice

CHAPTER I

ON THIS particular morning, it was only just 8.30. And the tall man in the black overcoat and cravatish sort of tie obviously shouldn't have appeared in public before about 9.15 at the earliest. Simply didn't belong. Too opulent-looking altogether. Chauffeur driven, yes. But strap-hanging, no. He didn't really mix with Underground society at all. From his air of aloof magnificence, he might have been the President of Overseas Missions, the founder of a long line of Sunday Schools.

And he wasn't being seen at his best either. Could hardly be seen at all in fact. That was because it was the rush hour. Stampede and congestion time. Dignity, modesty, hygiene, nice feelings and all the rest of it had been left behind on the platform in the mad rush to get crammed into the train at all. If the cargo had been steers instead of human beings, one of the Animal Protection Societies would have been serving out summonses by the fistful.

As it was, this big, distinguished-looking man had got an unknown female bosom crushed practically flat against his left elbow, there was somebody else's hip pressed into his right thigh, and immediately under his nose was a lot of yellow hair that looked as if it had just been washed in an enthusiastic, amateurish kind of way and then not given time to set properly. Indeed, if it hadn't been for his height, he would have been smothered by the blonde several stations back, suffocated in a living jungle of shampoo and peroxide. There was one little wisp in particular that just reached his chin. But what could he do? His right hand was jammed flat to his side, and the other was imprisoned by that uninvited and unwanted female bosom. Short of biting the curl clean off, he was defenceless.

But in any case this was where he got out. It was Bond Street. At least, it was called Bond Street. Really it was only Oxford Street. But, even so, it was indisputably one of the better stations. It was exactly right for a man of six-foot-two with a cravat. And his behaviour was exactly right for his appearance. He didn't fight and scramble the way passengers do at other stations. He just inclined his weight forward, and said " Pord'n me. " Then when he finally got his foot on to the platform, he moved slowly and serenely. And why not? There was obviously no one waiting in the world up above to mention it if he was a few minutes late. He could afford this unhurried, polar-bearlike saunter.

And it was the same when he emerged into the open air. Along Oxford Street he went. Into New Bond Street. Down past Bruton Street. Past Davis Street. Past Conduit Street. Into Bond Street itself. And finally to Downe Street, where the whole block—all four sides of it—was taken up by Rammell's.

There isn't anywhere in the world a more dignified emporium of retail commerce than Rammell's. Or a more varied and extensive one. It isn't just one shop. It is an entire streetful of shops. Complete with side arcades. And a restaurant. And two snack bars. And a bargain bazaar thrown in. All piled one on top of another, and with a specially big front door like the entrance to a Town Hall or a Bank Headquarters. A whole civilisation all to itself. Practically a State.

The flag—plain white with a green " R " on it—can be seen high over the main entrance in Bond Street. And—but only on Saturday afternoons, of course—over the pavilion at the sports field out at Neasden. What's more, the telegraphic address— Rammellex, London—is known to cable clerks the whole world over. Even the afterthought, " London, " isn't really needed. Letters addressed simply to Rammell's, England, find their way to Bond Street all right.

In short, Rammell's is famous. It's got everything. Take the Fur Salon, for example. As the highly decorative climax to what must have started up rather messily in Beaver Bay or Bear Creek, there isn't another fur salon that can match it. Not for minks or sables. Or the Library and Ticker Agency. Without it, most of Mayfair would simply sit at home looking at TV. Or Chinaware. Two floors up, there is nearly half an acre of hand-painted china and the more expensive kinds of cut-glass. Or Sports. That department brings Wimbledon, Lord's, and St. Andrews all together in one blaze of coloured cat-gut, pure ivory willow and stainless steel, and keeps them there in perpetual artificial sunlight and an

14

equable temperature all the year round. Then again, on the Provision floor (with the separate entrance in Downe Street) Rammell's potted shrimps are as good as anything that ever came out of Morecambe. But there's no point in trying to enumerate all the departments. Too many of them. Put simply, you could be clothed, fed, furnished, kept amused and ultimately buried entirely by Rammell's. Always provided that you are in the right income bracket, of course.

The tall man with the cravat had just turned the corner of Downe Street so slowly and majestically that he might have been standing still, waiting quietly for Downe Street to glide past him. But even so, as the corner was turned, the scene changed abruptly. Rammell's shop windows ended and Hurst Place began. Polished bronze and plate-glass gave place to grimed brickwork. And swing doors with metal kick-plates at the bottom were substituted for the revolving crystal cages on the Bond Street side.

In Hurst Place, too, the fleet of Rammell's delivery vans in their distinctive white coachwork were drawn up at the dispatch-bay like a floe of grounded ice-bergs.

It was a quarter-to-nine by now. And the staff entrance was crowded. The whole Rammell family was assembling. Rather a lop-sided family, admittedly. About two dozen girls to every man. But that's the way it is in these big shops. Rammell's alone ran to over five hundred and fifty on the distaff side. And there they were, all surging in, like novices turning up at the gates of some vast non-residential nunnery. Past the clocking-in machines they trooped, up to the staff cloakrooms. And, after a quick peep in the mirror and a pat here and a dab there, down they surged again into the main shop where the dust-cloths were waiting to be whisked off the counters, and the hat stands in the Millinery department were all bunched together on one of the side tables without so much as a hat in sight anywhere.

The man with the cravat had turned in with the rest of them. But clearly he was in a class apart. He didn't even say good morning to anybody. Merely inclined his head. And he didn't go through to the long rows of coat-hangers like the rest of them. In the corridor outside the staff cloakroom he had his own private locker. It might have been a safe deposit the way he opened it. First he hung up his black hat and umbrella. Next he removed

15

his overcoat. Then he took off his jacket as well, and stood for a moment in his shirt-sleeves. But not for long. There was some quick change magic going on by now. For, a moment later when he emerged, he was more majestical than ever. It was a tail-coat that he now had on. He might have been the Colonel representing the regiment at a Royal funeral.

And still with the same placid, mastodon-like tread, he advanced through the ribbons and the laces, past the veiling and the hat ornaments, into the gloves and the evening handbags, and out again into the little foyer that gave straight on to Bond Street. Once there, he squared his shoulders and rocked backwards and forwards once or twice on his feet like an athlete loosening up. Then clasping his hands behind his back, he remained motionless, apparently unbreathing.

It was still only five-to-nine, and Mr. Bloot, Rammell's senior floorwalker, had arrived on duty.

2

So also had a lot of other people. There was Mr. Eric Rammell, for instance. He was another regular five-to-niner. To the dot almost. But he got dropped by car at the Downe Street entrance, and went straight up by lift to his private office suite. The keynote of that suite was excellence. It was furnished (all by Rammell's, of course) in best Mayfair Chippendale and red Morocco. Only the other directors and one or two of the senior managers had ever been inside the room at all. That was because the ordinary day by day business of the shop was looked after by Mr. Preece, the general manager. Mr. Eric remained remote and invisible. Until 11.15 that is, when he made his regular quick tour of the main departments.

Then, particularly to new members of the staff, he came as a bit of a disappointment. It was Mr. Rammell's stature that was against him. Only five-foot-four. And with a bulge like a teapot. There was no getting away from it: he was tubby. And his colouring was bad. Too many shades of grey. Not enough pink or tan. Altogether, he looked as though he needed a good Nannie to take him in hand, keep him off sweet things, and see that he was in bed by seven-thirty every evening.

16

And that was not far wrong either. There was one drawer in the Chippendale bureau that was like a small chemist's shop. It was stocked solid with Alka-Seltzer, Milk of Magnesia, bismuth tablets, old-fashioned bi-carb., and charcoal biscuits. That was because Mr. Eric nursed a raging volcano inside him. The threat of a duodenal had been hanging over him for years. And it was worry, sheer rush and worry, that had done it. That was why he was always promising himself a long sea holiday. A cruise. Somewhere into the sunshine. With no business correspondence. No telephone. No directors' meeting. And above all, no Mrs. Rammell.

She was half his trouble, Mrs. Rammell. She spent her time feeding the volcano, shovelling in fresh coals just when the furnace seemed to be dying down a bit. That was because she was a born hostess. And a discoverer of talent. There was a young Indian dancer, Swami Lal, whom she had just found. He was due to give a dance recital in Mr. Rammell's own drawing-room. And so far as Mr. Rammell was concerned, even the threat of young Swami was pure anthracite.

Compared with Mr. Eric Rammell, Mr. Preece, the General Manager—one floor down and lodged in a room as bare and bleak as an operating theatre—led a life of placid and uneventful harmony. Home to Carshalton every evening, and back again to the surgical ward by 8.45 next morning, Mr. Preece asked nothing more of life. He was a thin, patient-looking man with rather beautiful hands. He had a memory like a comptometer, and slight catarrh that lasted from May until September when his regular winter colds began. Acute anæmia seemed to be his trouble. If he had accidentally cut himself with his garden sécateurs it didn't seem likely that he would bleed at all. Just a clean white incision like a carved veal. But that couldn't really be the case. Because the blood was there all right. And, once a year, when at the Annual General Meeting Mr. Eric referred to " the invaluable and selfless devotion shown by our General Manager, Mr. Preece," up it came straight from the heart and Mr. Preece blushed a deep, schoolgirl red.

Mrs. Preece, a soft, motherly woman with pale, dust-coloured hair, felt that her husband ought to be made a director. And, particularly towards Christmas, when he didn't get home till nine o'clock or ten o'clock at night, she made a point of saying so. But it would have made things much easier for both of them if

17

only she could have held her tongue. Because the plain fact was that Mr. Preece was simply not director-grade—not for a house of Rammell's standing that is. Nor was Mrs. Preece right for a director's wife. Socially there was a chasm. When Mrs. Rammell did try the experiment of asking Mr. and Mrs. Preece to one of her recital evenings, Mrs. Preece nearly ruined everything by glancing anxiously at her watch all through the Scarlatti and then, with a lot of hissing apologetic whispers, left right in the middle of a Chopin étude because she was afraid they would miss the 11.43 from Victoria.

At this moment, Mr. Preece was addressing another senior member of staff, also tail-coated like Mr. Bloot. But a very different type of man. Practically a separate species. You could never mistake this one for anything but a floor-walker. But rather a seedy one. That was because his tails were just a shade too large for him. There were mysterious folds down the back as though when he had originally bought them he had intended to share them with someone else, and had been doing a double act single-handed ever since. But, in any case, he hadn't really got the figure for tails. He was not much taller than Mr. Eric. And without the girth. There was a slightness and triviality about him. A wispiness.

But he knew his stuff all right. He presided, two floors up, over the household china, bed linen, slumber kit, towels, motoring rugs, leather goods, radio and television. It was quite an empire for a man of his physique to have conquered, subdued and now be ruling over.

In the presence of Mr. Preece, his whole attitude was one of respect and attention. He was leaning forward, and that made his striped trousers go into a whole lot of extra folds and creases around the knees as though he had just been paddling.

" Ah, Privett, Mr. Bloot tells me you want to get your daughter into the firm," Mr. Preece had just said in that precise, clipped voice of his.

Mr. Privett bent forward still farther.

" That's right, sir," he replied. " Very kind of you to take the trouble."

This was the moment that Mr. Privett had been waiting for, dreaming of, ever since his daughter's last year at school. But now that it had come, he found himself embarrassed, confused somehow.

18

He felt that in some strange way he was actually letting her down, being insufficient. So he went on hurriedly.

" You'll find she's a good girl, sir," he said. " Quite inexperienced, of course. But . . . but a really good girl. She'll do us all credit."

He was rather surprised with himself as he said the words. He was very proud of his daughter, but he had never discussed her with strangers in this way before.

" Well, we must get her to come and see us," Mr. Preece replied in his smoothest, office-velvet kind of voice. " Then if we *can* do anything, we'll fix her up."

" Thank you very much, sir."

Mr. Privett straightened up as he said it. That was because it was practically impossible to draw in a deep breath of sheer relief while he was bending so far forward.

" Of course, she'll only be a learner at first," Mr. Preece reminded him.

" Oh, naturally, sir. That's . . . that's all she'd expect."

But there was no time for any further conversation. Mr. Preece had already rung for his secretary. And he began dictating before the secretary had even got herself properly seated.

" Memo to Staff Supervisor. ' Please arrange to see Miss— you'll get the full name from Mr. Privett—of—Mr. Privett'll give you the address—with a view to filling one of the forthcoming learner vacancies. Kindly let me know the result of the interview.' That's all, thank you."

Mr. Preece gave a swift, colourless nod to the secretary and, another in Mr. Privett's direction. That indicated that he had done all that could be done. Indeed, he had already gone rather too far. There was a waiting-list the length of a Royal petition up in the Appointments Section. And in any case it was a strict rule that everyone must write in. There was a very strict protocol about application letters. And Rammell's believed in observing it. It all turned on the simple test of neat handwriting, orderly expression and a proper knowledge of punctuation—as judged by the Staff Supervisor. Only last week the younger daughter of a well-known Peer had failed on all three counts. Cheltenham and Somerville had been turned down flat by the Ilford Secretarial College.

That was why Mr. Privett was so pleased with himself. Thanks

19

to him, his daughter had jumped the whole lot of them. But no child of his could really have been expected to *write*. After all, he had been with Rammell's for nearly thirty years.

Mr. Preece caught Mr. Privett's eye for a moment.

" What *is* your daughter's name by the way? "

" Ireen, sir. Ireen Privett," he added idiotically. And because he could not think of anything else to say he repeated himself. " You . . . you'll find she's a good girl, sir," he said. " A really good girl."

3

Mr. Privett was still so pleased when he got back to his own floor that for once he almost seemed to fill his tails. He looked a larger man altogether. And he was thinking of nothing but Irene. How excited she would be. How pleased. And how he would buy her some little starting-off gift—a new handbag, or something. Because he was thinking only of Irene, he even misdirected an important-looking lady who had asked for fitted picnic cases, and had to go chasing after her as though she were a shop lifter.

It was nearly eleven by now. And at eleven o'clock precisely he always slipped up to the Staff Canteen for a cup of coffee. That meant that he would be able to tell his news to Mr. Bloot. Mr. Privett and Mr. Bloot were old friends. Natural inseparables. As would have been expected, Mr. Bloot took the lead in everything. It was a sort of knight and squire relationship that existed between them. Deference and devotion were mingled in equal proportions. And with every year that passed, Mr. Privett's admiration for the larger man grew more complete and unquestioning. Nowadays, simply to be in Mr. Bloot's company gave Mr. Privett a delicious feeling of the fullness of life. Of being in the very centre of things. That was why eleven o'clock was so important. He and Mr. Bloot usually managed to fit in a few minutes together at eleven o'clock.

When Mr. Privett arrived, Mr. Bloot was already there, seated at his usual table. He had his cup in his hand, and he was leaning forward so that no drops should get on to his cravat. Unlike Mr. Privett, he was a tea drinker. And he took tea drinking seriously. Just to look at him with his eyebrows going up as his chin went down, you could see that he brought an impressive ardour and intensity to the whole process.

Mr. Privett was so excited that he went straight over to Mr. Bloot instead of taking his place in the service line.

" Mr. Preece spoke to me about Ireen," he blurted out a little breathlessly.

" Yurss? "

Mr. Bloot's face was very pink, flushed by the heat of the tea. But he was still remarkably handsome. Quite noticeably imposing, in fact. Mr. Privett felt proud at having such a man for his friend.

" They're going to see her."

" Aaah! "

Mr. Bloot finished his tea and put his cup down. He was naturally a heavy breather. And at that moment he seemed to be doing nothing else but breathe. But that was not so. Really he was thinking. And thinking was always rather a slow business with Mr. Bloot.

" Ah'll drop a word mahself in the raht quarter," he remarked at last.

His voice was muffled-up and padded. It seemed to come from deep inside him like a ventriloquist's.

" Yurss," he repeated slowly. " That's what Ah'll do. Ah'll drop a word mahself."

Having spoken, he licked his lips as though he relished the idea. But that moistening of the lips didn't really mean anything. It was only a habit that he had got into. Like breathing.

There was a pause.

" Mum's going to be ever so pleased about this," Mr. Privett said suddenly.

Mr. Bloot turned graciously towards his friend.

" How is Ahleen? " he inquired.

" Eileen's fine," Mr. Privett replied. " She's . . . she's been asking for you."

Mr. Bloot made no comment. Merely pursed up his lips. And Mr. Privett did not press the point. Both men knew that Mrs. Privett did not like Mr. Bloot. And in a way Mrs. Privett's dislike was an additional bond between them. It served to put the seal of secrecy upon their friendship.

But even if the tactless lie had upset Mr. Bloot, Mr. Privett was saved from any further embarrassment. Elevenses were now over. And he had missed his morning coffee altogether. He rose obediently and followed Mr. Bloot who was marching slowly and majestically back towards the main shop.

Then Mr. Bloot spoke again.

"Areen's er lucky girl," he said, "coming into Rammell's. Ah wonder if she reahlahises."

CHAPTER II

IRENE PRIVETT herself was lying stretched out full length on the bed. Her chin was resting on her hands. And her feet were spread out across the pillow. Her two shoes had gone slithering across the floor when she kicked them off. One was lying half-way over to the fireplace. The other almost underneath the chest of drawers.

It was her dress that had saved her right shoe from disappearing completely. Taken off hurriedly and simply slung into a chair, the dress had gradually straightened itself out and collapsed limply on to the strip of Axminster. Not that Irene had yet noticed. Or would notice, even when she came to pick it up again. Most of her things seemed to be on the floor when she wanted them.

That was because she was only seventeen. Still living in the full turmoil of adolescence. Life opened out in front of her down a long corridor of chaos and confusion. With Mrs. Privett following silently behind, picking up, smoothing out, putting away. Any drawer that Irene ever went to looked as though someone had been burgling it. And even when the drawers were shut up again, the ends of all sorts of things, stockings, slips, corners of handkerchiefs remained sticking out like book-markers.

At the moment Irene was wearing simply the foundations of dress, the pale pink brassière and pants which she had bought for herself and of which Mrs. Privett had disapproved. She had a good figure. Still only schoolgirlish, of course. Nothing mature or magnificent. But supple and healthy-looking. Against the whiteness of her skin, her hair seemed darker than ever. And it was her hair that was the trouble. A thick lock of it kept falling forward, slanting across the book that she was reading. But that again was Irene's fault. Until a couple of years ago she had worn her hair in two long plaits. It had always been sleek and neat and tidy. Mrs. Privett had warned her what would happen if she allowed it to be slashed about by a hairdresser. But Irene had been determined. She detested long hair she had said. It was ghastly. And now every time she bent forward to read she had to pay the penalty.

23

The book open on the bed was paper-covered. It was an acting-edition. One of Mr. Samuel French's. Indeed, when you came to look at the room carefully you could see that the whole place was practically a sub-stockroom of Samuel French's. The wall-bracket bookshelf with the fretwork ends was packed full of the small grey-blue booklets. And even at the back of the dressing-table, amid to-day's harvest of hair brushes and screwed-up handkerchiefs and empty chocolate papers, there were more of the same little volumes. These were wedged in loosely between a pair of elephant book-ends, the rumps of the animals leaning purposefully against Gordon Daviot and Dodie Smith, James Bridie and J. B. Priestley.

The play that Irene was reading at the moment was one of Christopher Fry's. For the whole of the last month she had been going round in a stupefied daze of Fry. She had the taste of his words in her mouth when she woke in the morning. And she kept going back to him for further doses between regular mealtimes. She was at that moment cut off entirely from the rest of life. Suspended somewhere in a coma of medievalism and Mars bar. Even with her mouth full of the sweet chocolaty stuff, she was uttering Mr. Fry's words aloud. They came out as a continuous sticky mumble.

From down below, she heard the front door shut. That meant that her father had come home. She glanced for a moment at her wrist watch. It showed 6.20. And as she looked at it she remembered dimly, as a kind of shadow from the unreal world, that she had promised her mother to do something. Lay the table. Or light the gas. Or turn it out. Or put the kettle on.

The outlines of the shadow were far from clear. A mere blurred impression in her mind. But, in any case, it was probably too late by now. Whatever it was, Mrs. Privett would have seen to it herself.

It was, indeed, only because her mother was dressmaking that Irene had been asked to attend to things at all. When Irene listened, however, there was complete silence in the room beneath her. That in itself showed that everything was all right. If Mrs. Privett had still been working, there would have been the low, intermittent whining of the treadle machine, grinding away like a distant lawn mower. Consoled by the silence, Irene went on reading.

But not for long. It was Mrs. Privett's voice that called her. " Ireen."

Irene looked up. The voice somehow did not belong. There was no one in the whole of Mr. Fry's hag-ridden household who was called by that name.

Mrs. Privett called again.

" Ireen. Your dad wants you."

Irene swung her legs off the bed.

" Coming, Mum."

It took Irene some time to get dressed. For no particular reason she did not like anything that she had been wearing. And she couldn't find what she wanted to wear instead. Then her hair needed doing. And at the sight of a nail file lying on the dressing-table, she began idly going round her nails, pushing down the quick with the blunt end of the file. It wasn't that she was deliberately keeping her father waiting. Merely that she was distracted. She had been interrupted while she was busy. And her mind was still knee-deep in Mr. Fry's world of words and witches.

" Ireen, can you hear me? Your dad's got something to tell you."

Mrs. Privett's voice had risen by a semi-tone. It now had a sharp, rasplike edge to it. It probed.

Irene still did not hurry. She went across slowly and opened the door like a sleep walker.

" What's the matter, Mum? " she asked with the purely mechanical part of her mind. " I heard you."

It struck Irene as soon as she got down to the kitchen that her father was looking unusually pleased about something. He seemed pinker than usual. And it struck Mr. Privett that Irene was looking unusually pretty. She was just the kind of daughter for whom any father would want to do little things.

Mrs. Privett looked across at her husband, and gave a little nod.

" Well, Dad," she said. " You tell her. It's your news."

Mr. Privett straightened himself. He wished that Mr. Bloot could have been there. Mr. Bloot would have made the announcement sound so much better. There would have been real dignity and grandeur about it. Coming from him, it would really have sounded like something.

"It's all fixed," he said smiling. "They're going to write to you. They said so this morning."

"Who did?"

Mr. Privett opened his eyes wider in astonishment.

"Why Rammell's, of course."

"What about?"

"About you."

The smile had almost left Mr. Privett's face by now. He had been looking forward all day to this moment when he got home. And somehow it wasn't turning out as he had expected.

"What do Rammell's want to write to me for?"

Irene had taken a step away from him as she put the question. She was leaning up against the wall by now, her shoulder pushing the hanging calendar crooked. Her head was to one side, and she was frowning. Mr. Privett remembered that she always used to frown like that when she was a little girl. It made him love her still more.

"They want you to go and see them," he said, chasing up a smile again. "There may be a vacancy coming along. Nothing definite, of course. But this is your opportunity."

Irene drew herself up sharply. She was standing quite clear of the wall by now.

"I don't want any Rammell vacancy, thank you," she said. "They can keep it."

There was silence. Then Mrs. Privett spoke.

"That's no way to speak to your father. And what's wrong with Rammell's I should like to know?"

They were the first words that Mrs. Privett had uttered. And having uttered them, she stood there facing Irene with her mouth drawn in at the corners. The resemblance between mother and daughter was at that moment unusually striking.

"Don't be silly, Mum," Irene answered. "Nothing's wrong with it. You know I don't mean that. It's simply that I don't want to go there. I've told you so all along."

"And why not, pray? Isn't it good enough for you?"

Mrs. Privett had been a learner herself in Rammell's when she had first met Mr. Privett. And Rammell's in consequence was a good deal more than a source of living to her. It was life itself.

26

The polished avenues of the counters were sylvan groves where she and Mr. Privett had discreetly done their courting. The whole of that end of Bond Street still glittered in a mist of girlish and romantic memories. And she wasn't going to have her daughter spoiling any of it.

That was why it was so painful, so unthinkably wounding, when Irene answered back. It showed that suddenly the invisible cord between parent and child had snapped completely.

" No, it isn't if you want to know," was Irene's reply. " It may be good enough for you. It isn't good enough for me. I'm not going to be a shopgirl. I've told you so before, and that's flat. I'm going to be . . ."

Irene checked herself. Her lips came together again just the way Mrs. Privett's had done. She had already said all that she intended to say. Had said too much, in fact.

But Mrs. Privett was merciless. She was exactly the same height as Irene and now she was clearly sparring for an opening.

" Going to be what? " she said bitterly. " An actress, I suppose! "

Irene braced herself. It seemed somehow that this no longer concerned herself alone. The quarrel had ceased to be a mere family row. The smell of persecution was in the air. With martyrdom just round the corner. There in a back kitchen in Kentish Town Irene Privett, aged seventeen, was going to the stake for her convictions. She wished that Mr. Christopher Fry could have been there to see her.

" Well, what if I am? " she demanded. " Is there anything so very terrible in that? "

It was Irene's first open declaration of her intentions. Up to now there had been nothing more serious than school theatricals and the Samuel French acting-editions. But this was the real thing. It was a contest between adults.

Seventeen, however, is a bad age for challenges. Or for being adult. The glands at that age don't always work properly. And the nervous system is notoriously unreliable. The mind, noble and sublime, promises one thing—and the body, feeble and treacherous, does something quite different. At that very moment, Irene conscious of being freer and older and more self-possessed than she had ever been before behaved like a small child. She burst into tears. And because she couldn't stand there like that in front of her parents, she turned her back on them and slammed out of

27

the room banging the door shut after her with the noise of a gun going off.

Mrs. Privett started to go after her, and then stopped. She turned and faced Mr. Privett. Neither of them spoke.

Then Mr. Privett swallowed. There was an audible choke somewhere in the back of his throat.

" You've made her cry, Mother," he said idiotically.

It was a constrained, awkward sort of meal with just the two of them. The toad-in-the-hole—usually one of Mr. Privett's favourite dishes, with the crust golden-brown like fresh cornflakes and the sausages themselves glistening with a rich amber radiance—was left almost untouched. The rice pudding was simply toyed with. Neither of them did very much talking. There was one point, however, on which they were in complete agreement. Each said emphatically that it would be silly for the other to go upstairs and attempt to reason with Irene while she was in that state. In consequence they sat there dutifully sipping at their tea together and trying to pretend that nothing had happened.

Of the two, Mr. Privett's emotions were the simpler. He was merely sad and disappointed. But Mrs. Privett's were more complicated. She was sad for his sake. She knew what his piece of news had meant to him. And she couldn't forgive Irene for spoiling things. It was like being cruel to . . . to, yes, that was it, to a child. Mrs. Privett wanted to throw her arms around her husband and tell him that at least one of his womenfolk still loved him. It was merely her upbringing that prevented her. She had been married for over twenty years and never once had she given any sudden demonstration of affection. She despised women whose emotions were on the surface.

From upstairs there came the sound of a door opening. Mrs. Privett immediately began smoothing out her skirt as though there had been crumbs all over it. Mr. Privett thrust his cup and saucer away from him.

" That'll be her ladyship," he said.

Mrs. Privett merely drew in her lips again.

" You leave her to me," she replied.

" Perhaps she's coming to say she's sorry," Mr. Privett suggested.

But Mrs. Privett was paying no attention to him.

" Ireen! " she called.

" Yes, Mum."

Irene was half-way down the stairs by now. Going purposefully in the direction of the front door, it seemed.

It was a relief to Mr. Privett that Irene even answered. An absurd fear had suddenly flashed across his mind that Irene was running away, simply bolting from the house without another word to either of them.

" Where you going? "

" Out, Mum."

Irene's voice certainly sounded steady and composed enough. There was no trace there of tantrums or hysterics. A deliberately casual and indifferent note seemed, indeed, to have crept into it. It might have been a chance and unintimate acquaintance whom she was addressing.

" Where to? " Mrs. Privett asked.

The same note of coldness, of aloofness, was in her voice also. It was the kind of voice that staff-managers and personnel superintendents use.

" With Madge. Like I said."

" Don't be back la . . ."

But the end of Mrs. Privett's sentence was cut off by another loud explosion. It was the front door this time. The whole house recoiled from the violence of it. Then there was silence. A deep, unnatural silence.

Mrs. Privett got up and began stacking the dishes, piling the half-eaten toad-in-the-hole and the merely pecked-at rice pudding on to the tray along with the teapot and the cups and saucers.

" Why don't you go and do something with your boat? " she said.

It was at moments like this that Mrs. Privett was glad that her husband had a hobby to take his mind off things. At other times, even the mere recollection of the hobby faintly annoyed her.

One of the extraordinary things about all hobbies is that they should be exclusively male affairs. You don't find grown women flying model aeroplanes. Or bending over gauge OO trains. Or collecting toy soldiers. Or even sticking-in stamps. Or arranging coins. Openly confronted with her husband's hobby, there is hardly a woman who does not feel some embarrassment. And when

29

the hobby is open and exhibitionist, like kite-flying or butterfly hunting, the wife tends to keep away from the front door-step when her husband sets forth.

That is the way it was with Mrs. Privett. Model yachts were Mr. Privett's hobby. And in the whole range of hobbies there is nothing more open and unconcealable than a model yacht. It is bulky. Immediately identifiable. Unfoldable.

There are two schools of thought about transporting large boats through the streets. There is the perambulator school. And the bicycle school. Mere distance or the dimensions of the craft itself has little to do with it. It goes deeper. Rouses the old basic controversy of walking v. cycling. Every Sunday morning there are severe, earnest enthusiasts who live within half-a-mile or so of the various boat-ponds hitching themselves up into saddles and pedalling off with the boat-trailer lurching along behind them like a gun-carriage. And there are other men, just as severe, just as earnest, trundling a converted perambulator half-way across London.

Mr. Privett had never really been in doubt about the matter. He cycled. In one respect Mrs. Privett was glad about this. It meant that her husband's shameful passage to his playground was kept as brief as possible. But, in another way she deplored it. Bicycles are awkward things to have in the hall at all times. They take up room. They hurt ankles. They fall over. And a bicycle with a kind of home-made milk float on the back is nothing less than a menace. Mr. Privett's contraption cut off one whole section of the passage like a barricade. It was the first thing you noticed as you came in. The last thing you bumped against as the front door was opened for you as you went out.

To-night, however, it seemed not to be without its uses. Mrs. Privett felt almost grateful for it.

" Well, why don't you ? " she asked again.

Mr. Privett, however, only shook his head. His mind was turning naturally to his other solace, Mr. Bloot.

" Think I'll walk round and see if Gus is in," was all he said.

It was fortunate that Mr. Bloot lived so near. Within easy walking distance, that is. Just up to the end of Fewkes Road. Then turn right. And straight on to The Boston where you turn right again and then sharp left. At the outside, fifteen minutes door to door. Or about twelve travelling hard if it's raining.

Admittedly, it was Mr. Bloot who knew the route even better than Mr. Privett did. That was because it was usually Mr. Bloot who came. Ever since poor Emmie had died, leaving Mr. Bloot a helpless, floundering widower, Mr. and Mrs. Privett had naturally both done what they could for him. It was Mr. Privett who had deliberately set out to prove that there was someone who still loved Mr. Bloot. Wanted him. Needed him. And it was Mr. Privett who had shown that there was someone ready to listen. Mr. Bloot wasn't the kind of man to be rushed in anything. The recital of the last phase of poor Emmie's illness always took time. And it was Mrs. Privett who always made him the cup of tea that he needed at the end of it.

As usually happens at times of bereavement, the Privetts had probably piled it on a bit. It might have been Mafeking and not merely loneliness that they had been relieving. They had practically adopted Mr. Bloot.

In a sense, this had been their mistake. After the first month or so, even the most desolate of widowers can usually come to some sort of terms with life. There is, for example, always the wireless. But Mr. Bloot was not a radio fan. Never had been. The B.B.C. was all a bit too restless. Too frisky. Too quick-fire for him. Cinemas weren't in his line either. The films usually upset him. In the old days when Emmie had liked to go once a week, sitting there contentedly spooning up a tub-ice in the darkness, Mr. Bloot had been forced to shut his eyes because of all the dreadful things that were going on upon the screen. And afterwards, while Emmie was curled up sleeping peacefully, Mr. Bloot would lie, rigid and sweating, thinking of all that violence and cruelty and suffering that he had just been made to pay for.

That left only the public house. But Mr. Bloot was naturally a tea drinker. And, as public houses don't sell tea, even The Nag's

Head, the Boston Hotel, the Archway Tavern and all the rest of them couldn't help. He passed by them, austere and disinterested, hankering after Brooke Bond's or Lyons's.

Indeed, if the Privetts hadn't insisted that Mr. Bloot should come round to Fewkes Road every Sunday, he would have been left entirely high and dry. There were his budgerigars, of course. They had always meant a lot to him, those birds. And never more than since he had become a widower. But even prize budgerigars are not a full-time occupation. And on Sundays after Mr. Bloot had cleaned out their cages, changed the water, put in fresh millet seed, seen that the piece of cuttle-fish bone was firmly in position between the bars, there were still about fifteen hours to go before bedtime.

The first hour was always easy. He spent it in conversation. Budgerigars have to be kept alone if they are to say anything worth listening to. And they respond to attention. They thrive on it. That was just as well because Mr. Bloot was doing more than simply gossip with them. It was speech-training and elocution that he was engaged on. Serious and intensive stuff like " Pretty Billy " and " Kiss me, " said over and over again until his brain was reeling.

On the whole, however, progress was disappointing. No matter how much Mr. Bloot constricted his throat and pursed up his lips he still could not bridge the immense, the yawning gap, between his own deep baritone and their miniature piping treble. At times, the budgerigars didn't even seem to recognise the incessant rumble as being conversation at all. Even with Mr. Bloot's face pressed up against the bars and breathing hard over them, they just buried their beaks among their cape feathers and slept.

There was no denying that Mrs. Privett's hospitality had done a great deal towards preserving Mr. Bloot's reason. Even his life possibly. But life-saving can be very exhausting. Especially when it has gone on for nearly five years. And, after all, it was Emmie Bloot, not Augustus, who had been Mrs. Privett's special friend. They had grown up professionally together, the two girls; first in a general draper's in Brixton and then in Rammell's itself. Emmie in the dress lengths. And Eileen in the layette and baby clothes. They had become bosom companions. Intimates. Like sisters. There wasn't a thing that they wouldn't have done for each other. And, more than once since the bereavement, as she washed up Mr. Bloot's teacup, Mrs. Privett had reminded herself that it was for Emmie's sake rather than Augustus's that she was still doing it.

To-night, however, Mrs. Privett was spared the washing-up. Even spared Mr. Bloot. It was to be exclusively a men's evening. Just two old friends together, discussing life and its surprises. What's more, as it was Mr. Bloot's house, it was Mr. Bloot's turn to make tea. And after the emotional upset earlier in the evening Mr. Privett felt that he could do with a cup of it.

That was why it was so bleakly disappointing when Mr. Privett got there to find that Mr. Bloot was out. And more than out. Had not even got home, in fact. It gave Mr. Privett a chilly feeling right down his spine to hear this piece of information. Because it confirmed Mr. Privett's fear that there was something fishy somewhere. Mr. Bloot had been behaving strangely of late. Sometimes he was there. And sometimes he wasn't. He either came round on Sundays. Or he didn't. It was as simple and unpredictable as that. And it was the same with going up to the Ponds. No excuses afterwards. No apologies. No explanations. Just absence.

" It doesn't matter," said Mr. Privett diffidently, to the landlady who had come down in answer to his knock—a loud one and a sharp double rat-tat, which was the private code between the two friends, " It doesn't really. I was only just passing. Sorry to have brought you down."

CHAPTER III

EVEN THOUGH it was a real failure of a morning—black skies, dark pavements and a wet sticky look to everything—Mr. Rammell was sitting in his car with a kind of private sunshine of his own seeping in through the windows. The fact that he didn't feel well no longer mattered. He had felt worse yesterday. What really mattered was that he had got a particularly niggling little problem that had irritated him for days—something about soft furnishing discounts—all sorted out in his mind overnight. That was why he was glowing, while the rest of London just steamed.

Mr. Rammell carried this mood of well-being into the office with him. In consequence, everything seemed just right. The peace and calm of the office itself was something straight out of paradise. His desk was exactly as he liked to see it. Clean blotting paper on the pad. Jotter and diary close alongside. Dictaphone on the side-table. Two fountain pens, one for red ink and one for blue-black, stuck out invitingly from their heavy plunger-holder. Even the desk calendar had been set at exactly the right angle so that Mr. Rammell had merely to glance sideways for an instant to make sure that it really was to-day and not yesterday or to-morrow in which he happened to be living.

The flowers on the window table were something else that pleased him. They showed that the floral department had been up early doing some good buying. The flower trade is exclusively a dawn affair. There is very little that is worth having in the petal market after about 7.30 a.m. As it was, the big white vase was filled with the sort of dark red roses that look as if they have been growing in big white vases all their lives. But there was one thing better even than the roses. A glass of hot water with a thin slice of lemon in it had been brought through to him as soon as he sat down. Altogether it was being a perfect heaven of a morning.

And, as usual, he had started work immediately. At this very moment up in the mail room on the floor above there were twelve letter-sorters, presided over by the secretariat supervisor, all slitting open the day's post. They were part of the 8.0 a.m. shift, and they were working flat out, letter openers flashing like rapiers, removing the contents and pinning the letters, cheques, postal orders, samples for matching, back on to the envelopes in which they had come.

In the retail trade the date of the postmark can be important. It may make all the difference between a happy customer or a closed account. And as soon as the bits and pieces had been safely skewered together, they were pitched into the row of green metal trays marked Counting House, Travel and Tickets, Stock Sizes, Children's, Hardware, China and Glass, Hairdressing, Toys, Perfumery and Cosmetics, Pianos and Radio, Sports-goods, Model Gowns, Millinery, Furs, Dress Lengths, Furnishing, Groceries, Jewellery, and all the rest of them. There was a whole battery of these trays. And even in their emptiness they represented Rammell's livelihood. Homes and gardens and seats at the cinema and birthday presents and summer holidays for all the staff depended on getting those trays piled up and overflowing.

But it was the red tray beside each sorter's left elbow that really counted. The other trays were just so many bottomless tanks being filled up with the steady daily surge. The regular morning flow down the public pipe-line. The fuel that kept the firm going. The red trays were special. Anything that had explosive in it, the least little hint of fire, went straight into one of the red trays. As the red trays were filled, the supervisor emptied them. And, every five minutes or so, the whole collection of them, practically solid dynamite by now, were passed on to Miss Underhill for Mr. Rammell.

They were a particular pet of Mr. Rammell's, these complaints trays. He didn't, of course, attend to any of the complaints himself. At least, not at this stage. He wasn't an extra-department fiddler, a do-everything-myself kind of man. But he always liked to know what the dissatisfied customers were saying. It was the quickest way of keeping his finger on the pulse of the business. Or rather on the pulse of a hundred different businesses.

And there was another advantage to be gained from glancing through the complaint trays. There was his personal stamp " Seen by the Managing Director " that his secretary, Miss Underhill, affixed afterwards. That stamp had a tonic effect on the entire store. It kept other people perpetually on their toes and up to scratch.

Mr. Rammell was more than half-way through the first trayful already. The letter that he had just read was from someone complaining that one of the springs of a new sun-lounge had snapped clean in two the first time anyone had sat on it. The circumstances had evidently been violent and dramatic. And socially shaming into the bargain. According to the evidence, it had been a vicar and a doctor's wife that the treacherous contrivance had been temporarily supporting. A wicker table with teapot and hot-water jug had been standing immediately in front. Only by the mercy of providence had the vicar escaped a terrible scalding; and, as it was . . . there was a great deal more in the same vein. But Mr. Rammell merely jotted down the words " sun lounge, " and reached for the next letter.

He never attempted to keep an exact record of what he read in the complaints tray. There were plenty of other people, hordes of them, analysing, cross-referencing, double-checking everything. And it was enough that he had seen it. It lit a tiny red lamp somewhere in his brain and reminded him that there had been two other complaints about sun lounges last month. Either the buyer didn't know where to go for sun lounges, or Birmingham had been letting down the buyer. Later on in the morning he would ask Mr. Preece which way round it was.

The next half-dozen letters were nothing. Simply nothing. A china tea-service had arrived in Northwood with the milk jug shattered. The electric motor of a newly delivered washing machine had fused all the lights in a house at Camberley as soon as the contraption had been turned on. Six pairs of stockings had been posted off by Rammell's all half a size too large despite the fact that the correspondent had most particularly said " fives, " and didn't Rammell's assistants ever listen to anything that was said to them? A lady from Cheltenham had been violently ill in the 3.7 from Paddington after eating minced chicken in the Rammell's restaurant. The assistant with red hair and an offhand manner in model millinery had been " grossly offensive "—Mr. Rammell had long ago noticed that nobody ever used just the word "offensive" —to someone who was transferring her account immediately to Harrod's because she disliked being spoken to by any shopgirl as though she were a common shoplifter. A bottle of perfume purchased last Tuesday had given the customer and her husband a peculiarly violent kind of hay-fever. . .

36

Mr. Rammell passed them all across to Miss Underhill for stamping. Then he paused. Here was something. A watch, guaranteed for ten years, had stopped dead on the third day, and if that was what Rammell's meant by a guarantee . . . Mr. Rammell broke off and wrote the single word " watches. " There had been another watch complaint yesterday.

Mr. Rammell worked quickly, spending only a few seconds on each complaint. And he never read the last paragraphs at all. They were all entirely standard, these last paragraphs. Practically interchangeable, in fact. The stricken Cheltenham resident might have collaborated with the woman who had been addressed as a common shoplifter, or the owner of the cracked milk jug could have contributed the last few sentences for the lady with small feet. It was always in the last paragraph that the big rudeness, the real sting-in-the-tail venom came. It was the last paragraph that made the writer swing round from the desk, and in the glow from the shaded lamp say quietly to the family circle: " You might just care to hear what I've said to them . . ."

Not that Mr. Rammell minded these bits of fine writing. After all, he was in business with the object of indulging people. And if what they really fancied was a piece of virtuoso invective on the best note-paper, it didn't worry him. Rammell's was quite big enough and old enough to be able to ignore it. In any case, the rude bits were entirely silly and unnecessary. A simple statement of the facts would have had the same effect. Rammell's wasn't the sort of shop to let its customers down.

But it was nine-thirty by now. There was no time for any more uninvestigated complaints. He pushed the tray from him, and rang for Miss Underhill.

" Just stamp the rest," he said. " And let me have the Board of Trade papers. The carpet file."

There was a tap on the door and Mr. Rammell's other secretary, Miss Winters, stood there. She was a newcomer. A dark intense kind of girl, who seemed to have been born for the delivery of bad news. She was still on probation, and Mr. Rammell was far from sure about her. It was her eyes that troubled him. Too fixed and staring for his liking. They made him feel as though he were taking part in a verse drama, and had just heard that Troy had fallen. This morning that feeling was stronger and more overpowering than ever.

" A phone message from the Chairman, sir," she said, speaking right past him and out into the auditorium. " Sir Harry is on his way round now, and wonders if he can see you straight away . . ."

Mr. Rammell felt the whole calm of the morning suddenly evaporating. Because it was an understood thing that his father never came into the office on Tuesdays. Thursday was his day. And then only for a couple of hours around lunchtime. After all, the old boy was nearly eighty. But that wasn't the worst of it. He was somewhere in the teen-age of his second childhood. And spry. Spryness was Sir Harry's chief failing.

An aura of ghastly good health surrounded him. He emerged from his hotel suite in the morning—the house in Hill Street had been closed when Lady Rammell died—looking as pink and white as a big albino baby. He always wore a flower in his buttonhole. And his head was perpetually buzzing like a beehive with all the nonsense that he had been thinking up the night before.

Like most old people he didn't sleep very much. And some mornings he would have hatched up as many as a dozen different ideas, all revolutionary, all cock-eyed, and all requiring endless work, research, figures, before the Board could quietly turn them down.

This morning, moreover, Sir Harry felt simply marvellous. Having ordered the car for nine-thirty, he sent it away again—and set out to walk from Piccadilly to Bond Street. This, however, was a mistake. Too much to see on the way. Too many distractions. He was like a schoolboy. He hung about shop windows. He lingered. And, in consequence, he kept Mr. Rammell waiting. From the moment of that first impetuous telephone call, an air of suspense had hung over the office like a gale warning. It was nearly eleven-fifteen before the storm finally broke.

But even if Sir Harry was late he certainly got down to things as soon as he reached his room. He sent for his son straightaway. And it was obvious from the start that he was right at the top of his form. He had his little note-book open on the desk by the time Mr. Rammell arrived, and he was pouring over the mass of jottings

38

that had been so clear to him when he had made them, and were now somehow so puzzling.

It was apparently the staff pensions fund that was exercising him most this morning. Some time during the night he had thought up a scheme for a vast new rest home somewhere on the South Coast outside Bognor Regis, and he wanted his son to hear. But why Bognor? Mr. Rammell kept asking. Why a new rest home at all? Why even mention pensions when they had all been agreed by the Staff Association only last year? There was no time, however, to go back over that now. The old man's mind darted back and forth across the conversation like an intoxicated butterfly. It was off again on another of its zig-zags. Why didn't they sell more billiard tables? Had the game gone out of favour, or was there something wrong with the department? Was the Dramatic Society right in doing *Hay Fever*, or shouldn't they stick to things like *The Quaker Girl* which had been their first big success? Wouldn't escalators throughout the whole store save the cost of lift-attendants? Why were Jamaican cigars such a terrible price? Could he have by to-morrow please a list showing how much everything in the Fur Salon had gone up since 1939?

But this was only the small stuff that had been passing through Sir Harry's mind. He was only now getting to the real point of his visit.

" I've been thinkin'," he began.

Mr. Rammell felt a new area of coldness developing inside his stomach.

" When's Tony comin' into the firm? " Sir Harry went on. " Time the boy did somethin'. No good bein' soft with the lad."

Mr. Rammell did not reply immediately. The one subject that he did not want to discuss with anyone, least of all with his father, was Tony. The young man was altogether too mysterious. Too unaccountable. Too much like his mother. He seemed to have inherited none of the real Rammell qualities at all. He was twenty-three. And he might have been born yesterday for all the sense of family responsibility that he showed. And what made it so particularly maddening that the old man should have chosen this moment to ask him about Tony was the fact that only last week he and Tony had had a real set-to about the same thing. Neither of them had properly recovered from it, in fact. Apparently there were at least two people in London—Tony Rammell as well as

Irene Privett—who didn't want to go into Bond Street on any terms.

But already Sir Harry was off again.

"Got to be someone to run the place," he said. "You and I aren't so young as we used to be."

Mr. Rammell raised his eyebrows, but said nothing.

"You don't look so good. Ought to give yourself a holiday," Sir Harry continued.

Mr. Rammell stirred uneasily.

"I'm all right," he answered. "Nothing wrong with me."

It was a particularly delicate point this, the subject of Mr. Rammell's health. He knew how bad his digestion was. And so did his doctor. There, however, so far as he was concerned, was where Mr. Rammell felt that the matter should end. He wanted other people to make allowances for his weakness. Not refer to it.

"Look at *me*," his father advised him. "I take care of myself."

Mr. Rammell looked. Sir Harry was sitting right on the edge of his chair snipping the end off a cigar. The cutter was a brand new one. He had, in fact, discovered it that very morning on the counter of the Wine and Tobacco Department as he sauntered through. There was something special about the patented spring cutting lever. And, as he sat fiddling with it, his resemblance to an elderly schoolboy was more marked than ever. If the cutter had been something that he had just invented and built out of Meccano he could not have been more intense or preoccupied.

But already he was off again.

"What's Tony say about it?" he asked.

"He doesn't want to come into the firm," Mr. Rammell told him. "Says he won't, and that's that."

Sir Harry gave his son a wink.

"Leave him to me," he said. "I know how to handle 'im."

"It won't do any good . . ." Mr. Rammell began. But he was interrupted by the telephone. It was the verse-drama student who was on the other end of it.

"Mrs. Rammell to speak to you, sir," she said, sounding as though she was on her way to bury Polynices.

Because his father was there, Mr. Rammell spoke into the instrument carefully, diplomatically.

"Yes, dear. Yes. What is it?"

Mrs. Rammell's own voice came through very loud and clear.

It was naturally a little high-pitched. Urgent-sounding. And on the telephone it was always singularly penetrating.

" What's the matter? " she demanded. " Am I interrupting ? Is someone with you? "

" No, dear. No. Go on."

" Then why are you using your business voice? "

" I'm not, dear. Really, I'm not."

" Oh, yes, you are. But it doesn't matter. I only wanted to remind you about to-night," Mrs. Rammell went on. " It's not eight. It's seven-thirty. We'll have to eat afterwards."

" After what? " Mr. Rammell asked. He felt his strength ebbing away from him.

" After the concert," Mrs. Rammell told him. " You said you'd come. You can't let me down as late as this." Mrs. Rammell was fairly shrieking by now. " There's a box reserved for us. Constance'll be there . . ."

" All right, dear. I'll be back in good time, dear. Good-bye, dear. Good-bye."

As Mr. Rammell hung up the receiver he congratulated himself. There had been nothing for his father to get his teeth into from overhearing that conversation. Not a hint that he felt that he would go stark raving mad if he were ever dragged off to another concert anywhere. Last time it had been madrigals of all things. Part-songs and bleatings, like musical and demented sheep. His wife, Mr. Rammell realised gloomily, somehow belonged among such goings-on. And he didn't. That was the whole trouble. He didn't even look as though he belonged. Anyone seeing the pair of them sitting up there in the box would probably assume that it was the lady patroness being kind to the man who had landed the refreshments contract.

He looked up and caught his father's eye.

The old man winked again. Evidently Mrs. Rammell's voice had been louder than he realised.

" You singin' to-night? " Sir Harry asked.

CHAPTER IV

BUT MR. RAMMELL wasn't the only person connected with the firm who was having a bad day. There was also Marcia. And even though it was getting on for midday the curtains of her little flat were still not drawn back. Nothing very remarkable in that. In any large city there will always be plenty of late ones, night birds and other odd misfits who get home with the milk and try to make up for it afterwards. But for a member of Rammell's staff to be down under the bedclothes at this time was certainly a bit of an exception. Because among the whole of the one thousand and eleven employees there was only one—Staff No. 737—from whom such behaviour would have been tolerated.

That was because No. 737 was one of Rammell's big assets, their ambassadress. While there were five other mannequins in Rammell's, there was only one Marcia. Indeed, there was only one Marcia in the whole of England. Other houses had their models. Girls pretty as powder puffs. Or tall and dignified like Marchionesses. Or sun-tanned and smelling of the heather. Those girls were trained. They emerged. They walked beautifully. They were photographed. They married stockbrokers or a friend of the chief buyer. They disappeared. But Marcia remained.

And with every year that passed her position became more firmly established. More unassailable. She was like Royalty. She went everywhere. And, when she stayed away she was missed. Ascot, Wimbledon, Roehampton, Henley, Lord's—but only on the day of the Eton and Harrow match—the premières of big film shows, the more important first nights, the charity balls—she turned up, exquisite, delightful, smiling. Conscientiously bashing her way through an engagement diary that she dared not allow to grow empty. Her picture was in all the papers. In consequence, seven-pound-a-week typists learnt from Marcia the right way to drape themselves in two or three thousand pounds' worth of mink, so that there was an easy, almost nonchalant informality to the whole effect. Mothers with young children, and all the ironing still to do, saw just how they should stand when they next found themselves up against the radiator of a big Rolls-Royce in front of Blenheim or of Chatsworth.

Wherever you looked, she was there. Superb. Serene. Indisputable. The steeply arched eye-brows. The long curve of the cheek. The deep indecipherable eyes. The wide gentle mouth. The face smiled imperturbably on the public from all sides. From boxes of face powder. From the shiny pages of expensive magazines. From Mayfair pageant programmes. From the walls of Underground platforms.

That face, and the figure that went with it, represented everything that the race was always reaching out for. It was elegance. It was poise. It was correctness. But there was more to it than that. There was also an indefinable spiritual quality to it. A placidity. Even if it were a new strapless evening-gown that she was displaying, or a Longchamps ensemble with a hat as flat and wide as a Chinese umbrella, there was still the same ethereal, faintly surprised air of a discreetly fashionable Madonna.

But even a face and a figure must have some kind of private life. And it was the private life that wasn't so good as the public one. Not nearly so good. A proper mess-up, in fact. To be honest, it was hardly worth living. She had known better, too. Much better. At the time of her first marriage she had lived in the country. Quite a large house as she remembered it. With lawns and paths and shrubberies. And an awful lot of rain. But Marcia, against a purely agricultural background, had never made much sense. That was something that she had come to realise within the first few months of trying it. And, in the end, because her husband had refused to do the gentlemanly thing, she had allowed herself to be divorced for desertion. Had simply turned her back on the house, the stables, the kennels, the dove-cot, the goddam awful rain, everything . . .

Then there had been the suite-in-Claridges period when she had married her American. But that, too, had proved a disappointment. He had moved out one night in a great flurry of fancy-looking suitcases, clasping his World Airways ticket-folder in his hand and begging her to wake up just once before she was really dead. That had come as a great shock to her. She never had been able to understand the American way of putting things. But he had behaved very decently. For a start, he was the sort of man who understood divorces. He had realised that a woman can't live on

43

old memories. And the settlement had been generous. Even lavish. But his health had been shocking. He had died suddenly in a dude-ranch somewhere outside Houston—taken his own life she learnt afterwards—just when the bottom had fallen clean out of his particular corner of the stock market. And because it had always been a hotel suite that they had lived in, there wasn't even a house and furniture that she could sell. For all the good it had done, that marriage might simply never have occurred.

Luckily, she had kept up her modelling. And it was round about this time that, always beautiful, she had suddenly assumed the Madonna expression. What's more, finding that it suited her, she had stuck to it.

She had been with Rammell's for nearly eleven years now. That was what was so alarming. There aren't really that number of years in a model's life. And there certainly wouldn't be eleven more. Or ten. Or nine. Something more like three or four, probably. And, after that, a steadily descending scale. The sunset period. Free-lancing. Trips into the provinces. Autumn collections in the seaside towns. Going to places as one of the second best-dressed women. Or, worse still, not going at all because another brand-new Marcia had turned up from somewhere.

She had left it too late now to do any of the other things that had once been enticingly dangled before her. Films, for instance. Naturally, all the agents in turn had been after her. They could hardly afford to have neglected anybody who was so much photographed. So eminently photographable. There had been screen tests. Conferences. Auditions. It was the auditions that had been the stumbling block. Because at auditions you have to speak. And this was Marcia's weakest side. It was something that she had never properly got round to. She had been too busy ever since she had left school, getting married, being divorced, divorcing, standing in front of cameras, wearing clothes that didn't belong to her. There had been no time for amateur theatricals. Or verse reading. Or anything like that. No time even for ordinary elocution lessons. And this was a pity. Because Marcia's was by no means the kind of voice that could be allowed to speak for itself. Apart from a slight huskiness that might once have been possibilities, there wasn't even anything to work on. It was pure Kilburn. In the pursuit of refinement she had gone over her vowels so frequently that she had trodden them quite flat. There was scarcely a breath

44

left in one of them. When she did speak which was rarely because Marcia couldn't usually find very much to say—it was like someone murmuring under an anæsthetic. Not that this was surprising. There was a distinctly coma-like quality to Marcia. She had been going about in an elegant daze for years.

2

She glanced at her watch. Eleven-fifteen. Time to be getting on with things. The first parade at Rammell's was at lunch. And there would have to be a big change in her appearance, a complete transformation of everything, by then.

Slowly, gracefully, in the smooth undulating way in which she always moved, she slid out of bed. Then she drew her wrap around her, and went over to the dressing-table. Because it had been late when she had got back last night and because she had been tired, things had rather a messy, flung-about appearance this morning. She had upset a powder-box when she put her bag down. The black velvet of the bag was now all smeared and grubby looking.

It was to avoid that kind of thing that, she kept telling herself, she should have had a lady's maid. It was having had one once that had spoiled her. Because since she had lost her, she had never really taken proper care of anything—unless, of course, it was something of Rammell's that she had on loan. It was because she never remembered to put things away that she had to spend such an awful lot on herself. It wasn't that she was particularly extravagant. Or indulgent. Or even changeable in her tastes. It was simply that she couldn't manage. And all the time at the back of her mind there was that horrid shadow. The knowledge that the time would come when it wouldn't be so easy to go on like this. A voice from nowhere kept reminding her to be careful.

She sat for some time in front of her mirror, turning her head this way and that like a canary in a cage. Not preening. Merely looking at herself. Sideways. Full-face. Sideways again. On the whole, the effect wasn't so bad as it might have been. Not nearly so ghastly as she had feared. The new mud massage that the Rammell Beauty Parlour was providing had freshened her skin quite remarkably. It might have been the skin of a girl of twenty. The only thing that worried her was the fact that the full course was only six treatments. And she had taken five of them already.

45

Apparently if anyone took more than six in a row it was the skin as well as the mud that came away afterwards as soon as the scraping began. And she couldn't afford to go back to the old flat complexion with which she had been getting along for the last six months. It had been one of the fashionably sallow periods then. All pretty women had been looking slightly Asiatic. But that was over and done with now. The blood was being worn much closer to the skin this season.

Then her hair. It was the fineness of it that was the difficulty. Other girls—the phrase " other women " would have seemed all wrong to Marcia: she wouldn't have realised that she was included in the conversation at all—had hair like wire. The hairdresser's scissors could scarcely get through it. But her own was as soft as floss. That was why it had to be soaked in oil so often. Otherwise it would get ruined every time a wave was put into it. It was dark hair. And she was wearing it at the moment a little shorter. Ever since February, the lobes of the ear had been left showing.

Dressing was always rather a slow business with Marcia. She examined everything carefully before she put it on. Compared with her manner at night-time, it might have been a different person who was handling her clothes in the morning. She held out each garment at arm's length and went over it seam by seam, practically stitch by stitch like a wardrobe mistress. But this was only to be expected. It was the public Marcia, the one who was going out, who was preparing herself.

And once in the street, she felt better already. It was only in that pokey little flat that she felt so awful. So suicidal. Out here, life was going on all round her. And she was part of it. Contributing to it. Before she had reached Knightsbridge she had felt herself being looked at. Recognised. Desired. Thought about. She became reconciled to life again. Happily conscious of being permanently twenty-three.

Then at the corner of Sloane Street she stopped suddenly. The Madonna expression faded. And a frown that belonged to a different kind of fact altogether appeared beneath the veil. She felt for her handbag.

" Oh, God," she said. " Mum's postal order. I've forgotten all about it . . ."

Mum was another of Marcia's troubles. They hadn't lived

46

under the same roof for years. Not since Marcia was sixteen. Practically never saw each other nowadays. Didn't correspond very much, either. And never telephoned, because Marcia's mum wasn't on the phone. So it couldn't be said that Mum was a nuisance. Or even difficult. Just a drag.

And in a dim vague sort of way Marcia was still fond of her. Needed her at times. Would have liked to visit her. Take her out somewhere. But that was impossible. Their lives had grown too far apart. Old Mrs. Tutty in her back bed-sitter in Kilburn and Marcia in her flat off Cadogan Gardens didn't belong in the same world any longer. Simply couldn't be seen about out together.

That's where the tragedy lay. It was harder on Marcia than on most girls who have a poor widowed mum tucked away somewhere. Because other girls could always slip in during the week or pop across on Sundays. And Marcia couldn't. She hadn't got the right kind of clothes to wear. The last time she had made the attempt and had gone toiling up the Edgware Road by bus all the way to Pitter Street, it had been disastrous. It was a simple mink stole that she had on. And in those parts, mink stoles, real or artificial, meant only one thing. People who passed her kept thinking terrible thoughts. In short, the gulf was too wide. It was unbridgeable.

In consequence, she had been reduced to show her love, her devotion, by sending little gifts. But even that was difficult. Because she didn't like giving Mum's address at Rammell's. Or at Fortnum's. And Marcia wasn't the kind of girl who could buy the things and make them up in a parcel afterwards. Never had been any good with brown paper. And knots. And all that kind of thing. Cheques were no use either. Mum had never had a private banking account. So postal orders were really all that was left. And now Marcia had forgotten even that. All the week she had been reminding herself to send a couple of pounds. One for luck. And one because she had completely overlooked Mum's last birthday . . .

Not that there was anything that she could do about it. She had just got time to get along to Rammell's for the luncheon salon. It was lucky that the only food she ever allowed herself at midday was cinnamon toast and a cup of black coffee. Otherwise she would have been late even for the dress show.

47

CHAPTER V

SUNDAY HAD come round at last. The weekly miracle had occurred. And London had died in the night. The City, from St. Paul's to Liverpool Street, was simply for archaeologists. Fleet Street and Ludgate Hill might have been a deserted mountain pass. Bond Street itself was a smooth, unencumbered stream—practically a lagoon—meandering past curtained windows. With only the cats and the caretakers peering out.

Like one vast flock of homing pigeons some two or three million Londoners, all simultaneously released and all urged forward by a common impulse had popped out of their week-day imprisonment and made a bolt for their ancestral dove-cots.

Some of them, moreover, were doing quite nicely in their new surroundings. Mr. Preece, for example. Wearing a pair of smartly-pressed grey flannels and a sports coat obviously cut only for the mildest kinds of sport, he was sauntering round the garden in his idlers, feeling simple. Primitive. Bucolic. One of the Carshalton peasantry. In his left hand he carried his sécateurs, and in his right a tin of patent ejector insecticide with which he gave each rose bush a little friendly death blast as he passed by. He was in fact an entirely happy man. His new denture was bedding down at last exactly as the dentist had said it would. His eldest son had just won the school economics prize for an essay on Trade Balances. He kept remembering a strangely poignant and beautiful dream of cycling with an attractive but unknown girl through Portugal, a country which he had never visited. Mrs. Preece's new Swiss girl seemed positively to like washing-up. His petunias, after rather an anxious and uncertain start, were now safely established. He had done his exercises. And he had not thought about Rammell's once since breakfast when he had jotted down two little entries, one about gloves and the other about travel vouchers, in the small leather note-book which he carried even in his sports coat. All in all, life seemed very nearly perfect.

Not so with Mr. Rammell. At this moment he was standing in the bathroom bending forward over the basin and peering into the mirror to inspect his tongue. It was horrible. A pale, white-flannel tongue. And bundled up in his scarlet silk dressing-gown, with his hair still sticking up like feathers, the whole appearance that he presented to himself was obnoxious. This, the regular morning disillusionment, saddened him. And he stood gloomily reflecting. For a start, he had not slept well. At one-thirty he had got up and mixed himself a dose of Bisodol. Then, once awake, he had not been able to go to sleep again. He had lain there in his tall bedroom in Eaton Square thinking unquiet thoughts.

He kept remembering that last visit his father had paid him. Nearly two hours completely written off. Destroyed. Wasted. It was a severe nervous strain even having the old man in the office at all. So far as Sir Harry was concerned, life was one long conspiracy nowadays. Keeping things from him. Concealing future plans. Innocently deceiving him. If only he would finally agree to throw in the sponge and retire gracefully. . . . But it wasn't only his father who had kept sleep away from him. It was Mrs. Rammell as well. She was the prime cause of his dyspepsia. Not intentionally, of course. There was nothing deliberately malign about her slow-murder treatment. It was simply that she couldn't relax. Couldn't for one single moment ease up like other women. Simply had to go on and on tormenting him. Last night, for example, she had invited two Hungarians to dinner. And, as though she were actually proud of it, she had explained that one of them was a sculptor who did flower pieces in stainless steel and the other a film director engaged exclusively on abstracts. Mr. Rammell recalled, these two unheard-of émigrés from old Buda, all bortsch and botched accents, lapping up his claret and flattering the one woman in London fool enough to have been taken in by them. And in his 2 a.m. mood would have been ready to commit homicide, cracking the abstract film director over the head with one of his fellow-conspirator's cast-iron daffodils.

And in the stillness of the night, with the startling clarity of all-night thoughts, he realised suddenly how like his mother Tony really was. Artistic. Musical. Restless. The boy was completely indifferent to everything that went to make up responsible adult life. And more than indifferent. Openly hostile. He lived, hermetically sealed off from the world. A chrysalis inside a cocoon of pure selfishness.

Mr. Rammell felt better when he had breakfasted. The coffee had been particularly good. And the toast was excellent. Of exactly the right thickness, and a clear chrysanthemum bronze in colour.

As he left the table with *The Sunday Times* neatly tucked under his arm he felt that life was re-opening. Blandness enfolded him. And peace. He was, he realised, in exactly the right frame of mind for pondering on the future of his son. Not immediately, that is. But during the morning. In the meantime, he wanted to be alone. To finish reading the Sunday papers. To smoke a cigar. Even to doze possibly. He was still thinking about Tony and the way he would have a fresh shot at putting things to him, even more quietly, more reasonably than last time, when he reached the library.

That was why it was so unfortunate that he should have found Tony himself already installed there. And the boy certainly looked comfortable. His legs were dangling over the arm of Mr. Rammell's own chair, and a portable radio, like a pale cream cosmetics set, stood on the carpet beside him. Mr. Rammell knew that radio set well. And he hated it. Ever since it had come into the house, his son hadn't been alone with himself once. Wherever he went, he was followed by voices. Low, crooning voices. Husky, suggestive voices. Voices whispering in American accents of love and women's lips, and the moon.

To Mr. Rammell's relief, Tony turned off the set as soon as his father came into the room. But the relief was purely temporary. Compared with what Tony had to say, Mr. Rammell would have preferred the B.B.C.

" I say, Dad," he began brightly. " I've just had a brainwave. I've thought what to do with this bloody awful room."

Mr. Rammell started. The cigar, his first of the day, remained unlit between his fingers. This room, the library, with its quiet dark panelling and its deep red carpet and its heavy tapestry curtains had come to be his one retreat. His refuge. With the mahogany door closed behind him, he was safe alike from Mr. Preece and from Mrs. Rammell. Even his indigestion seemed to vanish as he entered.

But young Tony was still speaking.

" If we got rid of all that phoney woodwork," he was saying, with the same kind of dreamy insistence that Mr. Rammell knew in his wife's voice when she was planning a concert, " we could scrap the curtains altogether and begin getting down to things."

Mr. Rammell tried hard to feel amused.

" What sort of things? " he asked indulgently.

" I should junk the books for a start," Tony continued. " It isn't as if you ever read them."

" And then? "

" Why not offer the furniture to the V. and A? " Tony asked him. " Pity to disperse it. ' Hotel Lounge. English style. c. 1900 ' —that kind of thing. They'd rather like it."

" And if I did, what the hell should I sit on? "

" Plastic mostly," Tony told him. " Plastic. And moulded ply."

Mr. Rammell gave a little involuntary shudder.

" Any upholstery? " he asked.

Obviously there was nothing to be done but to humour the boy. And, up to the present, Mr. Rammell had been congratulating himself on the way he was keeping things going just as though it were a normal conversation between two sane, healthy people. But Tony's absorption in the project was already beginning to alarm him.

" Foam latex," he replied. " Sprayed on. Choose your own colour."

" That the lot? " he asked.

Tony paused.

" I've been wondering about the ceiling," he said. " With the chandelier down, it would make a rather nice expanse. Could be plain silver. Then you could throw the light up at it."

" And the walls? Don't forget you've stripped the panelling."

" Why not pink? " Tony asked. " Pink for the two sides. And apple-green for the ends. Then it wouldn't look so much like a bloody undertaker's. You'd find yourself breathing again."

Mr. Rammell took up a position on the carpet in front of the fireplace. He was still calm. That was the great thing. Hadn't

51

lost his temper yet. But he knew from long experience of talks with Tony that it was liable to go at any moment. And he particularly wanted to avoid any kind of upset this morning.

"I think I'll just keep things as they are for the time being," he said quietly. "If you want to go mucking about with the furniture why don't you start on your own room."

He smiled a little as he said it. If only his wife could have heard him she would have realised how patient—God only knew how patient—he really was with the boy.

But already Tony was speaking.

"I have," he said.

Mr. Rammell uttered a long, deep sigh.

"Does your mother know?" he asked.

Tony looked surprised.

"Oh, yes," he said. "She likes it. It was her idea about this study. That's why I came down here."

That was all that Mr. Rammell needed to hear. He could feel his temper, his carefully suppressed temper, suddenly boiling over inside him like a milk saucepan!

"Why the devil can't your mother leave things alone?" he demanded. "And you, too. It isn't like a reasonable home. It's just one long bloody madhouse. When it isn't music, it's ballet. And when it isn't ballet it's some goddamn-awful sculpture." He paused for a moment. "Just you listen to me, young man," he went on. "When I was your age I'd done nearly three years in the business. I knew enough to earn my own living. I could . . ."

But Tony was no longer listening. He had got up from the chair and was bending down to pick up the portable radio. Then he walked slowly across the room without even looking at his father. When he reached the door, however, he turned.

"Oh, my God," he said. "No wonder Mother gets sick of it."

3

For Mr. Bloot it was being a very different kind of Sunday. A unique, exciting sort of day. Easily one of the most intriguing and stimulating Sundays he had ever known.

He had shaved once already. But being dissatisfied with a small scrubby patch that he had just discovered beneath his chin, he was now hard at it again. Hot water. Soap. Shaving brush. Everything. In matters of shaving, Mr. Bloot was strictly orthodox. Never used anything but a cut-throat. It was like the beginning of a sabre charge every time he really got down to it. And, by the time he was through he usually had one or two honourable gashes.

This morning, when he came to put his collar back on, he noticed that his cravat was unworthy of him. Not exactly messy. And certainly not stained. Nevertheless, it was still too creased and rubbed in places to be suitable. And this itself was significant. Because in the ordinary way he usually let up a bit on Sundays. For years now he hadn't worn anything better than his second-best when off-duty.

This morning, too, he spent nearly ten minutes in bringing his shoes up to real Guardsman standard. He stood there beneath the budgerigar cages sawing away with the Nugget brush. The toe-caps now glistened like gun-metal. And to avoid soiling them, he placed the shoes carefully side by side under the sink, with a sheet of newspaper on top in case of drips.

On a shelf above the sink stood a small white vase. And standing up in the vase was a tea-rose. It was saffron-yellow in colour. And ingeniously wired by the florist so that it would die of sheer old age before it could open up beyond the bud state. Mr. Bloot had chosen it carefully for his button-hole. And he made a special point of trying out the holder to see that it was still water-tight. This was important. Because, although there was a patent rubber ring near the top of the holder to prevent spilling, it was not always reliable. Very much the reverse, in fact. Once when he had leant forward in the shop to pick up something the water had come squirting out as though it were some sort of carnival novelty that he was wearing.

Mr. Bloot glanced at his watch, and compared it with the kitchen clock. Eleven-fifteen. Everything ready. And no matter how slowly he walked, or how long he was kept waiting for a bus, it couldn't take him more than thirty minutes to get to Finsbury Park.

The Tufnell Park Road is one of the straightest highways in London. Probably the Romans made it. Or the brewers. Because, like most London thoroughfares, it runs quite simply from one pub to another. Slap down the Tufnell Park Road, in fact, is the very

53

shortest cut there can be from the Boston Tavern at the Archway Road end to the Nag's Head at Holloway. But for most people its straightness is also one of its defects. About half-way along, it begins to pall on the pedestrian. He becomes aware of his feet. Mr. Bloot however, scarcely noticed anything this morning. He was walking rather fast for him, with high springy steps like a Scoutmaster. Even though there was no likelihood of rain, he was carrying his umbrella. And not merely carrying it. With his hand held loosely round the handle, he was swinging the umbrella round and round in circles. His naturally florid complexion gleamed in the sunlight because of all that shaving. And, because he had been walking quickly for the last ten minutes, his nostrils were dilated. There was an air of conquest and adventure about him. He was like a superior kind of Viking on his way to sack a nunnery. If anyone from Rammell's had seen him they would have been amazed, incredulous. But that was only because no one had ever seen him really jubilant before.

This was Mr. Bloot in love. He was courting.

CHAPTER VI

IN A SENSE, it was all Mr. Bloot's fault. And, in a sense, it wasn't. He was perfectly entitled to live his own life. Especially his love-life. No one could deny him that. On the other hand, without him Mr. Privett was left lonely and unattached. And a couple of Sundays later Mr. Privett paid the penalty for his friend's unfaithfulness.

With no Mr. Bloot to keep him company, Mr. Privett simply stayed at home and moped. He hadn't the heart to do anything. He just sat in the kitchen in his shirt-sleeves, reading the *News of the World*, and getting in Mrs. Privett's way. The thought of going up to the Highgate Ponds crossed his mind more than once. He felt rather guilty about not going. He knew that the others up there would be expecting him. For years now a fair wind and fine sailing weather had found him there on Sunday mornings, taking his place on the bank along with the owners of the Sunbeams, Irises, Swallows and the rest of the fleet. If he didn't go this morning, it would be the third Sunday in succession that he had missed. But somehow without Mr. Bloot to keep him company he hadn't the heart to set out.

Not that Mr. Bloot was anything of a model yachtsman. He didn't know a spinnaker from a jib. But he liked to take the fresh air. And he made an impressive figure simply standing there, waiting for the winner to come in.

This morning there wasn't even Irene for Mr. Privett to talk to. She had plunged out of the house just after nine-thirty as though on the way to an emergency. At one moment she was still in bed, obviously over-sleeping. At the next, she was downstairs, dressed all in her tennis things and gulping down a cup of tea that was too hot for her. Then, just as Mrs. Privett caught up with her and asked if she would like something proper—a rasher of bacon or a grilled sausage—Irene had gone again. The one-gun salute from the front door was all that was left of her.

Her departure saddened Mr. Privett more than it did his wife.

55

Mrs. Privett merely winced a little as the door shut, and then began clearing away the breakfast things. But Mr. Privett was left staring into space. It was this morning that he had set aside for a special talk with Irene. He had promised himself that he would reason with her, gently and lovingly, about the Rammell's vacancy. Admittedly, the Staff Department hadn't actually written to Irene yet. But Mr. Privett had a strong psychic presentiment that there would be a letter in the morning. Then it would be necessary to strike. And strike instantly. So long as Irene was merely being difficult within the family, it didn't really matter very much. But suppose she persisted in her attitude, and wrote back a snubbing off-hand kind of note to the Staff Supervisor? That was what really alarmed Mr. Privett.

For once, the *News of the World* was not much consolation to him. It told him that Tuesday was a poor day for engaging in financial transactions, and warned him vaguely of domestic troubles later in the week. Journeys also, he learned, were better avoided. The whole paragraph was vaguely alarming. Even with no financial transactions in prospect and no journeys that he could possibly want to make, the bit about domestic troubles was obviously addressed to him. He put down the paper and called through to Mrs. Privett who was washing-up in the scullery.

" You don't think we've done anything to upset Gus, do you? " he asked. " He didn't use to keep away like this."

But Mrs. Privett was busy.

" Why don't you go and sail your boat? " was all she said.

2

As it turned out, Mrs. Privett could hardly forgive herself. It seemed that only by a last-minute whim of Providence had she been saved from being her own husband's murderess. Because when she spoke to him, Mr. Privett was so thoroughly dispirited that without a word he went upstairs to get ready.

Not that the matter of getting dressed for model-yachting was ever simple. There was so much to be remembered. First there was the pair of old grey trousers, the warm ones. Then the pair of long rubber Wellingtons into which they fitted. They were practically compulsory, the Wellingtons. Part of the uniform. And finally there was the blue, faintly nautical-looking jacket. The only thing that Mr. Privett drew a line at was the peaked cap.

Because Mrs. Privett was still washing up the breakfast things, Mr. Privett was left helpless and unaided in the difficult task of getting trailer and bicycle backwards out of the narrow hall. To-day it proved even more difficult than usual. The pedal of the bicycle was in the upright position and kept catching on things. It was one of the legs of the hat-stand that it finally got hold of. And having got hold it would not let go. In trying to shake it off, Mr. Privett very nearly brought the hat-stand down on top of himself.

It was the noise that brought Mrs. Privett out of the scullery.

" It's no good losing your temper like that," she said as she came forward. " You'll only smash something."

But she had spoken too late. The last jerk that Mr. Privett had given the bicycle dislodged the small potted palm that stood on the centre shelf of the hat-stand. It rolled along the floor, its leaves swishing.

Mrs. Privett did not move. She stood there surveying the mess, and drew the corners of her mouth down as she looked.

" I'm sorry . . ." Mr. Privett began, and bent down to begin picking up the pieces.

But Mrs. Privett would have none of it.

" Don't you start trying to tidy up," she said, " or we'll have everything else smashed. I'll attend to this."

She pushed past while she was speaking, and held the front door open for him. Mr. Privett sidled carefully through, drawing the long awkward trailer after him. Then when he had got safely over the doorstep he paused and looked back.

" If Gus should turn up, tell him I've gone on, will you? " he asked.

But there was no answer. Mrs. Privett simply slammed the door in his face.

That was at 10.35.

And less than half an hour later—at 10.57 to be precise—Mr. Privett had returned. He was on foot. He was torn. He was dusty. He was bloodstained. Beside him he supported a buckled bicycle. And in the partially demolished trailer behind rode the wrecked remains of *Daisy II*.

57

At the sight of her husband, so badly damaged and so woe-begone, Mrs. Privett's anger vanished instantly. She became wife, nurse and mother. And Mr. Privett surrendered himself. Seated in the arm-chair in the kitchen and with his feet up on the fender he allowed her to bathe his poor bruised forehead, and tried manfully to tell her what had happened.

The facts were certainly terrifying enough. Death, it was clear, had been avoided by inches. Possibly by as little as one inch. As far as the end of Fewkes Road, everything had been quiet and normal. Admittedly, Mr. Privett may have been pedalling a shade too fast, because all the way from No. 23 he had been haunted by fears of lateness, of missing the first heats. The road, however, had been empty and deserted. But there is a world of difference between the inner-suburban quietness of Fewkes Road and the arterial throb of the main thoroughfare that joins Camden Town to Highgate. The Kentish Town Road, though narrow, is important. The traffic in it is fast-flowing and imperious. Even on Sunday mornings there are motor cycles, cars, lorries, buses, trolley-buses, coaches. And it was a coach that had been Mr. Privett's undoing.

Enormous, stream-lined, decorated in white and chromium like an ice-cream parlour, it had borne down upon him from the King's Cross direction, bound importantly north for Bradford. Mr. Privett had seen it coming. He had observed the lighthouse-like headlamps, the bizarre savagery of the frontal design, the driver perched high in his glass cubicle. Mr. Privett had seen all that. And there had still been time, he reckoned, to cut across. Nippiness, in his view was what had been demanded of him. Nothing more . . . Indeed, as he had explained to the policeman, was it likely that anyone in his senses would risk putting up a bicycle and trailer against something that looked as if it could successfully have rammed the *Queen Elizabeth*?

It was merely the near-side mudguard that had touched him. A mere nip. But it was enough. With a single flick it had ripped up the trailer, and sent Mr. Privett flying into the gutter, his bicycle on top of him.

The crowd that collected magically, as though by bush telegraph, had been visibly edified. It was agreed that it was a miracle that Mr. Privett had not been killed. But by the time the driver of the coach had come back and someone had found a policeman, the entire perspective of the episode had begun to alter. Mr. Privett was still in the principal role. But the role itself had changed disturbingly. He was no longer the object of misery and compassion, the tragic victim of circumstances. He had become someone who was sinister and malign, a saboteur of immense coaches. The policeman had stationed himself close beside Mr. Privett as if to forestall lynching . . .

But Mrs. Privett could bear to hear no more. She told him not to exhaust himself further with conversation and helped him upstairs to the bedroom. Then, swift and masterful, she took off the nautical-type jacket. Stripped him right down. Popped him into bed. He was to stay there, she said, until she had fetched the doctor.

Mr. Privett felt better already. The anguish, the sense of shame, the pain even, had all ebbed out of him. In their place flowed in warmth, love, security. He felt at peace with the world.

Then suddenly he remembered something. He jerked himself up in bed.

" Do you think somebody ought to go along and tell Gus? " he asked. " If he's up there waiting, he'll be wondering what's happened to me."

CHAPTER VII

MONDAY, of course, was entirely out of the question. Mrs. Privett had to ring up Rammell's and explain. Nor was it easy. The last thing that she wanted was to get caught up in a long rigmarole about toy boats. A *cycling accident* was how she described it.

The doctor was dubious about the rest of the week as well. No man of Mr. Privett's age, he said, can run slap into a motor-coach and expect to feel the same afterwards. It was a wonder, he added, that no bones had been broken.

But even if Mr. Privett's skeleton was still intact, the rest of him soon began to show the effects of that header into the gutter. What revealed itself at first merely as a mild brownish discoloration developed rapidly into a whole pattern of bruises shot through with vivid colours like a sunset. They became magnificent. Sensational. Gratifying.

Whenever Mrs. Privett slipped out of the room for a moment, Mr. Privett would slide back the bedclothes and, going over to the long mirror in the wardrobe, would stand with his pyjama jacket held open admiring himself.

2

The accident brought out everything that was best in Irene. The sight of Mr. Privett lying there, pathetically small among the pillows, made her want to cry. She felt sorry that she had ever been beastly to her father.

And that was just as well. Because it was on that same Monday that Rammell's wrote to Irene. The letter was there on the door-mat, along with a postcard from the M.R.Y.O.A.—the Model Racing Yacht Owners' Association—reminding Mr. Privett that next week's rally was at the Round Pond in Kensington Gardens.

Naturally, Mrs. Privett recognised the Rammell letter the instant she saw it. It was the embossed " R " on the back of the envelope that gave it away. And even before she had turned it over she was certain that it would be for Irene.

But it wasn't to Irene that she took it. Not immediately, that is. First she showed it to Mr. Privett.

" There! " she said triumphantly. " It's come."

Mr. Privett, however, was only half awake.

" Give it to me," he said. " Let's have it."

And then, having inspected it carefully, he looked up at her. " That's it," he said. " It's from Rammell's all right."

The back of Mr. Privett's hand bore a large criss-cross of sticking plaster. And, at the sight of it, Mrs. Privett's heart leapt. She realised suddenly that Mr. Privett's accident was a blessing. Downright providential. It could not have been timed more perfectly. Because up to that moment she hadn't quite known how Irene was going to take the letter. As it was, everything would be simple.

". . . and with your father in that state," she told her, " we can't do anything to upset him. He knows it's come because he's seen it. Just you open it. I want to know what it says."

But Irene was only half-awake, too. She was still flushed with sleep. And a bit sulky.

" Oh, you open it, Mum," she said. " I can't be bothered."

Using one of Irene's own nail files, Mrs. Privett ripped it open. And having read it through once, she read it over again just to make sure that she hadn't missed anything.

It told Irene to present herself at the staff entrance in Hurst Place at three o'clock next Friday. There was even a little map at the top right-hand corner of the notepaper with an arrow pointing to the staff entrance so that she couldn't go wrong.

In addition to the appointment letter itself, Irene was asked to bring along her school-leaving certificate and a copy of the same certificate made out in her own handwriting for the Rammell files. The bit about the files was, however, only a half truth. It was the handwriting rather than the copy that Rammell's wanted. Rammell's had been caught out before by young ladies who couldn't for the life of them make out a bill that anyone in the counting house was able to decipher.

Mrs. Privett suddenly stiffened. Friday at three the letter said. That in itself was a challenge. It gave Mrs. Privett precisely three and a half days in which to get things ready. And it would be touch and go. She had just remembered that Irene hadn't got anything that was suitable for a staff interview.

There was the plain blue dress that she had worn for the Eleanor Atkinson school-leaving party. But that was too simple. Too plainly cut. It would make Rammell's underrate Irene. Regard her as no more than some sort of infant apprentice. Then there was her flowered one with the short sleeves. But that was completely wrong. It would give the Staff Supervisor the impression that Irene wasn't really serious. Only a sort of socialite playgirl from Kentish Town. Of course, there was always Irene's brown. But Irene, heaven knows why, had never really liked it. And in any case it was old. That settled it. Because the one thing for which Mrs. Privett would never have forgiven herself would have been to send Irene along looking as if she actually *needed* the job.

There was clearly nothing for it, therefore, but to run up something. Nothing was ever made, or sewn, or stitched together in the Privett household. It was always run up. And Mrs. Privett was taking no chances. She went herself to the newsagents. In the result, copies of *Woman*, *Woman's Own* and little paper envelopes stamped with the names of Butterick, Simplicity and McCall were mingled with sheets of magenta-coloured note-paper bearing Irene's own idea of what a dress ought to look like. It was getting on for evening before a compromise was reached.

Then, first thing on the Tuesday, Mrs. Privett dashed out to Daniels' in the Kentish Town Road to buy the material. One way or another, she bought quite a lot of stuff at Daniels'. She was a valued customer. But she was never able to admit to Mr. Privett that she so much as went near the place. That was because, at the first whisper of anything like a dress length, Mr. Privett would have told her to leave it all to him. Then, with the air of someone engaged on counter-espionage, he would have given her a trade card with somebody else's name—that of Rammell's wholesale buyer— on the front, and the name of some wholesaler or other pencilled across the back. And eventually she would find herself at a counter in a side lane somewhere off St. Paul's Churchyard, hemmed in by people buying great cascades of damask and velvet and gold brocade which would make her three and a half yards of cheap cretonne sound silly anyway. It was to avoid all this fuss that Mrs. Privett made a point of never telling her husband when she was buying anything. What she lost by way of trade discount, she made up in peace of mind.

The dress that Mrs. Privett finally made for Irene was from an American pattern called Miss Manhattan. Mrs. Privett was secretly very pleased with it. It had a certain discreet flair. Irene, however, disliked every single thing about it. In her view it was all too young-looking. It was distinctly teen-age. But it was late on Thursday by now. There wasn't time to do anything about it. And in any case mother and daughter were scarcely speaking to each other. Mrs. Privett had said twice already that next time Irene found herself in need of a new dress she had better try running one up for herself. And Irene had replied that every other girl she knew got hers ready-made.

That was the last straw. It was one of Mrs. Privett's proudest boasts that up to now nothing ready-made except winter overcoats had ever come into her house.

3

Irene was a bit disappointed with the back view of Rammell's. Something seemed to have gone wrong somewhere. It was as though the firm had overspent itself badly on the Bond Street frontage. Been forced to cut down on everything, even essentials, by the time it got round to Hurst Place. Compared with all the burnished copper and the embossed " R's " of the main doorway, the staff entrance itself was no better than a gap in the brickwork. There wasn't even a porch to it. Just a metal shutter that came down sealing everything off at night.

And inside things weren't much better. At the top of a little flight of concrete steps stood the clocking-in machines. It was like an Underground platform but without the advertisements. Then, again, the colour scheme was all wrong. The dark green dado with the thick black line along the top of it had an unpleasant police station sort of look. It might have led straight through to the cells instead of merely to the evening bags and the cosmetics.

Irene suddenly felt sorry for her father to think that he had been coming in and out of such a doorway all his life. Whenever she had been to Rammell's before, she had gone in by the Bond Street entrance and straight up in the lift. And there had been her father dressed up in his tail-coat as if he were receiving guests at a wedding. That was what she had imagined it was like everywhere inside Rammell's—all mirrors and satinwood panelling and thick Wilton pile.

There was a notice marked " Inquiries " just in front of her. Below it was a sheet of plain glass that suggested the front of an aquarium. And as Irene went over to it, the glass front silently slid back. She almost expected a cascade of cold water and pond-weed to come splashing down over her new stockings. But that must have been simply the effect of so much dark green paint and the subdued lighting.

And in a glass-eyed, fishy sort of way the man behind the desk tried his best to be friendly. As soon as he saw the official interview form, he pointed to the foot of a further flight of stairs. The stairs, Irene noticed, were plain concrete like the corridor. Straight up to the third floor and knock on the door, he said. The name " Supervisor " was on the outside, and it was the third floor up. Three floors, and she'd see the notice on the door. There'd be no mistaking it because it said " Supervisor " . . . He went on saying it over and over again, and then withdrew into his aquarium, gasping visibly because of all the neat oxygen that he had just been inhaling.

Suddenly there was another transformation. Irene recognised it as soon as she was shown into the Supervisor's room. This wasn't Rammell's at all. Irene was back inside the Eleanor Atkinson once more. The woman, who glanced up as soon as she came in and then ignored her after she had sat down, was like every headmistress that Irene had ever known. She might have been the last descendant of a long line of them.

The desk was rather small as desks go. And very neat. There was one little wooden cup for the paper-clips and another for the pins. In between them stood an ink-stand with red ink on one side and blue-black on the other. There was a large blotter and a small calendar.

Miss Townsend was now ready for Irene. She looked up with a smile that was perfect except that it gave the appearance of having been used too many times before. She certainly knew her job, how-ever. There was the expertness that comes of having done exactly the same thing over and over again for years. Folding her white, very nicely manicured hands in front of her as though about to open the proceedings with a prayer, and still with that exhausted, played-out smile crinkling up the corners of her eyes, she addressed Irene.

"There is one question that we laike to ask all our gairls," she said. "What is it that made you decaide on Rammell's? Hed you always plenned your laife thet way?"

And from the way Miss Townsend put the question it was obvious that nothing less than a complete nun-like sense of vocation was going to satisfy her. Irene shuddered as she remembered the row there had been in Fewkes Road to get her here at all. If she had said one word against Rammell's to Miss Townsend, the little room would probably have had to be reconsecrated.

"Well, you see," she began. "My father's always been here. So naturally . . ."

There was no need, however, for her to go on any further. By now the Staff Supervisor was fairly beaming. She was like a stained-glass window that had suddenly been lit brightly from behind. At any moment it seemed possible that the window might come round and kiss her. There wasn't even any trouble about the handwriting of the carefully copied out certificate. In her present mood Miss Townsend would have been satisfied if Irene had chipped it out in cuneiform.

"Oh, I see," she said approvingly. "We wraite a very naice, neat little hend, doan't we?"

And at the first mention of "we," Irene wondered why there had ever been any fuss about Miss Manhattan at all. She might just as well have turned up wearing her old nigger-brown school uniform with the sub-prefect's stripe. She would have felt more at home in it.

"Now, doan't worry. You'll be hearing from us," Miss Townsend assured her. "It may take a little taime, but thet's quaite all raight. We know all about you neow."

Irene felt that she knew all about them, too. There was no escape now. She was practically on the staff already. It had all happened just the way Mr. and Mrs. Privett had always planned it. The doors of the prison-house . . .

CHAPTER VIII

A NEW MAN had just come into Marcia's life. Thrust his way right in, in fact.

There was, indeed, no other way in which he could possibly have got there. He wasn't the sort of man that Marcia would ever have admitted on her own account. Really quite unthinkable. And so common, too. Common in the bluff, hearty way that she particularly disliked in men. He had called her " sweetheart " the first time they had been introduced—at a Latin-American fashion night at Grosvenor House. She had, of course, ignored him. Had simply turned her long beautiful back, and moved slowly, undulatingly away, leaving him sitting there gaping after her.

But it had been impossible to be as cold as that the next time they met. And on the very next morning, too. Because by then he was going round arm in arm with Rammell's chief buyer, nudging him, winking at him, telling him little stories. And the chief buyer was treating him with all the indulgence that would have been shown to a visiting ambassador.

Not that Marcia at first had even recognised the man. He had been wearing tails and a white tie the last time she had seen him. And in tails every rather fattish man of about fifty looks pretty much the same. It is as much a uniform as a bus conductor's. It is only by day that these white-tie people become individuals again.

For instance, the man whose arm was now linked through the chief buyer's, was wearing a brown suit and a bow-tie. He didn't look as if he could ever have worn tails in his life. There was something remorselessly provincial about him. Something that suggested black puddings and Handel's " Messiah " sung lustily and bashed into subjection in some huge local corn exchange. Marcia had no recollection of ever having seen him before.

The barbarian, however, recognised Marcia immediately. He came forward. And he asked after her feet. His own were terrible, he said, because of all that dancing. Then finding that she did not

66

know who he was—and the simple fact of this seemed somehow to amuse him—he introduced himself. He was Neptune Swimsuits, he explained. Also Daffette Fabrics and Medici Brassières and Red Tag nylons.

He just stood there reeling the names out, and watching what effect they had on her. Nor was he disappointed. Marcia was a sensible girl. She could see now that it didn't matter a bit his being so provincial. There comes a point when success is the only thing that really matters. And this big, red-faced man with the dreadful spotted tie was obviously nothing if not successful. Besides, Marcia had always prided herself on not being a snob where manufacturers were concerned.

All the same, Mr. Bulping—she remembered now having seen the name all over the place—was a bit disconcerting. He was so breath-takingly prompt. He sent her a little tribute that same afternoon. Not that he could have been about much. Or he would have known that nobody ever sends orchids nowadays. The mere sight of so many of them made her feel terrible. Like some ghastly left-over Gaiety Girl. And they showed, too, that Mr. Bulping couldn't really be even the least bit sensitive. If he had been, he would have recognised that orchids went with a more flamboyant type altogether.

But having received such a token there was nothing to do but to say thank you. Accordingly, Marcia had written to Mr. Bulping in her big backward sloping script, using a J-nib to give character to the handwriting. And that had provided him with her telephone number.

From then on the calls were incessant. Simply incessant. They didn't even cease when Mr. Bulping was called away up north to look after Neptune and Daffette and Medici and Red Tag and all the rest of them. It was worse, in fact. Because the farther away Mr. Bulping was from her the more unavoidable he became. He booked personal long-distance calls. And to make sure of catching her he put them through very late at night or early in the morning. At Marcia's end it was overwhelming. Like being courted by Mr. Bulping and the Postmaster-General both at the same time.

And in the result, she was finally trapped. Unable to resist the keen northern pressure any longer, she succumbed. She promised to have dinner with him when he was down on Tuesday.

Naturally, he had offered to pick her up at her flat. She was prepared for that. She refused. For years now she had been avoiding anything of the kind. The last thing she wanted was to have a large enthusiastic male advancing into the tiny living-room, and bearing down on her with that dreadful expectant expression that all men wore on such occasions.

There would have been something too horrible about it. Whereas there was nothing in the least horrible about arriving at The Chalice. The only thing that surprised her was that Mr. Bulping should ever have heard of The Chalice. She had imagined that Park Lane and Piccadilly were about as much of London as Mr. Bulping would possibly have known. And it wasn't as though The Chalice was even right in the centre of things. Too far down at the wrong end of Duke Street for that. But select. Beautifully exclusive and select. Royalty and ambassadors and four-star generals dined there. Marcia always felt perfectly at home the moment she stepped on to the zebra-striped carpet between that long double row of mirrors.

Mr. Bulping was there waiting for her. And in a dinner jacket he looked considerably better again. The brown suit and bow tie faded from her memory. Looked at closely, too, she could see his face was really rather a fine one. There was strength in it. And purpose. He was the sort of a man who might just have bought a railway. She found herself wondering what he would have looked like without his moustache. . . .

But even though his behaviour was quite good, it was still not perfect. For a start, sitting up on the high stool in the discreet corner bar, he called the barman " Charley. " There was something so frankly vulgar, so bank-holidayish about it that Marcia shivered. And he had such a positive way of eating potato crisps. He munched them noisily like a schoolboy, perpetually thrusting out his great red hand for more. But what was worse, far worse, was the fact that he tried to patronise her.

" Best food in London here," he said between crunches.

Marcia smiled faintly. In this week's *Tatler* there was a picture of her sitting at her favourite table in the corner.

" A matter of fact I came to the opening," she said.

Mr. Bulping patted the back of her hand affectionately.

" Changed a lot since then," he told her. " Only place in London if you want a steak."

" I adore steak," Marcia replied politely.

But Mr. Bulping wasn't going to let it go at that.

" Don't have to have steak if you don't want it," he told her.
" Plenty of other things. Better have a look down the menu before
you make your mind up."

There was that quick, involuntary shiver again. She hoped
that Mr. Bulping hadn't noticed. But really his pronunciation
of the word was appalling. Simply appalling. It must be twenty
years since she had last been out with anyone who called it "meenu."

And she didn't like it any better when Emilio himself came
over. He greeted her very politely, and there was a lot of rather
professional Italian handshaking. But it was clearly Mr. Bulping
whom he was really pleased to see. And he seemed to know all about
him, too. He asked after his golf, his fishing, his race-horses. He
lit Mr. Bulping's cigarette for him. Then when Mr. Bulping had
finished both drinks and had patted his chest to show how fine he
was feeling, Emilio paid them the last courtesy. Waving the
manager, the head waiter, the assistant head waiter and the reception waiter all to one side, he conducted them to their table himself.

" Your table, Mr. Bulping," he said.

It was the corner table that Marcia had always thought of as
hers.

" Thanks, Emmy," Mr. Bulping said.

Marcia was rather silent during the meal. But Mr. Bulping
did not seem at all put out by the fact. Having come out to enjoy
himself, it was obvious that nothing was going to stop him. He
was good company enough for two. He ordered champagne.
He told funny stories. He insisted on caviare. He gave Marcia
his views on price controls. He called the waiter over, and said :
" Here, Charley, see what's 'appening to our steak. We 'aven't got
all night you know." He sent the toast back. He promised Marcia
that, if she'd give him her measurements, he'd send her a Neptune
swimsuit that wouldn't be on the market until next year. He said
that she ought to eat more. He blew his nose loudly. He mopped
his forehead. He demanded crêpes-suzettes. He asked what scent
she was wearing. He mopped the back of his neck. He bought a
packet of Turkish cigarettes and invited her to fill her case with
them. He unbuttoned. He asked the waiter to leave the Armagnac
bottle on the table. He lit a cigar. He began to tell her about his
oldest boy. . . .

69

Marcia wasn't really listening to him. She often withdrew into a dim, private world of her own while people were talking to her. But at least she was thinking about him. Thinking hard. There was a splendid self-confidence that she found rather stimulating. She could see now why the North Midlands usually feels such a contempt for London and the South. It was purely a matter of vitality. He had a way of looking round the room, taking her in as he glanced about him, that suggested that at any moment now he was ready to put in a take-over bid.

Then came that awful shiver again. And really this was too frightful. Because Mr. Bulping was banging with his spoon on the side of his coffee cup.

" Check, Charley," he called out loudly.

Marcia had her thank-you-so-much-for-a-lovely-dinner speech all ready by the time they got to the front door. But Mr. Bulping only laughed at her.

" What's the matter? " he asked. " Don't you like me? "

They were outside on the pavement by now, and Mr. Bulping's car came across the road to meet them. Marcia gathered her evening cloak around her. She stood there motionless, her hands clasped beneath her chin. It was one of her most beautiful attitudes.

But Mr. Bulping apparently hadn't noticed.

" Well, get in," he told her. " Let's go somewhere where we can dance."

It was as she climbed in that Marcia realised that she was lost. Nobody had ever really treated her like this before. She had come out, beautiful, distinguished, aloof, and now she was being rushed off her feet like a schoolgirl by this commercial gorilla from Wolverhampton. Either she was losing her grip, or it was Destiny.

A large, hot hand descended on her knee. " Show you the sights," Mr. Bulping said.

And still with his hand resting there as though the girls he took out naturally expected that kind of thing, he leant forward to speak to the chauffeur.

" Ivory Tower, " he said. " Make it snappy."

And the very fact that it was the Ivory Tower at all was provoking. Because Marcia had never been to the Ivory Tower before. Out of the whole score of night clubs where the manager would have come forward smiling, bowing from the hips, delighted to see her there again, Mr. Bulping had chosen the one place where she knew no one. It was so humiliating that she could have cried.

But once they got there it was all right. The first person they met was a young peer who had taken her out once or twice himself. She felt her poise returning as she introduced him. But somehow Mr. Bulping didn't seem to be impressed. Hardly seemed to notice in fact. He was talking over his shoulder to the waiter. " Usual table, Charley," he was saying. " And put a bottle in the bucket."

Not that they sat at the table very much. Mr. Bulping was a keen dancer. And a remarkably energetic one. When he got on to the floor he liked to remain there. They were right up against the band the first time it stopped, and Mr. Bulping looked up indignantly. " Come along, Charley," he said to the band leader. " What's the matter with you? Give us a number."

But the worse thing about the dancing was Mr. Bulping's heat. He seemed to be in a raging fever, as though she had caught up with him in the middle of a malaria bout. It was like dancing with a large hot-water bottle. The perspiration was fairly streaming off him by now. And he came of a school that holds its partners very closely. She suffered the sensation of being crushed to death in a tropic jungle. If the band had been armed with blow-pipes instead of saxophones it could not have been more terrifying. Marcia felt herself swaying.

" Tired, dear? " Mr. Bulping asked. " Why not go back to your place? "

Mr. Bulping looked larger than ever inside the tiny flat. And more possessive. It was like having the landlord to tea. He reminded her vaguely of her first father-in-law, the one who had bred short-horns. But what she hadn't been prepared for was Mr. Bulping's pipe. Without warning, without even having asked her permission, he suddenly brought it out, charred and sordid-looking, and was sitting there in her small boudoir chair, smoking as comfortably as if he had been in some bar-parlour in the Midlands. Not quite so comfortably perhaps. Because the chair was about two sizes too small for him. The arms creaked and bent outwards every time he crossed his legs.

And Marcia simply didn't know what to do with him. She had been prepared for, expecting, dreading, hoping for—she was tired, and her emotions were becoming a bit confused by now—something

71

entirely uninhibited the moment the front door closed after them. If he had broken two or three of her ribs in a passionate hug on the doormat she would not have been surprised. Or asked her to sit on his knee. Or become sentimental, and started kissing her hand. Anything, in fact, but this.

". . . mind you, there's no point in rushing it," he was saying, as though she were a meeting of the Neptune Swimsuit board. " The law's got to take its time, and the case doesn't come up until next session. That's why I've got to be so careful. But after September it'll be different. I shall be a free man again. And it isn't as if I 'adn't got something to offer. I 'aven't been doing so badly lately . . ."

From the hearthrug Marcia looked up at him. This was another of her poses, hands folded in her lap and her head turned three-quarters away from the camera to show the neck line.

" I don't know why you're telling me all this, Mr. Bulping," she said quietly.

But that was where Mr. Bulping was so masterful and disarming. He didn't allow a girl even to have any nice feelings of her own. Extricating himself from the flimsy boudoir chair and putting his pipe down on the polished satinwood table alongside the Dresden Shepherdess, he came over to her.

" Yes, you do," he said. " You're not daft."

And when she spread out her hands appealingly he caught hold of her wrists and pulled her up.

" Let's 'ave a kiss," he said.

And then Marcia knew that all her premonitions had been correct. His arms were right round her. One second longer and it would be the spine as well as the ribs that would be giving way under the pressure of this sex-starved Napoleon from Wolverhampton.

CHAPTER IX

Mr. PRIVETT was back at Rammell's again. But the doctor had been quite right. Three full days in bed. And then two more pottering round the house, simply sitting about in chairs and reading the paper. It meant one full week away from Bond Street. And what was so hurtful was that Mr. Bloot totally ignored him. Seemed unaware that anything had even happened to his friend.

That was why it felt so good, so reassuring, to be seated beside him again. Mr. Bloot was sympathetic but mysterious. Said he'd been busy and he hadn't heard. There, during the eleven o'clock break, Mr. Privett had to tell him everything. And Mr. Bloot, hot and flushed from the strong Indian tea that he was drinking, ran his handkerchief across his forehead and listened.

But, even though he was sympathetic, he seemed somehow to be disapproving as well. For when Mr. Privett had finished Mr. Bloot only frowned and shook his head.

" Yurss, I know," he said. " But it's bad just the same. Doesn't do to get mixed up with the police. Not men in our position. Cahn't afford it. Bahnd to leak aht in the long run."

As soon as he had finished speaking, he shook his head again. He had assumed the air of immense authority of a man who has studied the effects of even quite casual encounters with authority, and has been shocked and chastened by what he has seen. Mr. Privett felt a small cold rivulet of fear running down his spine.

" But there hasn't been a summons or anything like that," he explained hurriedly. " They only took down a few particulars. It isn't as if anybody had been killed. I probably shan't never hear from them again. Never."

Mr. Bloot thrust out his nether lip.

" Yur'll 'ear all right," he said. " Yur mark my words. Yur'll 'ear."

Then came that ominous head shake once more, and Mr. Privett glanced up nervously at the clock. It now showed 11.15. That meant that it was time for both Mr. Bloot and Mr. Privett to be getting back to their particular floors. Mr. Privett got stiffly to his feet.

But Mr. Bloot stopped him.

" Wot yur need," he said, prodding into Mr. Privett's side with his forefinger to emphasise the significance of the remark, " is er solicitor. That's what yur need. Er solicitor. Someone to represent yur. Yur didn't ought to have come back down into the shop at all. What yur ought to do is to walk straight out of here now, and find a solicitor before it's too late." Mr. Bloot paused. He was breathing heavily again. " But yur'd better make some inquiries first," he went on. " A divorce lawyer wouldn't help yur. Or a police court man. What yur need is er naccident specialist. The others'd be worse than no one."

Another small, icy drop ran down Mr. Privett's spine. It seemed that whichever way he turned he was faced by dangers. So, both to bring the conversation to an end and to keep up his own spirits, he tried to pooh-pooh the whole affair.

" I don't want no solicitor," he said. " It's making too much of it."

But Mr. Bloot would allow none of that.

" Wot about your counter-claim? " he demanded.

" My what? "

Mr. Bloot pursed his lips. He was really at the top of his form by now. Immense. Knowledgeable. Majestic.

" Yur want a new boat, don't yur? " he asked. " Oo d'yur think's going to pay for that? Yur or the motor-coach company? And how much d'yer think yur'd get out of the motor-coach company if yur wrote to them yurself? Nothing. They probably wouldn't even answer. But if it's ur solicitor. He'd take 'em in Court if they didn't. And there's damages, too." Mr. Bloot's eyes went misty and unfocused for a moment at the thought of the huge, almost unassessable damages that were Mr. Privett's simply for the asking. " Properly 'andled this ought to be worth 'undreds to yur. Literally 'undreds. But only if your solicitor gets in first."

Mr. Privett was silent for a moment.

" You're quite right," he said at last. " I see that now. I'd better do something about it."

He was ashamed, bitterly ashamed, to think how he had misjudged Mr. Bloot. At first, he had seemed merely off-hand. Disinterested. Even callous. Some of the time he had not appeared

74

to be listening at all, just sitting there concentrating on his tea. But that had only been Mr. Bloot's way. Because all the while he had been really worrying about his friend, working out wonderful schemes for him. Mr. Privett saw now that he owed a duty to his family. It was Mr. Bloot who had opened his eyes for him.

2

Mr. Privett, however, was only half right. In point of fact, Mr. Bloot had not been listening all the time. For the greater part of it, indeed, he had been thinking of someone else. It was his own love-affair that was absorbing him. It now obliterated every-thing. It had become obsessional.

It had not been an instantaneous flare-up, a sudden and compulsive affair of passion. Mr. Bloot had known the lady for some time. And, at least in the early stages, there had been nothing particularly romantic or tempestuous about their friendship. Simply a slow middle-aged ripening. A late Septemberish, even Octoberish affair. What had begun as no more than an exchange of retail courtesies across a shop counter had gradually softened into something gentler, with Mr. Bloot lingering helplessly at the counter after the transaction was over. The good-byes had, indeed, lately become almost meaninglessly protracted. For whole minutes on end the two of them would just stand there, not even speaking, merely looking at each other.

There may, of course, have been hidden fires on her side before even the first spark began to show. Certainly the lady had been kind to him. It was something to have been able to drop into the little tobacconist's at any time during those terrible war years, and come out with ten perfectly good Players, when the rest of London was smoking unheard-of makes that might still have been all right in Cairo or Stamboul but smelt distinctly out of place in Tufnell Park.

It may, of course, have been Mr. Bloot's good looks that had done it. His good looks and the natural distinction of his manner. He was easily the most imposing customer to patronise the tiny shop. Because no matter what allowances you were ready to make for its central position—next door to the Underground and exactly

75

opposite the bus stop—the shop was undeniably an extremely small one. Even pokey. Only half a shop, in fact. It had been scooped out of a frontage that still accommodated the collection office of a laundry. And the name H. FLORENCE over one side of the entrance had necessarily been lettered in the most slender and attenuated of scripts in order to get the full word in.

But what made the shop seem smaller still was the size of H. Florence herself. A large woman against any background, she seemed positively effulgent within the confines of this minute cubicle. Instead merely of occupying the shop, she seemed rather to be wearing it.

Mr. Bloot would have found it impossible to say what it was about Hetty Florence that had first overwhelmed him. Possibly the voice, that was still warm and caressing even when sending casuals and other wartime shop crawlers away from the shop totally unserved. Or the perfume that she used—a thick musky scent that conjured up visions of palm trees and bright moonlight after scorching sun. Or her hair—jet black and worn long, wound round the top of her head in a braid as thick as a ship's hawser. Or the white roundness of her bosom which showed up so provocatively beneath the open lacework jumpers that she always wore. Or the startling redness of her nails.

It may, of course, have been simply that the natural charms of Hetty Florence were all accentuated by contrast. Because poor Emmie had been quite the other type—small, thinnish, practically Chinese she was so flat-chested, and with hair that was mole-coloured and rather thin.

Whatever it was about Hetty Florence, the effect was over-whelming. Mr. Bloot now spent whole evenings thinking about her, dreamed shameless scarlet dreams that startled him, woke up only to start thinking about her afresh. Even the simple fact of separation was now agony. That was why he had come to the helpless, but still daring, decision to see her to-night even though it was only Tuesday, and he had six of Monday's packet still left.

As it happened, he could not have chosen a worse night. The store had never been busier. And he seemed to be the nerve-centre, the information-desk, of the whole place. "Outsize ladies' gowns, Mod'm, second floor "; " Plastic picnic-ware, third floor through

Household and Kitchen Utensils, Mod'm "; " Groceries, Mod'm, next shop through the archway "; " Grand pianos, end lift please, Mod'm, third floor turn right " . . . his diction remained perfect. But his mind was reeling. And all the time he was thinking: " Am I going to be too late to catch her? If she's gone, what'll I do? how can I wait till Wednesday? "

When five-thirty came, he didn't stop to say good night to anybody. Simply marched to his locker, changed out of his tails and snatched up his hat and umbrella. By the time he had reached the street, he was walking level with everyone else. And that, for Mr. Bloot, was hurrying. In his own mind, he was practically running.

If he was to see Hetty at all he had got to be there in Tufnell Park by six sharp. He realised now that he ought to have asked Mr. Preece if he could have left a little early. Say a mere five minutes. Or ten, to be on the safe side. But he hadn't felt able to screw up the courage. How could he have gone along and said: " Please may I leave at five-twenty this evening? I am a widower, aged fifty-seven, sixteen stone two, and helplessly in love. Somewhere in N. 19 there is a magnet that draws me irresistibly, a flame that compels me to it. I am steel. I am a moth. I must go . . ."

As it was, he looked like being in the Underground all night. There was the rush-hour at Bond Street to begin with. Then, at Tottenham Court Road, London Transport simply turned against him. First one Edgware train, and then another. By the time he had shoved his way into the train marked Barnet—and there was no old-world courtesy about him by now: he was barging and elbowing with the rest—the clock showed ten to six.

And when he got there it was all just as he had feared. The other half of Hetty's shop, the laundry collection office, was still open. Inside they were doing something with hampers. But on Hetty's side the shutters were already down. It might have been Bank holiday, they looked so closed. Mr. Bloot just stood there staring at them, his chest heaving. And then, even though he knew that it was useless, he started ringing at the bell.

It was when he had rung it for the second time that he thought he heard some sort of movement inside. A noise too faint to be identified. But he could not be sure. There was too much clatter from the traffic for him to be sure of anything.

Nevertheless, a strange feeling came over him. Something told him that Hetty was still there. Still there, only not opening the door. And a sudden panic took possession of him. Perhaps something was the matter. Perhaps she had gone back for a moment after locking up and had fainted. Perhaps at this moment she was lying there in pain and had been trying to make him hear, vainly struggling to attract attention . . .

So he did a desperate thing. Forsaking all appearances, he went down on one knee and put his mouth up against the letter-box in the middle of the roller-shutter.

" Yur there Hetty? " he asked. " Yur all raht? I's me, Gussie, Ah've come to see you. Ah'm sorry Ah'm so late."

He must have shouted rather louder than he realised. Because when he got up again, he saw that people were looking at him. Two children on the pavement had stopped incredulous, fascinated at the sight of a large man kneeling at a letter-box and apologising into it. The reception clerk at the laundry came round to her half of the doorway to see what was going on. But Mr. Bloot took no notice of any of them. What was happening behind the roller-shutter was far too momentous for that. For the noises were quite definite by now. Quick, busy little noises. The sound of boxes being dragged along and then shoved away somewhere. He even recognised the scraping, tinny sound as the curtain that cut off the back part of the shop was pulled along the rail on its brass curtain rings. Then he heard footsteps. Unmistakable, approaching footsteps. And the next moment there was the sound of a bolt being drawn back and the roller-shutter shot upwards. Hetty stood there.

She was flushed. And breathing rather hard, he noticed. But alive. My word, yes, alive. Alive as no other woman he had ever known was alive. At the mere sight of her he wanted to rush into her arms.

But, at first sight, Hetty Florence didn't seem to be any too pleased to see him.

" Well, I must say, you are a one," she told him. " Coming here at this time of night, and scaring me like that."

Mr. Bloot looked down at his feet for a moment.

" I didn't mean to," he said, quietly. " I . . . I only wanted to see you."

It was the fact that he was so humble, so contrite, that softened

78

her. There didn't seem any point in going on being angry with him.

"Oh, well, you'd better come inside to say it," she said.

As she was speaking, she caught sight of the two children and the laundry reception clerk.

"And hurry up, do," she told him. "You're just making an exhibition of yourself."

As Mr. Bloot stepped inside, she banged the shutter down again. He then realised that he was boxed up in the tiny shop with her. Their two bodies were practically touching.

"Well," she said.

"It's nothing important . . ."

"Isn't it?"

"Not reely. Ah just thought . . ."

He broke off, unable to continue. He felt confused. Foolish. Ashamed. But he need not have worried. If only he had been looking at Hetty instead of down at his feet again, he would have seen that she was holding out her arms to him.

"Kiss me," she said quietly.

And this was Mr. Bloot's undoing. He had not kissed seriously for over twenty years. There were two decades of passion to be released. He went straight for her lips. And he was surprised to find how soft and moist they were. When he finally released them nearly fifteen seconds later he uttered a deep, long, drawn-out "Aaah!"

The extraordinary thing, too, was that apparently Hetty felt just the same way about the kiss. Because instead of putting up her hands to protect herself she actually drew him forward towards her.

"Do that again," she said.

But this time, the strain, the tension, was too much for him. The kiss was all right. Even better than the first one. It was more full blooded. He felt her gasp beneath it. But his elbow had become caught on the little bracket that supported one of the shelves. There was a sharp ripping sound. Dummy packets of Craven 'A' and Gold Flake came raining down all over them. And worse. On the shelf as well there had been a stand holding fancy cigarette holders. Mr. Bloot tried hard to recover himself. As he did so, he heard beneath his feet the crunch of broken vulcanite, the grating of shattered imitation amber.

But he was past caring. His head was now on Hetty's bosom and he could even feel her heart-beats.

It was Hetty who spoke first.

" What d'you have to come and do this here for? " she asked. " What's wrong with my flat? "

CHAPTER X

THERE ARE some days that are sour and malignant from the early morning cup of tea onwards. Not necessarily wet days. Or very cold ones. Or days on which a major disaster, a calamity, occurs. Merely separate and isolatable chunks of existence in which the whole process of life suddenly presents itself as subtly hostile and sinister. Days when the Furies have moved in overnight.

Mr. Rammell's day, for instance. His digestion was even worse than usual. The first symptoms—a kind of mild sea-sickness—began to show up before his car had got even as far as Hyde Park Corner. He reached out instinctively for the bottle of dyspepsia tablets that he kept in one of the side pockets. And he was still chewing away like a G.I. by the time they reached Bond Street.

Then, when he got there, he found that there was no Miss Underhill. Only a telephone message to say that she was suffering from—of all things—a bilious attack. It was astonishing. To all appearances Miss Underhill had the innards of a goat. Indeed, before now, Mr. Rammell had frequently marvelled at her. Most busy secretaries, he knew, are inclined to be nibblers. But Miss Underhill was in a class by herself. She was in the habit of producing mysterious little pieces of milk chocolate out of her handbag almost as she sat down in the morning. While Mr. Rammell was sipping away at his hot water with a slice of lemon, Miss Underhill, surrounded by files and memoranda pads, would be busy lapping up a cupful of thick, creamy-looking breakfast cocoa.

It was certainly a master stroke on the part of the Furies, this bilious attack of Miss Underhill's. Because Mr. Rammell relied on Miss Underhill. Couldn't do a thing without her. He had tried hard enough. With that dark, intense, verse-drama student, Miss Winter, for example. But it hadn't worked. In sheer self-defence he had been forced to transfer Miss Winter and her gloom-tidings to another department. But her successor, Miss Lipscombe, was about as bad. In some respects, even worse. Alert, clear-cut and eager looking like a young Wren Commandant, and with hair cut very short to denote sexless and almost inhuman efficiency, she proved on closer acquaintance to be as nervous and jumpy as a kitten. A kitten, moreover, with a touch of the evil sprite and mad fairy thrown in. She sprang new surprises on him at five-minute intervals. She produced wrong documents by the basketful, and whisked away from under his nose the papers with which he was dealing, sending them down to Registry marked " Urgent ". It was like having a poltergeist about the place. And that was not all. She cut him off abruptly in the middle of important telephone conversations. She heard imaginary bells and voices. She would come darting into the room all sparkle and freshness to know if he wanted her. And then, when she was needed, she would disappear as completely as if she had handed in her resignation. She had, too, like Miss Winter, a highly developed sense of the dramatic. She could register the emotions—alarm, panic, remorse, consternation, bewilderment and the rest of them—simply by standing there in front of him, and saying nothing. It was all done by a quick intake of breath and clever use of the hands. R.A.D.A. would have given miss Lipscombe a gold medal at any time. And whenever Mr. Rammell saw the neat white shirt waist start heaving, he knew that out there in the mystery of the outer office something else that she hadn't told him about was going wrong as she stood there. Some message, dimly remembered for a passing moment, had passed clean out of her mind again for ever. Some urgent outgoing call had been remorselessly suppressed at source.

If she had come romping into the office blowing a tin trumpet and banging on a toy drum she could scarcely have got him jumpier. By 10.30 a.m. it was obvious that it was Mr. Rammell versus Miss Lipscombe, with Mr. Rammell hopelessly on the losing side.

And, as the day wore on, it became equally obvious that it was Mr. Rammell versus quite a lot of other people as well. A correspondence with the Board of Trade about carpets had produced the worst possible effect. In the result, some blasted Inspector from Whitehall was calling on the chief buyer that very afternoon to satisfy himself that all the other export-reject clauses were being properly administered. Then one of the Unions had discovered a technical breach in their agreement, and unless the Industrial

Relations Officer got down to some pretty heart-to-heart discussions with the Organising Secretary it looked as if all Rammell's vans would be off the streets by the following Monday. Two large consignments of American shoes had been held up by the Customs for a week already, and the way things were going they looked like remaining in bond for ever. By sheer mishandling at the Bond Street end, Rammell's had just lost a small but highly profitable contract with one of the better girls' schools. The licence for re-building the soft-furnishing section, the part that had been hit by an incendiary in '42 had just been turned down for the eleventh time. . . .

By the time Bond Street had closed down for the night, Mr. Rammell was a jumpy and exhausted man.

" Give up smoking," he told himself. " It's ridiculous. Simply killing myself. No digestion left. Sheer madness to go on with it. Can't imagine why I ever started. Wish Tony didn't. Cut it right out. . . ."

On and off, Mr. Rammell had been giving up smoking for the last twenty-five years. He had become an expert. He knew when he really meant to give it up—this was one of those occasions—and when he was merely telling himself that he meant to do so. He knew, too, about all the proprietary devices that help. The mouthwashes that make tobacco in all forms taste horrible. The injections. The little sugar-coated pills. He had even during some of his serious bouts of non-smoking tried playing at smoking instead —puffing away at imitation cigarettes. Things made of coltsfoot and herbs and dried dandelion. Little bundles of mixed weeds that reduced the inside of the mouth to a furnace and left the whole room smelling like Autumn.

Even so, from sheer force of habit he found himself with a lighted cigarette between his fingers as soon as he was inside the car. This annoyed him. He promptly stamped it out again. Then he told himself that it was not cigarettes that were the trouble, Cigarettes were nothing. Mere paper. Not so cigars. They were as dangerous as sticks of dynamite, those big Havanas of his. The sensible thing was to go on smoking cigarettes—in moderation of course—and cut out the cigars entirely. But that would be a pity. Because the pleasure of cigar smoking was something quite apart from all other smoking. Cigars belonged to the very highest order of things. As sex began to wane, the taste for a good cigar grew keener. Cigars were the one thing in life that had got better as a man grew older. Whereas he hadn't so much as properly tasted a cigarette for years. Just gone on smoking them one after another—forty a day—two hundred and eighty a week—and getting nothing from them in return.

But there was no point in being silly about it, in administering a shock to the system by giving up smoking altogether. Far more sensible to cut down on them gently. Thirty-five one day, thirty the next, twenty-five the day after, and so on. Stabilise the thing at ten or fifteen. Ten cigarettes a day had never harmed anyone. Satisfied that he was doing the right thing, Mr. Rammell brought out his case again and lit the first of the new ten. . . .

It was over a drink at his club that it occurred to Mr. Rammell that perhaps he ought to cut out drinking, too. Spirits particularly. No gin. No whisky. And easy on the sherry. Give his tummy time to settle down again. Then, when he was feeling really fit, he could start taking a little wine with his meals once more. Only the lighter wines at that. Stick to hock and claret. Leave the burgundies and the brandies alone for the time being.

By now practically a non-smoker and total abstainer, Mr. Rammell got into the car to go home. But the undeniable fact was that after a couple of whiskies he felt better already. Easier and freer all over. And it would clearly be absurd for any man to deny himself the very medicine that so obviously was good for him. He began to see things more clearly, get them into their proper perspective.

" It isn't smoking and it isn't drinking," he told himself. " It's over-work that's doing it. Too much of it. For too long. What I need is a holiday. Get right away from it all. Go somewhere quiet with Eleanor so that I can relax . . ."

As he said it, however, he realised how ridiculous it was. With a wife like Mrs. Rammell, there was no possible chance of relaxing. Mrs. Rammell was anti-relaxation. Ever since he had married her she had been growing steadily more tense and energetic. Talking louder and faster all the time. Sitting on more and more committees. Having nervous headaches. Being treated by more and more specialists. Rushing about from one party to another. Filling the house with hangers-on and acquaintances that he didn't even know by name. Fulfilling her own nervous and exhausting destiny.

"I'll go somewhere quiet this year even if I have to go alone," he promised himself. "My God, yes, that's what I'll do: I'll go off alone."

He put his feet up on the rest and settled himself firmly back against the cushions. At the mere thought of asserting himself, of walking out on Mrs. Rammell, even if only for a month in the summer, he began to feel stronger, more carefree.

But only for a moment. Already those two drinks that he had taken at the Club were boring holes inside him. It might have been nitro-glycerine that he had just swallowed. He could feel the drilling and blasting going on as he sat there.

"It's no use," he resumed. "I must watch myself. Must go carefully. Better skip dinner. Turn in early and try to get some rest. Haven't been sleeping properly. That's my trouble. One good early night, and I'll feel better in the morning."

2

"Darling!"

It was his wife's voice that had called him. And coming through from the hard, glazed walls of the bathroom on the other side of the interconnecting door, it sounded shriller and more metallic than ever. There was a note of urgency behind it that startled him.

"Yes, dear?" he said, aware how flat and weary his own voice sounded after the panic note in hers.

"What kept you?"

The door had opened by now, and Mrs. Rammell was standing there. She was undeniably a handsome woman. Tall, fine-limbed, distinguished looking. But distinctly unrestful. Too much of the race-horse about her. Even in the loose bathrobe that she was wearing there was something in the dark, observant eye, the distended nostril, that suggested the starting-gate and photo-finishes.

"Not . . . not going out anywhere, are we?" he asked.

But already Mrs. Rammell had turned her back on him. She was over at her dressing-table. And when he suddenly caught sight of her reflection in the mirror he could see that her face was now smeared all over with white stuff. It was like finding oneself married to a witch doctor.

85

"Don't say you've forgotten," she said.

She broke off for a moment because some of the cream had gone into her eye. There was a sudden grab for a tissue.

"It's Swami Lal," she continued, speaking indistinctly from behind the tissue. "That's why we're dining early."

Mr. Rammell felt the old, familiar trapped feeling returning to him.

"What time?" he asked.

"Seven-thirty."

Mr. Rammell braced himself.

"Think it'd matter if I don't show up?" he asked. "Feeling a bit under the weather. Thought I might turn in early."

From one of the drawers in the dressing-table Mrs. Rammell had suddenly produced a little rubber trowel and was violently smacking her own face with it.

Slap! Slap! "If you don't feel well," *Slap! Slap!* "of course, you ought to go to bed." *Slap! Slap!* "As a matter of fact," *Slap! Slap!* "I've got a raging headache myself." *Slap! Slap! Slap!*

There was a real viciousness about the last bout of slapping. Mr. Rammell winced as he heard it.

Mr. Rammell loosened his collar.

"Think if you don't mind . . ." he began.

But it was too late. There was a sudden whirring sound from Mrs. Rammell's bedroom. It was like a small vacuum cleaner. Mr. Rammell recognised it as the electric massage affair that she used on her chin. Attempting to speak against it was impossible.

Whrrrrrrrrmp! She stopped the motor for a moment.

"But only if you really feel well enough, of course," she told him. "I don't want you making yourself ill. Why don't you take something? Then you'd feel better."

Whrrrrr! She had started the motor up again.

Mr. Rammell stood there in the doorway.

"I'm not coming down," he said firmly. "I'm going to bed."

Whrrrmp!

"It's no use, darling," she said. "I can't hear you with this going on. And do start dressing. They'll be here in a moment."

Whrrrrr!

Mr. Rammell walked over to the fireplace and rang the bell. He felt he needed something. A whisky and soda probably.

There was silence in the room for a moment.

86

" I just told you . . ." he began again. But there he stopped.
It was useless. There was now a loud *hiss*, *hiss*, *hiss* coming through
the open doorway.

Mrs. Rammell was spraying herself.

Because of the whisky and soda, he felt better again. Much
better. He didn't any longer resent the fact that he had been
made to put on a black tie. After a day in the office—particularly
after such a day—it was really rather pleasant. The only thing that
irritated him was the fact that he had been compelled to take his
bath and get into a dinner jacket, all at the double. If it had been
an exhibition display the whole thing could scarcely have been
done faster.

And, apparently, without the slightest reason. It was 7.30
already. And so far there was no sign of anyone. Moreover, in
the lull, Mrs. Rammell had sneaked away somewhere. Whenever
she found herself with a spare moment on her hands, she always
rang up someone. She was probably in the morning-room at this
very moment fixing up for the ruination of another perfectly good
evening. Mr. Rammell poured himself out a drink, lit a cigarette and waited for his wife's friends to arrive.

Mr. Aubrey Burnett, very pink and extremely apologetic, was
the first. He was a thin, reed-like young man with a high, lisping
voice and big agonised eyes like a fawn's. He had a nervous habit
of glancing over his shoulder while he was speaking. If there had
been a large dog in the room he would probably have fainted.

But at the reassuring sight of Mr. Rammell he rushed forward.
He wathn't late, wath he? he asked. It had been thimply terrible
all day: really he hadn't known whether he wath on hith head or
hith heelth. Ath it wath, Felithity would be arriving theparately.
She had been athithting with an exthibithion over in Thouth
Kenthington, and wath ruthing over here. Whatever else Mr.
Burnett was not sure about, he was positively certain that Felithity
wath ruthing.

Mr. Rammell had Mr. Burnett all to himself for nearly ten
minutes. And if it had been one moment longer, Mr. Rammell
was afraid that he would do something terrible. Like kicking little
Mr. Burnett on the shins. Or *woof-woofing* at him. Ballet was the
subject of their conversation. And Mr. Burnett was firmly of the
opinion that in variouth athpecth of décor and dethign Mr.

87

Rammell's own son, young Tony Rammell, thowed more than promith, he thowed real geniuth. . . .

Mr. Burnett was saved from assault only by the arrival of Mrs. Rammell. She was apparently devoted to Mr. Burnett. They started talking together intimately. Mr. Rammell had the uncomfortable feeling of being an outsider. From time to time he caught odd snatches of conversation. Thkandinavian thoprano at the Wellth . . . thimply marvellouth—thuperb voith . . .

Then the Cuzzenses arrived. Judith and Mrs. Rammell were old friends. And rather demonstrative. Even though it was only last Monday that they had seen each other there was more than a hint of the pierhead and arrival platform about the embrace they got into. Mr. Burnett came dangerously near to being crushed between them as they flung themselves into each other's arms. He retreated cautiously until his back was right up against a bookcase, and remained there quivering.

Major Cuzzens himself kept right out of it. He was a big, gloomy man with immense dewlaps like a bloodhound. There was something essentially sad and forlorn about him as though he was aware that he was entirely superfluous and at a loose end unless he was given something to smell and go trailing after. Mr. Rammell rather liked him.

" D'you do," he said, in a deep melancholy bay, and then went silent again.

But Judith was never silent. She had, Mr. Rammell decided, the loudest voice that he had ever heard from any woman. Loud and hard and piercing. It was like the sound of a wireless set that had been turned up too high. Even the crackles and the atmospherics were there. It was as though at any moment she might start giving out police announcements and news bulletins.

Major Cuzzens turned to Mr. Rammell.

" Who's the fellah? " he asked.

Mr. Rammell tried hard to forget how much he disliked young Burnett.

" I beg your pardon," he said. " Weren't you introduced? "

" D'you do," said Major Cuzzens, thrusting out a large flat hand. " Goin' to dance for us, eh? "

Mr. Burnett gave a shudder. The hunted look was inescapable now.

" Oh, no," he explained. " Really, I athure you. That ithn't me. I'm not Thwami Lal. He'th bithy rehearthing. We than't be theeing him until after dinner."

Major Cuzzens turned a deeply-set, rather red-looking eye in Mr. Burnett's direction.

"Thought you couldn't be," he said. "Fellah's black, isn't he?"

Mr. Burnett started quivering again.

"Good grathiouth, no," he said. "Not black. Jutht paletht coffee. Nothing in the thlightetht negroid. He'th Perthian acthually."

Major Cuzzens gave a little sniff. It seemed as though he had got on to something at last and had no intention of being fooled by anybody.

"Same thing," he said. "I've been out there. I know 'em."

By now Judith and Mrs. Rammell had screamed their way through the arrangements for a charity party, and had joined the others in front of the fireplace. Then Felicity Burnett arrived.

Mr. Rammell wasn't really sure which of the two Burnetts it was that he disliked the more. Mrs. Burnett was young—not much more than twenty-two or twenty-three—and pretty in a china doll, fancy powder bowl kind of way. She looked as if she might have been first prize at a better class hoop-la stall.

Round her neck she wore a thin strip of black velvet ribbon, and another piece was tied round her left wrist. Her hair, which was ash pale and quite straight, was cut into a fringe in front. And she stared very straight and fixedly out of a pair of deep cornflower blue eyes. The eyes were so fixed, indeed, that there was just the suggestion that perhaps they didn't ever close. It could have been that the manufacturer, satisfied that he had produced a winner for looks, didn't care very much whether this particular doll could go to sleep, or talk, or even move its joints.

Mr. Rammell was instinctively suspicious. The Burnett affair didn't seem to him like a real marriage at all. It was more like a conspiracy. It was as though young Aubrey, all purple socks and amber cuff links, must have combed London to find someone more aggressively feminine than himself. And to show how right he had been in his choice, Felicity had developed a speaking voice that might have come from beneath a pink bassinette cover.

"I'm tewwibly sowwy, Mrs. Wammell," she said, her eyes larger and more fixed and dewy looking than ever. "Please don't be cwoss with me. I wushed all I could. Oh Mr. Wammell . . ."

She had swung round by now, turning her whole head so that her eyes did not have to move at all. And she was holding out her hand as though she were giving him something that he ought to treasure.

But Mr. Rammell was no longer even looking at her. He was staring at the door. And so was Mrs. Rammell. It was Sir Harry who stood there. He stood in the doorway beaming at everyone. "Was to-night, wasn't it, m'dear," he said cheerfully.

3

So far as Mrs. Rammell was concerned, the whole dinner party was dreadful. Quite dreadful. For a start, seven was such a ridiculous sort of number. And really her father-in-law was at his most impossible. His attitude towards sweet little Mrs. Burnett was one of practically adolescent infatuation. He hovered all round her like a big white moth. And talked! Talked incessantly. Talked about everything that didn't belong to her world and Mrs. Burnett's at all. Cricket, Newmarket, Cowes, city finance, scandals. It was like having some terrible old rip from the Press Club sitting at her right hand and showing off in front of everyone.

She hoped desperately that he would be a little quieter and more tractable as the evening wore on. But Sir Harry had spent most of the afternoon sleeping. He was now fresh with a healthy, mid-morning kind of freshness. And he and Major Cuzzens were getting on famously. When the men came up and joined the ladies in the drawing-room Sir Harry and the Major were linked arm in arm.

"Dirty business," Sir Harry was saying. "Naturally it finished him. Couldn't show his face in the City again."

"Fellah was a dago, wasn't he? " Major Cuzzens inquired.

He spoke in a tone that made it clear that he would have regarded that as explaining, even excusing, everything.

"Oriental," Sir Harry answered dropping his voice a little so that it now came as a hoarse carrying whisper. "One of those turban johnnies. Slit your throat as soon as look at you . . ."

Mrs. Rammell rose hurriedly.

"I've kept this chair over here for you, Father," she said. "Major, won't you . . ."

But Sir Harry would have none of it.

"Can't split us up like that," he said. "Only jus' gettin' to know each other. . . ."

The room was filling up rapidly by now. The six rows of gilt chairs had the cream of the Old English Madrigal Society and the Ballet Lovers' Group sitting uncomfortably upon them, alongside others from the Natural Posture Guild and the Yoga League. Aubrey Burnett began recognising people. There was a lot of polite social waving.

Sir Harry turned to Major Cuzzens.

"Rummy looking lot," he said, slowly and distinctly. "Can't think where she finds 'em."

Major Cuzzens leant forward confidentially.

"Do with a haircut most of them."

But the leaning posture had been a mistake. The words came out considerably louder than he had intended. Mr. Burnett looked nervous again as though he expected to be suddenly attacked with comb and scissors.

Then Sir Harry caught sight of the butler. He signalled to him to come over.

"Two whiskies and sodas over here," he said. "And better bring me another cigar before it starts. Can't jus' sit here doin' nothin' while it's all goin' on. You all right, Major?"

Before Major Cuzzens could answer, however, there was a sudden hush. Swami Lal had just been shown in. He advanced, wearing a red silk robe tied loosely with a sash round the middle.

"Fellah looks like a boxer," Major Cuzzens remarked from behind his hand.

Sir Harry inspected him for a moment. Then he shook his head knowledgeably.

"Not him," he said. "No hands. Nothing there. Now, there used to be a coon . . ."

Mrs. Rammell herself was leading Swami Lal over to a chair placed near the piano.

Major Cuzzens leant forward.

"D'you imagine the fellah always goes about like that?" he asked.

Sir Harry inspected him again.

"Ever see that 'I've-got-a-horse' chap?" he asked. "Prince someone-or-other. He does."

Because the rest of the room was in silence, everybody began looking in Sir Harry's direction. He acknowledged the situation with a little nod in Mrs. Rammell's direction.

"You go ahead, m'dear," he said. "Don't bother about me."

Mrs. Rammell spoke her piece with the easy charm of someone who has done the same thing endless times before. She told them how lucky they all were to have Swami Lal with them at all, and how double fortunate that he had agreed to dance for them. Mrs. Rammell and Mr. Burnett might, indeed, have been rehearsing the part for months. Because the timing was perfect. As soon as she paused for a moment, Mr. Burnett said "Hear, hear," and then everybody else said "Hear, hear," after him. It was only the phrase "world-famous" that caused difficulty. Major Cuzzens leant forward again and whispered in Sir Harry's ear.

"D'you ever hear of the fellah before?" he asked defiantly.

Sir Harry thought for a moment.

"Used to be a chap on the halls," he said. "Same name. Did a dance with a snake. Can't be that chap though. Too long ago. May have been his father."

Various members of the Yoga League and the Natural Posture Guild said "ssh! ssh!" very loudly, and Sir Harry turned round to see who was *sshing* him. Major Cuzzens turned too, and the *sshing* stopped instantly. The bloodhound look had suddenly become quite unmistakable, and two keen madrigalists edged timidly away.

"I'm afraid that Swami Lal has to leave us after only one dance," Mrs. Rammell was saying. "It is because of a charity engagement that he has most generously undertaken to perform."

The clapping had already started when Mrs. Rammell rose again. That was because of some rather agitated signalling on the part of the small man who had come in behind Swami Lal. He was the agent. The only bit he had come to hear had somehow been left out.

"And before Swami Lal dances his . . . er . . . dance," Mrs. Rammell resumed hastily, "I should say that I am sure that we shall all be meeting again many times at the Coronet Theatre during Swami Lal's season which starts next Monday. And please tell your friends. The Coronet Theatre. For one week from Monday."

The agent had relaxed by now. But a broad grin had come across Sir Harry's face. He nudged Major Cuzzens.

" See you there," he said. " Don't forget. Tell the other chaps in the club."

Throughout the whole introduction Swami Lal had sat there with eyes closed. Now when he got up, he opened them and looked around slowly as though surprised to find himself there at all. He might have been transported in a trance state straight from Benares. But he soon recovered himself. Slipping the red silk robe off his shoulders, he stood there gleaming, supple-limbed, flexible-looking. There was a sudden creaking of the little gilt chairs as the ballet lovers all leant forward to see him more closely. It was their magical moment. Like something at Diaghilev's.

Swami Lal was certainly a magnificently built young man. The splash of colour of the caste-mark on the forehead showed up the natural aristocratic paleness of his skin. And the lines of the face were set in an expression of arrogant contempt. It was like being regarded by a rock carving. First he outstared Major Cuzzens and then slowly, contemptuously turned towards Sir Harry. Sir Harry stuck it for a moment and then winked back at him. Swami Lal looked hurriedly away.

Twining his two arms as though they were made of rubber from the elbows to the fingertips, Swami Lal began to address them. His voice, however, came as a bit of a surprise, even to the ballet lovers. It wasn't like a man's voice at all. It was a schoolboy's voice. Or a schoolgirl's. Practically junior mixed. There was a piping quality to it that suggested canaries. But it was obvious straightaway that Swami Lal was not an English canary. On his lips, the language seemed to consist mostly of s's. It was as though at some period in history the Welsh must have gone storming and whistling through the Khyber Pass.

" The danss I danss thiss night iss the Lotuss-danss," he explained. " It iss a danss that hass been danssed in my country for many thousandss of yearss. It iss very ssacred. A princess walkss by a river. Sshee findss a lotuss. The lotuss speakss to her. It tellss her that sshe iss going to die. Sshe iss very sad. Sshe weepss. Then sshe throwss the lotuss to the ground, and sshe stampss upon it. The lotuss changess into a snake and bitess her toess. Sshe isss poissoned. Sshe sscreamss, but her ladiess do not hear her. Sshe faintss, and fallss headlong. Sshe liess unconssciouss upon the

93

ssnake. But the ssnake hass changed back into a lotuss and bloomss again besside the river. Sshe diess. The lotuss-danss. No smoking, pleass."

" What'd he say? " Sir Harry asked.

" Fellah said it changed back into a lotus," Major Cuzzens replied.

Sir Harry shrugged his shoulders.

" Thought he said something about smoking."

" Don't think so," Major Cuzzens replied, blowing out a great cloud of smoke in Swami Lal's direction. " Mostly about snakes. Can't be certain, though. Difficult to hear what the fellah says."

Swami Lal waited motionless. The gilt chairs creaked uneasily.

" What's he waiting for? " Sir Harry asked. " I'm ready."

" Bit of a hitch by the look of it," Major Cuzzens replied. " Always the same with these fellahs."

" I've got it," Sir Harry said suddenly. " Partner hasn't turned up yet. Don't wonder if she's wearing those sort of clothes. Police've probably got her."

" Damn bad staff work all the same," Major Cuzzens said severely. " Fellah ought to have thought of it."

Sir Harry leant back and crossed his legs.

" Looks as though it's all off," he said. " Got us here for nothin'."

A hand came forward from the row behind and tapped Sir Harry on the shoulder. The hand belonged to an elderly lady with very thick glasses and a length of black muslin tied over her head.

" Swami Lal dances all the parts himself," she whispered.

Sir Harry was grateful for the information. He remembered now that the chap on the halls had been a quick-change artist, too. And devilish clever about it. You never knew what he was going to turn into next. This evening was looking up a bit.

" Does he, by Jove," he said. " Good for him."

There was a pause.

" It's your cigar he's waiting for," the whisperer continued.

But this time Sir Harry shook his head firmly.

" Count me out of this," he said. " Too old. Haven't been up on to the stage for years. Give him yours, Major. This lady's in the turn with him. You go up."

In the end, Mrs. Rammell herself had to come over. And, for

94

a moment, it looked as though Sir Harry was going to be difficult. But Major Cuzzens revealed a sense of diplomacy that had come in very useful in Bangalore in the old days.

"Fellah's probably got a weak chest," he said. "Most of 'em have."

Sir Harry shrugged his shoulders.

"Hope he hasn't got a weak throat, too. I'm not giving up my drink for anyone."

After another pause, this time only to set the piece, Swami Lal started. And it was soon evident that it wasn't only his arms that were rubber. It was his legs and thighs as well. He was sinuous all over. He wove patterns with himself. He slowly melted before their eyes, and reset in impossible positions. He merged.

But so slowly. Very, very slowly. It was like watching high diving in slow motion upon a cinema screen. There was a strange, lulling quality about it. Sir Harry began to feel sleepy. Once or twice, he opened his eyes to make sure that it wasn't all over. But the sight of those languidly waving arms, those legs crossed over somewhere at the hips, made him irresistibly drowsy again. He hadn't felt so much at rest for years. He snored. His head slid over on to Major Cuzzens's arm. But Major Cuzzens did not stir. He was off too. Front paws folded beneath his dewlaps he was dreaming of man-hunts and murderers and long-buried bones.

Trapped between Mrs. Rammell and Swami Lal's agent, Mr. Rammell stared down at the toes of his patent leather shoes. He had taken rather a lot to drink at dinner. And, though he didn't feel ill yet, he knew exactly how he was going to feel next morning. He wished that he had gone straight to bed.

Then he glanced up. Over by the door, young Tony was standing. He must have arrived late because he hadn't changed. It was one of his older sports-coats that he was wearing. Mr. Rammell forgave him that. What he couldn't forgive him was his expression. It was dreamy and entranced. Practically hypnotised. Apparently he actually admired Swami Lal.

"Oh, God," Mr. Rammell told himself. "I've got to get the boy away from this somehow. It's ruining him. And it's killing me. If there's another blasted recital in this drawing-room, I'll shoot myself."

CHAPTER XI

THE COPY of *Hassan* was lying open on the bed with two dents on either side of it on the pillow where Irene's elbows had been. But she didn't want to read any more of it at the moment. She had been Yasmin for too long. Ever since last Tuesday, in fact. She now had that stale, used-up feeling that comes at the end of all successful runs. That was why she was so glad that she was going out to the pictures with the girls.

As soon as she got outside the house she felt better. It was extraordinary how closed-in, half suffocated she felt when she was at home. And it was steadily getting worse. On Sundays it reached asphyxiation point. Particularly when Mr. Bloot came. Because, having kissed her, he never let go until he had added: " Mahy, mahy! Quaht the young lady, aren't we? " She could foresee an endless future of it—the same damp, rather spongy kiss, the same unchanging lunatic comment.

But by the time she had reached the end of Fewkes Road, everything about Mr. Bloot and his Sunday visits was forgotten. Her own mother and father, too, were simultaneously blotted out. It was simply her friends that mattered. And she was obviously late. Because there they were, a close little huddle of girls all bunched together outside the Underground.

They were all dressed—just as Irene was—in short thickish coats over light thinnish dresses. They all had flat shoes with low wedge-shaped heels. They all had brightly coloured scarves tied peasant fashion around their faces. And they all had just enough make-up to set off the head scarves and still get by their own mothers. Even their handbags were the same. Whereas up till a year or so ago everyone of them would have carried something small and rather dainty with a snap-over clip on top, they were now carting everything about with them—their small change, their compacts, their combs, their lipsticks, old letters, theatre programmes, photographs, propelling pencils and all the rest of it— in massive leather cases slung over the shoulder like an old fashioned cartridge pouch. The sling bags were of chunky, undressed leather. They looked as though the girls had hacked the things out for themselves with a bush knife.

Being seventeen is always rather exclusive. Childhood is over. But maturity hasn't come. It is the emotions that are the trouble —too many of them, and not yet properly sorted out. But when seventeen-year-olds are not bending under the strain of religious devotion or school examinations or prospective suicide, they are usually a pretty cheerful lot.

To-night, for instance, as soon as Irene got there they all started giggling. They went on giggling. They could not stop giggling. They had to hold on to each other to support themselves. They were noisy. They were conspicuous. They were happy.

It was really the fact that they were all four so well educated that made them so badly behaved. If they had gone straight into the world from Yerbury Road Senior Girls they would have had some real experience of life by now. It would have sobered and chastened them. It is also more than likely that they wouldn't still have been going out together at all. One by one, sex would have made its claim upon them. Any sixteen-year-old from Yerbury Road would have driven to find herself a boy-friend simply to avoid the appalling prospect of lonely old age at seventeen.

But they weren't merely Yerbury Roadites. They had all left Yerbury Road behind them, and graduated to the grammar school. They were Old Eleanor Atkinsonians now. And between Yerbury Road and the Eleanor Atkinson there is the sort of gulf that divides Pimlico from Belgravia.

To be frank, they weren't in favour of sex up at the Eleanor Atkinson. Rather frowned upon it, in fact. The accent there was on Modern European History, New Testament scholarship and games. Any girl seen out with a boy of her own age, even at week-ends—let alone in the cocoa-brown school uniform—was regarded as something of an emotional outsider. A misfit. The portrait of Eleanor Atkinson herself, unmistakably a thoroughbred, gave the whole school its keynote. It hung squarely above the hall platform, this portrait, with a bracket light directly under it. And the long, sad face, with bit and bridle removed, dispensed an unmistakable message of breeding, training and plenty of good healthy exercise.

97

All Irene's friends had sat for the School Certificate in June. Were still recovering from it, in fact. And not one of them would even know whether she had passed or failed before it was too late to do anything about it. Because, in their various ways, they had already disposed of themselves. Madge, the dark, rather sullen one, was going into an insurance company. As what exactly she was not quite clear. The only thing that she knew for certain was that it was in Old Broad Street, and that there was an Express Dairy almost exactly opposite. But she was a trusting kind of girl. She felt sure that if she didn't lose her head and minded her nines, which sometimes came out a bit too much like sevens, everything was going to be all right. It was life insurance that the company dealt in mostly. And going steady seemed to be what mattered.

As for Sylvia, the fair pretty girl on the inside, she was starting next week at the Brecknock Secretarial College. She knew exactly what the next twelve months were going to be like. And she wasn't particularly looking forward to them. By the time young Sylvia emerged she would be expected to know everything that there was about Pitman's shorthand up to 120 words a minute, touch-typing, correct forms of address, Roneo stencil cutting, office-filing, simple double-entry book-keeping, and how to answer the telephone correctly. The fact that she intended to marry one of the partners in whatever business she found herself was the only thing that made the future tolerable.

Compared with Sylvia's tremendous syllabus, Esther, the third one of the party, was embracing life the easy way. She was going to join her father in some vague, undefined job that was obviously without prospects. But it didn't matter with Esther, because it was a family business that she was going into. She alone had no need to make her own way in the world.

" It won't half seem funny not going back to the Eleanor Atkinson," Sylvia said suddenly. " Not seeing anybody you know, I mean."

" There's the Old Girls."

It was Madge who had spoken. She was an almost model Atkinsonian. Quiet. Loyal. Dependable. She had never even considered cutting herself off from Miss Preston and Miss Harris and Mrs. Wells and the games mistress, and all her other friends.

But the Eleanor Atkinson had always contained both kinds,

the solid rock and the rolling stones. And it was evident that Esther was one of the rollers.

" I'm not joining," she said. " It's just a waste of money. Nobody ever turns up. Not after the first time."

She had a quick, clipped way of talking. And when she had finished she always threw her chin back. The gesture was an unconscious one. But it was emphatic in an uncontradictable, adult sort of way that always impressed the others.

" You'll join, won't you? " Madge asked. " I mean it's up to all of us."

She said the words as though she really believed in them. Obviously nothing less than natural affinity had brought Madge and life insurance together.

Irene shrugged her shoulders.

" I haven't made up my mind," she said. " In any case, I mayn't have the time. I may be going into Rammell's."

Instantly there was a pause. This wasn't just gossip any longer. It was important. A piece of news. Something to be passed on at home.

" Why ever are you going *there*? "

It was Esther who had spoken again. She always wanted to know everything about everything. The reasons. The motives. The facts behind any fresh decision. Wanted to make quite sure that she hadn't missed anything.

" Dad thinks it'll be a good thing. He's spoken to one of the managers."

" But I thought you were going to do acting."

Esther sounded hurt about it. It was as though Irene had deceived her.

" Dad says the prospects in Rammells'll be better."

" It's all right if you get into gowns," Esther said with that little tilt of the chin again. " My mum's best friend started in gowns. She's got a business of her own now. Outsize and children's."

But Sylvia was the one who minded.

" Well, I think it's a shame," she said. " You going into Rammell's. You're ever so brainy, you know you are. Miss Preston said you ought to be one of the ones who're stopping."

Irene paused.

" Oh, Rammells'll be all right," she replied. " Might be

99

worse. I haven't actually got the job yet. I've only been up for the interview. Probably won't be so bad. I'm not worrying . . ."

The last bit was untrue. But the very last thing she wanted was to go over all that again. Besides, they'd reached the Odeon by now. And suddenly everything seemed funny once more. It was the way the commissionaire held the door open that started them giggling. Then the girl in the box office looked funny, too. And the sight of Humphrey Bogart's beard in a poster completely overcame them. Madge and Sylvia had to hold on to each other.

It was only Esther who was silent.

" When d'you expect to start? " she asked. " What are they paying you? "

2

" Can't say whether you'll like it till you've tried," Sir Harry was saying. " Never try, never find out. Stands to reason. Pour yourself out some more brandy."

It had been an unusually good dinner. Sir Harry had ordered it with all the enthusiasm of a rich choirboy. And Tony Rammell on the other side of the table was already feeling consciously insulated from the whole world. He had perhaps taken just a trifle too much drink. But no more than Sir Harry, he kept telling himself. Less, in fact. A great deal less. Only, Sir Harry appeared to be impervious. Sherry. Pouilly. Burgundy. Brandy. It all went down as so much ginger-pop to him. Even now his hand was stretched out for the bottle as soon as Tony was ready to pass it to him.

" Wanted to be a minin' prospector myself," Sir Harry went on. " Gold and all that. Or show business. Circuses, y'know. That side of it. Not sorry now, I can tell you. Was at the time though. Very."

Tony put his glass down and folded his arms on the table. It would have been so much easier if only Sir Harry would stop talking.

" I've been thinking . . ." he began.

But Sir Harry was off again already.

" Used to know a young feller once," he said. " About your age. Sister shot herself. Shockin' business. Wanted to take up farmin'. Never did. Made boxes instead." Sir Harry broke off for a moment and with the flat of his hands drew boxes in the air in case the point of his story was eluding Tony. " Owns the whole thing now. Just raised a new issue. Half a million. Oversubscribed."

" What I said was I've been thinking . . ."

" And there was another chap. One of the Burneys. Bankers. Said he was goin' to paint. They saw to that. Handles all their foreign business. Big place off Mincing Lane."

" I said I've been . . ."

Sir Harry looked up, surprised.

" What d'you keep interruptin' for? " he asked. " Gettin' me mixed up now. Wasn't that chap at all. Confusin' him with his brother."

" Were you? " Tony asked helplessly.

" I should know," Sir Harry told him. " Lived just opposite for years. Dead now. Both of 'em."

There were a few seconds' respite while Sir Harry relit his cigar. Tony made straight for the gap.

" Lishen to me! "

But it was just as he had feared. The brandy had done its work. His speech was now ever so slightly blurred. The " t's " proved unaccountably difficult. But his mind was clear. Clearer than he had ever known it. Now, if never before, he would make Sir Harry see how he really felt.

" I don' liker shop," he said, speaking slowly and he hoped distinctly. " I don' like anything abow it. I don' even liker people who go there. Is boring. Very boring. I don' wanna have anythinger to do with it. I just wanna be lef' alone go my own way."

Sir Harry grinned across at him.

" When d'you start? " he asked.

" Never. Neverarra shop. Never," Tony told him. It suddenly seemed a particularly succulent sort of word, and he repeated it with relish. " Never. An' never. An' never."

" Got y'cuff in y'coffee," Sir Harry replied. He paused for a second—but not long enough for Tony to speak again. " Admire y'spirit," he said. " Plenty of guts. Like y'mother."

Tony roused himself with difficulty and addressed Sir Harry directly.

" An' lemme tell you," he said. " My mother entirely suppors me in m'attitude. She dishliksh "—for no reason at all speech was suddenly becoming more and more difficult—" the idea of commersh for me just ash mush ash I dishlike commersh myshelf. Jush ash mush. Commersh ish ri' out. An' thasher end of it."

As he finished, he drew his right arm scimitar fashion across his chest for emphasis.

But Sir Harry only winked.

" That's what she tells you," he said. " Ought to hear her with y'father. Breaks her heart y'know. Thinks you're just like him."

" I do not reshemble my father in the schlightesht degree."

With the exception of two of the words the statement was clear and emphatic. But Sir Harry would have none of it.

" Spittin' image," he said. " Frightened of y'own shadow. Not like y'mother. There's courage for you. Knew a man once . . ."

Tony was now leaning forward half across the table.

" Is that a challengsh? "

Sir Harry did not reply. Instead he leant across the table and gave Tony a nudge that nearly dislodged him.

" Look over there," he said.

Tony looked.

Coming in through the door was Marcia. She was wearing a long white dress with one of the Rammell midnight-blue minks. The young man who was with her—Mr. Bulping was far away in Wolverhampton manufacturing Neptunettes—seemed faintly self-conscious about the extent of the treasure that he was escorting.

" Who ish she? "

Sir Harry gave a little laugh.

" There y'are," he said. " Shut y'self away. Don't know the facts. One of our gals. Could be one of yours, y'know. Call her over if you like."

But Tony only shook his head. What he had just seen was loveliness. Real loveliness. He wanted nothing to disturb the vision in the doorway. Also, he was far too drunk. If she actually spoke to him, he was afraid that he might break down and cry or something.

CHAPTER XII

IT WAS one of those Sundays again. Bond Street was shrouded in dust sheets. And the cats and caretakers were in control once more.

For Marcia it couldn't all have been simpler. Everything had been decided for her. By Mr. Bulping, of course. He had been on the phone all Saturday evening arranging things. At this very moment he was somewhere on the Great North Road tearing down towards her. Lunch at the Ritz, he had said; adding that they could decide when he got there what to do afterwards. From the tone of his voice it sounded as though he had already decided. But Marcia was past caring. After all, love—particularly love on Mr. Bulping's scale—was elemental. Undeniable. And wouldn't anyone expect some reward after a hundred-and-twenty miles of fast Sunday motoring?

For Mr. Rammell, too, there were no problems. He was down in Torquay. Staying at the Grand. One of the best rooms, with a pleasant study-boudoir adjoining. And no Mrs. Rammell. Not that there was any real significance in that. No sudden domestic flare-up. No instantaneous separation. Nothing like that. Merely the annual conference of the Retail Trades Federation. Mr. Rammell was this year's President. He had chosen Government Interference for the theme of his address. And a pretty powerful piece it was going to be. Slaps and punches all round, with what amounted to nothing less than a broadside on the whole Board of Trade. Real headline stuff. TORY ATTACKS WHITEHALL. CIVIL SERVICE V. PUBLIC SERVICE—that kind of thing. Mr. Rammell would, as a matter of fact, have rather liked Mrs. Rammell to hear him deliver it. It would have revealed him to her in a new light. As someone vital. Dynamic. Unpredictable. But Mrs. Rammell had never really fitted into those trade do's. Somehow looked too superior. Which was fatal. The last time she had attended an annual conference Mr. Rammell had been forced to hang about afterwards giving an extra handshake all round just to show how much they had both enjoyed themselves.

And it had never so much as crossed Tony's mind that he might even have been expected to come. All that he had said when he heard where his father was going was: " God! How bloody for you."

Whereas, Sir Harry simply could not be dissuaded. It had been real touch and go with him. The long train journey, the late hours, the strain of meeting so many people—he would listen to none of it. Torquay, he declared, was precisely what he needed to set him up. He ordered a new grey suit specially for the Conference. He booked the best suite. He bought his ticket. And then, on the very eve, the colic took him. Nothing dangerous. Just two or three days in bed. But long enough. By the time Sir Harry was about again, Torquay and the retailers would have said good-bye for ever.

Not that Sir Harry cared. He had subsequently remembered that it was Newquay and not Torquay that he really liked. Besides, his new high-fidelity player had just been delivered. It was a lavish affair in figured walnut with a separate loudspeaker cabinet. And it played on and on for hours. Classical music mostly. Which Sir Harry didn't care for. But the tone was magnificent. It was like owning a whole Brass Band Festival, right there in the bedroom.

For Mr. Privett it was not so easy. That was because he had nothing to do. No model yacht. And no Mr. Bloot. But a load of anxiety. And all because he had taken his friend's advice about consulting a solicitor. He kept telling himself that he would have been better off without anyone. But he was no longer sure even about that. Ever since he had consulted a solicitor, in fact, he wasn't really sure about anything.

It may, of course, have been the solicitor's fault. Mr. Felix Hamster, on whom he finally picked, was not one of London's acknowledged leaders. He was, in fact, in no more than quite a modest way of practice. But he seemed a thoroughly conscientious and reliable kind of man. And so convenient too. His office was only about a couple of hundred yards from Fewkes Road, over a coal merchant's, practically next door to the Underground. That meant that Mr. Privett could drop in on his way back from Bond Street just to see how the case was progressing.

What's more, even though the man didn't look very much, he was a real fighter. Behind the striped shirt, that had been patched on both sides where the points of the stiff collar cut into it, beat the heart of a Haldane. Practically single-handed as he was in his small back office, he was fully prepared to defy even the largest of insurance companies. It was the Federated Equitable that he was up against. And every letter that he sent contained the authentic note of challenge. It was as though Mr. Hamster had not merely written but had called personally and slapped the recipient across the face with his glove.

The only disturbing thing from Mr. Privett's point of view was that the Federated Equitable was equally prepared to defy Mr. Hamster. It might have been Mr. Hamster's own twin brother who wrote back to him.

Already Mr. Privett had been accused of cycling to the public danger, negligence, endangering the safety of the motor-coach and making an impudent claim. He was half sick from the sheer misery of thinking about it, and dearly wished that he had never made a claim at all.

In consequence, he was having a perfectly wretched Sunday.

2

Not so Mr. Bloot. He was made for Sundays. And Sundays were made for him.

He had just set out from the house, wearing his mysterious Viking expression. And as he walked his lips were moving. It was not, however, the name of Hetty Florence that he was repeating. It was her address. The words " 23b Artillery Mansions, Tregunter Road, N.12 " had penetrated into his brain like a charm. The inexpressible beauty of the address overwhelmed him. But what was more bewitching still, he had actually been invited there.

When he reached The Nag's Head a happy thought came to him. On the opposite corner was a man selling flowers. And Mr. Bloot realised immediately that flowers would give just the right note to the occasion. Moreover, he felt in a lavish and spending mood. Hovering about the stall like a huge enthusiastic bee, he chose sweet-peas and gladioli. Six shillings' worth altogether. But it was not the price he minded. It was the size. Instead of the neat little bouquet that he had intended, it was enormous. And down at the thin end of the bundle, the stalks dripped obstinately. It was the sort of load that would have been better delivered on a barrow.

As soon as he had mounted the number 18 bus, however, a strange, dare-devil feeling came over him. There he was, with his ticket in one hand and a harvest festival sheaf of flowers in the other, cruising across London in pursuit of a woman with black midnight hair.

He was so deep in thought, marvelling at the sheer magic of the morning, that he nearly missed it when the conductor called out the name " Tregunter Road. " And the shock of the discovery startled him. He got mixed up with his own flowers. From inside the huge white paper parcel there came the sound of stalks snapping. But if he had left it a moment longer he would have been carried on. In the result, he came down the stairs so fast that he missed his footing. If it had not been for the conductor, Mr. Bloot would have fallen. The conductor, who was a good deal smaller than Mr. Bloot, resented the whole incident. Any more of that, he said, and he would report him.

But Mr. Bloot was safe. And past caring. The bus with its rude conductor was already receding. And Mr. Bloot took his bearings. He was able to identify Artillery Mansions immediately. It was a large, square block of red brick with a battlemented coping of fancy stone running along the top, for the mortars and cannon to fire through. A short tiled walk led up to the front door. And there was a row of polished brass " IN " and " OUT " plates just inside the entrance hall. Altogether, it was definitely upper-class. Even classy.

But Mr. Bloot need not have bothered. Dressed as he was, he looked more like the landlord than a casual visitor. He would have adorned anywhere. Artillery Mansions were mostly show anyway. The stairs, which had metal treads on the front of each step, were dark and steep. And the walls were of an unpleasant dark green colour. Nevertheless, they were definitely mansion-flats. And, remembering his own unself-contained state in Tufnell Park, Mr. Bloot felt a sudden qualm. Was he worthy of her? he wondered.

When he reached the doorway of number 23b, however, he saw to his astonishment that the milk bottle had not yet been taken in. This was surprising. Because it was already after midday. And when he rang there was no answer. Behind the panelled front door with its little diamond panes of frosted glass there was silence. Complete silence. The suspense was terrible. His palms went wet and sticky. After a moment, Mr. Bloot rang again.

Then somewhere inside the flat a door opened. And a moment later he heard the soft *swish-swish* of slippers. It took longer to open the front door than he had expected because it was apparently bolted at the top and bottom, and the chain was up. But, in a sense, this relieved him. He was glad to think that Hetty took such good care of herself. It must simply have been that she must have overslept.

And when, finally, she sprang the catch back he could see immediately that everything was all right. For there she was, wearing a pale blue dressing-gown with a lot of swansdown round the neck and cuffs. And—delightful touch of intimacy—her hair, her glistening, raven hair, was not yet wound across her head. Instead, gleaming and hawser-like it hung, schoolgirlishly over one shoulder, tied up with a piece of baby ribbon.

" My, you're early, aren't you? " she said.

Her voice sounded warmer and more vibrating than ever in the confines of the tiny hall.

Mr. Bloot started to reply. He tried to explain. Apologise. Excuse himself. But it was no use. He felt confused suddenly. Sheepish. That rich plait of hair resting on the swansdown had knocked him temporarily off-balance.

" Just lakh Ah said," was the best that he could manage.

But Hetty saved him.

" Was he looking forward all that much? " she asked softly.

As she said it, she reached out her arms. Mr. Bloot removed his hat and took hold of it in his left hand along with his umbrella. But there were still the flowers. These were particularly difficult. The bunch really was too large. Or the florist had not secured the stems tightly enough. Whatever the reason, as soon as Mr. Bloot loosened his hold for a single moment they began to undo themselves. Unless he were careful, instead of offering a neat bouquet, he would find himself simply thrusting a bundle of mere garden refuse upon her. So, in the end, he thrust the whole sodden parcel under his arm, and came towards her. But as soon as she touched him, she drew back.

"Good gracious, you're sopping," she said. "Whatever's happened?"

By now, however, Mr. Bloot had recovered himself. He produced the flowers from behind his back like a conjuror and, with a little bow, he presented them to her.

"A few flahs, m'dear," he said gallantly. "Jurst something smawl to go into a vawse."

Hetty Florence might never have received a gift before she was so pleased with it. And, despite the wetness of Mr. Bloot's hand, she took hold of it again. This time, moreover, she did not withdraw it. She clung on. And more than clung. She drew him near her.

"They deserve a little kiss," was what she said. "That's what flowers are for, aren't they?"

Remembering his disastrous impetuosity in the shop, Mr. Bloot was careful. But again because of his inexperience he bungled things. He did not know whether it was her cheek or her lips that she was offering. And finally it was on the side of her nose that he kissed her. Moreover, he kissed wetly. When he bought his mouth away again he could taste the strange, wicked flavour of her face cream.

"Pord'n me," he said.

He was about to try again, properly this time, when Hetty Florence stopped him.

"Now, now," she said. "Be a good boy, Gussie. Just you go into the room at the end and wait for me. I shan't be long. I'm only going to slip something on."

The room in which Mr. Bloot found himself was in partial darkness. That was because the curtains were still drawn. Even though it was brilliant midday outside it was no better than late evening in the drawing-room. But he didn't imagine that Hetty could really intend him to sit there in the dusk. And, after a moment's pause to get his bearings, he began to move over to the window. It was not so easy, however, as it had seemed while he was still standing by the door. There were so many things about. First he stumbled over a cushion, lying unaccountably upon the carpet. Then, in avoiding a tumbler which was beside the cushion, his heel came down hard upon an ash-tray. It must have been made of something quite thin. Glass or china by the sound of it.

And the scraping sound that his foot now made as it moved across the carpet showed that some of the pieces must still be sticking into the quarter-rubber of his heel.

When he had finally pulled back the curtain, he saw at once that one more breakage in such a room would pass entirely un-noticed. As it was, a tumbler with a half-moon snicked out of the rim stood on the piano. And with the light that now came pouring in through the window he saw several other things as well. There was a green baize table, heavily ringed where glasses had been standing. And left scattered across it as though the play had broken up rather suddenly was a pack of playing cards. Two more packs, one still in its paper cover, were piled neatly at one corner. There was a whisky bottle amid a lot of empty beer bottles on an occasional table over by the couch. And there were unemptied ash-trays everywhere.

What Mr. Bloot could not understand was that the ash-tray nearest to him contained the fat butt of a half-smoked cigar. Then he understood. It must have been some friends in the trade that Hetty had been entertaining. And it struck him then that they must have been rather a jolly, carefree set of chaps.

He was still wondering whether he would have liked her friends, when Hetty returned. She had changed into a pale blue dress with rather a lot of open lace-work about the bodice. The shoes that she was wearing were white and toeless.

" Oh, my," she began saying. " It smells terrible in here. Why ever didn't you open a window? "

Mr. Bloot, however, did not reply. He was standing there, silently admiring her.

Hetty meanwhile was going rapidly round the room. She picked up cushions. Emptied ash-trays into the fancy waste-paper basket. Collected the bottles, holding them one by one up against the light.

" All empties," she said at last, almost as though talking to herself. " I guess that's why they went."

By now she had crossed over to a very highly polished walnut cabinet that stood in the corner. When she opened the doors a little light came on inside. Mr. Bloot could see that the interior was filled with every kind of wine-glass, as well as with an ingenious sliding tray that held the bottles. Outside Rammell's furniture showrooms, he had never seen such a cabinet. It had certainly never occurred to him that one day he might actually know the kind of woman to possess one.

Hetty turned and faced him. She held an unopened bottle of Haig in her hand, and she had deftly detached two heavily-cut glass tumblers from the side rack.

" What about a short one? " she asked. " There's no point in eating anything yet. That is unless you're hungry. I've only just had breakfast."

A short one! Mr. Bloot's heart stood still. How was he going to explain that he didn't ever drink? That he was teetotal? Remembering the state of the room in which he was standing, he decided that he *couldn't* explain it. It just wouldn't be possible. She would think him queer. A crank of some kind. Besides, he felt in a reckless, playboyish sort of mood to-day. It was the kiss that had done it. He couldn't very well go back on that.

So reaching out to take the bottle from her he smiled back blandly.

" That's the ticket," he said, surprised and incredulous at the sound of his own voice uttering such words. " Let's 'ave er nappitizer. That's what we both need—er nappitizer."

And, as he said it, Emmie's ghost—pale, anæmic-looking, slightly catarrhal as in life—rose from the clay of Highgate Cemetery, and stood confronting him. Mr. Bloot tried to ignore the spectre. But it was impossible. He knew what was behind the visit. Because Emmie had always been a solid non-drinker like himself, a pledged total abstainer. The present moment was the nearest that he had ever come to being unfaithful to her memory.

CHAPTER XIII

MORE THAN once as the weeks passed Irene told herself that Rammell's must have forgotten. Either that, or had second thoughts. She saw herself an actress again. The house lights had long since gone down. The last bars of the overture—admittedly recorded, but who cares?—had just died away. The tabs were parting . . .

But it was no use. Rammell's had remembered all right. The familiar envelope with the heavy embossed " R " on the back, was there waiting by her place when she came down to breakfast. And Mr. Privett, already half-way through his corn flakes and his *News Chronicle*, was wearing the sort of happy birthday expression that Irene recollected from her childhood.

It was, indeed, largely because of the expression on her father's face that Irene pretended that she was pleased, too. Ever since his accident Mr. Privett had not been looking at all well. He seemed suddenly to have grown older. Older. And shakier. And more hurtable. She noticed for the first time in her life that his eyebrows were shaggy. And there was a little tell-tale quiver at the corners of his mouth when he was drinking. Not that any of this was surprising. The accident alone would have been enough. But coming on top of it, the strain of all this legal trouble had only made things worse. Nowadays, even the sight of any letter lying there on the breakfast table was sufficient to upset Mr. Privett.

And it wasn't easy for Irene. You can't chuck away a vocation just to keep a parent happy. She had it all worked out, too. Her life belonged in dingy little dressing-rooms. In agents' offices with photographs of Vivien Leigh and Peggy Ashcroft and all the rest of her friends round the walls. On board ship going out to Australia, with the scenery and props stored away somewhere in the hold. In front with terrific explosions of applause still coming down from the gallery. Back at her old school judging the end-of-term drama contest . . .

But already her father was addressing her.

" Tell us what it says," he demanded. " Then we can all breathe easy."

It was a Monday. It was raining. It was eight forty-five. And as Irene took her place in the stream of smart girls, all dashing up the staff staircase and all as eager as a pack of young tigresses to get their teeth into the first customer, she hated the lot of them.

But with her father beside her there wasn't anything that she could say. Anything more, that is. It had all been said on the evening of the big row. But Mr. Privett had obviously forgotten all about that. He had even tried to hold her hand as they set out. And that was something else that Irene didn't care for—this prospect of endlessly being taken in. And presumably waited for again at night. It would be like starting Kindergarten again.

But there was worse coming. Much worse. At the head of the staircase, with the men's cloakroom on one side and the ladies' on the other, Mr. Privett suddenly kissed her. In front of everybody, too. And he didn't even remember to drop his voice.

" Now don't you worry," he said. " You'll be all right."

If her father had lain awake all night thinking of some way of humiliating her in front of everyone he could not possibly have done better. But she need not have worried. All round her, a busy, feverish preoccupied sort of life was already going on. Even though it was still not ten to nine, there was as much noise as though Rammell's were throwing an early morning cocktail party. The guests were fairly pouring in. And Irene was the only one who had turned up alone. All the rest were arriving in twos and threes. Not that this was surprising. Because by now the rate of arrival was about one hundred and fifty a minute. They had met coming along Piccadilly. Or turning up Bond Street. Or in Hurst Place itself. There was a whole converging procession of them. And conversations were everywhere being taken up where they had been broken off before the week-end.

They were mostly rather rushed, scrappy sort of conversations. That was because there was so much to do. And so little time in which to do it. There were dust sheets to be snatched off. Folded.

Put away. Traysful of stuff to be arranged on the counters. Furs and dresses to be hung out on stands. Hats to be stuck about on the tall silver knobs in the millinery department. Bowls of flowers to be arranged. Cash books issued. Hands washed. Faces made up. Hair tidied. And all by eight fifty-five.

Admittedly nobody ever came into the shop at nine o'clock when the doors opened. That wouldn't have been Bond Street behaviour. More the way Marks and Spencer customers go on. But that wasn't the point. Mr. Rammell and Mr. Preece were both great believers in punctuality. They would still have had the store opened dead on nine even if there had been a bye-law forbidding any buying and selling before midday.

It was the noise of conversation that reminded Irene that she was a stranger. A new worker turning up for duty at an already over-populated hive. The whole honeycomb was full and swarming. The buzz was incessant. And what her antennae did pick up made no sense to her. All wrong wave-length stuff, or something.

". . . so naturally I didn't wait. Can you imagine me standing there like that waiting for *him*? "

". . . and when I got them home and tried them on you should have seen them. You'd have killed yourself. They must have been tens at least . . ."

". . . was there all that time. I didn't know. Last Tuesday it must have happened . . ."

". . . then I said, ' It isn't even as though it's a front room ' I said. ' You can't expect three guineas a week,' I said, ' not for . . .' "

". . . but the end was lovely. She's absolutely marvellous in the third act. I didn't care for . . ."

". . . well, it may be ' art, ' I said. ' But it's still photography. You don't catch me having any.' "

Irene had taken her place in the queue by now, and began passing her things over the cloakroom counter. The attendant was an elderly woman in a brown apron. And she had hands like a slick conjuror's. As soon as anything was put down in front of her, she snatched it up again, palmed it, tucked it under her arm, folded what was foldable, and handed over a little brass disc in return. She could carry as many as three coats, four umbrellas, a hat and an attaché-case at once and all with different owners, and still give everyone the right token.

With her elbow—it was the only part of her that wasn't carrying something—she slid Irene's handbag back towards her.

"You keep this, dearie," she said. "You'll be wanting it."

The girl behind Irene gave a smile. She was a pale, sad-looking girl.

"There's always room under the counter somewhere," she said. "You'll get used to it."

"Thanks," Irene said.

She hated all this new girl stuff. It made her feel silly. Younger than she really was.

"Which department?" the dark girl asked.

"I . . . I don't really know," Irene admitted. "I've got to ask for a Miss Hallett."

"Ground floor," the dark girl told her. "Over by the handbags."

"Thanks," Irene said again.

Then, because it was obvious that the dark girl was trying to be nice, she added: "Thanks ever so."

The dark girl smiled.

"Probably be seeing you," she said. "Good luck."

By now they were pouring out of the cloakroom at such a rate that at first Irene didn't see her father standing there.

"Come on, dear," he said. "I've just got time to take you down and introduce you. Then I'll have to be getting back. It's through here . . ."

But this time Irene stopped him.

"I know," she said. "I've asked."

Mr. Privett seemed hurt. Was hurt, in fact. He had looked forward to introducing his daughter to Miss Hallett.

Not that it really mattered. Sometime during the morning he would be able to step down for a few minutes to see how she was getting on.

There was no difficulty about finding Miss Hallett. No difficulty at all. Indeed, as soon as Irene got past the evening bags there was Miss Hallett looking out for her. She seemed a nice sort of woman, too. A bit worried-looking, Irene noticed. But that may have been only because she was getting everything ready. And she certainly went out of her way to be pleasant. But, for all the wrong reasons, it turned out. It wasn't because she appreciated that she was lucky having Irene working alongside her at all. She didn't

114

even seem to know that Irene had been one of the star pupils of the Eleanor Atkinson, that both Miss Preston and Mrs. Wells had said that Irene could have gone to the University if she had stayed on. It was simply because Irene was Mr. Privett's daughter that she was pleased to see her at all. In Miss Hallett's order of things a shopwalker, even though he didn't happen to be on her floor, was a person of consequence. A figure.

"So you're Mr. Privett's daughter, are you?" she asked. "Well, we must see what we can do for you, mustn't we? Put your bag down there, dear. And are your shoes all right? It's all standing remember. Get ever so tired if you haven't got the right sort of shoes. Feeling nervous?"

"I am a bit," Irene admitted.

It wasn't really true. But it seemed to be the answer that Miss Hallett expected. And Miss Hallett was certainly pleased by it. The worried look vanished, and she patted Irene's hand.

"If you're your father's daughter you'll be all right," she said. "Now you stand about here. Of course, if the other young lady's busy, you may have to cross over. But try not to get into each other's way. And here's your cash book. I'll sign it for you just at first until you're used to it. And don't forget the carbons. That's terrible if you forget them. If I'm not around, Miss Kent'll show you."

But so far there was no sign of Miss Kent. Even though it was already one minute to nine, Irene had the counter to herself. Then she really did begin to feel nervous. She wondered what would happen if a customer really did come in and want to buy something. But she need not have worried. Miss Kent was in sight by now. She was a large, dark, sullen girl. And not hurrying. She came in like a disgruntled black swan, quietly drifting when everything around her was rush and bustle. As soon as she got round behind the counter she began easing her feet out of her shoes.

"Oh, God," she said. "Another week of it." Then she looked up as if she had only just noticed that Irene was standing there. "Where did you spring from?" she asked.

"I'm new here," Irene told her. "I'm only just starting. Are you Miss Kent?"

Miss Kent was flexing her toes and bending her ankles, like someone getting ready to dive. "Call me Babs. It sounds nicer. First day?"

115

Irene nodded.

" I'll pray for you," Miss Kent promised.

There was a pause. Miss Kent was examining her nails, holding them up so as to get the light on them. There was an air of having only just discovered that she had fingernails.

Irene began to feel a bit out of it. She gave a little cough.

" My name's Irene," she said at last. " Irene Privett."

Miss Kent stopped examining her nails. The magic had evidently been broken.

" Oh, that's right," she replied. " I remember now. Poor you." She was winding a bit of her hair round her finger as she was speaking. " I need a new perm," she added. " That's what's the matter with me. I only had the ends done last time." She paused. " Your dad's here, isn't he? " she asked. " He was down all last week talking about you. How much do you think you'll be able to get away with? "

But Miss Kent had already forgotten about Irene. She was wetting her finger and running it up and down the calf of her leg.

" Laddered," she said. " Oh, God! My last pair, too."

Irene tried to look sympathetic. But it was really about Miss Hallett's last remark that she was still thinking.

" Would you mind showing me about carbons? " she said. " I don't know the first thing."

Miss Kent stopped rubbing her stockings, and brought out her sales book.

" Nothing to it," she said. " You just fold the top sheet over like this, and . . . somebody's taken my pencil again. Be a pet, dear, and lend me yours. I'll give it back to you . . ."

3

But on that particular Monday morning Irene wasn't the only person in Rammell's who was feeling lost. Resentful. Bewildered.

Upstairs in a little room leading off the managing director's office there was someone else who was whole-heartedly loathing every minute of it. Not that there had been many minutes for Tony to loathe so far. It was still only ten-thirty. And up to the present he hadn't really done anything. Admittedly, two traysful of letters had been put down on the desk in front of him. But he hadn't done more than glance at them. They seemed to be complaints mostly. Rather rude, too, some of them. They represented retail commerce at its most sordid. And then, just when he had begun to get interested comparing the handwriting, the trays had been whisked away by Miss Underhill. He had decided already that he didn't like Miss Underhill. She kept sweeping in and out like some kind of ageing ice-queen. And he felt a chill run through him every time she entered. But even she had gone away by now. Her small efficiency igloo was just across the passage.

Left completely alone for the last quarter of an hour, he had done nothing but stare out of the window. It was all as bloody silly as he had told his father it would be. He would have been of more use to everybody, certainly less of an aching misery to himself, if he had simply stayed quietly at home. He had made one last attempt to explain this to Mr. Rammell as they came along to Bond Street in the car together. But he had already discovered that there were two completely different Mr. Rammells. One was the Mr. Rammell who crossed his legs on the footstool in the study and kept pouring himself out whisky and soda—first a little more whisky, and then a little more soda—right on through the evening. Rather a boringly talkative type, Tony had always found him. And the other was Mr. Rammell with his feet up on the footrail of the car. This Mr. Rammell had his nose inside the *Financial Times,* and wasn't prepared to talk about anything. Tony had just got as far as: " Y'know, Dad, I still think we're both making a big mistake . . ." when Mr. Rammell interrupted him.

" Oh, for God's sake, boy," he said irritably as the first twinge of the morning's indigestion began cutting into him, " how the hell can I read if you're talking to me all the time? I'll leave you to find your own way in to-morrow."

That was rich, Tony thought. It was irony at its most subtle. Because one of the grimmest things about going into Rammell's at all was that he was being carted along in this way in the morning. If Mr. Rammell had hired a nannie to bring him it couldn't have been worse. He had come down this morning as usual wearing his suède shoes and his purple pullover, and his father had said flatly that they wouldn't do. Had sent him upstairs again to change, in fact. And told him to hurry. What Tony was now wearing was a double-breasted blue suit with a dark tie, and a pair of very ordinary black shoes.

" Oh, God," he was thinking. " I feel like some bloody awful bank clerk. Perhaps the old man'd like it better if I wore pince-nez . . ."

But he wasn't entirely wasting his time. His window staring at least had a definite purpose. He was making a social survey. And the results were certainly interesting. Because, whereas Oxford Street was packed solid with Austins and Morrises and Fords, Bond Street—which after all was only just around the corner—was equally jammed up with Rolls-Royces and Bentleys and Daimlers. A correspondent of *Pravda* could have drawn all the wrong conclusions about England simply by standing at that particular window and being observant. Tony was still counting cars when his father came in.

" Come along now," he said. " Time to go round the departments."

This was very much the other Mr. Rammell. The one whom Tony scarcely recognised. There was a new air of authority about him. Tony even felt rather respectful. Because this version of his father made sense. He seemed more at home, as it were. More at home in the shop than back in Eaton Square.

But all the same Tony didn't find the prospect of going round the departments very attractive. It was too public for his liking. Suppose he met someone he knew. That wouldn't be so funny. And as they got into the lift, he mentioned what he was feeling.

" I say, Dad," he said diffidently. " Don't want you to feel you have to do this, you know. Not on my account. No point in making a spectacle of ourselves."

But Mr. Rammell merely laid his hand on Tony's arm for a moment.

" Got to get used to being stared at," he said. " Doesn't do you any harm, and it's good for them. Great mistake to slink round. Bad for you, and they resent it. Say good morning, and remember their names. That's the chief point. Very important, people's names. They're the only ones they've got."

They had reached the ground floor by now, and the lift girl pressed the knob that slid the big fancy doors back for them. Tony had been observing her carefully on the way down. They held a mysterious fascination for him, these lift girls. The one in charge of their lift was clearly a twin of the girl in charge of the adjoining one—the one which was going up while theirs had been starting to go down. But that wasn't the end of it. There were two more of the family, apparently of exactly the same age, both sailing serenely up and down the lift shafts on the north side of the buildings, and another pair, twins, in charge of the main lifts by the front entrance. The only difference was that some of them wore fair hair, and some of them dark. It was obviously the same hair, however—rather long and very curly, and fluffed carefully up under the hat band at the back. It occurred to Tony that perhaps the hair was issued along with the uniform.

Tony was thinking vaguely about a ballet that could be made with Robert Helpmann for the shop-walker, and a chorus of little blonde and brunette lift-dolls, when he became aware that his father was introducing him to someone. It was to Mr. Bloot. It was, indeed, Mr. Bloot who destroyed the ballet in Tony's mind. Because Mr. Bloot was not in the least like Robert Helpmann. It would have to have been an all-police ballet to do justice to Mr. Bloot.

" Vurry per-oud to meet yur, sir," Mr. Bloot was saying, with the sort of bow that is usually reserved for Royalty. " Vurry per-oud, indeed, sir."

" Everything all right? " Mr. Rammell asked.

He had a quick, clipped way of speaking that Tony had not heard before. The thought that his father was possibly quite a brisk efficient sort of person surprised him. Certainly he seemed to know a lot about the place. And he gave the air of wanting to know exactly what was going on. Not that Mr. Bloot had very much to tell him.

" Vurry quaht, sir," was all he said. " Vurry quaht, indeed. Always vurry quaht of a Monday."

But already Mr. Rammell was moving on.

" Get his name? " he inquired.

Tony shook his head.

" Didn't catch it," he said.

" Then listen," Mr. Rammell said sharply. " And concentrate. No good coming round if you don't pay attention. Just a waste of everybody's time. It was Bloot. B-l-o-o-t."

Tony said nothing. That was because he was finding it difficult to keep up with Mr. Rammell. His father seemed to have collected a new store of energy from somewhere. He was stepping out like

119

a road walker. What's more, he had just seen one of the ground floor's real aristocracy. Someone to whom he was rather proud to introduce his son. That was because he had himself once been introduced to him. The man, in fact, was almost as old as Rammell's. Been there for fifty years. And beginning to look as though it had been longer. Practically quills and parchment it must have been when he had started.

"This is Mr. Barwell," Mr. Rammell said quickly. "Try to remember. B-a-r-w-e-l-l."

The letters were positively hissed at him, Tony noticed. It was the sort of voice that a frayed schoolmaster uses when up against a really stupid child. Tony resented it. And it hurt all the more because it was so strikingly different from the tone of voice that Mr. Rammell used when speaking to Mr. Barwell himself.

"Ah, morning, Barwell," he said, rather as though it might have been in the saloon bar that they were meeting. "How's the back? Got to take care of yourself, you know. Like you to meet my son. Just taking a look round for himself. Probably be seeing a good deal more of him. Wants to find out how it all works, don't you, Tony?"

This was even more embarrassing. Because his father seemed to have forgotten what age his own son was. From the way he was speaking he was practically inviting Mr. Barwell to come forward and pat him on the head. Not that Mr. Barwell looked the sort of man to be unduly familiar. He had been in the stationery trade for so long that he had gone a bit dry and papery himself. And he didn't say very much. Just stood there smiling like a polite mummy, and rubbing the ball of his thumb across his fingers as though sampling invisible weaves. Tony felt sorry for the old thing.

But apparently Mr. Rammell saw Mr. Barwell differently. There was no trace of being sorry when he referred to him. There was respect, rather. Open, unconcealed admiration. A reverence for this ancient wizard of diaries and note-paper.

"No flies on old Barwell," Mr. Rammell said, admiringly. "Knows the whole thing from back to front. Best buyer in the business. Good standing, too. He's this year's President."

"What of?"

"S.D.T.A.," Mr. Rammell told him in a tone of surprise, as though he expected everybody to know about the S.D.T.A. and Mr. Barwell's presidency. "You know, Stationery and Diary

Trades Association. Quite a figure, old Barwell." He paused, and then, dropping his voice a little, added more respectfully than ever. " He could *kill* a new line if he didn't like it."

Even so, the despotic, line-killing Mr. Barwell was only one of them. There were other figures all evidently in their own way as well-established and formidable as that desiccated figure under the illuminated " FOUNTAIN PENS " notice. There was Mr. Chubb, a very tall, sad man who kept bending forward like a flamingo and easing his knee-joints while he was talking. He, it seemed, was a complete master of neckwear. There was Mr. Gibson, fat and squat and damp-looking like a toad, who knew all about gloves. And Mr. Rawle, upright and military in appearance, who was an authority on shirts. There was Mr. Hamlin, Mr. Newby, Mr. Bridson, Mr. . . .

But it was none of these that Tony Rammell was thinking. The names were too many. The accomplishments too various. He had given up. He wasn't even listening any more. He was looking instead at the dress ornament counter just beyond the handbags. There was a big dark girl there that he didn't care for. She looked altogether too glowering and sultry for his taste. And she was apparently having some sort of trouble with her dress. A shoulder strap had gone, or something. It was the girl beside her who interested Tony. She was dark, too. But in a younger, fresher sort of way. She couldn't have been more than about seventeen or eighteen, he reckoned. Scarcely more than a child. Ought to have been at the seaside somewhere enjoying herself. Not standing about in a big shop looking agitated.

Because there was no doubt about it: she was certainly in a state about something. And he saw that the cause of all the trouble was a rather seedy-looking, undersized man who was talking to her. Tony supposed that he was finding fault with the girl. He moved forward to hear what the row was all about.

But the words he caught surprised him. It might have been Rammell's medical officer who was speaking.

" You'll take a glass of hot milk like I say," the man was telling her. " A glass of hot milk and a bun. It's nearly eleven. I'll show you the way."

By now, however, it wasn't only Tony who was interested. It was Mr. Rammell as well. He had just spoken a word to Mr. Higgett of smoking accessories, nodded to Mr. Sparkes who specialised in binoculars and opera glasses, and smiled warmly at Mr. Benskin (umbrellas and shooting-sticks). Then he noticed what was going on through the archway on the feminine side of the store. It was astonishing! Five minutes to eleven, and the upper floor shopwalker engaged in what looked like a rather stormy flirtation with a pretty girl whom he had never seen before. Mr. Rammell hurried forward. He was glad to observe that Tony, too, had spotted that something was amiss.

" Good morning, Mr. Privett," he said briskly. " What's going on here? "

The " Mr." was itself significant. There was a coldness, a sense of distance about it, that would never have been there if he had met him normally on his own ground two floors higher up. Then it would have been: " 'Morning, Privett. Leg getting on all right? "

But to his surprise, Mr. Privett did not seem to notice that anything was wrong. At the sight of Mr. Rammell he began beaming.

" Good morning, sir," he said as though he had engineered the whole meeting. " This is er nappy omen. Might I introduce my daughter, Ireen? First day here, sir. Just starting. Ireen, this is our Managing Director."

He was as a matter of fact showing off a bit. Building up the part to impress Irene. He didn't usually carry on quite such a spirited conversation when he met Mr. Rammell. Generally it was nothing more than: " Nicely, thank you, sir. Very kind of you to inquire." But Irene's presence gave him a new confidence. He wanted to give her plenty of confidence, too. Show her that her father was the sort of man who was on practically back-slapping terms with all the directors.

And he felt bound to say—he did, indeed, say it very frequently to Mrs. Privett that evening—that Mr. Rammell behaved very nicely indeed. Because even though Irene, apart from being Mr. Privett's daughter, was a nobody, a mere beginner, Mr. Rammell leant across and shook hands with her.

" I hope you'll be very happy here," he said.

And Irene, instead of remaining silent, or blushing or doing anything silly like that, delighted Mr. Privett by behaving in her best Eleanor Atkinson speech-day manner.

" Thank you, Mr. Rammell," she said. " I feel quite sure I shall."

That in itself would have been good enough. But it was nothing to what was coming. Because Mr. Rammell glanced over his shoulder and beckoned to the rather diffident, shy-looking young man who was standing behind him.

" Well, well, well Privett," he said. There was no trace of the " Mr." now. " Quite a family party, isn't it? This is my son, Mr. Anthony. First day here, too. Tony, this is Mr. Privett. Keeps the third floor in order, eh Privett? "

Like Mr. Privett, Mr. Rammell was over-playing *his* part a bit by now.

Tony shook hands.

" I shall be coming up to see you one of these days, Mr. Privett," he said. " Perhaps you could spare the time to show me round."

At that, Mr. Rammell was delighted, too. Absolutely delighted. The politeness was so exactly right. The " one of these days " had the authentic ring to it. Tony might have been on the managerial board already.

But what Mr. Rammell couldn't understand was Tony's behaviour when he was introduced to Irene Privett. Because then he did more than shake hands with her. He said something that Mr. Rammell couldn't quite catch. It sounded like a warning against hot milk.

CHAPTER XIV

MARCIA HAD been trying hard, desperately hard, to bring her interests in line with Mr. Bulping's. She now even tried to read the articles in *Country Life* instead of merely glancing at the advertisements. Because it turned out that Mr. Bulping was by way of being a country gentleman as well as a manufacturer.

Secretly, the prospect of country life still appalled her. The perpetual rain. The brogues. The incredibly doggy-smelling spaniels. The neighbours. But she had learnt her lesson the hard way. After two husband failures she was ready to identify herself absolutely with the third one. And if her new life had to include racehorses she was determined to do her best by them. That was why she sometimes read *The Field* as well.

It was because of her selflessness that she was so wretched at the present moment. Quite cast-down and despondent. Almost suicidal, in fact. That was because she had begun to doubt Mr. Bulping. If she hadn't been working for her living it would all have been so much easier. But professional engagements were after all her livelihood. There were whole regiments of debs. and generals' daughters simply sitting by the telephone day after day waiting for their agents to call them.

And Mr. Bulping's visits were always so sudden. A telephoned love message at four-thirty meant that the lover himself would be arriving at Euston by nine-thirty. And it wasn't always convenient. What was she to do if he clashed with National Silk Week or a B.B.C. Television Knit-Wear Gala?

Take to-night, for instance. She was modelling for charity in the Park-Mayfair from nine until ten fifteen. Mr. Bulping, on the other hand, wanted supper at ten sharp. When she told him about the fashion show he didn't even ask where it was. Just told her to be round at Quog's at 10.30, and rang off.

Had he flicked her across the face with one of his own swimsuits, she could not have been more offended. Because if he had really loved her—loved her, that is, in the way that she loved him—

he would have come along simply to watch her as she paraded. She especially wanted him there, too. All on account of one particular wrap. It was an electric-blue mink. With simply enormous sleeves. The price was three thousand guineas. But Marcia who knew about mink had to admit that it really was worth every penny of it.

Without Mr. Bulping there, however, it remained horribly impersonal. Merely another expensive wrap that she was displaying for other people. It was heartbreaking to reflect that sometime there would be someone somewhere else sufficiently devoted to want to make a gift of it . . .

And there was another cause altogether for her low spirits. For some reason or other she couldn't help remembering Tony. Mr. Rammell had brought him into the dress salon the other day and introduced him. He had seemed so young, she thought. And so delightfully shy. He had actually stammered when he spoke to her. She wasn't in love with him. Or anything like that. It was Mr. Bulping she loved. But all the same, his image would keep coming back into her mind. If she closed her eyes for a single moment, he was there. And always the same image, too. Rather tired and dishevelled-looking, with a single lock of untidy hair falling over his forehead as he bent forward.

That was why it was so maddening to find that Mr. Bulping was depressed and out of sorts, too. Apparently he had been having a quite peculiarly exasperating kind of day and he was intent on telling Marcia all about it.

". . . then when I got back to the office I found that the bloody fools had been waiting all the time round at the factory . . ."

"You poor darling," Marcia told him. "You must be absolutely all in."

Mr. Bulping gave her a long sideways glance.

"I was when I came down here," he said. "Not now. That's why I rang you. I felt I needed a bit of fun."

A bit of fun! She gave an little inward shudder at the words. If only for once Mr. Bulping would consider her feelings. It was his awful enthusiasm that she found so off-putting. And to-night it was more crudely apparent than ever. Locked in his bear-hug embrace while dancing she had to listen to the kind of endearments that are so much better left unsaid.

" So I said to myself ' Me for a night out,' and here I am . . .
I'm not saying you're the first, but I am saying I never felt quite
this way before . . . Talk about calf-love. Give me the middle-aged
variety."

And it was the same when Marcia let him take her home afterwards. Only by then he had drunk just a little too much and was
sentimental in a slow, maudlin way that reminded her of her first
husband.

" Unattainable, that's what you are," he kept saying. " Unattainable."

Marcia drew her wrap more closely round her, and gave him
her Madonna smile. She was still hoping that he would decide to
go.

" You really can't say that, can you? " she asked, without
looking up at him as she said it.

But finesse and Mr. Bulping had never been on other than the
most distant of terms.

" It's what I do say," he repeated. " Unattainable. The
eternal feminine. *Cherchez la femme.* Mysterious, that's what you
are. Mysterious. It's what I like about you."

It was getting on for one o'clock by now. She still hoped that
he would notice how late it was. But he gave no sign of it. Quite
the contrary, in fact. He had just undone his waistcoat.

" Would you care for another drink? " she asked.

Mr. Bulping shook his head.

" Not while I'm here," he said. " Not so long as I can just sit
back and watch you." He paused. " If there's anything you ever
want, anything in the world, just tell me. It's yours. That's the
sort of man I am. You tell me what you want and I'll get it for
you."

He got up as he was speaking and moved over to the little
Japanese side-table where the drinks were set out. While he was
pouring himself another whisky and soda, Marcia decided right
out to ask him for the electric-mink. It would have seemed altogether
too horrid to ask if he hadn't actually offered. As it was, it would
have been equally horrid to refuse.

" There is something . . ." she began.

But already Mr. Bulping had interrupted her.

" I know," he said. " And by God you shall have it. If any
woman ever earned it, you have."

Marcia paused, trying hard to bring out her smile again.

" Have I? " she asked. " Have I really? "

" You bet you have," he told her. " It's what I came down to talk about." He paused for a moment and stared down at his shoes. " What do you do with yourself when I'm not around? " he asked.

Marcia dropped her eyes again.

" I manage."

This was evidently the moment for which Mr. Bulping had been waiting. He got up and came over to her.

" You sit on my knee," he said. " Then we can discuss it properly."

It wasn't easy because all the chairs in Marcia's flat were so small. But Mr. Bulping seemed determined on it. There were sinister creakings in the framework as he settled himself.

" Now put your head on my shoulder," he said. " And don't upset the glass. It's just by your left elbow." He breathed deeply, seemingly content by this re-arrangement. Then he resumed. " Well, you needn't manage any longer."

" Needn't I? " Marcia asked, scarcely above a whisper.

Sitting on people's knees is always difficult. And for a tall girl it is practically impossible. Certainly uncomfortable. But in a way it was restful, too. She could have dropped off to sleep, all folded up as she was, if only she hadn't been so anxious to know what he was leading up to.

" I've found it at last," Mr. Bulping went on. " Just for the two of us. And that's all that matters, isn't it? "

Somewhere in the crook of his shoulder Marcia, still as much bewildered as ever, tried to nod her head. But it wasn't easy. The edge of Mr. Bulping's collar kept cutting into her every time she moved.

" It's nothing much to look at," Mr. Bulping told her. " Georgian. Nothing fancy. But it's all been done up. And there's a nice bit of land. Keep your own horse if you want to."

" My own horse? "

The words came out faint and incredulous.

" That's what I said," Mr. Bulping told her. " And it's only twenty-five minutes. Good road all the way."

" Where to? "

Marcia was sitting up by now.

" Wolverhampton, of course. Where d'you think? Timbuctoo? "

" Me live outside Wolverhampton? " Marcia asked.

Mr. Bulping took a sip from the whisky glass beside him.

" That's the idea," he said. " Then I could see you every day. None of this once a fortnight stuff. Be more natural about it."

" Do you . . . do you mean after we're married? " Marcia asked.

Mr. Bulping put his glass down again.

" That's the whole trouble," he said. " It's Mrs. B. Won't divorce me." He felt Marcia stiffen as he said it. And he went on hurriedly. " Now don't get mad at me," he told her. " It's not my fault. There's nothing more that I can do. I've done everything the solicitors said. There's enough evidence to divorce an army. It's simply that she won't have it. Religious. And spiteful. God how that woman hates me . . ."

Marcia got up.

" Hadn't you better go? " she asked coldly.

" Hadn't you better think it over? " Mr. Bulping replied.

BOOK TWO

Love and the Shopwalker

CHAPTER XV

WELL, there we are.

Mr. Privett had got his way. Irene was safely launched on a career behind the counter. And whenever he popped down from the third floor to take a look at her he felt in a warm, sunsettish fashion that his life's work was very nearly done. That was because there is nothing that consoles a parent so much as to know that whatever turn Fate may take his offspring is safe and provided for. A wife's different. There is always the insurance to take care of her. And Mr. Privett was well insured—nine hundred pounds *and* benefits.

All the same, he was a very worried man. Nothing physical. His leg was completely better by now. Not even a scar to show for that miraculous escape from death. It was simply that it was now obvious that in choosing Mr. Hamster he had made the wrong choice. In short, the man had shown himself to be a dud. A real bad egg among solicitors. Practically strike-offable if all the facts were known. Already there was a rift between Mr. Privett and Mr. Hamster. That was because Mr. Hamster wanted to sue the insurance company. And Mr. Privett didn't.

For a start, he couldn't bear to think of the costs. Mr. Hamster was such a prolific letter writer. Every time Mr. Privett saw an envelope with blue rather smudgy lettering that was the best that Mr. Hamster's typewriter could manage, his heart missed a beat. Because so far he hadn't paid Mr. Hamster anything.

And in the meantime, he was left spiritually stranded. He was like a watch without a mainspring. At first glance outwardly normal. But nothing going on inside. Mondays to noon on Saturdays were all right. Sundays simply terrible. He still went along to the Highgate Ponds as regularly as before. But without a model yacht to sail it all seemed rather silly and pointless. He just stood around, getting in other people's way and criticising. Already he could feel himself becoming unpopular.

Even so, Mr. Privett's state was not so bad as Mr. Rammell's.

Mr. Rammell was really up against it. He was contemplating the wreck of his whole marriage. There didn't seem to be even one point of contact where he and Mrs. Rammell ever really came together. They existed in the same house. But there was a gap the width of the Atlantic between the two of them. They were merely two strangers, with a roughly parallel life history.

It wasn't even as though Tony had done anything to bring them both together. On the contrary, it was chiefly about Tony that they quarrelled. Not that you must start getting the wrong ideas about the Rammells. There weren't rows. Scenes. Flare-ups. Scarcely even bickerings. Just a steady withdrawal from each other. A sort of emotional recession. Except where Tony was concerned. " Why? " Mrs. Rammell had demanded, her voice rising higher and higher. " Why drive the child into Bond Street when all that he wanted to do was interior decoration? " Mr. Rammell could still feel the palms of his hands growing sticky as he remembered everything he had gone through before he could get Tony safely behind that desk in the room next door to his.

Mrs. Rammell was pretty miserable, too. For a start, there were her headaches. And that mysterious pain in her spine that no specialist could diagnose. And her sinus. But she knew deep inside herself that really it was none of them. It was all because of Tony. She knew him. Knew more about him than his father could ever hope to know. And she could see that he was being wasted. Thrown away. Sacrificed. Not that this surprised her. She had seen so much of her marriage squandered and trampled on already.

In the end, there had been only two consolations left to her. Tony. And her music. If Tony was to be snatched away as well, surely Mr. Rammell could see that she must do more for music. Much more. Make it so that musicians and artists everywhere could feel that it was as much their home as hers and Mr. Rammell's.

But there were still some perfectly happy people left in the Rammell collection. Take Marcia, for instance. She was now living in that lulled, contented state that comes of having made an irrevocable decision. She had decided to dedicate herself to Mr. Bulping. Simply wait patiently for his divorce to come through.

It was wonderful knowing that, apart from delays on the purely legal side, her future was secure. God knew that he, poor darling, was doing all he could to get things moving. And surely that awful wife of his couldn't go on for ever being so downright wicked as to stand in their way now that their love was so apparent, so undeniable.

Marcia could make herself weep just by thinking how wonderful Mr. Bulping had been during all this awful period of strain. Always devoted. Always considerate. Always generous. Dotingly generous, in fact. He never really seemed to think of money. There was a magnificent casualness about him whenever the topic cropped up. And that was just how Marcia liked a man to be. Big. Impetuous, even, in a reckless, schoolboyish sort of way that Marcia found irresistible. What, for instance, could she do but accept when he turned up late one evening entirely unannounced—she didn't even know that he was in town—with a pair of pearl and platinum ear-rings. And after the pearls had come an evening beauty box from Paris. It was an enchanting little toy that turned itself practically into a small dressing-table when it was opened fully out. And after her dressing-table beauty box came a pair of long gloves studded right up to the armpits with rhinestones. The long gloves were particularly exciting. And reassuring. They showed that, as well as being generous, Mr. Bulping had some really astonishing flashes of good taste.

Yes, it was wonderful for Marcia having Mr. Bulping so whole-heartedly enthusiastic about her. And she didn't intend to let anything go wrong this time. Her two previous marriages had taught her that it wasn't safe to leave things entirely in the hands of the husband. In consequence, she was working really hard trying to be a sharer, a helpmeet. She was sinking her personality in his. Blending her exquisiteness to his robustness. She was still reading *Country Life* and *The Field* and had just started on *Horse and Hound* as well . . . Even her appearance was perceptibly changing. The last thing that she had ordered on her Rammell account was a rough, practically sandpaper tweed with a divided skirt. She was having trouble to find a pair of shoes heavy enough to go with it.

There was nothing very sensational that had happened to Irene so far. She was still having trouble with the carbon sheet in the cash book. Had established a new record, in fact, for three missing counterfoils all in one morning. But she was gradually getting things sorted out. She could carry a sale right through now without having to ask Miss Kent to help her. And, to her own surprise, she had found that she could add up shillings and pence correctly.

What pleased Mr. Privett so much was that she was entering into the social life of the place. She had joined the Sports Club (subscription, ten shillings) and the Dramatic Society (subscription, five bob). The Sports Club was somewhere right out in the Wembley direction, and Mr. Privett had never even been to it himself. But the Dramatic Society used the Rudolf Steiner Hall in Baker Street. Mr. Privett had seen two performances there—*The Pirates of Penzance* and *Dear Octopus* And he had enjoyed them enormously. He liked the idea of Irene appearing alongside the cream of Rammell's acting talent, Mr. Brittle from the Counting House, Mr. Thompson-Strong from Sports, Mrs. Alford from Post and Export and the pretty Miss Peggy Winters from Cosmetics.

Mrs. Privett, on the other hand, was afraid that Irene might be overdoing it. Taxing her strength too far. But there was no real danger of that. Irene still disliked Rammell's intensely. She certainly didn't intend killing herself for Mr. Preece. In the Autumn she was planning to go to the Polytechnic evening Drama School as well.

Tony Rammell, too, still felt himself to be an outsider. He intended chucking his job altogether as soon as he could find something that he could really get his teeth into. He was spending all his spare time learning Russian. The one thing that he really wanted was a visa. Then he would be able to see the Bolskoya Theatre for himself. But Mr. Rammell had declined to help him. Even forbidden him to write to the Foreign Office on the firm's note-paper. It was Sir Harry who was more sympathetic. He could understand the boy's restlessness. His eagerness for travel and adventure. As soon as Tony mentioned it, the old man cottoned on at once. He suggested that the two of them should go somewhere. Monte Carlo. Cannes. Nice. Anywhere in reason that Tony cared to suggest.

There was, however, more to it than his love for young Tony. There was photography. Sir Harry had just bought himself a Leica f.1.4, complete with a bag of tricks that a Press photographer would envy and never use. He wasn't very good with it yet. There were some knobs that he hadn't properly got round to. And sometimes he took three or four snaps all on the same piece of film. But what did it matter? Sir Harry was happy. He had made a lot of new friends, too, at Wallace Heaton's where he bought the camera. And he rather liked the red-haired girl at the chemist's where he took his strange multiple pictures to be developed. The last one showed Mrs. Rammell with Major Cuzzens's head in her lap and a spectral pianist, whom he couldn't even remember, brooding like a cloud over the pair of them. But Sir Harry didn't care. Wherever he went, his camera went with him. And Wednesdays now had a brand new thrill for him. That was because it was on Wednesday that *The Amateur Photographer* came out. The last issue had contained a whole article on Mediterranean lighting.

And that about accounts for everyone. Except Mr. Bloot. He was in a terrible state. He was being driven half crazy because he didn't yet know whether Hetty Florence really intended to marry him. Or whether she was just toying with his affections. That was why he couldn't sleep at nights. Why for the first time in twenty-seven years he had forgotten to change the budgerigars' water. He'd had eleven different budgerigars altogether. But the shame of forgetting to attend to Champion Billy continued to haunt him. It showed that under the strain he was beginning to break up. What's more, he was losing weight. He could now put a half-pound packet of bird seed into the waist-band of his trousers and still do up the top button. It was terrible.

CHAPTER XVI

Mr. Bloot's decision to go round to see Hetty was made without any proper planning or forethought. It was simply the compulsive action of an overwrought and desperate man.

Normally, he didn't ever see Hetty on Wednesdays. That, she told him, was the evening when she washed her hair. And remembering how much of it she had, the occasion had a semi-sacred significance. Sometimes, dreamily, at the moment of dropping off to sleep he had seen himself brushing Hetty's hair. He could hear the swish that the brush made as it swept through the long clinging tresses. Feel the caress of the hair upon his bare hands. Smell the rich fragrance of the real egg-shampoo. . . . But such intimacies, he told himself, should be reserved for the final mystery of marriage. Better not think about them. Or he would go mad.

And it wasn't merely the strain of a long engagement from which he was suffering. It was worse than that. Because he didn't even know what her intentions towards him really were. For all he could tell she was merely toying with him. That was why he had got to ask her. Put the question point blank. Real take it, or leave it stuff.

He heaved himself up suddenly.

" It's now or never," he said. " Ah just can't go on like this. Not even if she is washing 'er 'air. She 'asn't got the raht to arsk it of me. Ah'm only 'uman. Ah'm flesh-and-blood, even if Ah am fifty-seven. Ah'm not some sortover monk."

The fact that he had voiced such feelings, even to himself, showed how keyed-up he was. Not that he looked unduly perturbed as he set out. That may, however, have been merely because the weather had turned chilly, and he was wearing his knitted lining. It was a thick lining with padded sides. And knitted things and passion do not go together. There is something mutually irreconcilable. Also, his overcoat was of a cut that suggested social standing rather than romance. It was dark blue with a black velvet half-collar. A thoroughly distinguished piece of tailoring that had been made for a man only a few inches shorter than Mr. Bloot, it had reached him via a misfit specialist off Shaftesbury Avenue. And it showed its origin most distinctly. Every time Mr. Bloot wore it, he added something of Savile Row and Boodles's to the local landscape of Kentish Town and Tufnell Park.

It was only his gait that revealed that there was something urgent and imperative about the expedition. And there were no flowers this time. The period for bouquet and blandishment was over. A straight "yes" or "no" coming from the other party was what Mr. Bloot now demanded. And this was a pity. Because full-blooded, high-spirited women like Hetty Florence are often touched and left practically defenceless by some little attention, some small floral tribute. That original bunch of sweet peas and gladioli had very nearly won her the first time. But he was not to know that. Subtlety, particularly subtlety in matters of the heart, formed no part of Mr. Bloot's make-up. Nor had he ever needed it. Emmie had been demonstrably of the straightforward, no-nonsense school.

The Tufnell Park Road seemed unusually long this evening. And the bus up the Seven Sisters Road unnaturally slow. As he sat in the corner seat looking out anxiously for Tregunter Road, he kept muttering. His temper was up by now. He was angry and morose. "Wash 'er 'air, indeed," he said aloud as the bus trundled endlessly along. "If she isn't careful she won't 'ave no one to wash it for."

The woman next to him glanced apprehensively towards the well-dressed gentleman who was sitting beside her, and then moved over to the seat opposite. She was disappointed in him. He looked such a reliable, distinguished sort of man. And now she could see that he was just a drunken old reprobate like the rest of them. The words: "Ah'm not a bloody monk. Ah'm a 'uman being like the rest of them" had just reached her from across the gangway. But by then the bus had reached Tregunter Road and Mr. Bloot had got out. Just as well, too. Another mumble from him, and she would have rung the bell so that she could get out herself.

Still inwardly fuming by the time he reached the entrance to Artillery Mansions, Mr. Bloot's whole nature changed as he mounted the steel stair-treads. He was no longer angry. He was frightened. Frightened and contrite. He was afraid of losing Hetty altogether. Ashamed of the thoughts that he had just been thinking. When he reached the first landing he paused. In the course of climbing the last flight his courage had completely evaporated. He was no longer in any mood for an ultimatum. He was trembling too much for that. The utmost that he could go through with—and then only with an act of supreme self-control—would be to pretend that he had just dropped in. He was even working out in his mind some vague, improbable story about having been to see a man in Harringay about a budgerigar. . . .

Passing his tongue across his lips because they were dry, he put out his forefinger and gave the bell-push a quick, nervous jab as though the little porcelain button were red hot.

The abrupt ping of the electric bell made Hetty jump violently. She was not washing her hair. Or anything like it. She was wondering whether to play a seven or take another card from the stack. Her cards had been terrible all evening. She was therefore now concentrating really hard. She had already lost twenty-three-and-sixpence.

" You go, Chick," she said without looking up into the thick blue haze of cigar smoke that was swirling round the room. " It's only Hutch. He said he'd be here if Daisy'd let him."

2

It was not merely the presence of Chick that amazed Mr. Bloot. It was his appearance. For it had grown hot in the small front sitting-room. And Chick had been getting down to things. He had taken off his jacket. Nor had he taken the trouble to dress before going to the front door. His waistcoat—it was a fancy one covered all over with *fleur-de-lys* as though he were the last of the Bourbons —was over the back of his chair. This meant that his braces were showing. And they were like no braces that Mr. Bloot had ever seen before. They had pictures of ladies all over them.

But Mr. Bloot's surprise was no greater than that of Chick himself. He had expected to see Hutch. And Hutch was only a small man. A small man with a thin pointed wedge of a face resting on a polka-dot bow tie. He was a commission agent. And he carried about with him something of the unmistakable alertness of his profession. Whereas this ponderous, muffled-up mammoth with

138

his umbrella and his velvet half-collar suggested a different kind of world altogether. It was the world of church wardens and temperance leagues and boys' welfare clubs. Chick immediately felt suspicious. Gripping his cigar firmly between his teeth, he blocked the narrow hall completely.

" Yah? " he asked.

Mr. Bloot did not reply straight away. He was spell-bound, hypnotised by the ladies on Chick's braces. The thought that perhaps he had blundered, that possibly this was number 25b and not number 23b—there was a duplicate entrance to Artillery Mansions one door farther up the street—flashed into his mind. But one glance over Chick's shoulder reassured him. There on the corner on the mahogany hat-stand hung Hetty's magenta rain-cape. There could hardly be two women in one block of flats who would have chosen so rousing, so declamatory a colour. And even above the general odour of cigar smoke he could detect the elusive, penetrating fragrance of the scent that Hetty always used.

" Good eeverning," he said in his full, robust-sounding baritone. " Ah wonder if Miss Florence is at home. If so, perhaps Ah might be allowed to 'ave a word with 'er."

It all sounded civil enough, Chick admitted. But all the same he didn't like it somehow. There was the additional flavour of debt-collection somewhere in the background. And he wasn't the kind of man to see a good sort like Hetty shamelessly dunned in the middle of a quiet game of poker. He shook his head firmly.

" You're unlucky," he said. " Nothing doing. Oo shall I say called? "

Mr. Bloot felt his whole body go limp. He had been forced to brace himself to come at all. And in the result he was more bewildered than if he had stayed at home. Never a quick thinker he felt the need to play for time.

" It's not important, thank you," he said. " Ah'll call again. She wasn't erspecting me."

His voice was level and steady while he was speaking. But inside him, his heart was hammering. For all he knew the man in front of him might be a burglar. A breaker-in. He tried desperately to memorise his appearance. And he was just turning away, with Chick closing the front door inch by inch on him as he retreated, when suddenly through the half-open door of the sitting-room, he heard Hetty's voice.

Only it was not like her usual voice. Not soft, And husky. And vibrating. It was a torn, anguished voice. With the authentic note of desperation ringing through it.

" No, you don't," she was saying. " That's all you get out of little me. Try it again, and I'll start screaming."

In the ordinary way Mr. Bloot was neither a violent nor impulsive man. Compared with Hetty Florence's friend, Chick, his reactions were definitely lethargic. But sudden anxiety—above all, anxiety about a loved one—can change a man completely. Make a hero of him.

And Mr. Bloot undeniably had weight on his side. Before Chick knew properly what was happening, he found himself trapped behind the half-opened door as Mr. Bloot forced his way past him. The hall was only two foot nine and for a moment the pressure was terrific. The japanned letter-box on the back of the front door was rammed mercilessly into Chick's stomach. He was winded.

But only temporarily. Chick had been in tight corners before. In his time, he had emerged many times victorious and unscathed. From a rough-and-tumble in Harringay. A free-for-all in the King's Cross district. A full open-house down Walthamstow way when a policeman had cut his knuckles open on a razor. Even winded and compressed, he did not doubt that he was more than a match for this sinister, bundled-up figure armed only with an umbrella. But he had never before been up against a real master of umbrella fighting. For Mr. Bloot did not attempt to jab or poke or start hitting out. That would have been disastrous. Instead, finding himself in danger of being attacked from behind, he merely turned round and opened his umbrella.

The barrier was impenetrable. On the one side the spokes caught into the mahogany hat-stand and, on the other, they fixed themselves round the electric light company's main fuse-box. The frame of the umbrella bent and sprang back again. It groaned. But it held fast. Chick went down on hands and knees and began crawling underneath. But by then Mr. Bloot had reached the sitting-room, and flung the door wide open.

" Don't nobody move," he said, in a loud and terrible voice.

He got no further, however. Because at that instant Chick sprang on him from behind. And it was not an amateur attack. It was low. And classical. And rugger-like. It caught Mr. Bloot just below the knees and sent him pitching. At one moment there were Hetty's two friends sympathetically contemplating the wretchedness of her last poker hand. And at the next, sixteen stone of muffler and blue overcoat suddenly crashed down on top of them.

By their very nature, card tables are unable to withstand such strains. They tend to sag if one player even so much as rests his chin upon his elbows. And Hetty's table was by no means a new one. One of the legs was secured by an extra hinge of adhesive tape already. And, in the result, the table offered no resistance at all. Mr. Bloot went straight through it. Cards, glasses, an ash-tray full of cigarette-ends and cigar-butts, all went flying.

But Chick wasn't the only one in the little party to show himself resourceful. There was Sid as well. A bald, fat man, with a wide, expressionless face, he too was experienced in emergencies. Without even getting up from his chair he reached over to the side-table and picked up the lamp that stood upon it. It was quite a small lamp with a pretty flowered shade. But the base was of pottery with a thick rim running all round the bottom. And Sid knew just how to take hold of the lamp—round the narrow fluted neck. That gave him the leverage he wanted. He brought the base down hard on to Mr. Bloot's head as it went past him.

" O.K., Hetty," was all he said, and put the remains of the lamp back on to the side-table.

3

Of course, they all had a good laugh about it afterwards. And it was Hetty with that magnificent vitality of hers who led the laughter. It was an absolute scream, she said, thinking that they had been going to murder her, and Gus was a real darling to have come forward the way he did. There had never been anything like it in her life before. And she wouldn't have missed it for all the tea in China. It was as good as the movies. She went off into more peals of shrill nervous laughter at the memory of it.

Mr. Bloot laughed, too. Laughed more than he had ever laughed before. And louder. He was, in fact, rather surprised at himself for finding everything so funny. But that was probably because of the whisky that he had been given to revive him. Whatever it was, he saw the funny side of it. He fingered the bump on his skull, And laughed. He contemplated the ruins of the card table. And laughed again. He laughed at the ladies on Chick's braces. Sometimes he laughed simply because *everything* seemed funny. The only time he stopped laughing was when there was a ring at the bell. But it still wasn't Hutch—all Hetty's friends he had noticed had monosyllables instead of names. And that struck him as being funny, too.

The person at the door was the tenant of the flat beneath. And he was in a nasty sort of mood. Full of threats about writing to the landlord if this sort of thing went on. His wife had been alone at the time, he said, and he had come back to find her, head under the bedclothes, terrified. There had been screams and the noise of fighting. He had his wife's word for it. And now all this drunken laughter. If there was any more of it he would go round to the police station straightaway.

But Hetty handled him all right. She had a marvellous way with difficult customers. Then when Hetty returned, Mr. Bloot started laughing again. Only this time it was about the tenant of the flat below.

The others left shortly after eleven. Con was the last to go. He was the one of whom Mr. Bloot had seen least. Quieter than the others, he seemed. And in a way, superior. He wore a shirt with a stiff collar, and suggested a counting-house clerk who had got himself into rather mixed company. Because there was no denying it, some of Hetty's friends seemed more than a little beneath her. But that, Mr. Bloot told himself, was only another aspect of this fascinating woman. It was her natural magnetism. And now all that mattered was that he was alone with her. He was still a little dizzy from the force of the blow and the effects of so much whisky. He had, in fact, forgotten why he had come.

But with her beside him, it all came back.

" Marry me, Hetty," he said. " Please marry me."

There was something in the tone of voice, in the very simplicity of his proposal, that Hetty found deeply moving. She had received plenty of the other kind. Bold. Hysterical. Sly. Drunken. Salacious. Overwhelming. But never anything so straightforward and direct as this. For some reason, it made her want to cry.

" D'you really want me all that much? " she asked.

And Mr. Bloot, too much overcome to answer, merely nodded.

" But you don't know anything about me," she told him.

" Ah love you," he said simply. " That's all Ah need to know."

Hetty's heart gave a silly, girlish sort of bound as she heard the words. But it was no use pretending. She was not a girl. She was a mature, experienced woman of forty-five.

" I've been married before, you know," she went on.

Mr. Bloot politely brushed the point aside.

" Ah'mer widower meself, m'dear," he said with a slow, sad smile. " It's the same for both of us."

And as he spoke the words he found himself wishing that Emmie had been there to hear. It would have made her feel better about things knowing that he still valued the state of marriage so highly. Emmie had always been a very conventional woman.

" Well, I suppose you might put it that way," Hetty answered. There was a pause.

" Then will you? " he asked.

" What's the hurry? " Hetty asked gently. " Why's my boy got to know to-night? "

She had linked her arm through his while she was speaking and had led him over to the couch. He felt himself enveloped and wrapped up in a great billowy cocoon of feminine softness and fragrance. The old swoony feeling came over him again.

" Because Ah can't sleep," he answered, in a low mumble like a man talking in his sleep. " Ah can't sleep. Ah've turned against me food. And Ah'm forgetting things. Ah've gone all to pieces because of you, Hetty. Ah can't go on like this. Ah'm not . . ." He checked himself hurriedly. That was just the way things were with him nowadays. His mind kept playing tricks on him. He never knew what silly thing he was going to say next.

But Hetty was in no mood for noticing his sudden pause. She was lying there limply in his arms, her large dark eyes turned towards him.

" Have I really done all that to you? " she asked. " Perhaps I had better marry you. Just to make up for it."

As she said it she stroked the side of his face with the back of her big white hand.

" You mean you will, Hetty? "

She dropped her eyes for a moment. There was a pause.

" I mean I will, Gus," she said, at last. And, to her own

surprise, she found herself adding: "I'll try to be a good wife to you."

The sigh that went up from Mr. Bloot was so deep and long drawn out that for a moment Hetty feared that he had died there in her arms from sheer relief and happiness. But she need not have worried. Because a moment later he sat up again and pulled out his watch.

"Wot time does the last No. 18 go?" he asked.

But Hetty only pulled him down again, and kissed him.

"It's gone," she said quietly.

CHAPTER XVII

MR. BLOOT's arrival at Rammell's next morning was the cause of much comment. For a start, he was late. But that wasn't Mr. Bloot's fault. The doctor was entirely to blame. It was not until twenty to nine when the doctor finally got busy in the surgery. He went to work with a needle and surgical catgut and finally fixed a large criss-cross of sticking plaster on top of the wound that Hetty's ornamental reading lamp had made. Then he told Mr. Bloot to come back again at the end of the week to have the stitches taken out.

The sticking plaster was a mistake. It lent a strangely school playground-like air to Mr. Bloot's appearance. But that was not all that was wrong about him. His collar was not clean. And his clothes had a crumpled, almost slept-in look. This in itself was remarkable. Because usually Mr. Bloot's linen and the crease in his trousers were both irreproachable. Even his eyes—usually pale, glassy and expressionless—were different, too. They were noticeably bloodshot. And he had shaved abominably. That was hardly Mr. Bloot's fault. Arriving at Artillery Mansions entirely unprepared for a night's stay, he had been forced to shave next morning with the best that Hetty could produce in the way of a razor. It was very small. Practically pygmy-size. Straight out of Hetty's week-end beauty case, in fact.

There were two schools of thought on the matter of Mr. Bloot's appearance. Young Mr. Burton (Household Enamel and Aluminium Ware) winked knowingly across at Mr. Rufford (Electric Cookers, Refrigerators and Washing-machines) and whispered something about nights on the tiles and a bit of stray. But that was characteristic of Mr. Burton. He was low by nature. He wore a gold wrist watch with an all-metal bracelet. Mr. Rufford, married, with three children and an invalid mother-in-law, was a different cast of man altogether. He simply didn't believe that the things that young Mr. Burton was always talking about ever went on at all. But he was careful to conceal that he didn't believe in them.

So he winked back just as knowingly in Mr. Burton's direction and pulled the corners of his mouth down just as Mr. Burton had done. Miss Hambridge (Detergents and Stain Removers) took the opposite view. It was wonderful, she contended, that Mr. Bloot should have turned up at all after his injury. But Miss Hambridge had always admired men. Not any one man in particular. Just men.

And it must be admitted, the story that Mr. Bloot concocted was an unsatisfactory one. It was a window that had inflicted the wound. That much was constant. But he was his own worst enemy when he attempted to elaborate. In one version, he had been leaning out when the whole thing had come down on him. In another, it was he who had jerked up too suddenly. The window became sash and casement by turns. It was a front window. And a back window. It had occurred when he was going to bed. And again apparently when he was getting up. It had knocked him nearly unconscious. He had scarcely noticed it until he felt the blood running down.

Either it was the effect of the blow. Or it was the effect of trying to live up to an untruth. Whichever way it was, Mr. Bloot felt poorly. And at lunchtime he went out to buy some aspirins because his head was hurting. It was, indeed, a great tribute to his sense of responsibility that he should have taken the trouble to go outside at all. There was a perfectly good pharmaceutical section on the ground floor that sold aspirins by the hundredweight. But it would have savoured too much of weakness to be seen going there. Also, there would have been all that fiddling business about number and department. Because the assistant would be sure to think that Mr. Bloot was trying to get them at a staff discount.

Not that leaving the premises was entirely without its compensations. It meant that he could phone Tufnell 3246, and talk to Hetty. Even this was not easy, however. Because it was a call from her wholesalers that Hetty was expecting, and before Mr. Bloot could do more than ask if it was the number he had been accused of deliberately keeping back two thousand Players, the same number of Gold Flake, and what sounded to him like a whole lorry load of Top Score, Weights and Woodbines. That being so, there was nothing for it but to wait until she had finished. And then explain who he was. Hetty couldn't have been nicer about it. She told Mr. Bloot that he must have been teasing to allow her to go on like that. At the end of the call she even made kissing sounds into the mouthpiece of the receiver. But the whole incident left Mr. Bloot jangly and perturbed. He had not known that Hetty could get such an edge on to her voice. And her language! It was a revelation that such words were apparently part of the daily to-and-fro of the smoke trade.

And he was still as much in doubt as ever about his future. And hers. After last night, he assumed that they were going to get married, straightaway within a matter of months. Even weeks possibly. But he still didn't know exactly when.

Somehow amid all that laughter he had never got round to asking her.

2

The only thing that saved Mr. Bloot was the problem of young Tony. If it hadn't been for him someone from management would have been bound to notice the sticking plaster. The shagginess.

As it was, Tony was absorbing the whole attention of Management. The office that he now occupied was second from the end on the corridor marked " MANAGEMENT PRIVATE. " There was a plain frosted-glass door. On one side of the door it was all bustle and strip-lighting and card-index cabinets. And on the other, the Management side, it was blue Wilton pile and mahogany panelling and small Doulton ash-trays.

More than once, Tony had applied his mind to the matter of the Management décor. If only the blue Wilton could have been ripped up and the mahogany panelling torn down, then there would be distinct possibilities. It had occurred to him that walls of blue mirrors with a ceiling of pale silver might prove rather attractive. Or daffodil yellow, with chromium doors. Or, no doors or inner walls at all. Just one wide-open living and breathing space. Anyhow, he intended sometime to have a real good go at re-doing it.

For the time being, however, there was nothing to do but lump it. Sit back. And be grateful that even in the office he still had the leisure to do a little serious thinking. Take to-day, for instance. Compared with his father who had been as hard at it as ever from about 8.55, Tony had not done very much so far. He wouldn't, in fact, have minded doing a bit more. Indeed, in a vague, indeterminate fashion he would rather have liked to have something to do. Either buying. Or selling. He didn't very much mind which. But the place was so confoundedly well organised already that he couldn't quite see how to butt in. Not that he really minded. So long as he didn't get in other people's way and remembered the names of the assistants and paid cash if he bought any cigarettes at the tobacco counter, everybody seemed pretty well content to let him lead his own life. He was till leading it when Miss Underhill came in.

She seemed whiter-faced and more tense than usual this morning. She was clutching her shorthand note-book to her bosom as though she expected someone at any moment to try and snatch it from her. Three pencils, already sharpened, were fastened to the note-book in a kind of rubber band quiver. She looked harassed. And gloom-bearing.

" The Chairman would like to see you," she said breathlessly. " He's . . . he's in the Board Room."

She gave another quick little intake of breath. And showed the whites of her eyes as she said it. Then she whisked away again, note-book and pencils and all, as rapidly as she had come in. Even if he had wanted to say anything he would have been too late.

When Tony reached the Board Room he found his father there as well as Sir Harry. Mr. Rammell was seated in businesslike fashion at the table. But Sir Harry was standing at the window see-sawing up and down on his heels. He appeared to be in high animal spirits, and was wearing a new lavender-coloured waistcoat.

" Dam' fine woman," he was saying as Tony came in. " Married a planter fellow. Ruined him though, just like I said. Don't see many of her sort around these days."

Mr. Rammell looked up. He made little signalling movements in Sir Harry's direction, warning him to stop.

" Come in, Tony," he said. " We want to have a word with you."

Sir Harry turned and faced him. He seemed to be scrutinising him very closely, Tony thought.

"Y'look a bit washed out," he said at last. " What's the matter with you? Get to bed too late? "

" No. No. I feel fine, thank you," Tony told him.

Mr. Rammell took out a soda-mint tablet. Then he put it thoughtfully into his mouth.

148

" We've just been talking about you," he said.

The tone of voice was the one that Tony disliked intensely. It sounded ominously reasonable. He raised his eyebrows a little.

" Really? " he asked.

It was Sir Harry who answered. The old man had just lit another of his before-luncheon cigars and seemed to be in a brusque, rather truculent mood.

" Can't 'ave you mucking about all your life," he said.

" Mucking about? "

" That's about it," Sir Harry told him. " Asked y' father how you'd been settlin' down. An' he told me. How long you been here? "

" About four months."

" An' you haven't done a damn' thing, 'ave you? "

Tony paused for a moment.

" Oh, I don't know about that," he said.

Sir Harry gave a little chuckle.

" Well, we do," he replied. " Time we faced up to things. You're no bloody good, are you? "

Tony thrust his hands deeper into his pockets. He deprecated the sordidness of all family rows. And this promised to be even more distasteful than most.

" I didn't ask to come into the firm," he said.

Sir Harry spat out a piece of cigar leaf and then swung round on him.

" You didn't have no choice," he pointed out. " You belong 'ere. Same as your father does."

While Sir Harry was speaking, he continued to see-saw up and down on his heels rather as if he were enjoying himself.

But Tony noticed that there had been a most extraordinary transformation. Sir Harry had suddenly ceased to be a pinkish, rather benevolent old gentleman. He had become coarse. And fierce. And wolfish. It occurred to Tony that he was getting a glimpse of half a century ago. At last, he was seeing the original Mr. Rammell, founder of the firm.

" Suppose I walk out? " he asked.

" You won't," Sir Harry answered. " Or I wouldn't have given you the chance. If I was dead, it'd all be different. But I'm not. And I don't intend to die just to please any of you. If I see

149

you walking out, then it's y'father who suffers. Not me. If he's got no one to carry on where is he? "

Mr. Rammell's soda-mint tablet had now dissolved completely. He poured out a little sip of water from the vacuum jug beside him. Then he turned to Tony.

" It's for your own good, we're saying all this," he explained. But Sir Harry contradicted him. He turned on Tony.

" No it isn't," he said. " I'm thinkin' of m'self. After what I did buildin' up this firm, d'you think I'm goin' to chuck it all away again? That's where you come in. You're goin' to start in at the bottom the same as your father did. Then you'll be ready when the time comes."

Tony felt the sickness of real alarm.

" Start in at the bottom? " he asked.

Sir Harry nodded.

" That's what I said," he told him. " Get behind the counter. Meet the customers. I did. So did y'father. Start in on the ground floor. Shirts. We've told Mr. Rawle. 'E's expectin' you."

Tony pursed his lips up for a moment.

" I bloody well won't," he said at last.

Sir Harry's cigar had gone out. He took some time in re-lighting it. Then he looked across at Tony.

" Then that about finishes y'father," he said. " He's just sent off a note. Make 'im a bloody laughing stock if it gets round that 'e can't even control 'is own son. I tell you if that 'appened, I'd rather see that fool Preece sittin' there than him."

Mr. Rammell took another sip of water.

" Certainly make things very difficult," he said. " Make them very difficult indeed."

For the first time during the whole interview Tony spoke direct to his own father.

" Oh, God," he said. " Haven't you got any mind of your own? "

Naturally, Mrs. Rammell took Tony's side. It was fantastic —utterly fantastic—she said, that any son of hers should be expected to serve behind a counter. But for goodness' sake leave her out of it. Even if her feelings counted for nothing, at least remember poor Tony's. It would be martyrdom, she contended. Absolute martyrdom for anyone of his talents to be forced to sell shirts

150

whether they had his own family name on the neckband or not.

Altogether it was one of the worst evenings of Mr. Rammell's life. That was because he had to take full responsibility for everything. It would have been as much as his life was worth to confess for a single instant that the whole idea had been Sir Harry's.

3

Because Tony disliked emotional scenes intensely, he decided to go out to dinner. Moreover, he felt in need of good sober advice. That was why he went along to see a friend. He chose Derek in his small flatlet over the dress shop in Sloane Street.

" And now if you please the idea is," he finished up, " that I should start selling shirts for them behind the counter. So I bloody well told them where they both get off."

Derek filled Tony's glass and then his own.

" What d'you propose to do if you leave? "

Tony paused for a moment, twirling the stem of the wineglass round in his fingers.

" After all you must have *some* plans," Derek went on.

" Oh, I don't know," Tony replied. " Get back to ballet somehow. Do something worthwhile. I suppose you wouldn't like to have me in with you, would you? "

Derek shook his head. His line was interior decroation.

" No scope," he said. " You have to keep this game personal. It's such a racket." He stared for a moment into the space between the two gilt Cupids and the Venetian chandeliers somewhere in the direction of the mantelpiece. Then he resumed.

" In any case," he said. " I think you're making entirely the wrong decision."

" You mean about selling shirts? "

Derek smiled. It was his best feature, his smile. And certainly he had practised it often enough. It was superior. Engaging. Enigmatic. And now seemed to be exactly the right opportunity for using it.

" If necessary," he replied. " Not for always of course. Only for the time being. But think of the copy if you ever wanted to write a book. Blow the gaff completely. They could never hold up their heads again. It could be rather wonderful."

Tony shook his head.

" Not for me, thank you," he said.

Derek smiled again.

" It's absolutely the chance of a lifetime," he went on. " If you accept, you've got them exactly where you want them. And think of the publicity. They'd be terrified. Positively terrified. One word from you, and they'd be finished."

Tony stood staring at him.

" Can you imagine me behind a counter? "

This time Derek did not even bother to look in his direction.

" Can you imagine me on top of a step-ladder? " he asked. " But it has to be done, you know. If I were in your position I wouldn't hesitate. If you went about it in the right way you might even get them to stock a few decent patterns."

He shot out his own shirt cuffs as he was speaking.

" Look at these," he said. " Could I get anything like this at Rammell's, I ask you? Pure silk. And mauve. I get them from a little man in Knightsbridge."

Tony finished his drink and got up.

" Oh, go to hell," he said.

CHAPTER XVIII

IT WAS all Mr. Preece's idea that there should be any such thing as a Staff get-together.

Not that it was in any sense original. On the contrary he had first learned of the scheme in an American publication called *Sales Efficiency*. The magazine had just published a special supplement on department merchandising, and there was one section devoted entirely to staff relations. Mr. Preece had read the supplement on the way down from Victoria in the electric train. And by the time he reached Carshalton he had come to dislike everything about it. But it was there that his natural conscientiousness took over. Just because it was so American was that any reason why it shouldn't be tried in Britain? Even if he personally disliked meeting people, shouldn't he steel himself to overcome that dislike? And if it was really true that errors in stock delivery had declined by 7.2% after social contact had been established between the stockroom and other departments, wasn't it his duty to make the experiment?

The only thing that he drew the line at was the drinks. *Sales Efficiency* had made rather a special point of the drinks. " After the closure of the store, introduce a sunny home atmosphere," was what the editor had said. " Give your cashier a high-ball. Two if necessary. Breakdown the inhibitions born of long routine. Concentrate on contacts. Make people mingle. Be one of them. The part that the intelligent General Manager has to play at a good Staff get-together is to listen. Listen and learn . . ." Not knowing—scarcely daring to imagine—what he was going to learn, Mr. Preece called the first Staff get-together for the 17th.

Naturally, Irene Privett was there. She had no alternative. Miss Hallett told her that it would be expected. Indeed, from the whole department it was only Miss Kent who was absent. But what could she do? It was only at the week-end that she had met her own dreamy American. And, as he was going back on Friday—

all of 6,000 miles he had reminded her—she felt that she owed him the last few hours of her company for which apparently he was now craving. Besides with twenty-three other girls at the party she felt sure she wouldn't be missed. Not unless Mr. Preece began nosing round and checking-up, that is.

And Tony Rammell was there because there seemed to be no obvious way of avoiding it. Miss Underhill had given him the invitation personally. She had silently slid the card on to his blotter as though it were an ice-pack that she was delivering. Then Mr. Preece himself had rung up on the internal telephone. It was the first time since Tony had been there that anyone had actually used the instrument. And it was therefore rather flattering.

Finally, Mr. Rammell himself had put it to him point blank. Told him to go.

" You go along. And try and be of some use," he said. " Let them do the talking. Just keep your ears open, and pick up what you can."

Mr. Rammell, too, had read that month's edition of *Sales Efficiency*. He knew exactly how the game should be played. It was merely that he did not feel strong enough to play it himself.

" As a matter of fact," Tony began. " I was going out this evening . . ."

But Mr. Rammell interrupted him. This was not a moment when he felt like entering into an argument.

" Then go out some other evening," he snapped back.

But there he paused. Perhaps Mrs. Rammell was right. Perhaps sometimes he was unduly terse with the boy. Didn't make the effort to draw him out. He came across from the door.

" As a matter of fact," he went on, " I'd appreciate it if you looked in. Preece's idea, not mine. Like to hear what you think of it. Needn't repeat it if it's no use."

It was no good, however. That first remark of his had done it. On the other side of the desk Tony was regarding him with an expression that might have been not his son's but his wife's. And the most maddening thing about it was that on Tony's face lay the half smile that Mrs. Rammell always used when she was particularly irritated.

" You've already told me to go," Tony said. " Shall we leave it at that? "

Without the drinks that *Sales Efficiency* had so carefully recommended, the Staff get-together led off to a pretty slow start. Mr. Prescott of Stock Deliveries, a pale, heavily-spectacled young man with a lot of wrist and ankle, was the first to arrive. He shook hands with Mr. Preece in a quick, experimental fashion and then began furtively to move away. Not that Mr. Preece would have embarrassed him if he had remained. Mr. Preece couldn't think of anything to say either.

And when Miss Hallett got there she was frankly tired. It had been a long day already without this. Ever since five o'clock she had felt one of her headaches coming on. That was why she was so untalkative. Altogether Mr. Preece simply couldn't make it out at all. He had been listening hard ever since he got there. And so far, he was still waiting for something. Not that he need have bothered. Because up to the present, nobody had said anything.

There were about a score of them already assembled when Tony got there. And they had arranged themselves discreetly in the manner of all easy, carefree, English parties—the men on one side of the room and the girls on the other. There was an air of slightly nervous expectancy hanging over the company as though at any moment they were afraid that Mr. Preece might start addressing them.

" 'Evening, Mr. Preece," said Tony. " Sorry, I'm late."

" Quite all right, Mr. Tony," Mr. Preece assured him. " We're only just warming up."

The room that had been quiet before, now suddenly became silent. The men, as a body, moved apprehensively a little farther away from the women. And the women avoided each other's eyes. Instead they looked down carefully at their feet as though they had never seen them before. Mr. Preece wished that he had read *Sales Efficiency* more carefully. Then he would have known how long this rush of uninhibited revelations might be expected to continue.

It was Tony who spoke.

" Isn't it about the right time of day for a drink, Mr. Preece?" he asked. " Don't you think the ladies might like a glass of sherry? "

In the hush, Mr. Preece thought rapidly. It was, after all, precisely what the *Sales Efficiency* had specified. And nobody had told him not to serve drinks. Besides, if he refused, what would Mr. Tony think? Even though—or rather, because—he despised the young man, the last thing that he wanted was for young Tony to go away with the idea that he didn't know how to organise a Staff get-together.

"Just coming, Mr. Tony," he said hurriedly. "I was just about to order it."

Because it was so late—getting on for 5.45 already—Mr. Preece experienced some difficulty in getting the sherry. The bar of the public restaurant had been closed long ago. Ever since three o'clock, in fact. And in the end, it was the directors' sherry that had to be sent for. Mr. Preece felt rather self-conscious about using it. It was the best pale Amontillado. The kind of stuff that in the ordinary way was reserved for Board occasions, at which Mr. Preece was no more than in attendance.

But it certainly worked. It was not in the least that everyone in Stock and Haberdashery had suddenly been tormented by a craving for alcohol. Indeed, if it hadn't been for the Staff get-together, the most that any of the men would have had would have been a quick mild-and-bitter or light ale on the way home; and the girls wouldn't even have thought of it. But here at six o'clock in the empty lounge outside the main restaurant it all suddenly seemed rather fun because of it. Like a surprise present. And now that it was clear that Mr. Preece wasn't going to make a speech after all, everyone's spirits had noticeably begun to mount again.

Tony went dutifully right round the room. It surprised him a little that there should be so many people connected with the Stock side. And some of them seemed so important, too. Compared with his own future, there were two or three of them who looked as if they could have bought out Mr. Rammell to-morrow. Solid, massive men. Men with horn-rimmed glasses. And waistcoats.

And, now that he appreciated that this was simply an informal social occasion, even Mr. Prescott of Stock Deliveries allowed himself to relax. When Tony reached him, he shot out a red, bony hand in greeting and tried to show how much he was really enjoying himself. It was only that he couldn't think of anything to say. Just nothing at all. Not that it mattered. Because by then Tony was already on his way over to the ladies' side.

Naturally, Miss Hallett put herself out for him. She wanted to introduce him to all her girls. But things were not easy for her either. Coming so soon on top of her headache, the sherry had been a mistake. A bad mistake. It was now nothing less than a real migraine that she was suffering. Already she had bright spots like star-shells dancing about before her eyes. Mr. Tony kept appearing and disappearing in the midst of them. At any moment now there would be nothing for it but to go and lie down. And even that would be difficult. Because the ladies' rest-room had been shut up a good half-hour ago. But to her relief Tony scarcely noticed her. It was Irene whom he had just seen.

" You're the new girl, aren't you? " he asked.

" Not really," Irene told him. " Not any longer."

" How are you getting on? "

" Oh, I'm all right, thank you," she said.

" Enjoying it? "

" Oh, yes, ever so."

" They don't work you too hard? "

" Oh, no. Not a bit."

" Still glad when it's the end of the day, though? "

" Definitely."

It seemed to Tony quite one of the silliest conversations that he had ever had. And it was getting nowhere. For every foolish question he asked she had a foolish answer all ready. And she was worth more than that. She was looking at her very prettiest this evening.

" Come over here," he said. " Let's see if there's any sherry left."

It was quieter over there by the side-table, away from the main group. And it was rather pleasant having the dark, pretty girl all to himself for a moment. He poured out some more sherry for both of them.

" Did you want to come into Rammell's? " he asked.

" Not really," she told him.

" What did you want to do? "

" I wanted to go on the stage."

" Then why didn't you . . .? "

It was Mr. Preece who interrupted them. While Tony had been

talking to Irene, the restaurant lounge behind them had emptied mysteriously. The solid, important men, the ones with the chins and the waistcoats, had all said their good-byes to Mr. Preece. And poor Miss Hallett had made a bolt for it long ago. It was only Tony and Irene who were now left. But Mr. Preece was still listening hard. So far the only remark that he had heard all the evening was that Mr. Prescott had apparently already missed the 6.35 and was afraid that he would miss the 7.5 as well. All things considered, it hardly seemed worth six bottles of directors' sherry to have learned that. But he was still master of the situation. And he was thinking about his own train as well.

" Well, all good things must come to an end," he said brightly.

Tony, however, did not seem to be entirely convinced. He lingered. After they had both thanked Mr. Preece for his nice get-together, Tony walked down to the main floor with Irene.

" What about coming over to see the new film at the Curzon? " he asked her.

" Oh, thank you ever so. But I couldn't possibly," Irene told him. " Not to-night. Not now. It's frightfully late. Besides, Dad's waiting for me. He's been hanging about for hours."

Tony thought for a moment.

" Make it next Monday," he said. " It'll still be on."

" D'you really mean it? "

" Of course, I do."

" Oh, thanks ever so. I'd love to."

And she looked so pretty as she said it that Tony knew that he was going to love it, too.

The following day Mrs. Privett came down to Bond Street at closing time. It was her birthday, and she and Mr. Privett were going to make an evening of it. With Irene, of course. Nothing late. Just a bit of dinner. Somewhere nice. At the Corner House, probably. Mrs. Privett had been looking forward to it all day. It was as they were going up Bond Street together that Mr. Privett pointed to someone crossing the road just ahead of them.

" That's him," he said. " That's Mr. Tony. The one without a hat."

" He isn't much like his father, is he? " Mrs. Privett remarked. " I'd never have known him."

Irene herself said nothing.

CHAPTER XIX

EVEN NOW, after the night when he had missed his last bus, Mr. Bloot remained as perplexed as ever by Hetty. He felt himself to be neither one thing nor the other. Because, though she was ready to accept his advances, she remained obstinately opposed to any public linking of her name with his.

" People'll know soon enough," she said lightly. " Why start getting them worried now? "

" But suppose they see me coming here? " Mr. Bloot objected.

" They'd get over it," she told him.

Mr. Bloot, however, was not so easily reassured.

" Ah mean late. Late at naght," he explained. " Leaving the flat. Wot'd they think? "

" They'd be right, wouldn't they, dear? " Hetty replied softly.

She was seated on his knee at the moment, and his arms were around her. Or, at least, partly around. Because he could only half encircle her. And she was heavier than he had imagined. Heavier, in fact, than anything that he had ever imagined. He had pins-and-needles in both legs from the knee downwards.

" It's just that Ah'd rather have er nannouncement," he told her.

" Over the B.B.C.? "

Mr. Bloot shook his head.

" Inner noospaper."

He took a firmer grip of her as he was speaking, and tried to straighten out his legs. Even the pins-and-needles had ceased by now. Both limbs were entirely numb practically from the hips downwards.

But he was unprepared for the fact that Hetty suddenly wriggled free. She got up and stood facing him.

" No, you don't," she said. " I'm not going to have my name appearing in any newspaper, thank you."

" It . . . it'd only be to show people," Mr. Bloot explained. " Just . . . just so that they'd know."

He was, however, secretly more than a little relieved that Hetty wasn't in fact the newspaper kind. In a passing moment of panic he had looked up the social announcement rates in the best national dailies. And even the merest mention, " *The wedding has been arranged and will shortly take place between Henrietta Florence, daughter of* . . ."—who the hell was she the daughter of ? he wondered—"*of 23b Artillery Mansions, Tregunter Road, Finsbury Park, N. 12, and Augustus Archibald Bloot, eldest son of Archibald Augustus Bloot and Maud Caroline (both deceased) of 17 Tufnell Park Crescent,*" would have set him back by about five guineas at least.

But there was an unshakable single-mindedness about Mr. Bloot.

" Ah still think there oughter be some sorter er nannouncement," he persisted. " Ah'm thinking of mah friends."

" Then why not give a little party? " Hetty asked. " Break it to them that way."

Mr. Bloot paused. His lips began moving. But no sound came. That was because he was adding up in his head. And the total that he reached astonished him. Because up to now he had always seen himself as rather a sociable sort of chap. The kind of man around whom other men inevitably gather. Whereas, in reality, he was practically alone.

" There's only two," he finally admitted. " Only two that matter."

But Hetty did not seem unduly put out.

" Then have 'em here," she told him. " Ask 'em round. Isn't this good enough for you? "

Mr. Bloot felt his whole mind lighten. He knew that he had behaved badly to Mr. Privett in having kept his romance concealed. And this would make it all right again. He tried to struggle to his feet. But it was not easy. The circulation had not yet properly returned. And he had difficulty in balancing.

" That's what Ah'll do," he said jubilantly. " Ah'll ask 'em."

He was close beside her again, and his arms went out towards her.

" Yur're er nangel," he said. " That's what yur are er nangel."

Breaking the news to Mr. Privett proved easier than Mr. Bloot had feared. It was all done the following morning over a cup of tea. And Mr. Privett was delighted. Absolutely delighted. The fact that he now shared his friend's confidence again was all that mattered.

" I'll tell Eileen to-night," he said. " She'll be ever so excited. You say which evening. And we'll come over."

But Mrs. Privett was not so delighted. Nor was she logical. Merely loyal.

" No, we don't," she said firmly. " Not until he's brought her here first. I'm not going chasing over to Finsbury Park just to please her. Think of Emily."

That made it very awkward for Mr. Privett. He hardly knew how to put it to Mr. Bloot.

" It's . . . it's just that Mother," he explained haltingly, " wants you to come over to us first. She . . . she feels it would be friendlier."

And that made it awkward for Mr. Bloot, too. Because he had already learnt enough about women to know that they do not like having their arrangements questioned.

But if Mrs. Privett had been obstructive, Hetty was nothing if not forthcoming. She enjoyed all parties. And naturally she was excited at the prospect of this one.

" I hope you said ' yes,' " she told Mr. Bloot when he had delivered the invitation. " I could do with a bit of gaiety."

2

It was the following Monday they finally fixed on. Indeed, urgency had seemed to be of the very essence of the arrangement. But now that everything was settled Mr. Bloot began to suffer misgivings. He wondered what Hetty and Mrs. Privett could possibly find in common.

It wasn't even as if the Privetts played cards. Whereas as soon as Hetty sat down for relaxation with a few friends, out would come the pack and she would begin shuffling it with that fascinating whirring movement that always had such a strangely hypnotising effect upon him. Then again Hetty smoked such a lot, leaving the Cornish pottery ash-tray full to the brim after each rubber with inch-long stubs thickly daubed with rich gleaming lipstick. And neither Mr. Privett nor his wife ever smoked at all.

Mr. Bloot reminded himself that he would have to put a packet

—or even possibly two—into his pocket before they set out. He even wondered if there were not some simple game, about midway between Ludo and Canasta, that he could buy in the toy department and take with him as a surprise.

But it was the memory of all those pots of tea that Mrs. Privett used to make that really alarmed him. He panicked. He knew that Hetty could not be expected to survive an evening of the Privetts without something in a glass beside her. And he began making desperate plans. He would take her first into The Nag's Head and give her a little something before they got there. Or he would invent an imaginary ailment—pernicious anæmia possibly—from which his loved-one suffered, and ask Mr. Privett if a little Australian Burgundy or Invalid Port could just for once be laid on specially for the patient. Or a hip flask, and keep smuggling it across to her during the course of the evening . . .

Mrs. Privett's misgivings were of an entirely different kind. She wanted everything to be nice, she kept telling herself. And, now that she came to review her surroundings, she was dissatisfied with them. The curtains in the front room, for instance. They were old and faded. And the repairs which she had made on them, though skilful, were still unmistakably repairs. Then the rug in front of the fireplace. It was all right at the sides. Still thick and plushy, in fact, but worn right down in the middle where Mr. Privett's heels—and Mr. Bloot's for that matter—had rested. The covers, too. They had a limp, sagging look as though having just managed to reach the chairs they had simply collapsed there.

As Monday drew nearer, tension mounted appreciably on both sides. At elevenses Mr. Privett and Mr. Bloot continued to see each other regularly. But there was now a brooding sense of foreboding that hung over both of them. They kept catching each other's eye and looking down at the tablecloth again.

On the day itself Mr. Privett could stand it no longer. He blurted out exactly what was in his mind.

" I . . . I hope to-night's going to be all right," he said. " I . . . mean I hope the lady's going to enjoy herself."

Mr. Bloot was in the middle of drinking. The tea was exactly right for once. Right temperature. Right strength. Right sweetness. Not too much milk. And it showed how keyed-up he was that he should interrupt himself to speak at all.

"Yurss," he said. "Let's 'ope so."

Mr. Privett would have liked something more affirmative. But he was in no mood for false sentiment.

"Of course, it's bound to be on the quiet side. Just the four of us."

By now, Mr. Bloot had finished his tea. He wiped first his mouth and then his forehead. Then he stared glazedly at the sugar basin. Nothing that Mr. Privett had said had done anything to reassure him.

"Ah know, Ah know," he replied.

Mr. Privett took a sip at his own tea.

"Ireen's going to be out," he went on. Then he paused. "She asked me to apologise," he added untruthfully.

Mr. Bloot made a gesture with his hands that was at once gallant and dispirited.

"Ahr lorss," he said. "Ahr lorss entirely."

But Mr. Bloot was not thinking of Irene. He was still thinking of Hetty and the drink problem.

And Mr. Privett was not thinking of Irene, either. He was secretly preoccupied by what he had discovered when he got home last night. For, going into the front room as usual to make sure that the windows had been fastened properly, he had found himself fumbling about in thick folds of something that he had never encountered before. What he had expected was merely the smooth surface of rather threadbare cretonne. And when he had put the light on he could see that the window was now framed in thick drapes of russet-coloured velvet. They gave the whole room a new and slightly theatrical appearance. As though when drawn, they would reveal some startling transformation scene, and not merely the houses on the other side of Fewkes Road.

This shock was followed closely by finding a new Axminster hearth-rug in front of the fire. The two of them together had left him strangely unsettled. It was evident that Mrs. Privett had been keeping things from him.

And this was doubly disturbing. Because, without telling Mrs. Privett, he had already bought a half bottle of gin, a bottle of lime juice, a bottle of Sauterne and four glasses in readiness for the evening so that Mr. Bloot should really feel welcome and know that his old friends had been trying to make things a success for his sake.

That was why it seemed that someone had been overdoing it a bit when he got home and went into the front room. Because the pair of easy chairs that had been dark red for as long as he could remember now had blue covers with white piping. And on the couch were two bright pneumatic-looking cushions that he had never seen before.

Mr. Privett was now too curious to restrain himself any longer. "What's been going on in the front room, Mother?" he asked. "All those new cushions . . . and things."

Mrs. Privett, however, was busy in the kitchen. She merely gave a little wriggle of annoyance.

"It's nothing," she said. "Just a few odd bits and pieces I had by me."

If Mr. Privett had shown even the slightest discretion he would have left it at that. But he went on.

"Because you needn't have put yourself out that way, Mother," he said. "Gus knows all about us. And just because he's bringing . . ."

But Mr. Privett got no further.

Mrs. Privett rounded on him.

"If you think I've been doing it because that woman's coming you'd better think again," she said. Her voice rose shrilly with scorn at the sheer outrageous absurdity of such a notion. "Re-furnishing for her, indeed! I'm doing it because this house isn't fit to be lived in. And I'm not prepared to live in it any longer like that, even if you are."

This time Mr. Privett had the good sense to say nothing. In any case, he had just remembered that he hadn't put out the cigarettes that he had bought.

They were still in the pocket of his raincoat.

3

Mr. Bloot, too, had been buying cigarettes. He had thought of asking Hetty if he could buy two packets of twenty from her at cost price. But in the end he had decided against it. It might seem to savour too much of meanness. There was nothing for it therefore but to put a good face on it, and behave as though he were a confirmed chain smoker himself. Then, having invested

164

more than seven shillings in tobacco, he went along to the Off Licence.

It was a bit of a rush because he had promised to call for Hetty. And he could not make up his mind. But the young lady behind the counter was the understanding sort. And in the end she sold him a bottle of South African white wine, called " Voortrekker, " and a small bottle of very bright red port that she added cryptically was just the thing. Then Mr. Bloot remembered that Hetty always liked to end up the evening with whisky. So he bought a half bottle of that, too. By then, it was nearly ten-to-seven.

As Mr. Bloot came away from the Off Licence he thought gloomily about the way he was spending so much money. All courtship, he supposed, was costly. But living up to Hetty was positively crippling. At least he had the manner of the presentation all worked out.

" Er little something for the ladies," he was going to say. " Ah'm not muchuvver drinker mahself. Ah'd be glad if you'd relieve me of 'em. . . ."

Mr. Privett had remembered more than cigarettes. He had remembered flowers as well. Two bunches of purple asters. And one of white. They made a rather fine display even all crushed together in the long spill of white paper that the florist wrapped round them. He could just see them arranged nicely in a vase.

But when he went to arrange them, they were already there. White and purple asters standing on the side-table in the front room. He stood blankly regarding them. His own bunch drooped in his hand.

Mrs. Privett came in carrying something, and he caught her eye.

" I . . . I just thought I'd buy you a few flowers," he explained lamely.

But Mrs. Privett was too busy even to say thank you.

" Put 'em in the blue vase with the others," she said sharply. " And then come with me. I need you."

It was to bring down the little table out of Irene's room that he was needed. Then he was to put the remains of the yacht-trailer out of the hall. The old mat out of the front room was to go at the bottom of the stairs. And, when he'd seen to that, she wanted him to put a new bulb in the hall light.

"You don't have to bother yourself, Mother . . ." he began. But there he stopped abruptly. Not that Mrs. Privett had heard. She was far too busy. Out in the scullery she was washing four Woolworth wine-glasses, and scratching the little "Made in Czechoslovakia" labels off their bases with her fingernail.

A taxi would have been better. Because there is no direct bus route between Artillery Mansions and Fewkes Road. And, with Hetty's heels, serious walking was out of the question anyway. But Mr. Bloot was being economical. There was nothing for it therefore but to make a public transport zig-zag, changing first at The Nag's Head. Then travelling due North to The Archway. And finally doubling back in a South-Westerly direction to Kentish Town. Hetty said afterwards that via Camden Town would have been quicker. But Mr. Bloot was taking no risks. A Tufnell Parker himself, he believed in keeping to routes that he knew.

It was while they were waiting at The Nag's Head that Hetty suggested that it would be a nice idea if Mr. Bloot took the Privetts a few flowers. Every woman liked receiving flowers, she said. For a moment, Mr. Bloot thought of refusing. He was already making the Privetts a present of various expensive liquors. He did not see why he should start giving them bouquets as well. But the last thing that he wanted was to upset Hetty. So he merely gave a little nod of assent and went over to a flower-seller in the doorway of the Fifty-Shilling Tailors opposite. It was asters that he chose. White asters, with surprisingly little foliage. Hetty said outright that they gave her the creeps. If he had to buy asters at all, she explained, he should have bought the dark purple ones.

She was still going on about the flowers when they reached Fewkes Road. But by then it wasn't about the flowers that Mr. Bloot was worrying about. It was about Hetty. As he followed her up the short, flagged path to the Privett's front door it occurred to him that possibly she was a shade too fashionable. It was the flounce of nutria around the hem of the skirt, as well as around the collar and cuffs, that did it. And, as he looked at her, he had misgivings. He could not help remembering the plain brown dress with pearl buttons that Mrs. Privett had worn almost for as long as he could remember.

But he was wrong. It was Mrs. Privett herself who opened the door. She was wearing a smart, obviously new, black dress with

166

white collar and cuffs that gave her a brisk, rather waitressy appearance.

"Erlow me to introdoos mah friend, Hetty . . ." Mr. Bloot began over Hetty's shoulder.

But he got no further.

"We were expecting you earlier," Mrs. Privett told him. "Fred was wondering what had happened to you."

The first part of the remark was not strictly true. Because, as they moved into the narrow hallway, Mr. Privett appeared in his shirt sleeves. He had, in fact, been straightening the new pelmet. And, by the time he had got down from the step ladder, he was trapped. His jacket was in the kitchen. And before he could shake hands, or even say how glad he was to see them, he had to sidle out of the room carrying the step ladder with him.

When he got back, Mr. Bloot was already making his presentation.

"A few flahs for you, mah dear," he was saying to Mrs. Privett.

Hetty, however, had already glanced appraisingly round the room.

"You've certainly come to the right place," she said. "They collect 'em."

It was as she was saying it that she remembered her own little present. Just before setting out she had thrust a box of fifty Players into her handbag as a kind of goodwill token.

"I say ' never go into a new home without a little something,' " she explained.

Mrs. Privett was on the point of refusing. The twenty that she had bought already were in the china box on the mantelpiece. And she had just discovered that Mr. Privett had been wasting his money, too. Two packets of ten apiece were arranged in strategic positions round the room so that no matter where Hetty was sitting she had only to extend a hand.

"Thank you very much," she said coldly. "It was kind of you to think of it."

But Hetty was determined not to allow formalities to spoil the evening.

"Don't mention it," she replied. "I'm in the business."

As Mr. Bloot realised that the room was practically full of cigarettes already, he decided to say nothing about the supply

167

that he had brought along himself. Instead, he produced the parcel that he had been saving up for Mr. Privett.

" Er little something for the larder," he said. " Ah'm not muchuvver drinker mahself. Ah'd be glad if you'd relieve me of 'em."

Mr. Privett received the parcel with astonishment. It was, in point of fact, the first present that Mr. Bloot had ever given him. And when he found it contained nothing but drink he was more amazed than ever.

" Well, that's very nice of you, Gussie," he said as he unwrapped the bottles. " We'll have to . . . to drink it, won't we? " He paused. " Excuse me a moment I . . . I've just remembered something."

This was quite true. He had just remembered the half bottle of gin and the bottle of lime-juice that he had bought so that Gus's friend should be able to make a good start to the evening. He blamed himself for not having thought of it earlier.

" I'll be back later," he promised, as he reached the door.

Mrs. Privett watched him go. Then she turned to Hetty.

" You'll take a little something? " she asked.

It was in the corner cabinet that Mrs. Privett had been hiding the bottles. There was a small bottle of gin and a large green looking lime-juice bottle. The glasses were on the shelf beneath. She had just finished arranging them on the table out of Irene's room when Mr. Privett returned. He was just in time to hear Hetty refuse everything.

" Not for me, dear," she said " Not after last night. I'm not touching a thing. But don't let me stop you. Give one to Gussie. He needs it."

The supper table with Mrs. Privett's bottle of Sauterne and Mr. Privett's Moselle as well as Mr. Bloot's Boerish vintage from South Africa looked festive. Even overladen. Hetty herself drank nothing but water. Mrs. Privett resentfully sipped a little of her own Sauterne. But it was left to the men to finish it. And because the Sauterne was so sweet it made Mr. Privett feel a little sick. But Mr. Bloot was content. He rather liked it. And he would in any case have needed something to wash down the huge quantities of food that Mrs. Privett kept putting down in front of him. He had already spooned up a plateful of fruit salad and now he was being

168

offered little cheeses in silver paper as well. The profusion astonished him. It seemed that since he had last visited the Privetts their whole standard of living had gone up beyond recognition.

Hetty herself, however, did not seem to be eating anything. And Mr. Bloot was suddenly glad after all that he had got a cigarette to offer her. Despite the number of cigarettes in the other room, it did not seem to have occurred to Mr. Privett that ladies like Hetty who went about a lot were accustomed to light up while still sitting at the table.

He beamed across at her.

" Have one of these, mah dear," he said, producing the packet suddenly like a conjuror. " Ah know your brand."

But Hetty only shook her head.

" Not me," she answered. " You have one. I've got a mouth like a bird cage."

Because of Mr. Bloot's half bottle of port, the small party lingered indolently over the supper table. And because the word " Invalid-type " appeared on the bottle, Mrs. Privett allowed herself to be persuaded. But it was a mistake. She was not accustomed to drinking. And she had already taken one glassful of Sauterne. Coming so soon on top of it, the port was too much. It immediately gave her a hot, angry flush as though someone had just said something deliberately offensive . . .

Between them, the two men finished up the bottle. They even seemed surprised when they found that it had all gone. But they felt better for it. Much better. A rather aimless little smile began playing round the corners of Mr. Privett's mouth, and Mr. Bloot simply beamed. Large and pink looking, he glistened. Unable to imagine why he had ever been so anxious about the outcome of the evening, he blamed himself for having kept Hetty away from Fewkes Road for so long.

Only Hetty remained entirely abstinent. Neither drinking nor smoking, she sat back observing her companions. And she found the sight strangely consoling. More than once just lately she had told herself that she would have to go easy, and miss every other round. And it came as a relief to discover that other people took just as much as she did. One glance at the Privetts was enough to show that they were practically pickled. And there was a smile on Gus's face that she had never even seen before.

The film that Tony and Irene were seeing was at the Curzon. It had been on for weeks already. And judging by the queues outside it would be on for ever. What was so remarkable was that it was all in French, too. Indeed, the whole atmosphere of that end of Curzon Street was so thoroughly continental that it was obvious that if an English film should have been booked by mistake, the management would have had to add French sub-titles before their patrons would have been able to follow it.

Irene was not merely happy. She was blissful. The seats in which they were sitting did not seem to have been made for ordinary cinema-goers at all. She had never before sat in anything like them. They were obviously designed for an exclusive race of luxurious, movie-loving satraps.

But it wasn't merely a matter of the upholstery. It was the fact that she was holding hands that counted. When she had felt Tony's hand come stealing up out of the semi-darkness she had thought at first that it was by accident that it had touched hers. She had expected it to go away again. But it hadn't. It had taken hold. And stayed there. At first she felt a strange electric tingle run through her at the contact. Then came the hot, rather sticky period. And finally she had reached the dumb, inert, stage.

The film itself—the wildly popular one—was rather sad, Irene thought. It was set in the Canebière district of Marseilles. And it was all about a deaf and dumb girl who murdered her illegitimate baby when it turned out to be blind like her lover. But the photography, everyone agreed, was out of this world. It was shot mostly at night. Or in rain. With only the outlines of things showing. These, however, were enough. Rubbish bins, urinoirs, public wash-houses, sewers, horse-abattoirs—they were all there. In short, the film had Cannes Festival Award written all over it.

When it finished, everyone dutifully stood up. But it was the National Anthem that was played. For a moment, Irene had half expected that it would be the " Marseillaise. "

Tony helped her into her coat, and they made their way out into the night scene of Mayfair.

" Thank you ever so," Irene told him. " I loved it. Really, I did."

Tony glanced at his watch.

" Better come and get a drink," he said. " We can just make it."

Because it was so near to closing-time, it wasn't much of a drink. But that didn't matter, because Irene wasn't much of a drinker. She asked for gin-and-lime because it was the only thing that she could think of. And Tony himself drank only beer. Five minutes after they had gone into the pub, they were outside on the pavement again, right in the middle of Shepherd Market among the antique shops. And the poodles. And the ladies who looked as though they had somehow remained over from some previous attraction.

Tony and Irene walked round as far as Hertford Street where the car was parked.

" I'll run you home . . ." he began.

But Irene stopped him.

" No, please don't bother," she said. " I'll just pop into the Underground."

" Get in," Tony told her.

Irene hesitated.

" Well, only as far as Piccadilly," she said. " It isn't really out of your way."

" Where d'you live? " Tony asked.

" Kentish Town."

" Where's that? "

" Oh, it's miles. Really it is. It'll take hours. You mustn't think of it."

Tony leant across her and tried the door to make sure that it was shut properly.

" Come on," he said. " There's no traffic at this time of night."

It was as they were going along the Hampstead Road that Irene kept telling herself how silly she had been to get into the car at all. Because now that she was in, Tony obviously intended to drive her all the way. And she didn't want to be driven all the way. There was no use in disguising it. The Curzon and Fewkes Road just didn't belong together. And she wanted them left separate. Part of the fun of the whole evening had been the fact that she had been able to forget all about everything. What she had been enjoying was a glorious girl-from-nowhere kind of feeling.

She made one more attempt to save herself when they got to Camden Town.

" Do drop me here," she said. " Then I can get a bus."

But it was no use. Tony was intent on taking her. There was nothing for it, therefore, but to tell him to go half-right and keep straight up the Kentish Town Road.

She wished more than ever by now that she hadn't allowed him to come at all. The Kentish Town Road is not on any showing a particularly pretty sort of thoroughfare at the best of times. It needs people to give life to it. And at eleven-thirty at night it was neither pretty nor lively. Compared with Curzon Street, it might have been somewhere down in the dock area.

" It's here," she said at last. " On the right. Just past Woolworth's."

Tony glanced up at the side of the public house on the corner.

" Fewkes Road? " he asked.

Irene nodded.

" Second lamp-post," she told him. " Before you get to the pillar-box."

Now that they had arrived, there was nothing for it. She certainly wasn't going to let Tony know that she was ashamed of where she lived. Moreover, now that she came to think of it, she wasn't ashamed of anything. Just happy.

" Come in for a moment," she said. " They'll all have gone to bed."

Tony gave her a little smile.

" Well, just for a moment," he said. " Just to say good night."

Irene had her own key. And Tony did not need to be reminded to be quiet. He tip-toed in. He was so quiet, indeed, that it seemed to Irene that he must be used to tip-toeing. He came up close behind Irene and put his arms around her.

" Kiss," he said.

But quiet as he was, he had not been quiet enough. They were just outside the front room door when it suddenly opened. It was Mrs. Privett who stood there.

" Who've you got there, Ireen? " she began.

Then she stopped. She could see perfectly well who it was. And she was astonished. But not nearly so much astonished as Irene. That was because over Mrs. Privett's shoulder she had an unobstructed view of her own sitting-room. And it might have been someone else's. That was because when Mr. Privett had been told to bring through the drinks, he had brought everything. There seemed to be bottles everywhere. And cigarettes. The room was littered with cigarette packets. But what was most astonishing of all was the table. There were cards spread out on it. Not that they had been played with so far. It hadn't got as far as that. The game was still merely in the tuition stage. It showed, however, that Hetty must have been feeling better. Indeed, as soon as her headache had cleared away she had begun wondering what to do. And naturally her mind had turned to the pack of cards in her handbag . . .

Mrs. Privett steadied herself.

" Good evening, Mr. Rammell," she said loud enough for the name to reach the company behind her. " Come in, won't you? "

She stood back for him to pass. And then to show how much at ease she was, she added. " I expect you'd like a drink."

And as she said it, she fixed Irene with her eye.

The one problem in Mr. Privett's mind was that though he had got a half bottle of whisky practically untouched he had not remembered to buy any soda. His chief emotion, however, was one of warm gratification that Tony should be there at all.

" Come in, Mister Tony," he said slightly indistinctly. " Thish ish a gray pleasure frollofush."

Naturally Hetty was delighted to see a newcomer. And in the face of such cordiality as hers it would have been impossible for Tony not to feel at home. She patted the empty chair beside her.

" Thank God you've come," she said to him. " Perhaps if we both take a hand we can show them. Don't tell me you can't play either. Or I shall scream."

It was only Mr. Bloot who was not at ease. Hetty's headache had somehow transferred itself to him. He was feeling slightly sick. And very sleepy.

Not so sleepy, however, that he could not size up the situation. He glanced from Tony to Irene. And then back to Tony again. Finally he caught Tony's eye. And he held the glance longer than he should have done. Finding himself being stared at by a pair of fixed incredulous eyes popping out of a pink shining face, Tony winked.

And it was fatal. Mr. Bloot immediately misunderstood it. He came across to Tony and loomed respectfully over him. Then he dropped his voice.

"Yur can rahly entahly on mah discretion, sir," he told him. "Sahlence Ah assure you."

CHAPTER XX

SIR HARRY had been on about it again. On and on. Incessantly.

How much longer was young Tony going to be allowed to waste his time up there in the Management Suite? Was it Mrs. Rammell who was standing in the way? Why not put him in the Stock rooms for a spell? Or Dispatch? Or attach him to one of the buyers? Or better still, like he'd said, get him down into the shop so that he could meet his first customer?

Sir Harry had been on the phone three times already this morning. And practically all day yesterday.

It was Mr. Preece who agreed with him. There was something extraordinarily unattractive in the whole idea of having the young man messing about in Stock. Or Dispatch, for that matter. Anything could go wrong there. And probably would. But no harm at all that Mr. Preece could see in letting him have a go on the Sales side. Provided that he was properly supervised, of course. And that was where Mr. Rawle of Shirtings would come in so useful.

Mr. Rawle was flattered. But unimpressed. He had been the Napoleon of shirts for nearly twenty-seven years. And an entire pageant of shirt history had passed across the counter over which he presided. First he had seen stiff shirts for day wear succeeded by soft ones. Some even with collar attached. And then, since revolutions run always to extremes, he had watched gentlemen buying themselves soft shirts for evening wear as well. Then substitute fabrics, home-washable and self-ironing, had become popular. There was, he had often felt, not much more that could possibly happen to the downfall of shirtings during his lifetime.

In a sense it was a personal tribute to him that, of all the hundred and seven other departments, the managing director should have chosen his. But no Napoleon likes the feeling of being patronised. And after a brief spell of elation to think that he, Mr. Rawle, would now have the privilege of ordering a Rammell of the blood royal to perform the various little menial duties—

spreading out dustcloths, picking up bits of string, restacking boxes and so forth—that go with all retail shopkeeping, he was feeling resentful.

Nor when it happened, did it make things any easier that young Mr. Rammell should be confoundedly civil. Not ordinary straight-forward civility either. It was a kind of jaunty humility which left Mr. Rawle powerless.

" Now I'm entirely in your hands, Mr. Rawle," he began. " Entirely and absolutely. Remember I know nothing. And you know everything. I want you to teach me. And I'm here to learn. I shall make mistakes at first. All beginners do that. But I shall expect you to jump on me as soon as you see things going wrong. No half measures, mind. No making allowances. And above all no favouritism, please . . ."

He had gone round to Mr. Rawle's side of the counter while he was speaking. And he was already brushing imaginary specks of dust off the plate glass counter.

" Well," he continued in the same staccato fashion that Mr. Rawle found so unnerving, " I'm sure there's plenty of work to be done. You show me what it is. And I'd better make a start with it."

Because it was only 9.10, the store at the moment was still entirely empty. The long blue-carpeted aisles had a bare and lonely look, as though they were set for a play that had not yet started. Only the figure of Mr. Bloot at the far end of one of the aisles gave even a hint that the audience might soon be there.

Mr. Rawle turned towards the glass-fronted shelves behind the counter.

" First of all, sir," he said. " I suggest we run through the ranges. Then I can take you through the sizes afterwards."

But even that did not satisfy Tony.

" Now Mr. Rawle," he said. " No ' sir ' when addressing me, please. Remember you're the principal. I'm only the assistant."

It was while Tony was being shown the sports shirts that he made his one blunder. He ran his hand over the patterns. Then he turned to Mr. Rawle.

" Bit grim, aren't they? " he said.

Mr. Rawle stiffened.

176

" I beg pardon, sir? " he asked.

" Grim," Tony repeated. " Do they expect you to be able to sell these? "

Mr. Rawle avoided Tony's eye and stared down the empty corridor ahead of him.

" I do sell them, sir."

" Good for you," Tony answered. " They must take a bit of selling. Look at that one."

Mr. Rawle turned his head for a moment.

" That, sir, is one of our most exclusive patterns . . ." He paused. " Forgive me a moment, sir."

Already he was moving slowly, almost furtively away. His face had assumed a new expression. At once polite and predatory. Tony started to fold up the sports shirt. Then he turned and watched. On the other side of the counter, the day's first customer was approaching. He seemed quite a reasonable sort of person, Tony thought. A bit hot and rushed-looking, perhaps, and carrying an over-large suitcase. But still civilised. And from the way he was bending down he seemed to be looking at price tickets. It was obvious that he was avoiding Mr. Rawle's eye, while Mr. Rawle was trying to catch his.

As he drew level, Mr. Rawle addressed him.

" Can I show you something, sir? "

The stranger paused.

" No thanks. I was just looking."

Mr. Rawle drew back to make it plain that Rammell's was the last shop in London where anything so vulgar as ordinary salesmanship was ever practised. He took out a drawer of soft evening shirts and began studying them as though purely for his own relaxation.

The man with the suitcase hesitated.

" Er . . . how much are those evening shirts? " he asked.

" Evening shirts, sir? "

There was just the right note of surprise in his voice as he asked the question. He tilted the box forward as he spoke.

" This is one of our regular shirts, sir. Special uncreasable front. Fifty-five and nine."

The man had put his bag down by now. He began examining the shirt.

" You haven't anything cheaper, have you? " he asked.

Again Mr. Rawle seemed surprised.

" Oh, yes, sir."

He brought out another drawer.

" This is a very popular shirt, sir. Forty-two and sixpence."

" Anything between the two? "

Already Mr. Rawle was bringing out a third drawer.

" Two-ten, sir," he said. " Only just come in. The cuffs are nylonised."

He had spread all three shirts out in a kind of fan on the counter. Now he was standing back again so as not to rush his man. He had the air rather of a collector showing his prized pieces to a cherished friend.

The customer glanced for a moment at his watch and then stared down at the shirts again.

" Which do you recommend? " he asked.

Mr. Rawle seemed almost embarrassed.

" Well, of course, this is the shirt, sir," he explained. " The others are very good value. But this is the shirt."

The customer glanced down at his watch for the second time.

" I'll take one of those," he said.

Mr. Rawle came round to the customer's side of the counter to measure his arm-length.

" Are you all right for bow ties, sir? " he asked, confidentially as though he knew that the question was verging on the indiscreet.

The customer nodded. And Mr. Rawle ignored the nod.

As he was wrapping up the shirt he deftly thrust out a third arm from somewhere behind his back and placed a long Cellophane packet behind the shirt.

" These are the pattern that are being worn," he said almost diffidently. " You notice the new thin outline . . ."

A few moments later, Mr. Rawle had returned to Tony's end of the counter. He had sold a shirt and an evening tie.

" How d'you know he wanted dress shirts? " Tony asked.

" The suitcase, sir," Mr. Rawle told him. " And the time of day. Quite a lot of gentlemen drop in on the way to the office when they have to dress and go out somewhere. They frequently forget something. You'll come to recognise the type, sir."

" And how did you know he'd buy a tie? "

Mr. Rawle lowered his voice a little.

" He wasn't quite sure of himself, sir. If he had been, he wouldn't have asked my advice."

Mr. Rawle broke off, and slid a box of sports shirts along the counter.

"Suppose we go through these, sir," he went on. "And allow me to show you. It's the collars that require attention. Points always nicely down. And mind the pins. Never forget the pins, sir. And never drag one shirt across another. Lift them, sir. Lift them. Like this."

It was shortly after ten when the first of the Press arrived. The news of Tony Rammell's staff appointment had only just broken. But it was obviously a good story. RAMMELL JUNIOR SERVES BEHIND COUNTER would be bound to catch the eye of every woman reader. Already in the glass panelled row of offices over on the Hurst Place side a whole company of rather smart young women with note-books concealed in the handbags and large sagging men with camera cases over their shoulders were now assembling. Mr. Thorpe of Publicity was trying to keep them all at bay while Mr. Robson of Public Relations got through on the phone to Mr. Preece.

"The Press? Here? Why?" Mr. Preece kept repeating. "And photographers? I'll speak to Mr. Rammell about it. Tell Thorpe to keep them where they are. We don't want them wandering all round the store, until we know who authorised it."

Mr. Rammell was not at all pleased at being interrupted. He was dissolving a new kind of charcoal-and-bismuth tablet in his mouth. And he did not want to talk to anyone. Just suck.

"The Pless?" he said, indistinctly because the tablet was an unusually large one. "No, of coulse not. Shlend them away." He paused. "Shtlay where you are. I'll ling you back."

Mr. Rammell poured himself a sip of water from the vacuum jug beside him. He had somehow managed to swallow the charcoal tablet. His speech was suddenly clear again. But his whole mouth now tasted dismally of late autumn.

"Get me Sir Harry," he said.

When at last Sir Harry came through he seemed even at that hour in the morning to be in remarkably high spirits.

"What's that?" he asked. "Havin' your photograph taken, you say?"

"It's *Tony* they've come to see," Mr. Rammell told him. He spoke very slowly. Slowly and distinctly. As though he were speaking to a child. He had explained it to Sir Harry at least twice already.

And gradually, very gradually it seemed, Sir Harry was getting round to the real nature of the problem.

" Well, why did you ask 'em if you didn't want 'em? "

" Nobody asked them," Mr. Rammell replied. " That's the whole point."

Sir Harry gave a little chuckle.

" Somebody must of. Stands to reason. Perhaps it was his mother."

" I thought," Mr. Rammell continued, still in the same quiet patient tone, " that perhaps you . . ."

But Sir Harry interrupted him.

" Leave me right out," he said. " Too old. Don't photograph so good."

As Sir Harry replaced the receiver, he shook his head sadly. Lack of decision. That's what his son's trouble was. Sheer lack of it. Couldn't make up his mind about anything. Sending for a lot of Press photographers, and then telling them to go away again. Finally trying to drag his own father out of bed just to make up a group . . .

Sir Harry was only thankful enough that he was still active enough to be able to step in when needed. Like this morning, for instance. If he hadn't intervened goodness knows what sort of muddle they would have been getting themselves into round in Bond Street.

2

It was while Mr. Robson was holding the main body of the Press at bay that a small free-lance photographer slipped past him. He was a thin, shabby-looking young man with rather long hair, who came and went as he chose. Going straight through to Shirtings he got exactly what he wanted. And he was out of the shop again before anyone could stop him. Before anyone had really noticed him. Anyone with the exception of Tony, that is. And he was incredulous. Simply incredulous.

Because he was really responsible. It had all happened the

other night at a party. He had found himself talking to a rather distinguished-looking young man. One of Derek's better friends. The young man with a pale waistcoat and a jacket with folded-back cuffs. " To do with publicity " was how he described himself. And as soon as he heard that Tony was really going to work his way through Rammell's he stopped being languid. Instead, he became tremendously interested. He even brought out an apparently nibless fountain pen—the pen was so streamlined that it might have been made for writing in space-ships—and made a note of Tony's name on the back of an invitation card.

Moreover, the air of languidness must have been merely a veil. A deception. The young man was nothing if not thorough. When the picture appeared in all the evening papers, there was nothing missing. ". . . whose mother is, of course, the well-known hostess and musical patron," the caption rambled on. " Sir Harry, 82, the original Chairman, is in excellent health and is a familiar figure on the racecourse."

Tony, who was going out that night, entirely forgot to look. Mr. Rammell made a point of looking. And was appalled. Sir Harry was delighted. Simply delighted. Mrs. Rammell wept.

3

And next day there was a real first-class row up in Management Suite. With last night's evening papers spread out on the desk in front of him, Mr. Rammell banged his fist down on the offending pictures and threatened to make a clean sweep of the Press, Publicity, Public Relations. The whole lot. Every damn' one in the department. Start again. Get rid of dead wood. Find people who knew their jobs. Clear out the duds.

Mr. Preece sat beside him, silent and dismayed. He knew what Mr. Rammell must be thinking. Because he was already thinking it himself. There was no getting round it. He was one of the duds. He had shown himself to be that worst of all things, a General Manager who couldn't manage. After the others had gone, Mr. Rammell would be bound to keep him back. Put it to him point blank. Resignation or dismissal. . . . Like most professionally calm men, Mr. Preece had his private moments of panic.

Mr. Rammell meanwhile was still threatening and banging.

He was, indeed, so much caught up in the sheer enjoyment of being beastly that he refused to take a telephone call from Sir Harry. Flatly refused. In front of the staff, too. But there was more to it than mere annoyance at the interruption. The one thing that Mr. Rammell feared was Sir Harry's voice crackling out of the receiver full of congratulations over the Press coverage.

Meanwhile, two floors below, Tony knew nothing of the row. He was busy behind the Shirtings counter. Busy and dutiful. It was the latter quality that dumbfounded Mr. Rawle. He had been prepared for anything. Idleness. Frivolity. Inattention. Condescension. Rudeness, even. But not what he was getting. It was like having the industrious apprentice always at his elbow. He was so much impressed, indeed, that he mentioned it more than once to Mrs. Rawle. " It's hereditary," he said. " That's what it is, hereditary. If there's shirtings in the blood it's bound to come out."

Mr. Rawle, however, was only partially correct. Because Tony was not being dutiful. He was only being bloody-minded. He had worked the whole thing out to his own satisfaction. Revenge and masochism were nicely mingled.

The first that Mr. Rammell had known of it was this morning. The car had turned into Bond Street at the usual point. But at the Downe Street entrance Tony had said good-bye.

" I go in round the back," he had said. " Staff entrance. Got to clock in."

" No need to do that," Mr. Rammell had begun.

But that was as far as he got. Because by then Tony had already waved good-bye, and turned the corner.

Not that the arrangement was altogether without its compensations.

It meant that a Rammell was seeing the staff side of things for the first time in more than a quarter of a century. And already it was beginning to occur to Tony that perhaps the store wasn't quite so well run as it seemed to be from the directors' floor.

Take the time-machines, for instance. There were four of them just inside the front door. Everyone, with the exception of the buyers and a few people like Marcia who led irregular hours anyway, had to get the exact minute of their arrival stamped on to the small buff card. It wasn't the sheer impersonal tyranny of the machines that irritated Tony. It was the simple fact that they were in the wrong place. Around 8.50 a.m. there were two or three hundred people all arriving in Hurst Place at the same time. And on wet mornings the rear end of the queue had to stand outside getting steadily wetter. And later.

" I'll mention it to Preece. Get him to do something about it," Tony promised himself.

In point of fact, he forgot. Simply forgot all about it. The remarkable thing was, however, that he should even have thought of remembering. And, in any case, by then he was already busy on something else. By the end of his second day he was re-organising the whole method of replacements. That, he had decided, was in one hell of a mess. Positively bloody awful, in fact. Because if any line—Tony had learnt by now to refer to everything as a " line "— started selling at all briskly, the head of the department sent one of the juniors along to the stock room with a requisition slip. The stock room was in the basement at the Downe Street end. And on some mornings Tony had counted as many as twelve juniors all standing about, waiting for their fresh supplies.

" My God," Tony reflected. " This is medieval. If there was only a decent internal phone system they could ring through for things as they wanted them. Then the stock department could pick up the requisition slip when they delivered the goods."

But it was around then that something happened that put departmental management and re-organisation clean out of Tony's head. He met Irene again.

Irene worked in quite a different part of the building altogether. She was separated from him by three aisles, seven counters and a double row of imposing marble-looking pillars. Practically in the next parish, in fact. One hundred and seven departments is about a hundred too many when it comes to meeting people.

But despite all those departments, even Rammell's had only twenty-four windows. And men's shirts, ladies' handkerchiefs, beach wear, furs, sports good, refrigerators, jewellery and all the rest had to share the displays. The windows were decisive. Merely to be allotted one was enough to put a whole department on trial. And it was these display weeks that brought the departments together.

Not that the department itself was ever allowed actually to dress the window. That was the preserve of Mr. Banstraw. And of his assistant, Miss Defoy. Mr. Banstraw was tall, stooping and sedate with a preference for plain labels, plenty of top lighting and what he called " general straightforwardness. " Miss Defoy on the other hand wore a snood, inclined to Perspex cut-outs and abhorred overcrowding.

Mr. Banstraw in turn abhorred Miss Defoy. He prided himself that, with careful arrangement and a lot of standing about on the pavement peering in at the windows with his eyes screwed up and head on one side, he could manage to get as many as six different dress models into a single window frame. Left to herself, Miss Defoy would have preferred one. Her most successful window, she always contended, had consisted simply of a flight of white papier-maché steps with a single evening bolero draped over the balustrade on the top landing.

In consequence, there was always a lot of coming and going between principal and assistant, with Miss Defoy whisking things away as soon as Mr. Banstraw's head was turned, and then Mr. Banstraw carting them all back again.

Because it was soon to be Shirt Week, Mr. Rawle was moody and preoccupied. He still served his regular customers with as much care and attention as if shirts were something that he had personally invented and was still interested in promoting. But his mind wasn't really on collar bands and cuff lengths. It was busy planning. Mapping things out. Devising the ground strategy.

In the end it was stripes he decided on. Soft, with button cuffs and collars attached. There was only one objection. Mr. Banstraw insisted on ties to go with the shirts. That upset Mr. Rawle. He didn't see why he should have to share his window with the un-pleasantly flashy Mr. Clarkson from the next counter. But Mr. Banstraw was adamant.

" Too bare," he said firmly. " No finish. You just leave it to me I know what I want. Some nice checks and foulards. And plenty of shirts. Dozens and dozens of 'em."

It was because the first requisition on the stock department was too small that Tony was now on his way over to the window with a fresh supply. Mr. Banstraw seemed relieved to see them.

" I may need some more still," he said. " No point in wasting valuable space These windows cost money. . . ."

At the same moment in the next window, Miss Defoy was speaking to Irene.

" I shan't be needing these," she said. " Or these. Or these.
It's not a jumble-show we're managing. It's a window. And
windows are what people go by. I always say they're our
ambassadors, these windows. . . ."

That was how it was that Tony going back towards the stock
department for more, met Irene as she was carrying away a
collection of belts, fancy buckles, dress ornaments and every kind
of flower except real ones.

Miss Defoy had examined the velvet roses, the artificial
violets, the sham camellias, the pink feather carnations. And
being artistic, she had rejected the whole lot in favour of some small
and rather nondescript budlets of dried beech husks and a bunch
of flowering sea-shells. The rest were going back into stock. And
Irene with her chin pressed down hard on to the top box lid to
give steadiness to the pile was making her way as best she could.

Tony and Irene met head on.

" Here. Let me take those."

" No, really. Please don't bother."

She felt herself blushing as she said it. That was what was so
humiliating about being only seventeen. Because you found yourself
blushing when there was nothing to blush at. Simply because
someone spoke to you, for instance.

And it would have been better if she had not attempted to
resist. Cardboard boxes, especially the white shiny kind, are
notoriously slippery. Handling them calls for a good firm grip.
And no fumbling. Two lots of hands are usually fatal. A moment
later the marble parquet was littered with multi-coloured fabric
petals and sprays of fiercely curled synthetic foliage.

" Clumsy," Tony remarked.

Between them, they picked up the whole lot. And then Tony
slammed the last box lid back into place.

" Well, that's that," he said.

Then he glanced at his watch.

" What about elevenses? " he asked. " Come and have a cup
of coffee."

They stood side by side at the long staff counter with the words
Horlicks and Oxo and Kia-Ora staring down at them.

" When are you coming out to another flick with me? "

" You haven't asked me."

That was better. She wasn't blushing now. She was easily holding her own with him.

" Well, I'm asking you now."

He took out a limp little diary and began consulting it.

" Can't to-night," he said. " Or to-morrow. What about Wednesday? Why not come on Wednesday? "

" D'you really mean it? "

" Of course I mean it. Why not come Wednesday? "

" I . . . I'd love to."

So that was settled. Then the stupid business of being seventeen suddenly cut right across everything. She felt herself blushing again.

CHAPTER XXI

IT WAS because of Irene's second visit to the cinema with Tony that Mrs. Privett decided that she must act. And act now.

She had been on the point of it before. Had nearly done something after that first time when Tony and Irene had surprised them all during the evening party for Mr. Bloot and his fiancée. That had been a warning. A danger sign. But she had checked herself. Tried to pretend that it was nothing.

But twice in one month was too much. It was more than a danger sign now. It was the peril itself. Right on top of them, too. There was only one thing that it could mean. Young Mr. Rammell was serious. And Mrs. Privett could see no good coming of it.

Other mothers might have been flattered. Dazed. Bowled-over. And even for Mrs. Privett there was an element of bewilderment in it all. To think that her own daughter and one of the Rammells . . . But that was precisely what she was determined not to allow herself to think. For a start, what did she know of his intentions? With young men of Mr. Tony's age they were frequently of the worst. But that wasn't all. Supposing he came to the point and actually proposed, what chance would there be of a match like that lasting?

The real trouble was that Tony and Irene hadn't got so much as a single piece of background in common. Fewkes Road and Eaton Square might have belonged to different planets they were so different. Mrs. Privett held strong views that the Fewkes Road planet held the better promise of a steady life. There had never been a divorce on either side of the family. And she wasn't going to be a party to preparing for one now.

Mr. Privett, however, held other views. Simpler ones. If it was love, he contended, wasn't that all that mattered? And wasn't his Irene good enough for Mr. Tony? Or for anyone else for that matter? Besides, at seventeen, she might change her mind. Most girls did. Quite a lot of times some of them. Besides if they tried to influence Irene in any way it would be bound to lead to trouble. Trying to influence Irene always did.

Mrs. Privett had listened to her husband many times. And despised him. There was a weakness and lethargy about the middle-aged male that she found contemptible. That was why she kept on about it so. Kept on urging him to do something.

She was at the moment sitting up in bed rubbing cold cream into her hands. And Mr. Privett was over by the dressing-table taking out his front and back studs. This was the time of day which the Privetts usually reserved for most of their really serious conversations.

" Well, did you say something to her? " Mrs. Privett demanded.

Mr. Privett did not even turn round.

" I did try," he said weakly. " But she didn't seem to want to discuss it."

" You should have made her," Mrs. Privett replied, replacing the lid of the cream jar with a snap.

" That's not so easy," Mrs. Privett told her. " Not with her. Not when she's in one of her moods."

As he said it he was aware of something like duplicity. He was very fond of Irene. And she was practically a grown women by now. It seemed sometimes as though he had two wives instead of the one. And he was always siding either with one or with the other. To-night it was Irene's turn.

" Well, what d'you propose to do about it? " Mrs. Privett asked from the bed.

Mr. Privett did not reply immediately. He unscrewed the last metal stud cap, forced the shank out of the collar band with his thumb and then screwed the cap on again.

" I don't think that there's very much we can do," he said. " After all, it isn't as though there was anything wrong with it."

" How do we know? " Mrs. Privett asked. " What makes you think she was the first? "

Mr. Privett had not considered this aspect of it before.

" I . . . I just meant that I didn't see any particular harm in it. It isn't as though it's gone very far."

" It's gone quite far enough," Mrs. Privett retorted. " Are you going to speak to Mr. Rammell, or am I? "

Mr. Privett spun round.

" We aren't neither of us going to speak to Mr. Rammell,"

he said. " It wouldn't be fair to Ireen. Or to me for that matter."
He paused. " You can't mix up business and . . . and the other
thing. It . . . it only leads to awkwardness."

Mr. Privett was relieved that his wife attempted no reply. He
climbed into bed beside her, kissed her gently on the forehead and
reached up to put out the light.

" These things always settle themselves," he said. " Far better
not to worry."

As he settled himself down on the pillow in the pleasant darkness,
he felt rather pleased. He had been firm. And calm. It occurred
to him that this was the great difference between men and women.
Men were able to take a longer view. And a saner one. Whereas
women, especially the quiet sort like Mrs. Privett, tended naturally
to get a bit worked-up and fidgety. It was a pity. But there was
nothing that could be done about it.

He was asleep before Mrs. Privett.

2

As soon as Mr. Privett had left the house next morning, with
the cause of all the trouble walking demurely beside him, Mrs.
Privett took things in her own hands. She rang up Mrs.
Rammell.

It requires courage to ring up anybody on a personal matter.
And it requires all the more courage when the call has to be made
from a public call box. Mrs. Privett, moreover, was not an experienced telephonist. She had a tendency to dial too many
numbers. And the buttons A and B had always confused her. By
the time she did get through to Eaton 4537, the operation had cost
her sixpence already. And by then she was so exhausted that she
could scarcely answer.

" Who wants her please? " the voice kept asking.

" It's Mrs. Privett," she said, adding by way of explanation,
" Mr. Privett's wife. And it's personal."

There was a pause, during which Mrs. Privett grimly watched
the buses passing along the Kentish Town Road. Then the voice
at the other end spoke again.

" Mrs. Rammell isn't in," it said. " Could you leave a message,
please? "

Mrs. Privett, however, wasn't having any of that sort of stuff. "Tell her it's important and it's urgent," she said firmly. "And tell her I want to speak to her myself."

The voice went away again. Mrs. Privett counted six more buses and a hearse. Then the voice came back.

"Would you hold on please?" it said. "Mrs. Rammell's just coming."

By the time Mrs. Rammell did come, Mrs. Privett was in a private flurry of her own. She seemed to have been in the little glass-and-steel cabinet for hours. And she was afraid that the operator would begin asking for another threepence. She was therefore brief. Even peremptory.

"I've got to come round to see you," she said. "It's urgent."

"But what about?" Mrs. Rammell asked. "Who are you, please?"

"I'm Mrs. Privett. I've got to see you."

She realised now how foolish it was to have allowed herself to be trapped.

"It's about Ireen," Mrs. Privett told her.

"About what?"

Mrs. Rammell sounded more incredulous than ever.

"About Ireen," Mrs. Privett repeated. "Your boy and my Ireen."

For a moment, Mrs. Rammell very nearly rang off. The only possible explanation was that the poor women at the other end really must be mad.

"Did . . . did you say 'my boy?'" Mrs. Rammell asked.

"Yes," Mrs. Privett answered. "That's why I want to see you." The conversation seemed to her to be getting somewhere at last. She felt calmer. And she remembered her manners. "So if it's convenient I'd like to come round to-day," she said. "I don't want to intrude. But it oughtn't to wait."

There was a thin, gasping sound at the other end.

"There isn't any mistake, is there?" the voice asked. "You did say you were Mrs. Privett, didn't you?"

This time it was Mrs. Privett who gasped. They seemed to be right back at the beginning again.

"Yes, that's me," she answered. "It is Mrs. Rammell, isn't it? I mean Mrs. Rammell of Rammell's?"

Cornered, Mrs. Rammell had to admit it.

" Then you're the one I want to see," Mrs. Privett continued. " And I'd like it to be this afternoon, please."

" But . . . but what about? "

" About your boy and my Ireen."

" My boy and your what? "

" My Ireen."

Mrs. Privett heard the same, exasperated intake of breath at the other end.

" I'm afraid I still can't hear. It must be the line."

" Ireen," Mrs. Privett repeated. " *Ireen.*"

She was getting annoyed herself now.

" And you want to see me about it? "

" Yes, if you don't mind, please," Mrs. Privett told her. " It'll be better for everybody. Would four o'clock do? "

Mrs. Rammell glanced automatically at her diary. There was the Anglo-French Ballet lunch at the Embassy. And there was a private view that she had meant to go to afterwards. Then there was a cocktail party at six. Apart from that there was nothing. Nothing except for all that telephoning she had to do for next Wednesday. It was as though this strange, agitated woman at the other end had been secretly spying on her engagements.

" Yes," she said weakly. " I . . . I could see you at four."

" Then I'll be there."

Mrs. Privett had a feeling as she said it that Mrs. Rammell wasn't quite ready to ring off just yet. And she was right. Mrs. Rammell was making one last effort to collect herself.

" You are Mrs. Privett, aren't you? " she asked. " I . . . I mean your husband is on Mr. Rammell's staff? "

Mrs. Privett very nearly lost her temper at that.

" I told you," she said. " I'm Mr. Privett's wife. He's my husband. And I want to see you about Ireen."

When Mrs. Privett left the call-box she was exhausted. Even the palms of her hands were wet. She had to wipe her face all over with her handkerchief. But there was no turning back now. She had done what she intended to do. And she would have to go through with it.

But because she had never been to Eaton Square before, she miscalculated. She didn't want to arrive at the last moment, rushed and breathless. And in the result she was nearly fifty minutes

191

too early. By five minutes past three she had found Eaton Square —not too easy with Belgrave Square looking so much like it just beside—and she had located the house. And it was worse even than she feared. It wasn't even one of the terrace houses. It was the big detached one over in the corner with the two carriage gates and the portico like a corn-exchange.

To pass the time, Mrs. Privett drank a cup of tea that she didn't really want at a tea-shop right over by Victoria. Then she doubled back. And this time she only just made it. Four o'clock was actually striking as she made her way over the cobblestones of the crescent drive and up to the big front door.

Even though the maid seemed to know all about her, Mrs. Privett was a bit taken aback when she was shown into the drawing-room. There was no Mrs. Rammell. Simply a desert of large empty chairs and couches and rather a lot of expensive-looking flowers. Mrs. Privett couldn't understand it at all. If anyone had telephoned to her about Irene she would have been down by the front door. Ready and waiting.

She was just beginning to grow angry at the delay when Mrs. Rammell came in. She looked unusually cold and distinguished.

" It is Mrs. Privett, isn't it? " she began.

But there was no need to ask. She recognised her perfectly. " I'm afraid I must have been keeping you waiting."

" That doesn't matter," Mrs. Privett replied. " Not now that we can talk."

It was not quite so easy, however. Because at that moment tea was brought in. The cup of tea that Mrs. Privett had already drunk at Victoria very nearly made her refuse everything. But though she intended to remain firm, she still wanted to appear friendly.

" No sugar, thank you," she said. " I don't take it."

There was a brief pause.

" As I was saying we can talk now," she resumed.

" But you still haven't told me what about," Mrs. Rammell reminded her.

" It's about your boy," Mrs. Privett said bluntly. " He's been taking my Ireen out. And it's not right. He never even asked us if he could. And she's not his kind anyway. They're quite different. She's a good girl, our Ireen. But she's not eighteen yet. And she won't listen to reason. That's why I want you to say something at your end."

Mrs. Rammell had put her cup down and was staring hard at Mrs. Privett.

"Are you telling me that Tony is going out with your daughter?" she asked.

Mrs. Privett pursed up her lips and nodded.

"I am," she said. "And I don't approve of it. Some mothers might be pleased, but I'm not. It's my girl that I'm thinking of. And I don't think it's good for her."

Mrs. Rammell was still confused by this outburst. Numbed rather. She could not make out what exactly it was that this small intense woman opposite to her was trying so hard to say.

"You don't mean that anything's actually happened, do you?" she asked.

"I don't like to think about it at all," Mrs. Privett replied. "Not at her age, that is."

It was then that Mrs. Rammell realised that it was she who would have to speak plainly. Not that the fact was altogether surprising to her. She had noticed before that women of Mrs. Privett's class never would come to the point when it was a matter of mentioning anything unpleasant.

"You don't mean there's anything wrong?" she asked. "There isn't a baby or anything?"

This time it was Mrs. Privett who spoke out.

"She'd never have let him!"

The reply was fairly snapped back. Mrs. Privett was sitting bolt upright by now. Simply perched there. Like an angry female kestrel.

"She's not that type of girl, thank you," Mrs. Privett said emphatically. "Not my Ireen."

Mrs. Rammell was so much relieved to hear it that she leant forward and laid her hand on Mrs. Privett's arm.

"I'm sure she's not, Mrs. Privett," she said. "It's just that I wanted to know everything, so that I could help you." She paused. "So that we can both do the right thing, I mean."

Mrs. Privett was not, however, so easily placated.

"The best thing we can do is to stop it," she said. "Our Ireen won't listen to us. So perhaps you can make your Tony listen to you. There's no good can come of it. Not with your son."

This time it was Mrs. Rammell who stiffened.

"What's wrong with my boy?" she asked.

She realised as soon as she had said it how ridiculous it was. At this rate she'd be down on her knees next begging the Privetts to have her Tony as a son-in-law.

And it made it worse, not better, that Mrs. Privett should be so deliberately polite about it. Because this time it was Mrs. Privett who leant forward.

" There couldn't be a nicer young man," she said. " There's no complaints about him. It's . . . it's simply "—here Mrs. Privett seemed to be groping for her words again—" that it isn't right. They're not the same sort of people. We've brought up our Ireen very simply. And your boy's always been brought up to have everything. I don't think they'd make each other happy. That's all I'm thinking about, my Ireen's happiness."

Mrs. Rammell had recovered her poise by now. She was trying to enfold Mrs. Privett again.

" I think you're being a very sensible woman," she said. " I admire you for it."

" So d'you think you could get his dad to say something to him? " Mrs. Privett asked.

" I'll make it my business," Mrs. Rammell promised.

" And you won't let my husband know I've been to see you," Mrs. Privett asked.

" We'll keep this entirely to ourselves," Mrs. Rammell promised her. " There shan't be a word of it to anyone."

She had got up from her chair by now and was moving round the room arranging things. At the bowl of chrysanthemums she paused, tugging the big obstinate blooms into position. By now Mrs. Rammell was completely in possession of herself again. She addressed Mrs. Privett from across the flower bowl.

" I'm sure your daughter is a dear, dear girl," she said. " I can see it in you. And my Tony's a dear boy. But you're so right. They *couldn't* possibly make each other happy. And that's why we've got to step in. We older ones can see it even if they can't. They haven't got anything in common—except being young, of course."

Mrs. Rammell broke off because the door had opened. It was the maid again. She stood there as though determined to interrupt her.

" Miss Parkinson, Madam," she announced.

And then Mrs. Rammell remembered. She had been certain

all the time that there was something that she should have put in her diary. It was only because it was her own sister that she had forgotten. Somehow she always did forget her sister.

She rose hurriedly and went towards the door.

" Nancy, dear," she said. " How nice."

She broke off for a moment. Then she recovered herself.

" Come over here," she went on. " You must let me introduce you to my friend, Mrs. Privett. Mrs. Privett, this is my sister, Miss Parkinson."

Mrs. Rammell wished as she said it that Miss Parkinson looked a bit more probable for a sister. Not that it was her fault, poor dear. Things had always been difficult for darling Nancy. And she had been far, far too proud to accept assistance. All the same, that coat. And those shoes. Or rather, that coat and those shoes in conjunction with that hat. Poor dear darling Nancy, Mrs. Rammell reflected, might at least have *tried*.

A moment later, however, it was not about Nancy's clothes that Mrs. Rammell was worrying. It was about everything else as well. For Mrs. Privett and Miss Parkinson were regarding each other with a kind of fixed fascination.

" Eileen! " Miss Parkinson said at last in a voice that might have been speaking from a tomb.

" Nance," Mrs. Privett answered.

" You know each other? " Mrs. Rammell asked blankly.

But the answer was obvious. And horrifying. For Mrs. Rammell could feel the tentacles of her own past reaching out for her. She was no longer in Eaton Square at all. She was back in that dreadful little house in Streatham where they had moved after Papa's last long illness.

It was horrid and degrading even to think about it. Because Mamma had been left so unexpectedly, disastrously poor in her widowhood. She had even been forced to let rooms to pay for her daughter's music lessons. And Nancy, brave unselfish little Nancy, had taken a job in a draper's shop over at Brixton. It had been the only thing to do. Because Mamma alone couldn't afford to support both her dear girls.

Mrs. Rammell gave a little shudder as she recalled it. It was terrible, unthinkable, what Nancy had been through for their sakes. But also in a way unforgivable. Because she had never quite been able to throw off the experience. She had become stained by it. Even when Mrs. Rammell was still only engaged to Mr. Rammell she had been ashamed—yes, that was the only word, ashamed—of the sheer shoppiness of her own sister.

It wasn't as though the Parkinsons had been brought up to retail trade. Far from it. Papa had been a general merchant in the City. And if Mr. Rammell's father had been in a smaller way of business Mrs. Parkinson wouldn't even have considered him. It was simply the scale of Rammell's that had somehow purified, sanctified even, the inescapable retailness of shopkeeping. That had been what had made her so terrified lest Mr. Rammell, while still only in the engaged state, should discover that his fiancée's own sister was a common shopgirl. Together with Mamma, they had concealed the whole shameful secret. And at the time oh how thankful she had been to think that, even if the journey was tiring for young Nancy, it was also sufficiently long for none of their neighbours ever to have seen Nancy actually serving . . .

But already Nancy and Mrs. Privett were in each other's arms. And worse than that. They had not merely embraced. They had kissed as well.

" It must be nearly thirty years," Nancy was saying, her voice trembling on the edge of tears.

" Well, twenty-five anyway," Mrs. Privett told her.

" I can't believe it. Really, I can't," Nancy went on. " And do you ever see Emmie? You remember? The little pretty one."

Mrs. Privett paused.

" Dead," she told her. " Nearly ten years ago. And now her husband's just going to get married again."

" Well, I never," Nancy replied. " Isn't it wonderful the way time flies. It only seems yesterday . . ."

Mrs. Rammell began to move over in their direction.

" Now, Nancy dear," she said. " We mustn't keep Mrs. Privett. She just came over to see me. And I know she's got to be getting back." She turned to her visitor. " I think we'd quite finished, hadn't we, Mrs. Privett? "

It was Mrs. Privett now who was struggling with her past. While Mrs. Rammell was speaking she had been far away. She was young again. Young as the others were. Standing behind a counter

196

over in Brixton between Nancy, who wore her pretty gold hair all piled up on top, and Emmie who wore her brown hair screwed securely into a bun. Mrs. Privett remembered suddenly that her own hair had been raven in those days. Absolutely raven and with a wave in it that defied even the rain . . .

She jerked herself back into the present.

"Yes, thank you, Mrs. Rammell," she replied. "That is if . . . if you'll do what I asked."

Mrs. Rammell was so relieved that she gave Mrs. Privett a real smile instead of her regular social one.

"I feel sure we understand each other," she said. "Good-bye. And thank you again for coming."

But even then silly, impetuous Nancy couldn't take a hint.

"Well, I'm going as far as the bus with her," she said. "Eileen and me have got such lots to talk about."

CHAPTER XXII

For Mrs. Rammell that untimely reunion between Mrs. Privett and poor sister Nancy had proved the last straw. It represented humiliation. Nothing less. She could never hold up her head again.

If only Mr. Rammell would have listened to her. If only he hadn't been so brutally pig-headed about insisting that Tony should go into the shop at all. Couldn't he have foreseen the consequences? Wasn't it exactly what anybody might have expected with someone so young, so inexperienced, so fatally attractive as her Tony?

And because Mrs. Rammell was so angry, so inwardly seething, all her self-control went from her. She broke every promise of secrecy that she had made to Mrs. Privett. As soon as Mr. Rammell returned home that evening she blurted it all out to him.

". . . and would you listen to me? " she asked. " Did you take the slightest notice of what I said? Do you ever listen to anything I say to you? " Despite her polite upbringing Mrs. Rammell had a distinctly vulgar side to her nature when disturbed. " And now see the mess that you've made," she went on. " You and your father. I hope you're proud of yourselves, the pair of you."

Mr. Rammell poured himself out another whisky that he didn't particularly want. Then he waited patiently for Mrs. Rammell to subside. If there was one thing that he hated it was talking to a woman who had red rims to her eyes and a catch in her voice that threatened a complete breakdown at any moment.

" All right. All right," he said at length. " I'll . . ."

Mrs. Rammell had clearly reached the danger point. Logic, reason, argument counted for nothing any longer.

" It's not all right," she said. " It's just like you to think so. It's all wrong. As wrong as it could be."

" I was only going to say that I'd have a word with Tony," Mr. Rammell replied quietly.

But it was no use. He had made the mistake of using his soft reasonable voice. Mrs. Rammell had always found even the mere tone of it maddening. It was as though he were trying to treat her as no better than a silly child.

"You can't. Don't you see?" she almost screamed. "He hasn't come in. He's out somewhere *with her*."

Mr. Rammell, however, was not unduly concerned by the delay. Unlike Mrs. Rammell he had managed to retain his composure. He wanted to make a few discreet inquiries before saying anything.

He therefore avoided Tony altogether next morning. Simply didn't appear at breakfast and sent down a message that he was not going into the office at the usual time.

When he did arrive at Bond Street, the first thing he did was to work through the shop. And in Haberdashery, he lingered. He remembered the girl perfectly. He knew for whom he was looking. And there she was. Younger and prettier than ever. Very neat, too, in the black Rammell costume with the white collar and cuffs. At the thought that she was the cause of all the trouble Mr. Rammell almost smiled. It was ridiculous. Like being blackmailed by an unusually attractive schoolgirl.

But his mind was made up. And as soon as he got upstairs to his room he sent for Mr. Privett. This was something that he wanted to handle personally. Besides, he rather liked Mr. Privett. He was so much a part of the place. When he came in, Mr. Rammell invited him to sit down as though he were an important visitor.

"Everything going all right up on your floor?" he asked.

Mr. Privett smiled contentedly.

"Oh, yes, sir, thank you. A bit on the quiet side. But very smooth, sir. Everything going very smoothly."

Mr. Rammell paused.

"Now about that daughter of yours."

It seemed to Mr. Rammell that Mr. Privett leant forward a little nervously.

"Yes, sir?" he asked.

"Very good girl," Mr. Rammell told him. "Excellent reports. Does you credit, Privett."

"I'm so glad you think so, sir."

"Time for a transfer, you know," Mr. Rammell went on. "Can't have a girl in Haberdashery all her life. I'll speak to Mr. Preece about it."

" I'm sure she's very contented where she is, sir," Mr. Privett began.

But already Mr. Rammell was speaking again.

" Oh, and there is just one other thing. She and Mr. Tony have been seeing rather a lot of each other just lately. Not a good thing. Starts people gossiping. I just thought I'd mention it to you."

Mr. Privett swallowed for a moment.

" I . . . I understand, sir."

" Thank you very much, Privett, I felt sure you would. Good morning."

So that was that. Mr. Rammell felt like congratulating himself. If there was one thing which he really knew it was how to handle staff. Friendly, without being familiar. Firm, but not a trace of harshness. Brief rather than curt.

And the idea of a transfer was sheer genius. If they put the girl up in Gowns, or better still, Teen-age or Children's, that would mean that she was as much separated from Shirtings as if she were working in another store.

2

Indeed, everything would probably have been all right if only Mrs. Rammell could have left things alone. But it was too much to ask of her. Ever since Mrs. Privett's visit, she had lain awake at night listening to the heavy sound of Mr. Rammell's breathing, and thinking of that dreadful, scheming girl lying in wait for Tony as soon as he reached Bond Street. And by day the thought was never from her.

In the result, she did the one fatal thing. She conspired to get Tony alone with her. She appealed to him.

". . . don't you see that it would be throwing your life away? " she pleaded. " She may be pretty. She may be amusing. She may be anything you like *now*. But think of how it will be in a few years' time. Think of her, too. Cut off from anything. No friends. Not really belonging. Out of her depth socially . . ."

Mrs. Rammell broke off.

" Tony, dear, put that magazine down while I'm talking to

you. It's rude." Here Mrs. Rammell screwed her two hands together until the knuckles showed white against the skin. " Can't you realise? It's your whole future I'm talking about. It's everything that matters. It's . . ."

It was at this point that Mr. Rammell came in. The day, like most days, had been long. And, like most days, tiring. At the sound of voices in the room he had nearly drawn back. But it was too late now. Mrs. Rammell had seen him. She was beckoning to him. Begging him to come in.

Tony looked up to see why Mrs. Rammell had broken off so abruptly. And at the sight of his father, he gave a little smile almost of sympathy.

" Oh, God," he asked. " Are you in this, too? "

The discussion, though long, was inconclusive. Tempers were lost. Recovered. Lost again. And this time it was Mr. Rammell who blundered.

" I've a very good mind to get rid of the girl altogether," he said. " Just give her back her card and see the last of her."

" I call that bloody unfair," Tony replied. " And I tell you this now. If she goes, I go too."

" No."

It was Mrs. Rammell who had spoken. The word had simply been forced out of her. Because this was too dreadful. It showed how far things had really gone. Her Tony was being loyal to someone else.

Mr. Rammell took out his cigar cutter and began fiddling with it.

" I haven't said I will," he pointed out. " I'm only reminding you."

And then, because it wasn't a conversation that he had wanted to start in the first place, he suddenly felt his own temper rising.

" And let me remind you of something else," he added. " It's gone quite far enough. Her father knows. The staff know. And . . . and your aunt knows. If you want to have the whole of London talking about you, I don't."

Tony got up slowly and put the magazine that he had been reading under his arm. Then he walked over and kissed Mrs. Rammell on the forehead.

" Don't let Father keep you up too late," he said quietly.

CHAPTER XXIII

MR. BLOOT had always assumed that it would be a white wedding. St. Asaph's, the large red-brick block of Victorian medievalism at the end of Artillery Row was the nearest church to the bride's home. And, in his mind's eye, he had frequently pictured the whole scene. The organ pealing. Mr. Bloot himself wearing his best tails and the practically new pair of striped cashmere that he had bought specially for the Rammell anniversary celebrations. And, above all, Hetty, smiling and effulgent, with a wreath of orange-blossom in her hair and a long expensive-looking train supported by tiny local bridesmaids.

Not that his wedding to poor Emily had been in the least like that. On that occasion he had worn his blue serge with four buttons. And Emily herself had looked thoroughly sensible, but still appealing, in a plain white shirt waist and her going-away costume. But then Emily was not Hetty. And Mr. Bloot simply could not imagine Hetty bringing herself down to his own simple level.

That was why he was so astonished when she refused even to consider a church wedding at all.

" Us? In church? " she asked. " You can if you like. I'll wait outside, thank you. What's the point of advertising it? "

" I . . . I just thought you'd rather," Mr. Bloot explained weakly.

He was surprised as he said it to find how strongly he felt about church weddings. He had, in fact, not been inside a church since Emily's death. And then only to the cemetery chapel. Nevertheless he had not even considered the possibility of any other place in which to get married. Marriage at a Registrar's Office savoured too much of film stars. And run-away society couples. And divorcées. And fly-by-nights generally.

" Then if you don't want a church wedding," he asked, " what do you want? " and his heart chilled as he put the question.

" Why a Registry Office, of course. Same as normal people," Hetty told him. " It's just as legal."

Mr. Bloot shook his head.

" But it's not the same thing," he said.

" Of course, it isn't," Hetty answered. " It's less fuss. Go
along at nine o'clock, I say, and get it over quickly."

Mr. Bloot drew in his lips. They were trembling.

" Ah can't make you out," he said at last. " Really, Ah can't.
Anybody'd think you were ashamed of marrying me."

" Not ashamed, dear," Hetty replied. " Just doing it the easy
way."

And when he asked her what she meant by that she did not
answer. Instead she opened her arms and pursed up her lips at
him.

" Oh, stop worrying," she said. " You make me tired. Come
and kiss me. You haven't given me a single decent kiss all the
evening."

The kiss, though long and rather moist, was unecstatic. Mr. Bloot
had too much on his mind to give himself over freely to his own
rapture.

" You're not going back on it, are you? " he asked, almost as
soon as they had separated. " You still mean next month? "

" Of course I do, silly," Hetty replied.

She was speaking now in the low throaty voice that always made
Mr. Bloot feel utterly yearning and entirely helpless.

" It's just that I don't want you to fuss yourself. Don't get so
worked up about me. I'm not worth it."

" Oh, yes, you are," he told her. " Yur're everything in the
world to me. Yur're mah ahdeal." He paused. " Shall Ah put
up the banns? "

" Yes, if they have 'em in Registry Offices," Hetty replied.
" They probably need a fortnight's notice or something. Better
make it a Thursday. That's early-closing."

" Early-closing? " His heart missed a whole beat. " But . . .
but we are to 'ave er nunneymoon, aren't we? "

" If my boy wants one."

Hetty by now was stroking his cheek with the back of
her hand. " Does he want one? With me? Is that what he
wants? "

Mr. Bloot nodded helplessly.

" Ah do," he said. " Yur can't know how ah feel or yur
wouldn't even ask. It's all Ah want."

He paused again, and seemed to be working things out in his mind.

" And there's one other little matter we ought to talk abaht," he added. " If Ah move into your flat which of mah little bits and pieces would you lahk me to bring round? "

As it turned out, the matter of Mr. Bloot's bits and pieces had to be decided even before he went along to put up the banns. That was because he was so excited about getting remarried that he had to tell somebody. And like most naturally reticent men he made a mess of it. Instead of waiting for a proper opportunity, he told his landlady when he happened merely to meet her accidentally on the stairs.

" Ah've got a piece of news for you," he said, adding in the vein of jauntiness that so often conceals deep emotion. "Ah'm goin' through the 'oop again."

" Going through the 'oop? "

Mrs. Gurney regarded him cautiously. She had been conscious for some time that a change had been coming over Mr. Bloot. For close on twenty years, an ideal lodger, either married or single, he seemed suddenly to have developed flighty tendencies that had hitherto lain unsuspected. Drink, she decided, might prove to be at the bottom of it.

" Yurss," Mr. Bloot went on. " Gettin' married. Next month."

" Have I met her? " Mrs. Gurney asked.

It occurred to her as she put the question that with the exception of Mr. and Mrs. Privett—and Irene Privett as quite a little girl— she had never met any of Mr. Bloot's friends at all.

Mr. Bloot shook his head.

" Nevah," he said. " That is because the lady 'as nevah been here."

" Then when's she coming? " Mrs. Gurney asked.

There was caution in the voice. Almost alarm. What would she be like? Would she be the right sort? Would she be difficult over things like stairs? Would she be trustworthy about locking up and about electric lights? Having Mr. Bloot under her roof was one thing. But a newcomer. A woman. And a totally unknown woman at that. The natural hostility of the sex began bridling.

And Mr. Bloot's reply left Mrs. Gurney aghast and speechless.

" She's not coming," he told her. " Ah'm goin' there. To 'er place."

" Is she a widow? "

Mr. Bloot nodded.

" Yurss," he said. " Very comfortably provided. Very comfortably, indeed. Wouldn't like it 'ere at all I'm afraid. Er mansion flat. That's what she's got. Er mansion flat . . ."

" Wouldn't like it here? " Mrs. Gurney repeated. " You mean we're not good enough? "

It was then that the simple honesty of Mr. Bloot's mind betrayed him. He had no diplomatic reserves whatever. It was the truth, the plain flat-footed truth, that broke from him.

" That's abaht it," he said. " That's the way it is."

" Well, I like that! "

This time Mrs. Gurney's voice—and until this moment it had never occurred to Mr. Bloot that Mrs. Gurney even had a voice—sounded strangled and choking. Mr. Bloot regarded her with astonishment.

" Ah didn't mean that," he said. " It's all raht for you and me. Very nahce in fact. Very snug. It's just that it wouldn't be raht for her."

But he got no further. For Mrs. Gurney, aged fifty-five, herself contentedly married and therefore in no sense jealous and unnaturally possessive of her lone lodger, had burst into tears.

At one moment she was standing on the stairs beside him; and, at the next, she had shot across the landing and gone into her and Mr. Gurney's bedroom, slamming the door after her.

Mr. Bloot stood where he was for a moment. Then slowly he resumed his climb to the second floor.

" Ah can't understand it," he kept telling himself. " No feelings. Didn't even wish me luck."

CHAPTER XXIV

It HAD been a brave decision on Mrs. Privett's part to go to Mrs. Rammell's in the first place. But no matter what the consequences, she knew that she had done the right thing.

And when Mr. Privett came back and broke the news that Mr. Rammell had spoken to him about Irene, she was more than ever convinced. Convinced and gratified. Because it showed that Mrs. Rammell had kept her word. She had respected Mrs. Privett's secret.

For Mr. Privett, however, there remained all the bitterness of disappointment. Secretly, he had felt from the outset that Tony and Irene would make a lovely pair. He had boasted of it openly to Mr. Bloot. But he did not feel disposed to challenge Mr. Rammell. After all, Irene was still young. It wasn't as though Tony were her only chance.

And, in any case, things were happening. It was too late now to start protesting. Irene herself announced the news. Innocently, as though she hadn't guessed the full significance, she told her parents that very night at supper.

" I'm getting a transfer," she said. " Right out of Haberdashery. Into Children's. Sounds awful."

Mr. Privett caught his wife's eye as Irene said it. It proved that the wheels were turning. Showed that Mr. Rammell was tackling the problem the quiet, sensible way.

And then Irene said something that made both Mr. and Mrs. Privett suddenly sit forward.

" If I don't like it," she said, " I shan't stay."

" Not stay? " Mrs. Privett repeated.

" Why should I? " Irene asked. " It's not fair about that transfer. I never asked for it."

It was there that Mr. Privett intervened. As he was speaking he wished that Mr. Rammell could have been present to hear him.

" That's not the point," he said. " There's more than you to be

206

considered. You couldn't run a store if everybody chose for themselves. They're only doing what they think best."

" Well, I don't see it," Irene replied.

She got up as she said it and went over to the door. Then she paused for a moment.

" And Tony doesn't either," she added as she went out.

" No," Mrs. Privett said firmly. " You leave me to handle this. I'm going to have a word with that young lady."

2

That was at about seven-fifteen. At seven-thirty Mr. Privett took his raincoat and umbrella and said that he was going over to see how Mr. Bloot was getting along. He would be back again shortly after ten he said. But by then it was too late.

" That you, Ireen? " he heard his wife's voice call out as the front door closed on him.

" It's only me, Mother," he answered.

But, as he said it, it struck him that Mrs. Privett sounded unusually strained and anxious about something. Alarmed, even.

And a moment later, Mrs. Privett came out to meet him. Then he could tell at once that there was something wrong.

" Why, what's the matter? " he began. " Is . . .."

But he got no further. Mrs. Privett interrupted him.

" She's gone," Mrs. Privett told him. " Our Ireen's gone."

Because it was so unexpected he found some difficulty in understanding. The words simply did not make any sense to him.

" Gone where? " he asked.

" Gone away," Mrs. Privett replied. " Packed a suitcase and gone."

" I don't believe it," he answered. " I just don't believe it. She'd never do a thing like that."

" Well, she's done it, I tell you."

But Mrs. Privett could get no further. Quiet, controlled, unemotional as she normally was, she broke down and sobbed on Mr. Privett's shoulder.

With his free arm Mr. Privett managed to get rid of his umbrella in the hall-stand. But there was nothing that he could do about his raincoat. All wet and steamy as he was he led his wife back into the living-room.

" You tell me what's happened," he said. " You tell me all about it."

It seemed that it had occurred almost immediately after Mr. Privett had left. That fatal reference to Tony was what had started it. Mrs. Privett had warned Irene. Spoken to her frankly as any mother should. And, thereafter, so far as Mr. Privett could judge, the fault had been all Irene's. She shouldn't have been so rude. Shouldn't have told Mrs. Privett to mind her own business. Because that was what had made Mrs. Privett tell her that it was everybody's business by now.

Bit by bit it had all come out. Mrs. Privett's misgivings. Her fears. Her patience. Her anxiety when she saw how things were developing. Her visit to Mrs. Rammell.

And it was the last that had done it.

" You never," Irene had said. " Not about us. You wouldn't have dared."

" I did dare," Mrs. Privett had assured her. " And let me tell you another thing. That's why you're being sent up to Children's. So as to separate the two of you."

That, it seemed, was what had decided Irene. According to Mrs. Privett she had jumped to her feet, knocking over a teacup that was on the arm of her chair beside her, and had said something —Mrs. Privett couldn't remember exactly what—about not stopping there any longer. Then, some ten minutes later, when Mrs. Privett went upstairs to look for her, she had gone. And she had taken her attaché-case with her. The brown leather one that she had always used for school. She had packed pyjamas. Bedroom slippers. Tooth brush. Everything.

The whole lot. And then disappeared.

" You've got to find her. Now. Before it's too late," Mrs. Privett wound up. " She can't stop out. Not all night. Not at her age."

" But . . . but how do we know where she's gone? " Mr. Privett asked idiotically.

" We don't," Mrs. Privett told him. " But the police'll find her. That's where you've got to go. To the police station. I'd have gone myself only I was afraid that she might come back and find nobody here."

At the thought of such a return to a house left silent and empty Mrs. Privett began crying again. Mr. Privett stood there, regarding her.

" The police? " he repeated doubtfully. " How'll they find her? "

But already Mrs. Privett had recovered herself. She was pushing him out of the room in front of her.

" You go straight round there," she said. " They've got their ways. They'll find her all right. Only hurry." She paused. " Before it's too late," she added significantly.

3

Irene herself at that moment was just getting into bed. It was a small bedroom. Rather like the bedroom in a nursing home. With white shiny walls and white painted woodwork. And the corridor outside was made of some kind of composition stuff that curved up at the sides and looked as if it would be very soft and yielding to walk on, and wasn't.

Up to now, it hadn't been so bad. Not bad at all, in fact. She had been in such a temper when she left Fewkes Road that nothing had seemed to matter. And for the last couple of hours she had been among friends. There had been two girls from Stationery, a middle-aged woman whom she didn't know from Woollens. And another girl of her own age from Classical Records. The brother of the Classical Records girl was there, too. He was a tall, rather serious young man, who didn't say very much. But he seemed to be listening all the time. And he had a nice laugh. He was something in Travel he told her.

Because there was so much chatter going on, Irene had found herself forgetting all about the trouble at home. It had been rather fun sitting there as one of a group that was ready to accept her as a grown-up person who could be talked to sensibly. Not treated as a schoolgirl the way her mother did.

But then 10.30 had come round. The young man from Travel had been forced to leave them. And the whole party had just broken up.

Now she was alone with herself in that white, clinical-looking little bedroom. Really alone. So much alone that she felt like the last person left awake in London. And immediately it all came crowding back on her. The row with her mother. The way she had dashed out of the house without even saying good-bye. The consternation that she must have left behind her. The thought— the perfectly horrible thought—of what people had been saying behind her back. The thought of what they would begin saying after this had happened.

Somewhere nearby she heard an unfamiliar church clock strike eleven. It was a thin, melancholy chime. It reminded her that in less than twelve hours' time she would have to face it all again.

She began crying. Crying very softly, with her head right down among the pillows, so that all the girls in the other white, clinical-looking little bedrooms wouldn't be able to hear.

4

Mr. Privett had just reached the end of Fewkes Road. The police station was a couple of hundred yards away on the right-hand side. And he was going straight towards it.

But something kept holding him back. All the way from the house he had expected to meet Irene. He was certain, in fact, when he got to the Kentish Town Road that he would see her coming back. That was why he was walking so slowly. Giving her time to catch up with him. And, because there was no sign of her, because the whole street was just so much emptiness, he felt lost. Utterly lost and bewildered. Mrs. Privett, it seemed, had not been exaggerating.

He had reached the police station at last. But even then, with his foot on the bottom step, he still hesitated. His opening sentences, " I've come about my daughter. She's run away from home," were all ready on his lips. It wasn't even the shame of saying it that he minded. He was long past caring about that sort of thing by now. All that mattered was finding her.

And then, just as he got to the door with the blue lamp shining over it, he stopped dead. But only for a moment. Because turning round, he came back down the steps again. He was walking very quickly. And this time there was no looking over his shoulder to see if Irene were following. He just went straight along to the Underground Station and into the nearest telephone box.

It took him a long while to find the number. But that was partly because the light was bad. And partly because his hands were trembling so. Even then, after he had dialled, the pause seemed an unduly long one. He was just beginning to think that he had blundered with the noughts or something when a voice answered.

" Rammell's Staff Hostel."

" It's Mr. Privett here," he began. " You know, Fourth Floor. Is my daughter . . ?"

When he got back to Fewkes Road, he naturally expected Mrs. Privett to go along to the Hostel with him straight away to bring Irene home. They'd be sure to get a taxi, he said, if the Underground had closed by the time they got there.

But Mrs. Privett only shook her head.

" Not if that's where she is," she said. " She'll be all right there. Better leave her to herself."

She paused.

" I only thought . . ." Mr. Privett began.

" No," Mrs. Privett told him. " It wouldn't be fair on her. It'd only make her more conspicuous. There's been enough talk about her as there is. I'll go along by myself in the morning. First thing."

Mr. Privett let out a deep sigh and sat down. He suddenly felt tired. Very tired. It had all been too much for him. And he felt hurt as well. Mrs. Privett hadn't so much as congratulated him once on having thought of ringing up the Hostel in the first place. She had simply accepted the news without question. Calmly, sensibly accepted it.

" You go to bed now," she said. " You won't be fit for anything in the morning." She hesitated for a moment. " Don't wait for me," she went on. " I haven't even looked at the paper. I'm going to sit up for a bit."

Mr. Privett made no reply. He was too shocked. This was more than calmness. It was downright callous, he reckoned, sitting down to read at a time like this. How she could . . .

A faint sound on the other side of the fireplace made him glance up. Then he understood. The evening paper lay beside her untouched. Mrs. Privett had got her handkerchief up to her eyes. And her shoulders were shaking.

" Oh, my little Ireen, why did you ? " she was saying.

CHAPTER XXV

It was difficult nowadays for Mr. Bloot. Merely going on living in Tetsbury Road was a strain.

Resentment was no longer limited to Mrs. Gurney. She had confided in her husband—told him of the slur on the house—and he had sided with her. The two of them down there together in the rather dark front basement had whipped themselves up into a fury. They no longer spoke to Mr. Bloot when they met him on the stairs. Simply brushed past him silently as though one or other of them was a ghost.

And the rent was now no more than a formal, real-estate transaction. Mr. Bloot left the book with the pound note, the ten shilling note and the half-crown in an envelope marked " Mrs. Gurney " on the little ledge of the hall hat-stand. And by next morning, as though mute impersonal genies had been in charge of the whole operation, the money was removed, the rent book receipted and the same envelope with " Mrs. Gurney " crossed out and " Mr. Bloot " substituted for it, was back again on the same little ledge.

Even without this unpleasantness, Mr. Bloot's spirits were at a low ebb already.

Admittedly there was the excitement, the rapturous anticipation of the wedding night ahead of him. But, hanging over everything was the grey, tremulous sadness of remembrance. It is always a painful, heart-tugging sort of business breaking up a home. And 17 Tetsbury Road was the only real home he had ever had. Before he and Emily had moved there, they had lived with her mother at Stoke Newington. And though it had been placid, comfortable, undifficult, he had never known exactly that real Englishman-in-his-castle kind of feeling.

And now he was planning the deliberate destruction of this great part of him. To say that he had loved Tetsbury Road would have been pitching things too high. But, until he had met Hetty, he had never imagined anything else. Tetsbury Road and Mr. Bloot had seemed practically indissociable.

"Bring round any little things you like, silly," Hetty had said to him. "We'll find a place for them."

But what little things? He was, for instance, almost inordinately fond of a bow-fronted mahogany sideboard with a bevel-edged, oval mirror at the back. In the old days Emily had kept it polished like bronze. And with the Jubilee biscuit barrel, the cut-glass cruet stand and brightly-painted cheese cover with the design of roses on the top, he had sometimes passed his hand sensuously along the woodwork simply because he liked the sheer security of good living that the piece represented.

Only it wasn't, by any means, a little thing. And Hetty had her own sideboard. A small almost boudoirish affair in light fumed oak with chromium handles.

And it was the same with his dining-room table. It was undeniably large. Large even for the spaciousness of Tetsbury Road. But good. Good and strong. And solid. But, again, Hetty had her own table. Fumed oak like the sideboard. And built refectory-style with one of those magic sections that jump up in the middle when you pull at the two ends.

Nor was she in any need of a bedroom suite. Again, she already had a suite in bright, palpitating satinwood with glass knobs on all the drawers, and a low dressing-table stool that looked as if it had been designed for child pianists. And though Mr. Bloot's suite was more comprehensive—it included a marble-topped washstand complete with jug, basin, soap-dish and tooth-brush stand, it would clearly be impossible to crush it into the bedroom in Artillery Mansions.

In short, as Mr. Bloot went round his little home, he realised sadly that it would all have to go. All of it. By the time he had moved in with Hetty he would simply have submerged his life in hers.

In the end he decided to make an exception of three things. A small bamboo table which he always kept alongside his bed at night. A practically new ironing-board that he used when pressing his trousers. And a glass-fronted corner cupboard that he refused to believe couldn't be wedged in somewhere. Apart from that, nothing. Nothing at all preservable from the possessions of a lifetime.

If Hetty had rescued him from the very gutter itself he could hardly have seemed more destitute.

Except, of course, for his budgerigars. Even if the rest of his furniture was a bit on the old-fashioned side there was nothing to be ashamed of about them. No matter how you looked at it, champion budgerigars in specially sprung, pavilion-shaped cages really were something worth acquiring.

And all the things that went with budgerigars—the millet seed, the grit, the vegetable salts, the cuttlefish bone, the sack of refined sand, the tin water-jug—could easily, he told himself, be stored away somewhere in the kitchen quarters, leaving the birds themselves, free and unencumbered for their social life.

Because the Gurneys were being so horrid to him, it was with a feeling of glorious relief when Sunday morning came round again, and Mr. Bloot went round to Hetty's.

Indeed, as he shut the iron gate of the front garden behind him with its familiar, insistent screech, he felt better. By the time he had reached the Tufnell Park Road he was whistling.

And Hetty, as it turned out, was in the same mood of jubilation herself. Even though it was only eleven-thirty in the morning, she was already dressed and her face all made up. She suggested a cocktail as soon as he got there.

Mr. Bloot accepted it. He had grown used to cocktails. And then, because Hetty kept pressing, he lit a cigarette as well. Sitting there, glass in hand, watching the swirl of blue smoke coil upwards he felt like a big recklessly wicked Latin kind of lover.

" I like a man to smoke," Hetty told him. " Seems more manly somehow. And after all it's only natural. Everyone smokes cigarettes. . . ."

She came over and refilled his glass. And from sheer coyness she rubbed the cold frosted side of the shaker across the back of his hand as she did so.

" Not that you need to," she went on. " Not really. You're all right as you are. It's just that it's more friendly."

" Ah love you," Mr. Bloot told her, somewhat mechanically. " Ah will 'ave 'er noccasional smoke if you'd rather."

It was after all the very least that he could say after Hetty had been so nice to him. And if she was happy he wanted to keep her happy. He would have agreed to smoke cigars if necessary.

215

" Ah've found out where to go," he told her. " And they take three weeks. Ah couldn't actually do anything yesterday because they'd shut. But Ah'll go in on Monday. Ah've explained the position at Rammell's. It'll be all raht."

" What will? "

" The registry yoffice. It's in the Town 'all, Finsbury Park. Just round the corner. It's er nomen. Er nappy omen."

But Hetty only laughed.

" Don't bother about it," she said. " I've seen to it."

" Seen to it," Mr. Bloot repeated incredulously.

Hetty nodded.

" Done it all myself," she told him. " And fixed the time. On the 26th, at 9.30. We're the first that day."

At the thought of such devotion Mr. Bloot's eyes filled with tears. He was deeply, uncontrollably moved. But his sense of the proprieties remained.

" You shouldn't of," he told her firmly. " It's not raht. It's the man's prerogative."

" Don't give it a thought," Hetty told him. " After all, it was nearer for me, wasn't it? "

Mr. Bloot reached out his hand and began fondling her wrist, thrusting in his fingers between the thick slave bangles that she was wearing.

" Yur're such a dear," he answered. " Saving me all that trouble. But it's still wrong. All wrong. It makes me despahs mahself."

He paused for a moment, his wide, pink face clouded with apprehension.

" But 'ow did you know the facts? " he went on. " About me and Emily, I mean. Things like 'er second name. And the date. And which church it was. They need all that, you know."

" I asked Mrs. Privett," Hetty replied. " That night when we went round there."

She had removed his glass from his hand while she was talking, and now sat herself heavily upon his knee. He gave a sharp, involuntary gasp as her weight came bearing down upon him. But he still had enough breath left to kiss her. It was a real, full-blooded, rousing kiss. And he felt quite exhausted at the end of it.

" Now let's talk about the honeymoon," Hetty suggested. "I still think Bournemouth. It's more select. And it's warmer. Not that I mind so long as it's just us."

Because of the little additional squeeze that she gave him as she said it, Mr. Bloot could not reply immediately.

" Bournemouth it is," he said breathlessly. " You've done the lahcence. Ah'll look after the 'otel."

" Make it a front room," Hetty said softly. " So that we can lie there listening to the sea."

" Leave it all to me," Mr. Bloot told her. " We'll 'ave the best."

He paused, as his strong sense of the practical regained possession of him.

" After all," he added, " it's only for three days. And it's not the season. If Ah knows anything abaht 'otels they'll probably be very glad to 'ave us."

They sat there in silence for a time, Hetty gently squeezing his ear and Mr. Bloot allowing his hand to stray upwards until it was toying with the thick coil of her hair.

" Ah've made up mah mind what Ah'll bring round 'ere," he said at last. " It's nothing really. Just two useful bits, and one ornamental."

Hetty gave him a little kiss on the top of his head.

" Whatever you say," she told him dreamily.

" And then there's mah budgies," he went on.

" Your what? "

" Mah budgies."

" You're teasing."

" If you'd ever been round to mah place you'd 'ave seen 'em," he said. " Flying abaht, too. Not just in cages."

He broke off for a moment as though wondering whether to disclose a secret.

" Ah'm teaching Joey to say your name," he confided.

Hetty, however, did not seem reassured. He could feel a little shudder run right through her. Then she got up.

" Birds," she said. " I can't abide them. Give me the shivers. Even sparrows."

Mr. Bloot shook his head.

" But not budgies," he said. " They're more like little 'umans. They can think."

Hetty did not reply immediately. It was obvious that she was still battling with her feelings.

"Horrible smelly things," she said at last.

Mr. Bloot himself had got up by now and was on his way over to her.

"Budgies aren't smelly," he blurted out.

But before he could reach her, she had turned round.

"Well, smelly or not, they're not coming here," she said. "And that's flat. What sort of place d'you think this is anyway? A menagerie?"

CHAPTER XXVI

Considering what the consequences might have been, the Staff Hostel incident passed off very quietly.

Mrs. Privett had gone along at breakfast time as she had promised. And that was all that Mr. Privett knew. What had actually taken place when she got there was a secret between the two of them. And had remained a secret.

Mr. Privett had peeped in at Children's on his way back down from coffee. And he had seen Irene. There she was, standing underneath a sign marked Zipperwear. She certainly appeared to be all right. Showed no signs of the drama of the night before. But he couldn't be certain from that distance. And, above all, he didn't want her to know that he had been spying. There was nothing for it, therefore, but to wait until he could see Mrs. Privett when he got home. Not that this helped him very much either.

" We're not going to talk about it," Mrs. Privett told him. " Irene knows she's been silly. And it's not going to happen again. We're just neither of us ever going to refer to it."

Even so, Mr. Privett couldn't help worrying. He knew how Irene must be feeling. And he tried to be extra nice to her to make up for it.

That was why he was so glad when the Staff Association Ball came round again. Not much of a dancing man himself, he knew nevertheless that it would be something that would take Mrs. Privett and Irene right out of themselves. Because, even including the Summer Outing and the Dramatic Society's Annual Performance, the Staff Association Ball was easily the biggest thing in the whole Rammell year. Attendance was practically compulsory. Everyone from Sir Harry downwards was there. And not to have turned up would have been the cause of a lot of raised eyebrows next morning. Might have stood in the way of promotion, in fact.

From what Mr. Privett had told her about previous Staff Association Balls, Irene could tell that it was going to be a pretty fashionable turn-out. And the one point on which she was determined was that she wasn't going to wear anything that her mother had made. She hadn't forgotten the Miss Manhattan dress for the staff interview.

In consequence, she spent all her lunch hours in looking at dresses. She had never bought a dress in the West End before. Didn't really know how to set about it. For a start, there were all the small shops, some of them not much more than a mere window with a door let in somewhere at the side. They looked very nice in their fancy paint work. And they had pretty names like Isobelle and Jacinth and Margueretta. Sometimes, too, the note of real class, ancient and hereditary, crept in with Christian name and surname as well, like Cynthia St. Cyr, or Gloria Grosvenor.

But the trouble with all small shops was that there was no selection. Unless they happened to have exactly what you wanted, you were stuck. Irene had peeped in through some of those discreetly frosted doors and had caught sight of the chief salesladies, a race of large, experienced-looking women like Assyrian priestesses, with sleek black hair parted in a straight white line down the middle. And she knew perfectly well that if it came to a tussle of wills with one of those Old Testament abbesses she might find herself bewitched into buying something entirely different, like a new tweed costume or a long padded house-coat or any other damn' thing that the lady abbess happened to want to get rid of.

There was always Oxford Street, of course. She could have got exactly what she wanted if she had gone to somewhere like Bourne's. But that was precisely what she couldn't do. What none of the girls in Rammell's could do. It wasn't actually printed in the Rammell Staff Handbook that you mustn't buy your clothes in Oxford Street. It was simply understood. To have gone openly into anywhere at all in Oxford Street would have been sheer defiance. And to have gone secretly would have been treachery.

That was why, in the end, Irene decided to do what she had been trying to avoid. She went along to Rammell's own staff stores. If you were lucky you could get last year's models—particularly if they were the sort that faded or got crushed easily—for as little as two or three pounds sometimes. They were such bargains, some of them, that the assistants were allowed to buy only one dress apiece. That was to prevent the more ingenious ones from going into the misfit gown business on their own account.

To safeguard against anything like that, the girls had to take their Staff Association card along with them so that the transaction could be properly marked up.

The only trouble was that Irene had left everything so late. While she had been hanging round the Isobelles and Jacinths, all the real bargains had been snapped up. There was now nothing left except a great trailing gown of black velvet that a prima donna might have fancied for a contralto solo at a public memorial service, and something in lace and sequins that looked as though it had come straight out of a musical comedy of the twenties.

Miss Sulgrave, who had charge of the dresses, was broken-hearted about the poor selection. Because she knew exactly the sort of dress that Irene wanted. There had been an absolute little pet of a dress from the Débutante's Salon. It would have suited Irene perfectly. But it had gone now. Someone from Towels and Bed-linen had positively pounced on it. . . .

She was a thoroughly nice woman, Miss Sulgrave. Warm-hearted and sentimental. She spent her whole life doing little things for people. Just for the sheer pleasure of it, too. She didn't even expect thanks. But she did like recognition. Basked in it. Became suffused and radiant whenever she heard the words: " Ask Sullie. *She*'ll help you." Then she fairly glowed. And no wonder. Because hers wasn't a very happy existence outside Bond Street. She lived with an elder sister, invalid and unmarried, somewhere in the wilderness out beyond Penge. The two of them quarrelled incessantly up till the moment when Miss Sulgrave left in the morning, and started again as soon as she got back again in the evening. . . .

Irene was just going away when Miss Sulgrave called her back again.

" Now, I've got your measurements, haven't I, dear? " she said. " I'm not promising anything, mind you. But if something should turn up . . ."

It was worse, too, because Miss Kent had made arrangements to get herself all decked out in oyster satin. Irene hadn't actually seen the dress. But she had heard a great deal about it. Had heard about nothing else for days, in fact. It was strapless with a divided skirt, and two perfectly darling little diamanté clips that looked just like the real thing. It wasn't hers really, which was why she had got to be so hideously careful with it, and the last dance had been simply ghastly with everybody half tight towards the end. But it might have been made for her it fitted so marvellously. There was six yards of satin in the skirt alone. The girl she had borrowed it from had been able to get it only because her boy-friend was in the wholesale gown trade himself. All completely open and above board, of course. But the very moment the dance was over this exclusive oyster satin dream had got to go back on to the hanger in the back of her chum's boy-friend's car.

That night Irene took out her old party frock and looked at it. There was nothing really wrong with the dress. It just belonged to a different world. A world of bridge-rolls and paper-napkins and one and threepenny blocks of Wall's ice-cream cut into slices and served up on saucers. It was lemon squash and ciderette, that dress. Whereas what Irene wanted was something that was pure champagne.

All the same, unless Miss Sulgrave found something Irene knew perfectly well that, somehow or other, she would have to make that dress worthy of the Staff Ball.

There were plenty of things that she could do with it. Buy a new sash, for instance. Flame colour always looked well on black. And she could always try a rather dashing vivandière effect. Or, alternatively, she might get hold of a length of tulle with sequins on it. Wear it over her head and shoulders in a mysterious Eastern manner, remembering to look downwards all the time as though she had just slipped out of a zenana in Benares and would have to get back before the eunuchs started searching for her. But she knew in her heart that every other girl would recognise it for what it was. She had seen enough of those emergency ballroom jobs to know that they deceived nobody but the very youngest of young men. And they weren't the ones with whom she hoped she would be dancing.

But there was nothing else for it. The Ball was less than three weeks away. And Irene simply had to do something. She had saved three pounds of her own money. The time had now come to begin spending it.

In the end she wasn't quite sure that she could carry off the Eastern zenana look. So she bought the scarlet sash instead. In point of fact, she went one better. She bought a scarf of the same colour, too. They weren't cheap, the sash and the scarf together. They cost twenty-five shillings for the two of them. But at least they were effective. And, above all, they were new. They added a great vivid flash of sheer recklessness to the old black dress. And Irene was grateful for one thing. At least, the dress *was* black. It had been her mother's idea entirely. There was nothing like black, Mrs. Privett had always contended. You could wear absolutely anything with it.

And even with something over a pound gone on decoration, there was still enough left over for an evening bag. And it was rather a nice one that she found. Black, shiny plastic with a modern design stamped into it. And the clasp was striking. Also of plastic, it finished up with a large square knob practically the size of a door handle. And like the sash and the scarf, it had the supreme merit of being new-looking. Irene wouldn't have minded going anywhere with a bag like that hanging over her arm.

It had been a bit of a rush getting all those things in one lunch hour. It was like the last-minute arrangements before Judgment Day. And she had been forced to go as far as New Oxford Street before she could find a shoe shop with the right shoes. There hadn't been time even for a cup of coffee. But at least she had got what she wanted. And she had overspent her three pounds by only one and ninepence. That was just about the amount of overspending that she could easily put right again. For once, the personal budget of Irene Privett was nicely under control. In consequence, she felt cheerful. Courageous. Independent. A bit empty and wobbly inside. But still gloriously free. It was her own money. And she had used it well. Thanks to no one but herself she was going to be a success at the Staff Ball.

Then, when she reached the counter, Babs Kent told her that Miss Sulgrave had been asking for her. It was surprising that Babs remembered to mention it at all. Because Babs herself had rung up at lunchtime only to find that her chum's boy-friend had let her down. He couldn't let her have the oyster-satin after all. There was nothing but a ghastly cerise affair that clashed with every single blasted thing she'd got. It made Babs want to scream simply thinking about it. She had practically decided not to go to the Staff Ball at all. . . .

Because Irene had been a bit late getting back from lunch, she couldn't go along and see Miss Sulgrave until tea break. And, when she got there, she found Miss Sulgrave in the last stages of agitation. She had very nearly made herself cry, she said, just imagining how Irene must be feeling.

In the result, she had gone through everything in the Débutante's Salon to see whether she could find even the slightest excuse for drastic marking-down. What's more, it was just as she had expected. There was a sweet little silver grey one with distinct lipstick stains on the collar. And it is the waking nightmare of the gown saleswoman, this lipstick business. That is because all the tissue paper in the world, no matter how carefully wrapped round the inside edges of the collar, won't save the dress if the customer is a squirmer, a wriggler. What is more, the lipstick manufacturers are distinctly on the side of the despoilers. There are whole research laboratories doing nothing but ensure that the modern lipstick is kissproof, wetproof, chemical remover-proof.

That is not to say, of course, that a lot can't be done with a bottle of Ronsonol and a pad of cotton-wool. Or even with a saucerful of hot water and a clean handkerchief. And the dress that Miss Sulgrave selected was very clearly on the borderline. At any other time she would have seen what could be done about it. But the memory of Irene was too strong for her. The temptation was there. And she succumbed. She rubbed the stains in a desultory smearing fashion with her forefinger, and then agreed with the Supervisor that the dress was unsaleable. Not that there is anything very astonishing in her behaviour. Dishonesty is one of the commonest by-products of compassion. The cells of prisons are full of sentimentalists.

And, at the sight of Irene, she swooped.

" Ah, there you are, dear," she said, her voice rising with her excitement. " I was beginning to get so worried about you. I wondered where you were. I've got just the thing. Come round here and pop it on."

Irene felt a sudden little chill run through her.

" Thank you ever so much," she began, " but . . ."

Miss Sulgrave, however, was in no mood for excuses.

" No need to thank me, dear," she said patting Irene's hand affectionately. " I *like* doing things for people."

Already her arm was round Irene's shoulders, and she was leading her towards the dressing cubicle.

Miss Sulgrave was so excited by now that she had ceased to behave like a normal woman. She didn't merely walk any longer.

She fluttered. With her head bent sideways and her little beady eyes fixed firmly on Irene, she kept up a shrill chirruping.

And the dress that she had discovered was beautiful. Simply beautiful. Irene had to admit it. Better than anything that she had imagined. It was pale silver. "Moonbeam," Miss Sulgrave called it. And it made all old black dresses with fancy scarves tied round them look like old black dresses with fancy scarves.

As soon as Irene saw the dress, she knew that she was going to have it. It was paying for it that was going to be difficult. She had been along to the cashier after lunch. And had come away with her small buff envelope containing the pound notes. And the silver. And the strip of paper, that was like a robot's rough note-book, showing all the deductions. By the time the robot had finished its homework there was only three.pounds two shillings and sixpence left. And the dress that Miss Sulgrave had set aside for her was priced at a full four pounds. Miss Sulgrave would have liked to make it less, she explained. But how could she? Only twenty-four hours ago it had been standing in Rammell's balance sheet at eighteen guineas. And there are limits beyond which even sentimentalists can go.

Irene decided to borrow the extra pound from her father. The mere sight of that milky moonbeam creation had reduced her to the morals of the bankrupt and the common gambler. She was ready to pledge everything. There would be no contribution that Friday to the family house-keeping. Nothing for fares. Nothing for lunches. No weekly hair-do. Simply a new dress. And an unexpected overdraft. But at least she would be brilliantly set up for the Staff Ball.

Not that there was any difficulty in getting the money out of Mr. Privett. A shopwalker is singularly defenceless in such matters. The one thing that he can't risk while on duty is anything in the way of a scene. Mr. Privett paid up at once. Felt rather flattered, in fact. And he understood perfectly. Most women usually did need something when they were going out. He had known his own wife suddenly not able to show herself in public without a new pair of evening gloves.

And that had been merely for the ladies' night at the North London Model Yacht Club in the Archway Rooms at Highgate.

Mr. Privett waited just inside the Hurst Place entrance so that he and Irene could go home together. And to-night he had to wait longer than usual. That was because Irene was picking up the new dress from Staff Stores.

This was one of the things about which Rammell's were really strict. Positively sharp, in fact. There had been an unpleasant case, only a few years back, when an assistant in Model Gowns had been discovered in the act of running what was practically her own second-hand misfit department for the benefit of a private clientèle of trusted customers. It was after this incident that Mr. Preece, with the help of the Personnel Supervisor and the Legal Department, had produced the revised Manual of Staff Instructions. Now all staff purchases had to be collected after closing time. And not brought back into the shop unless the assistant was actually wearing them.

But everything was all right this time. The box alone was sufficient to prove it. Ivory white, it had the decorative Rammell "R" printed all over it. Mr. Privett felt proud and happy simply to see Irene carrying it. It wasn't every night of the week that a box like that got taken by Underground all the way to Kentish Town.

When they reached Fewkes Road, Mr. Privett guessed that there was something brewing. That was because he saw Mrs. Privett looking out from behind the lace curtains as they came in. She withdrew hurriedly at the sight of them. But it was enough that she should have been there at all. Mrs. Privett wasn't the sort to keep a look out if she hadn't got something pretty big on her mind.

And when they got inside Mrs. Privett continued to behave just as mysteriously. She just stood there in the hall, staring. Not at both of them. Not even at Irene. Just stood there, staring at the Rammell dress box.

"Hallo, Mum," Irene said to her.

But Mrs. Privett did not answer.

"You never," she exclaimed at last.

And with that, she turned her back on both of them. Didn't say another word. She went straight along to the kitchen, and slammed the door behind her.

Mr. Privett and Irene stood looking at each other.

"What's upset your mother?" he asked.

He felt bewildered. Completely bewildered. And Irene's reply was just as baffling as all the rest of it.

"She can't have," Irene exclaimed.

" Can't have what? "

But already Irene had run along the passage and shut herself inside the kitchen with Mrs. Privett.

They were in the kitchen together for some time. And when they came out Irene had her arm round her mother. She was busy talking. But, as it was the same mystery language, Mr. Privett could not make head or tail of it.

" You shouldn't have. Really, you shouldn't," he heard her say. " Why did you ? You didn't have to. Then I wouldn't have."

Because they went into the sitting-room, Mr. Privett followed. Then he understood. In the centre of the room stood the dress-maker's dummy that Mrs. Privett used for all her serious work. And on it was draped a long silver evening gown with nothing but a pair of straps at the shoulders and a great billowing skirt like a half-folded parachute.

CHAPTER XXVII

IT WAS the sale of the furniture that broke Mr. Bloot's heart.

It was one thing to think about it. But it was quite another to see it actually go. And the second-hand dealer in the Archway Road who bought the lot was so frankly disparaging. Definitely interested at first, even eager it seemed, he palpably lost interest from the moment he saw the stuff. And his manner did nothing to raise Mr. Bloot's spirits. A small sad man in a bowler and raincoat, he cast his own gloom over Tetsbury Road. He went round the two rooms with pursed up lips, tapping doubtfully on the table top, the sideboard, the marble washstand with a small stub of pencil that he held between thumb and forefinger. The tap-tapping began to get on Mr. Bloot's nerves. It was so hostile. From the way he behaved he might have been suspecting worm even in the marble washstand top.

And after it was all over he offered thirty-five pounds for the lot. Mr. Bloot had been expecting a round hundred at least. He would have been prepared to close on eighty. But thirty-five! If he had been living all those years in a horse caravan the fittings alone would probably have been worth that much.

But he had left it too late to get in counter-offers. He had already given notice. And if he left the stuff there, he would have to go on paying rent.

In the end, the little man tilted back his bowler and agreed on forty-two-ten if the china and glass were thrown in as well. And as a kind of makeweight he offered to deliver the bits and pieces to Artillery Mansions free of charge next time he was sending over in that direction.

Not that Mr. Bloot was entirely downcast. For with the quixotic generosity which was so peculiarly a part of her nature, Hetty had relented over the budgies. They could come with him, she agreed. There were terms, of course. She still wouldn't have them actually in the flat. But they could go in the little, cupboard-like room beyond the kitchen, the one that had been a coal cellar before the gas fires had been fitted.

It had brought a tear into Mr. Bloot's eye when she told him. He saw immediately how foolish—unfaithful almost—he had been to allow himself to worry when he was dealing with anyone as kind and loving as Hetty.

But he couldn't simply shove the birds in there on the floor along with the empty bottles and the carpet-sweeper. He would have to put up some strong hooks for the cages. And make sure that the shelving was safe, because, even though the budgies were mere pigmies, their food weighed a terrible lot. The last thing he wanted was for them to see their lunch, tea and dinner go crashing to the floor while they, caged and helpless, were powerless even to raise the alarm.

Besides, he knew from experience how difficult it was to sweep up millet seed. He didn't want Hetty to have any cause for complaint. Least of all about mice.

2

Originally, it had been Mr. Privett's idea that the staff should give Mr. Bloot a wedding-present. But it caught on so fast that it was soon everybody's idea. There was a house rule that Mr. Preece had to give his permission before the collection box could actually go round. But naturally in a case like this Mr. Preece raised no objection. He even said that he thought that some of the directors might like to give a little something themselves. And it was the same everywhere. There wasn't a soul in the store who did not know Mr. Bloot. He was practically part of the fixtures. The only odd thing was that he should be getting married. In its way it was as astonishing as if one of the caryatids on the Bond Street frontage had suddenly announced that she was going to have a baby.

Odd or not, the money certainly flowed in. When Mr. Chilvers in Accounts came to empty the boxes and add in the directors' personal donations, the total stood at twenty-eight-ten already. And that wasn't counting the fifty pounds—minus P.A.Y.E. of course—that the Board voted.

Because of the Board's generosity towards him, Mr. Bloot was naturally in a very bland and complacent frame of mind. He had known about the collection, of course. But he hadn't known how much. And, when he heard, he gave a great sigh. A sigh of sheer happiness. Life, after all, had not always been kind to him. He had known what it was to walk down long avenues of steadily darkening depression. And now, suddenly, everything was radiant again.

" Ah suppose Ah cahn't be such a bad sorter chap affter all," he confided in Mr. Privett. " Or they'd neverer done it, would they ? "

" Well, that's how much it is," Mr. Privett told him. " So you'd better make up your mind, and tell me what you'd like."

For a moment Mr. Bloot's face clouded over. All decisions presented difficulties. It was the making-up-his-mind part that he found so trying. And obviously this decision was a vital one. No one had ever before suggested giving him a great enormous present like this.

" Ah'll have to think," he said cautiously. " That's what Ah'll have to do. Ah'll have to think."

" There isn't much time," Mr. Privett warned him. " Only another week."

But Mr. Bloot was in no mood to be rushed.

" Ah know. Ah know," was all he said.

He took out his watch while he was speaking and glanced down at it. The watch, which was rather thick and slightly lemon-coloured round the rim, showed 10.32. Whereas the restaurant clock plainly showed 11.16. Mr. Bloot shook the watch for a moment and began playing with the winding key. But there was nothing wrong with the winder: he knew that. It was simply that the watch itself was old. Old. And overworked. And exhausted. He began shaking it again.

Then his face cleared.

" Woterbouter watch ? " he asked eagerly. " Er watchun chain. Something good. Er reel *gole* watch."

Mr. Privett hesitated.

" Don't you think that perhaps it ought to be something for both of you ? " he asked cautiously. " Cutlery, for instance."

Mr. Bloot looked astonished.

" Wot would 'etty want with cutlery ? " he asked. " She's gotter 'ole canteen of it."

" I was only suggesting cutlery," Mr. Privett explained. " Perhaps . . ."

But Mr. Bloot shook his head.

230

"It's no use," he said. "She's got everything. Everything er woman could want."

Mr. Privett was silent for a moment.

"Why not ask her?" he inquired. "There may be just some little thing. Something she's never actually got round to."

The smile had gone entirely from Mr. Bloot's face by now. But so had the anxious look.

"Ah see wotcher mean," he said. "Something personal perhaps. Joolery, for instance."

And by next morning Mr. Bloot had the answer all ready. For again Hetty had shown the warm side of her nature. It was not anything for herself that she had chosen. It was something for both of them. She had decided on a television set.

"Only do be careful," she had warned him. "Don't let them give you one without doors. They look terrible. And make sure it's walnut, not mahogany. I can't bear the dark kind."

Mr. Bloot would have liked Hetty herself to come along and choose it. But with the shop on her hands, there was no chance of that. And, finally, he went down himself to Rammell's Radio Salon. It was lunch-time. And he had Mr. Privett with him. But because he hadn't given any warning, Mr. Gore, the real electronics chief, was out. Mr. Asplett, his second in command, was there. Programmes rather than engineering was Mr. Asplett's forte. And naturally with Mr. Bloot for audience he showed off everything he knew. He went reeling through lists of celebrities and famous artists of whom Mr. Bloot had never heard. And he described sporting events—ice hockey, table tennis, badminton, swimming galas and the rest—that Mr. Bloot had never thought of attending. The TV had them all, Mr. Asplett assured him, as well as guessing games and classical plays and weather reports and visits to big engineering works and Church Services and political discussions and variety programmes from Forces' canteens.

Mr. Bloot listened in amazement. And he suddenly realised how right his clever Hetty had been to ask for television instead of joolery. Without television, a man was only half-alive, it seemed.

In the end, it was a light walnut table model, so highly polished that the case might have been made of satin, that he selected. It had white Bakelite knobs with a narrow gold ring round them that he felt sure that Hetty would appreciate. But what really decided him was the picture in the glass front. Instead of being empty and staring like the rest of them there was a view of a cathedral or something pasted into the frame. It was almost as though the thing had somehow started working before the man had even connected it and switched it on.

Mr. Bloot was excited all day thinking about the television set. And, even though Hetty had begged to be left alone so that she could do what she referred to mysteriously as getting herself ready, he went across that same evening to tell her all about it.

" It's worlnut just like you said," he began breathlessly. " And it gets table tennis and visits to engineering works and swimming galas and weather reports and everything. It's mahrvellous. That's what it is. Mahrvellous. Mr. Asplett says so. He looks in every night. Every single night."

" What's it called? " Hetty asked.

Mr. Bloot looked up in astonishment.

" Television," he told her.

" No, silly. The make."

Mr. Bloot paused.

" Ah don't rightly remember," he had to confess.

" Has it got a guarantee? " Hetty demanded.

" Oh, yurss," he replied. " It's gotter guarantee. If anything goes wrong . . ."

" It will," Hetty interrupted him.

The remark seemed tc Mr. Bloot to be querulous and in bad taste. But it only showed how much on edge she must be.

" If anythink goes wrong," he repeated, " we'll 'avver nother one 'ere the same day. Ah give you mah word."

" Oh, it's not that," Hetty answered. " It's just that I couldn't bear to think of you being diddled."

Mr. Bloot was aghast. He saw the golden gates that were ajar already about to close on him again. Visits to big engineering works had sounded very interesting.

" Give me the pictures every time," Hetty went on. " I like to go out to enjoy myself."

Mr. Bloot's voice began to tremble.

" Then . . . then why did you ask me to buy it for you? "

Hetty got up and came over to him.

" Because we'd look such fools not having one," she said. " It

232

doesn't follow you've got to use it. Besides, I shall have you, shan't I? There won't be time for anything once we've got each other."

And before Mr. Bloot could uncross his legs she had sat herself upon his lap.

"Aaah!" he exclaimed in a gasp in which pain and delight were mingled. "That's more lahk it. That's more mah girlie."

CHAPTER XXVIII

THE STAFF BALL was really on them at last. And there is nothing
like a Staff Ball for upsetting the normal smoothness of life. By six-
thirty that evening some four hundred and fifty homes in all parts
of London were seriously affected. There was a tense, keyed-up,
D-day sort of atmosphere in everyone of them.

Not that Rammell's could be blamed for that. Most marriages
proceed smoothly from one week's end to another until they are
put to the supreme test of husband and wife going out together.
It is the common bedroom, the shared dressing-room, that is at
the root of the trouble. By the time they are ready to set out for
the evening, most wives have the feeling that they have been
responsible for dressing two entirely different people.

For a start, things weren't going any too well inside the Rammell
household. Tempers were badly frayed already, in fact. That was
because Mrs. Rammell had a headache and didn't want to go to
the dance at all. It had been like that last year, Mr. Rammell
reminded her. And, in the end, in sheer exasperation he mixed her
up one of his own magic draughts—two aspirins in half a tumbler
of warm liver salts—and told her brutally to drink it. As he did so,
he let slip the remark that for once she knew how he felt when she
had one of her blasted musical evenings. That was why the
Rammells weren't even speaking to each other when they set out.

And it didn't help to raise their spirits that Tony was with them.
He had made a mix-up with the dates. And right up until he had
left the office he had imagined that he was going to spend the
evening at Covent Garden. In consequence, he was silent and sulky.

Nor, for that matter, were Mr. Preece's arrangements any
smoother. Going out anywhere was always an ordeal for the
Preeces. That was because Mrs. Preece disliked setting out alone.
Mr. Preece, therefore, always had to make the effort of slipping
down to Carshalton by an early train, and then returning to town
by a slightly later one.

234

He had made the effort to-day. And now he was sorry. Sorry that he hadn't simply gone along to the Staff Dance alone and told Mrs. Preece about it afterwards. It was his daughter, Julia, who had ruined things. A large, athletic girl, with a fondness for horses, she had been promised the dance for a special treat. But Mrs. Preece had insisted that first she must do something about her hair. She seemed to have more hair than most girls. And there was an untameable healthiness about it of which Mrs. Preece did not quite approve. What might have been all right with the wind rushing through it on the Downs would clearly have been unthinkable on the dance floor. Mrs. Preece and daughter had therefore spent nearly two hours at Isobel's Beauty Parlour in the High Street while the assistant snicked away and thinned it out and finally waved and set it.

Mrs. Preece had been really quite delighted with the result. But she had been reckoning without Julia's highly developed open-air talents. It had rained that same afternoon. And Julia had gone out without a hat. There was now nothing left but dense dark fuzz. Miss Preece looked like a princess from one of the Solomon Islands. She carried with her a strong hint of hibiscus and roasted missionary.

In consequence, Mr. Preece who hadn't been late for anything in years, kept walking up and down the hall. He went from the front door to the wall-bracket barometer and back again, click-clicking with his tongue as he went, and reminding his wife that they had missed the 8.2 already, and the way things were going looked like missing the 8.17 as well. But Mr. Preece was not thinking of himself. He was thinking of Mr. Rammell. " Can't turn up after Mr. Rammell," he was saying. " Look very bad."

And at that moment Mr. Rammell was thinking of Mr. Preece. Thinking of Mr. Preece and talking to Mrs. Rammell. " Wear whatever you like," he had just said to her. " Nobody'll notice. Only hurry. There's Preece coming right up from Woking or somewhere. Look all wrong if the Preeces get there first."

Things were bad, too, in Sloane Square where Marcia lived. She was tired already. She had been on her feet all day showing off what was left of the Rammell Autumn Collection. The one thing that she wanted was to be left alone. In any case, she hated these staff dances more than anything else in the whole world. Unless you were careful, you found yourself becoming familiar

235

with all the wrong people. Awful young men from Hardware or Provisions cut in during the Excuse-me dances, and moved off jubilantly, leaving a wake of violet haircream and cheap shaving soap behind them.

Of course, if Mr. Bulping had been available there would have been no problem. Any girl can relax if she has arrived in a Bentley. But Mr. Bulping was not available. Very much the reverse, in fact. It was his son's twenty-first birthday. And he had explained—rather callously, Marcia thought—that he had to be present for appearance's sake.

That was why Marcia had accepted Mr. Preece's invitation to sit at his table. It would scarcely be exciting. But it would at least be respectable. And remembering the company, Marcia decided on her beige dress. The beige dress. And her moonstones. It promised to be a pretty pale colourless kind of evening. And Marcia decided to fit in perfectly.

She had just finished dressing when the telephone rang. It was Mr. Bulping. He sounded large. Male. And uninhibited.

" How's my little girlie? " he asked.

" I . . . I thought you were in Wolverhampton," she told him.

" Not me when my little girlie's in London," he answered.

" But . . . but what about your son? " Marcia said.

She could have bitten out her tongue as soon as she said it. The last thing on earth she wanted was to remind Mr. Bulping of his first marriage. It was the sort of unfeeling remark that she had always been very careful to avoid.

Mr. Bulping, however, did not seem to be put out.

" Didn't need me," he told her. " Takes his mother's side in all this. That's why I'm here. Let's make a night of it. Coming round straightaway."

And before Marcia could explain, Mr. Bulping had rung off.

There was, however, one person who was thoroughly looking forward to the whole evening. That was Hetty. She didn't mind what dance it was so long as the floor was all right and the band leader really knew his stuff. There was, indeed, in Hetty a quality of enthusiasm, a sheer appetite for enjoyment, that Mr Bloot found vaguely disquieting. He had never known anyone get so much pleasure out of life. And he kept telling himself that he must not disappoint her. Nevertheless, the prospect sometimes scared him.

236

Because the more he saw of it the more he realised that being engaged to Hetty looked like being a very expensive business.

The ring alone had nearly ruined him. Eighteen pounds ten it had cost. The one disappointing thing was that the diamond solitaire still looked small on Hetty's hand. That was because she had a large hand. And because she couldn't bring herself to discard the other rings that she always wore. These were enormous. Not necessarily valuable. Just enormous. The new engagement ring could do no more than peep coyly through the great panes of amethyst, garnet, topaz and sheer ordinary coloured glass.

And it wasn't the ring alone that made him uneasy. This evening itself was going to set him back quite a bit. The tickets alone were twelve-and-six each. And that would be only the beginning of things. Because somehow or other he couldn't see Hetty keeping up her magnificent high spirits for the whole evening on the tall jugs full of orangeade and lemon that the management provided. Before he was through there would be Graves or Sauterne as well. Not to mention gins and tonic and probably whiskies and Baby Pollies, too.

Not that there was anything that he could do about it. He had invited her. And it was up to him to make a go of it. Vital, in fact. For yesterday evening, all because of one thoughtless remark, he had very nearly lost her.

It was over at her flat that it had all happened. She had been showing him her new evening-dress. Quite a striking looking model in orange-coloured satin, with a big feather flower on one hip. And Mr. Bloot knew at once that she would look magnificent in it. Even a little too magnificent. Opulent. Also a shade on the undemure side. Even though she hadn't actually got it on he could guess how much bosom would be left showing. And he very diffidently suggested that she should wear a little lace hankie or something, in front.

That was what had upset her. She had simply flung the dress down and told him that, so far as she was concerned, he needn't bother his head about her any longer because her mind was quite made up, thank you. To prove it, she had wrenched off the diamond solitaire that he had given her.

It may have been that the ring was tighter than she had realised. Or possibly she was a little overtired. Whatever it was, her reserve went completely. The niceties just left her. Instead of merely thrusting the ring into Mr. Bloot's open palm, she added that he knew what he could do with it.

In consequence, it had been a day of phone calls. And it had been nearly teatime before he got Hetty to listen to reason. She softened suddenly. " Silly boy," she said to him in the old purry-purry voice that he had always found so affecting. " What's the matter with him? " she asked. " Can't he even stand a little tiff without getting all worked up about it? Hetty's going to be cross with her Gussie if he starts behaving like a great big cry baby. Hetty wants her Gussie to be a big strong man. . . ."

There had been a great deal more in the same vein. Including some pretty remarkable baby talk. It was a staff line on which he was speaking. And the baby talk was so remarkable that the switchboard operator simply threw up all the other keys, and sat back to listen. All telephone operators have an uncanny ear for voices. This one recognised Mr. Bloot immediately. But, when the call was over, she had begun disbelieving herself.

It was not, in fact, until nearly five-thirty that she had the final proof. The call was an incoming one. A woman's voice, the same, deep, unmistakably husky voice, was there. And it was asking for Mr. Bloot. The operator put the call through to Main Foyer, and waited. It was worth waiting for. Because the caller didn't indulge in any silly baby talk this time. She got down to business straight away.

" Where's my ring anyway? " she asked. " I'm catching cold in my finger."

CHAPTER XXIX

The Medina Rooms certainly did their dances very well. That was something you had to hand them.

Admittedly, the entrance hall with the brass rails and the mosaic flooring and the sign-poster's fingers pointing in the direction of the separate cloakrooms were a little on the formal side. And there was a strange hot stuffiness peculiar to all entrance halls. The queer thing was that once you were actually inside the hall this smell vanished completely and was replaced by quite different ones. The thick, varnishy aroma of beeswax floor polish. Very efficient central heating. And the faintest possible trace of gas escaping somewhere.

But by the time you were in the hall itself it wasn't the smells you were thinking about. It was the decorations. And in them was displayed a streak of lavishness that had remained carefully concealed outside the big swing doors. Gold and silver were the two colours. The walls, which were dimpled all over in the very latest neo-cinema style, must have been sprayed from a variety of paint tanks. They started off near the floor with an opulent sunset lushness and finished up at the ceiling, pale and gleaming like winter moonlight. Alternate banners of gold and silver, some thirty or forty of them at least, hung down from the high roof. And the big chandeliers, apparently suspended from nothing, appeared at intervals between the banners like something that had drifted in through the air from old Versailles. The professional lighting—the coloured spots and the snowstorm reflectors—were up in the balcony along with the strings for releasing the balloons. It was gold and silver everywhere like the budget of a mad Chancellor.

Amid the gold and silver gaiety, the Preeces' table presented a sad, rather forlorn appearance that even the two bottles of South African hock did nothing to dispel.

That was because there were too many men. Too many men. And too few women. It was like a dance table in a monastery. But what else could Mrs. Preece have done but invite young men?

239

she kept asking herself. It wasn't as though there had been only Marcia to be considered. There was her own darling Julia as well. And the young man whom Mrs. Preece had rounded up for Julia was really a very nice young man. A bit on the silent side, perhaps. And slightly under average height. But extremely personable and well turned out. A kind of pocket prospective son-in-law, in fact. And how was she to know that her darling Julia, without saying a word about it, was going to invite someone on her own account?

What made it so peculiarly maddening was that Julia's young man might have been the twin brother of the young man whom Mrs. Preece herself had cornered. Same size. Same colour hair. Same silence. When they were not dancing—which was most of the time—they just sat there, quietly sipping their hock, saying nothing.

Mrs. Preece realised now what a mistake it had been to add their new family doctor to the party. He was young. He was handsome. He was a Scot. Every time he had swept into Two Gables she had been impressed. Even rather excited by him. He was always so vigorous. So quick. So incisive about everything. But it was extraordinary how much he seemed to have changed now that she saw him against the background of the dance hall. Rugged, rather than handsome, was the word that she would now have applied to him. Like a great block of Aberdeenshire granite. If a fine drizzle had sprung up on his side of the table it would not have surprised her in the least. And, compared with the other two young men, he might have taken a vow of silence just as he was leaving the surgery. He was mute.

Not that Mr. Preece himself was being any help. He was sitting with his back to the company and keeping his neck screwed round so that he could see towards the door. That was because Marcia had most mysteriously failed to arrive. Mr. Preece could not understand it. Simply could not understand it at all. The last thing that he had done before leaving was to ring down to Model Gowns. And he had spoken to Marcia personally. Nine o'clock was when she had said that she would be there. And it was now after ten, getting on for five past in fact.

But Mr. Preece was never really at his best on this kind of occasion. The heat. The noise. The lights. The people. They were all rather too much for him. Secretly, he wished that he had not come. Then he could have been sitting in his comfortable chair in

Carshalton, his beaker of Ovaltine within arm's reach on the table beside him, and that week's issue of *Popular Gardening* open upon his knee.

As it happened, Mrs. Preece too wished that she were back home. But for quite a different reason. A nervous woman at all times, she was convinced that at the last moment, just as they were ready to leave, she had gone back and turned on the gas fire in the bedroom. Turned it on. But not actually lit it. She could remember every-thing else. The bending down. The stiffness of the key. The hiss. Even the smell of the gas itself. But nothing, absolutely nothing, about the scraping of the match box on the match. In consequence, she was certain that the whole room, practically the whole house, must by now be full of gas. Simply one vast lethal chamber. With her loved ones, her cherubs, all peacefully asphyxiated in their beds. Or worse. For all she knew, the maid—deficient anyway—might already have struck a match somewhere in the kitchen or the scullery. . . . As Mrs. Preece sat there, gripping the sides of her small gilt chair, she could almost hear the whoosh, see the blinding sheet of scarlet flame, as Two Gables, Thirsk Avenue, Carshalton, dis-appeared for ever.

That was why she kept leaving the table to go out to one of the telephone boxes in the hall. And every time she came back she wondered whether it was merely the charred ends of a telephone cable that kept giving her the engaged tone, or whether the deficient maid was really talking to someone.

It was when she returned from the fifth attempt that she found that Marcia had arrived. And more than arrived, she had brought another man with her. That meant that there were now four sets of hungry male eyes all fixed on Marcia. And no one was paying even the slightest attention to her darling Julia. Marcia's friend seemed such a dreadfully coarse, vulgar sort of man, too, Mrs. Preece thought. Compared with Marcia, who was wearing her new, slightly corpse-like make-up this evening and looked too spiritual to be in a dance hall at all, her companion might have spent his whole life at race meetings and the wrong sort of hotels.

At the offer of a glass of hock, he gave Mrs. Preece a wink and explained that he never drank anything stronger than whisky. What's more, he was going to do something about it, he said. While Mr. Preece was still trying to attract his own waiter's attention, Mr. Bulping managed somehow to get hold of another one. There was the distinctive rustle of a note, and the waiter went off towards the service door while Mr. Preece was still futilely snapping his fingers and beckoning.

Mr. Bulping did not seem so far even to have noticed Julia. Or the three young men. Or Mr. Preece, for that matter. He leant right across and addressed Mrs. Preece.

" Nice of you to invite me," he said. " Marcia said you'd be short of men."

In Sir Harry's suite in the Royal Park Hotel, dinner was just being cleared away. It had been a good meal, and Sir Harry and his companion had a warm, comfortably full, slightly flushed kind of feeling.

" Eshtrornary woman, m'daughter-in-law," Sir Harry remarked suddenly. " Really most eshtrornary." He came up close to Major Cuzzens and tapped his forehead significantly. " Up there," he added. " Mental."

Major Cuzzens pursed up his lips, and took a long slow pull at his cigar before replying."

" Bad show," he said. " Very."

" Always been that way," Sir Harry went on. " If it isn't one thing, it's another. Like a kitten. Never know what'll be next. Can't tell for twenty-four hours. Remember that snake dancer? "

" Indian fellow, y'mean? "

Sir Harry nodded.

" Probably been murdered by now," he continued. " Got his throat cut or something. Happens to most of 'em in the long run. Wanted me to go over to dinner."

Major Cuzzens swung round in his chair.

" Who did? That snake dancer johnny? "

" No, m'daughter-in-law."

The ash from Major Cuzzens's cigar had fallen on to his waist-coat and he had to brush himself clean.

" Asked us, too. Remember now. Judith told me."

" What d'you say? "

" Said I'd got a prior engagement."

" Me, too."

There was so much natural good fellowship and understanding in the situation that both men instinctively raised their glasses. Then Sir Harry started nervously.

" Didn't mention my name, did you? "

Major Cuzzens considered.

" Don't think so," he replied. " Just said ' a chap.' "

Sir Harry looked relieved.

" Better that way," he explained. " Might have led to un-
pleashantness. No point in dragging the two of us in." Sir Harry
paused. " Mad as a tiger if she could see us now," he added.
" Don't like it if two men get along together. Makes 'em feel left
out of it. Shows we can do without 'em."

The remark struck Major Cuzzens as penetrating and profound.
He was frequently amazed by the sheer wisdom that Sir Harry kept
displaying. That was what made Sir Harry's company such a tonic.

But already Sir Harry was speaking again.

" Shouldn't have been having a little dinner party at all," he
said. " Not to-night. Firm's got a dance on. Ought to have been
there. Both of 'em. Can't neglect the business like that. Always used
to go when I was a bit younger."

" No use taking chances," Major Cuzzens agreed with him.
" Got to look after ourselves."

" Never did like those modern dances," Sir Harry remarked.
" Not my line of country. Give me the old-fashioned waltz every
time. That's what I call dancin'." He leant back and hummed a
few bars under his breath while his feet moved idly on the hearth-
rug. " ' Blue Danube.' That was a good one," he said at length.
" And *The Merry Widow*. Better than those blasted foxtrots."

" Can't stand 'em," Major Cuzzens agreed again. " Not like
proper dancin' at all."

Sir Harry glanced at the clock. It showed ten-fifteen.

" What about lookin' in for half an hour? Just to cheer 'em up.
Can't offend the Staff Association y'know."

" I'm ready," Major Cuzzens agreed for the last time.
" Does y'good to get out for a bit."

Sir Harry poured out another drink.

" Better have this first," he said. " Nothing much to drink
when we get there."

Because it was the big night of the year, Mr. Rammell had
ordered champagne for everyone at his table. It was so much sheer
poison for him. He knew that. But there was nothing that he
could do about it. It was just one of those things that were expected

243

of him. Like inviting senior members of the staff over to the table to share a glass. Mr. Bloot's turn, in fact, was just coming up.

Only this year, there was a difference. Hetty had asked for champagne at the table, too. And, when he arrived, Mr. Bloot showed an unusual degree of self-assurance.

Raising his glass, he toasted Mrs. Rammell as though she had been an ambassadress.

" Maht Ah say, ma'am," he observed, with a wide, shiny smile, " on beharf of the whole starf what pleashah it gives us all to have Mr. Rammell and his lady here to-naht."

Mrs. Rammell smiled back at him without rising. She was still in a thoroughly bad temper about having been made to come at all. And, above all things, she wanted to see what Tony was up to. Was he, or was he not, still fussing around that Privett girl? What made it so particularly maddening was that at the moment she couldn't see either of them. . . . Then, hurriedly, she recovered herself. Turning to Mr. Bloot, she assured him that this was an evening that she and Mr. Rammell had been looking forward to all the year. Ever since the same time last year, in fact.

It was with something of a flourish that Mr. Bloot drained back his glass and returned it to the table. He was, however, just a shade impetuous. The base of his glass caught the edge of an ash-tray that was already standing there, and there was a little tinkle of glass falling on the gilt table top.

Mr. Bloot drew his breath in sharply.

" Pud'n me, ma'am," he said. " Pud'n me."

And to show that he wasn't the kind of man who would allow broken glass to litter up the tables, he took out his handkerchief and began flicking at the chips. But table-flicking is an art. Only waiters can perform it with impunity. On the upward sweep of the handkerchief Mr. Bloot caught one of the red carnations in the tall vase in the centre of the table. At one moment, there was Mrs. Rammell, smiling up politely at a tall florid man whose name she had forgotten and, at the next, she was frantically backing away from a cascade of water and red carnations. . . .

Mr. Bloot was still saying " Pud'n me. Pud'n me," long after Mrs. Rammell had gone across to the Powder Room to dry herself. But he was not really thinking of Mrs. Rammell at all. He was thinking about Hetty. Something told him that she wouldn't like being left so long. And he was right. Hetty was sitting at a table with the Privetts. At that moment, Mr. Privett was retelling the story of his accident. And Hetty, with her shoes half-kicked off beneath the table, was wondering how in God's name she was ever going to be able to stick her future husband's friends.

But Mr. Bloot himself was behaving magnificently. He had overcome his embarrassment. And, in a mood of arch gallantry, he was now leaning over Mr. Rammell.

" Maht Ah presume to introdooce mah brahd-to-be? " he asked. " It's what you maht call her first public appearance."

Considering how much he disliked staff dances, young Tony Rammell was diligently doing his stuff. Under his father's directions he had already danced with a thin, hawk-faced creature who looked like minor European Royalty and really came from Handbags. With a pale, rather frightened-looking Elliot-Fisher clerk out of Invoicing—that was because his father had said that the behind-the-scenes girls never got any proper notice taken of them. With Miss Sulgrave who had fitted up Irene Privett with the new party dress that she wasn't wearing. And with a big motherly creature who turned out to be Corsets. On his own account he had managed to slip in a couple of dances with the tall, Cleopatra-like Miss Anson from Hairdressing, and two more with a small, pretty, nameless one who worked in Cosmetics.

So far he hadn't danced even once with Irene. That was partly because he had been kept working so hard by his father. And partly because the Privetts' table was so far away. Irene herself didn't seem to be missing him. She had danced the last two dances with the young man from Travel whom she had met that night at the Staff Hostel. And, Mrs. Privett was pleased to notice, she was looking her absolute prettiest.

Not that there was anything exceptional in that. There were pretty girls practically everywhere you looked. But that is the way it is with all staff dances. The transformation is sudden and complete. Generations of employers have been amazed because of it. It is always hard to believe that even the plainest girls can leave the office at five-thirty, dim and colourless and with hair all anyhow, and re-emerge two hours later looking like sleek professional beauties who would faint clean away at the mere thought of having to earn their own living.

245

And Rammell's, remember, had at least more than averagely presentable ones to start with.

Hetty's arrival at the Rammell's table coincided almost exactly with that of Sir Harry and Major Cuzzens. And altogether it was very nearly too much for Mrs. Rammell.

In the first place, Sir Harry wasn't expected at all. Nor, for that matter, was Major Cuzzens. And the big flamboyantly-dressed woman whom Mr. Bloot had brought over was a complete stranger to her. But it was not merely the matter of overcrowding that was worrying her. It was Sir Harry. She had detected a glint in his eye that seriously alarmed her. Apparently, at the mere sight of Mr. Bloot's lady friend, he had been bowled clean over. He stood there simply gaping at her. And, as soon as she had been introduced, he insisted on having her sit next to him.

" So you're a new girl, are you? " he said. " Don't expect you know a soul. But don't worry. I'll look after you."

A moment later, when Mrs. Rammell looked across, Hetty and Sir Harry were holding hands.

Over at the Preeces' table things were quieter. A great deal quieter. Altogether too quiet, in fact. Even Mr. Bulping's champagne had done nothing to raise Marcia's spirits. She sat there pale and spiritualised. Like a despondent lady-angel. Mr. Bulping felt more than a bit despondent himself. He didn't see what more he could have done for her. It had been all her idea to come to this god-awful dance in the first place. And it had been left to him to make more of an evening of it by buying the champagne.

He leant forward.

" What's the matter, girlie? " he asked. " Don't like the bubbles, eh? "

Champagne was exactly in his line, anyway. And he had just the thing for it. It was a dainty little toy that opened up like a flower as soon as the end was pressed down. He bent over and started twirling it in her glass in a bland, proprietorial manner as though anything that was hers belonged to him already.

" Drink it up and say ta-ta to everybody," he whispered as soon as his head was down close to hers. " You've made your number. Let's be getting back to your place."

Marcia smiled. But she seemed scarcely to have heard him.

And it was in any case purely her professional smile that she gave him. The one that had been photographed so often. It didn't mean a thing. She was far too depressed to do any real smiling. But she couldn't possibly explain. Didn't even know herself what it was that was depressing her so much. It wasn't anything in particular. It was everything. The staff dance. Mrs. Preece's fidgets. The boy-scout expression on the face of the Aberdonian doctor. The state of her bank balance. The way she wasn't sleeping. The fact that *Woman and Beauty* had just brought out a picture supplement for the *under*-twenty-fives. The sudden realisation that she still hadn't been to see her mother. The knowledge that she ought to go to the dentist. The pressure of Mr. Bulping's knee up against hers beneath the table. The size of his hands. The way he kept mopping his forehead after every dance. His breathing. Everything about him, in fact.

It was Tony who interrupted her thoughts. Sent over by his father, he came obediently across and asked Marcia for a dance.

For a moment it seemed to Mr. Bulping as though she were hesitating. So, cupping her pale white hand with his hot red one, he gave a little squeeze.

" O.K.," he said. " Have this one. Then we'll be getting along."

But it was not really hesitation on Marcia's part. It was simply her natural daze-state. She had hardly even no iced that anyone had spoken to her. Instead of replying, she rose slowly and grace-fully and started to go on to the dance floor.

It was usually at this moment that she felt happiest. Most sure of herself. Out there in the centre of the room people would be watching. Admiring. Other women would simply cease to exist as she came near them. But to-night it was different. It was this terrible despondency. This despair. At the sight of Tony, standing there waiting for her, she very nearly began weeping.

" Oh, God," the thought formed itself inside her. " How young he looks. I'm beginning to notice things like that nowadays. It shows what's happening to me. I must be growing . . ."

Just in time she managed to suppress the forbidden word. She even continued to brighten up enough to give Tony one of her really sweetest smiles. Smiled, while inside her there continued the same gnawing, the same heartache. Through a thick mist she heard

Tony asking what she thought of the band. And, through the same mist, came back the answer in her own voice that it was marvellous, simply marvellous.

It may have been because of her thoughts that Marcia looked so beautiful. All that emotion going on inside had definitely helped. Even Tony noticed the difference. In a sad, elemental fashion Marcia seemed suddenly to have come to life. She kept reminding Tony of something. Someone. Somewhere. He couldn't remember what. Who. Where.

Then it all came back to him.

" D'you ever go to the ballet? " he asked.

Marcia's eyes were half-closed already. She opened them, just for a moment.

" Of course," she replied dreamily.

What else could she say? It would have sounded too silly to explain that her kind of men somehow hadn't turned out to be the ballet-going sort. And she never went anywhere alone.

" Like to come to *Giselle* sometime? "

" Adore it."

" Next Tuesday? "

She began thinking round desperately in her mind. Was there anything on? Had she promised anything? Would Mr. Bulping be in town? Would . . . would he mind?

" I'll have to look at my book," she said safely.

" Let me know in the morning."

" Promise."

They were up at the quiet end of the room by now. Away from the band. And their heads were close together. Marcia's last words were almost whispered.

And as she danced, she could feel a change coming over her. She no longer felt sad. Merely ethereal. The way saints must feel. It was a kind of rapture that she hadn't known since she was first engaged. Only this was sweeter. Sharper.

" But how young he is," the thought kept coming back to her. " How inexperienced. I know that he'll be hurt sometime. Wounded. If only I could help him somehow. Shield him. Look after him. Show him that . . ."

The band had banged itself noisily to a close. Everyone started back towards the tables. But Marcia did not move. The trance-state had come over her again. She wanted the band to go on playing for ever. So that she and Tony could just dance. Just dance. And dance. And dance.

Anything, in fact, to postpone the moment when it was all over and, back at the flat, Mr. Bulping started to say good night in his own peculiarly enthusiastic fashion.

But this time the band had done more than simply stop playing. The boys had pushed their chairs back, and the saxophonist was wiping his mouthpiece. Up in the ceiling heights, the big gold and silver chandeliers were coming on. The moment had come for Mr. Bloot to take charge of things.

He had already reached the Rammells' table. And at the sight of him Mrs. Rammell nervously drew back a little. But it was not Mrs. Rammell whom Mr. Bloot wanted. It was Sir Harry. And this was difficult. Because Sir Harry was still too much engrossed in Hetty to notice anyone else. It was her ear-rings that seemed to fascinate him. He had already adjusted one of them. And he was now at work on the other. Because it was on the far side of her, he had his arm right round her neck. Mr. Bloot had to cough twice quite loudly before Sir Harry even noticed that he was there.

" Pud'n me, sir," he said, slowly and as distinctly as he could manage through the enormous smile that he was wearing. " The prahzes. The nuffelty and speshiulity prahzes. Would you be so kahnd as to excort our lady patron on to the plahtform? "

Already on the other side of the table Mrs. Rammell was gathering herself together, smoothing out invisible wrinkles in her long black gloves. But for Sir Harry there was only one woman in the whole roomful of nearly six hundred of them. And his mouth was close against her ear at this moment.

" What about my little kitten presentin' 'em? " he asked.

The words that Sir Harry had intended to be whispered had reached Mrs. Rammell quite distinctly. She immediately put her bag back down on the table again, and folded her hands in her lap in the attitude of a woman who has not been listening. Motionless, she sat there waiting for the impossibly big woman opposite to refuse.

But it was not left to Hetty. Already Sir Harry was hauling her up on to her feet. If she attempted to resist now there would be a struggle.

" Up's a daisy," he said. " Give 'em something worth looking at for a change."

249

CHAPTER XXX

THE WEDDING-DAY had come round at last.

Mr. Bloot, naturally, was feeling a bit keyed-up. Edgey. And it wasn't merely the solemn fact of matrimony that was worrying him. He was worried about Rammell's as well. Because, even though things were usually pretty quiet on a Saturday morning, he still didn't like the idea of no proper direction in the main vestibule.

To-day, moreover, Rammell's wouldn't have Mr. Privett either. That was because Mr. Privett had agreed to act as best man.

Mrs. Privett herself hadn't been any too sure about it. There was so much connected with the wedding of which she disapproved. In particular, register offices. Second marriages. Husbands who moved in on their wives. Wives in business on their own. Hetty herself. And Mr. Bloot for wanting to marry her.

And in the end, Mr. Privett had been forced to appeal unashamedly to pure sentiment.

" Think of Emmie," he had said. " She'd rather you were there. It . . . it'll be a link somehow."

Mrs. Privett had been thinking a lot about poor Emmie during the past few weeks. It was as though it had been yesterday she had last seen her.

" All right," she had finally said. " Just this once. But only for her sake. Not for theirs."

Even though the ceremony was not until ten o'clock, Mr. Privett insisted on setting out shortly after nine. Kentish Town to Finsbury Park via Tetsbury Road is rather a tricky little journey. And Mr. Privett guessed that Mr. Bloot would be in the need of company.

As it turned out, their early visit was just as well. They found a morose and disconsolate bridegroom, sitting in a practically empty apartment. The second-hand furniture dealer from the Archway Road had two jobs on hand that day. And he had made the collection from Tetsbury Road his first.

"Mah favourite chair," Mr. Bloot told them. "Raht from underneath me. And mah table. Before Ah'd even finished."

To keep him from brooding, Mr. Privett suggested that they should leave straightaway. Mrs. Privett, however, insisted that she should stay long enough to wash up. There was Mr. Bloot's cup and teapot that had been left standing on the mantelpiece. It was the only place that he could find when the table had been whisked away from him.

"It won't take a moment," Mrs. Privett said. "And it'll look better."

Mr. Bloot watched her go.

"There was another cupper tea there," he observed. "Ah'd only had one." He paused. "Seems funny to think Ah shan't never see Tetsbury Road again," he went on. "Ah could find mah way here with mah eyes shut."

The thought of permanent departure visibly saddened him. Even though Mr. Privett tried hard to cheer him up, it was plain that Mr. Bloot was drooping. And by the time they had left the house his spirits were even lower.

"Did you notice?" he asked. "Nothing from the Gurneys. Not even er nandshake. Ah wouldn't treater dog that way."

As much as anything else to take Mr. Bloot's mind off his last bitterness, Mr. Privett suggested that they should hurry. And he was so insistent on speed, that Mr. Bloot panicked. He began striding out. Disregarding his two smaller companions, he forged remorselessly ahead until Mr. and Mrs. Privett were almost running.

In the result, it was 9.30 sharp when they reached the Register Office at the Town Hall. The porter seemed surprised to see them. And slightly resentful. He had the air of a man who dislikes being caught unawares with mop and bucket. But the waiting-room was at their disposal, he said. They could make themselves comfortable in there if they liked.

Not that this was easy. The oilcloth was still damp under foot from its morning wash down. And the hard chairs and dark green dado round the walls might have come out of an infirmary. The only decoration in the room was a framed notice advertising local vaccination facilities.

"Well," said Mr. Privett brightly. "We've got here before the bride. That's all that matters."

But Mr. Bloot did not seem in any mood for brightness. He was still noticeably depressed about something.

"It'ser pity abaht that other cuppertea," he said broodingly. "Ah could 'ave done with it now."

Because Mr. Privett realised that it would be entirely up to him to keep things going, he crossed over and put his hand on his friend's shoulder.

"Cheer up," he said. "It's only for life."

Mrs. Privett winced at the sight. So long as she could remember she had always been irritated by the way her husband kept fussing over Mr. Bloot. He treated him as though he were some kind of gigantic toddler. And she felt suddenly that she could stand no more of it.

"Go and open the door," she said. "Otherwise they may miss us."

After that, they all three sat there in a draught as well. But at least they could see what was going on. And at ten minutes to ten when a tall, important-looking man went into the room opposite with his arms full of papers they knew that they had seen what they were waiting for.

"That's him all right," Mr. Privett observed over his shoulder. "Won't be long now."

But Mr. Bloot was past consolation. He might have been a condemned man having his own executioner pointed out to him.

"Not if the lady's on time, that is," he replied. "Not if she is."

But he need not have worried. It was still two minutes to ten when the glass doors at the end of the corridor opened and Hetty began to come towards them. At the sight of her, Mr. Bloot's heart gave a great bump. She was wearing a bright, peach-coloured coat, with a fox fur slung over one shoulder. But it was the little hat with a veil that did it. It added just that note of demureness that might otherwise have been missing. Mr. Bloot wanted to rush up and embrace her.

And, to Mr. Privett's relief, she was obviously in top spirits. She came straight in as though she were thoroughly accustomed to being married.

"Hadn't any of you got a shilling for the gas?" she asked. "This place is freezing."

It was not until she was actually inside the room with them that

252

they noticed that she was being followed. Hidden somewhere behind the peachiness came her escort. He, too, was dressed for the occasion. He was wearing a light, rather large check suit that showed beneath his brown overcoat. And his tie, all circles and lightning flashes, seemed to have come straight from California.

Mr. Bloot recognised him gloomily as one of Hetty's poker companions. And could not help wondering why he had been invited.

Not that there was any time for introductions. The porter had put away his broom and bucket and now presented a brisk, civic appearance. He asked if they would mind stepping into the next room, please.

It was the tall, important-looking man all right. A registrar of nearly thirty years' standing, he was doing holiday relief work for the resident Registrar. He exuded professionalism and efficiency. And he was quick in sizing up things. One glance at the little company and he knew that it was the light check that was marrying the pale peach.

" Here in the middle *if* you please," he said to Hetty and her companion. " And "—he turned to Mr. Bloot and the Privetts— " at the side *if* you don't mind."

Mr. Bloot was obediently making his way towards the fireplace when Hetty stopped him.

" Oh, no you don't," she said. " You can't slip out of it like that." She turned to the man beside her. " Hop it, Chick," she added. " You don't want to get mixed up in this."

The Registrar sat back in silence while the game of musical chairs went on before him. He was not taking any further chances. There is nothing that more easily makes a laughing stock of a good Registrar than for him inadvertently to marry the wrong couple.

" Are we all settled? " he asked finally.

But Mr. Bloot was too much on edge to reassure him. Now that the moment had actually come, he was feeling distinctly faint and swimmy. He hoped only that he would be able to sit through the ceremony without fainting. The premature arrival of the furniture dealer, the wastage of his second cup of tea, the pace of the road race through Tufnell Park had all been too much for him. He was sweating.

That was why he made such a seemingly reluctant bridegroom. Whereas Hetty each time answered up loudly and cheerfully, Mr.

253

Bloot might have been having second thoughts. He kept wiping his face and gulping audibly. Twice Hetty had to nudge him. And the second time the Registrar asked her quite sharply to let Mr. Bloot speak up for himself.

It was in the same mood of vacancy and dreamlike remoteness that Mr. Bloot signed the register and put out his hand for the certificate. " Aaah! " he said when he got hold of it. " Ut lahst." And he began to read. " *Augustus Archibald Bloot, widower, of* 17 *Tetsbury Road* . . ." that was him all right. And there in the next line his loved one. " *Amy Henrietta Florence, divorced, of* 23b *Artillery Mansions*. . . ."

Divorced! Mr. Bloot's heart missed a beat. Thank goodness that he had come to in time to save Hetty's good name.

He leant over and addressed the Registrar.

" Wot's the meaning of this Ah'd lakh to know? " he demanded, pointing at the offending word. " Oooze rersponsible? "

The Registrar bent anxiously forward over the sheet of paper, and even Chick came round and peered across his shoulder. Only Hetty herself and the two Privetts were temporarily out of the discussion. That was because Mr. Privett, to Mrs. Privett's great astonishment, had suddenly become remarkably skittish and had announced that he was about to kiss the bride.

It was not much of a kiss, however. For no sooner had Hetty pushed up her veil than she heard the one word, " divorced," being indignantly repeated by Mr. Bloot. And she immediately thrust Mr. Privett away from her.

" Give it to me," she demanded, going up to the table and snatching the certificate clean out of the Registrar's hands. " It's my marriage so I suppose I'm entitled to it, aren't I? "

Then folding it up as though it were a circular she prepared to thrust it into her handbag.

" But it says you're . . ." Mr. Bloot began.

He got no further, however. For Hetty kissed him. And it was a real kiss, this time. The little man in the check suit looked on, aghast and incredulous. He had merely read about such kisses. Never actually seen one. When she released him, Mr. Bloot was too exhausted to speak.

" Why don't you stop worrying? " Hetty asked. " You've got me, haven't you? "

It was early for a wedding breakfast. But after the cold of the November day outside, the interior of the flat seemed unusually warm and welcoming. And Hetty had thought of everything. She'd even got the daily woman to come in two hours before her usual time so that it should all be ready.

In the result, it was a spread that was waiting for them. Running her eye hurriedly over the table Mrs. Privett noted sausage rolls, three kinds of sandwich and a plate of shrimp vol-au-vent as well as mixed gateaux and a white wedding cake. But she also noted something else. Nothing on the whole buffet was home-made.

Not that there was much time for reflection, however. Chick had been put in charge of the drinks. And he was undeniably quick. They had scarcely fitted themselves inside the room when there was a loud plop. The first champagne cork had already been prised out. Then, at an hour in the day when Mrs. Privett would normally have been still tidying up the home, she found herself glass in hand preparing to drink the bride's and bridegroom's health.

It was Mr. Privett who proposed it. And for the second time that day his social jauntiness amazed her. It was a side of his nature that he normally kept concealed. But there was a simple explanation. It was merely that he wanted to do his best for Mr. Bloot and not let him down in Hetty's eyes. He was therefore deliberately arch and facetious. He referred to "the young couple." He predicted that Hetty would be the making of Mr. Bloot and complimented them both on the snug little home that they had waiting for them. He even said that he was afraid that the front stairs might prove a bit tricky for the baby carriage. And in the result, Hetty was delighted. Simply delighted. She hadn't known that the little man could possibly have had it in him. Mr. Privett was rather pleased, too. But not Mrs. Privett. She was remembering poor Emmie. And she could not imagine how Mr. Privett could apparently have forgotten her so completely.

The other person who did not seem to have appreciated the toast was Mr. Bloot himself. He seemed hardly to have heard it. He just stood there beside Hetty, dazed, incredulous, uncomprehending. Every time Chick handed him a glass of champagne he took it automatically. But without enthusiasm. It might just as well have been medicine that he was accepting.

Not so Mr. Privett. He took it. And he liked it. And took more of it. In consequence, he became talkative. Putting his arm round Chick's shoulder, he confided in him.

". . . thass why I'm so glad iss all worked out this way," he went on. " Comfobly settled for life. He d'serves it. Iss no more than his due."

Here he dropped his voice and taking a firmer grip on Chick's shoulder he lowered his face until he was speaking confidentially into his listener's ear.

" I don' mind telling you," he finished up, " he's had a hard life. No home comforss. I only hope she makes him ver' ver' happy."

But Mr. Privett was forgetting that Chick was Hetty's friend, not Mr. Bloot's. It was evident from the way in which he reacted that he didn't give a damn for Mr. Bloot's happiness. All that he was thinking about was Hetty. And from the way he kept glancing from one to the other he might even have been jealous. In any case, he was certainly loyal. He was also more accustomed than Mr. Privett to taking an occasional glass or two of champagne out of hours. He was not in the least garrulous. Merely a shade touchy.

" What about her? " he asked. " Doesn't she deserve it? My God, she had a hell of a time with her first one, I can tell you. I wonder she was prepared to go through with it again. . . ."

They broke off because Mr. Bloot was already sidling over in their direction. He still wore a look of complete unconsciousness as though he were sleep-walking. But it was evident that somewhere behind the mask the wheels were again slowly turning.

" Don't forget about the budgies," he said brokenly. " It's . . . it's not just the food. It's company they need. Someone they can trust. Someone to . . . to talk to."

Then, as soon as the others had gone, Mr. Bloot threw his arms around Hetty. And holding her in an embrace so fierce that she cried out involuntarily, he unburdened his heart.

" You should er told me," he said brokenly. " Ah never even guessed. Ah've never known anybody who was divorced before."

256

There is always something faintly depressing about a holiday resort out of season. Bournemouth is easily one of the best. The resident population sees to that. And the hotels are the kind that keep open all the year round. But it was still cold. Undeniably cold. The little clump of pine trees at the end of the road looked pinched and frost-bitten.

In the circumstances, Mr. Bloot would not have minded if the Royal Meadway had been a little farther inland. The wind came in straight off the sea. And the hotel, protected only by a low hedge, seemed to be getting most of it. As he stood outside paying off the taxi driver, he could hear it—practically solid ozone—whistling past him to flatten itself against the uninhabited balconies and the deserted sun lounge. Even the hotel itself was not quite so warm as he had hoped. Or so airtight. Inside the lounge, the only really comfortable-looking person whom he had seen since he had left London was the receptionist. Dressed in a knitted jumper with a thick cardigan on top, she was crouched inside her small glass cubicle over a portable electric fire, drinking tea.

But she was expecting him all right. And she could not understand why he seemed to be in such a state of indecision about signing the register. With the hotel pen on its little captive chain held firmly in his hand, he just stood there doing nothing.

That was because he was still in a daze. He scarcely recognised himself. It seemed that since getting up that morning he had become someone else. The Mr. Bloot whom he knew was a widower who went quietly home every evening to bachelor apartments in Tufnell Park. Whereas this Mr. Bloot, the new one, stayed with divorced women in private suites in expensive hotels. Twice the other Mr. Bloot put the pen down and wiped his forehead.

" Forgotten your name, dear? "

It was Hetty. Tired of waiting for him by the lift, she had come over.

" Well, go on," she said. " Put down anything you like. I don't mind. I'm frozen."

It was because he was being so rushed that Mr. Bloot made the silly slip of writing down his own name first. But, having started, he had to go through with it. And with a little mumble of apology he passed the pen over to her. But she ignored it.

"Just put ' Mr. and Mrs.' in front," she said. " It saves paper."

The alteration, however, was not a success. On the clean, orderly sheet of signatures it had a strangely illicit kind of look. The receptionist by now was obviously doubtful of the whole episode.

Hetty, however, was not put out. The one thing that she wanted was to get up to the suite and kick her shoes off. And because Mr. Bloot was still scratching and blotting, she picked up the key and went ahead of him. If he hadn't hurried, he would have missed the lift altogether.

As it was, the sight of the bedroom with its twin beds was almost too much for him. He felt dizzy again. And he found it strangely embarrassing the way the porter went round switching on lights and opening cupboards as though he were going to move in along with them.

He wished that the man would go away. So, apparently, did Hetty.

"Well, why don't you give him something?" she asked rather irritably. " How'd you like to have to carry up four suitcases? "

Even after the porter had left and the door had been shut on them, Mr. Bloot remained there, motionless.

"It'ser rum go," he said at last. " That's what it is. A proper teaser."

"Whatever's come over you?" Hetty asked.

She had gone over to the dressing-table and was carefully smoothing out her hair.

But still Mr. Bloot did not move.

"Wot was he lakh, your first?" he blurted out suddenly. " Wot *was* he lakh? "

"What was he like?" Hetty repeated. " He was no good. That's what he was like."

She paused.

"And for goodness' sake ring down for a drink," she told him. " This is supposed to be my honeymoon."

BOOK THREE

Private Affairs
of a Leading Model

CHAPTER XXXI

MARCIA did not forget. On the contrary, she remembered all that night. While Mr. Bulping was still with her, in fact. But when morning came she didn't see how she could very well do anything about it. Not unless Tony came back and asked her again, that is.

And the astonishing thing was that Tony did ask her again. Long after she thought that he had forgotten. They met quite casually. Just as Marcia was coming out of the Salon. Up to that moment, the one thing that she had wanted had been to flop down somewhere. Simply to get off her feet. But at the sight of Tony, she remained standing, one hand on hip, model fashion.

" Weren't you going to ring me, or something? " he asked.

It was quite extraordinary the effect even his voice had on her. As soon as he began speaking, she might have been back on the dance floor with the band playing somewhere away in the distance. And the gold and silver lights. And her dreary old beige dress that she had chosen specially for Mr. Preece. And all those endlessly refilled glasses of champagne.

" Was I? " she asked. " Tell me. What about? "

She lowered her eyes while she was speaking. And then raised them again. As she did so, she realised with a start that it was a mannerism that she hadn't used for years. Not since she was a girl. A mere beginner.

What was so annoying, however, was that Tony did not seem to have noticed. Possibly hadn't even been looking. His voice still sounded entirely casual. Matter-of-fact.

" I asked if you'd care to come along to *Giselle* he told her. " Can if you like. I'm going."

She was a little disappointed that he should put it like that. It didn't sound as though he minded either way. But it was definitely being asked again. And that was all that really counted.

" I'd adore it," she said.

She was using her husky voice by now. It practically came natural to her when she was tired.

261

" O.K.," Tony replied. " See you at six then. I've got the car."

Because it was all so rushed and sudden, Marcia was in a difficulty. It was nearly a quarter to five already. And she had nothing to wear. The dress in which she had come to Rammell's that morning was a strictly plain black one. Not even the dress for a cocktail party. And, of course, her shoes were all wrong, too. So was her bag. And her ear-rings. If it had been anyone else but Tony, she would simply have refused. But there was something in the sheer thoughtlessness that she found rather touching. It showed how impetuous he was. How boyish.

And with another walk-through in Model Dresses at five-thirty there was no possibility of going back to the flat to change. She therefore had to do what she simply hated doing. She was forced to borrow something from stock.

The dress she chose was one of the new Italian models. With a single shoulder-strap. And just absolutely no back at all. Definitely the kind of dress that required wearing. And definitely the kind of dress that she knew that she *could* wear.

She stood regarding herself in one of Rammell's tall mirrors. And really the effect was quite lovely.

" But somehow it's not . . . not me," she was forced to confess to herself. " It . . . it might be anyone."

There was no time, however, for regrets. It was nearly ten to six by now. She had managed to find a pair of shoes that weren't too terrible. And Furs had sent her up the familiar, overinsured mink that she always wore when she was representing Rammell's anywhere. The fact that it was old did not matter. There is something about mink that is always reassuring. Marcia felt a warm, suffusing glow of satisfaction beginning to run through her.

" Oh, God, have you gone and changed? "

She noticed as he said it that Tony himself was looking even untidier than usual. It was something to do with his shirt. The corners of his collar did not lie down properly. And his hair was all anyhow.

" I thought you'd rather," she told him.

" I don't mind, if you don't," he replied cheerfully. " I was only afraid that you might get knocked about a bit."

It was not until they reached the car that she understood what he meant. Then it was obvious. Up to that moment, she had somehow expected it to be Mr. Rammell's Rolls that they would be using. Or a taxi. Anything, in fact, but this low awful red thing to which Tony was leading her. The sides were cut away sharply. And the seats were nothing more than two little rubber cushions with curved backs.

"Thank God, it isn't raining," Tony remarked.

This time she saw at once what he meant. The horrible little car had a mackintosh sheet that could be pulled over it. But no hood. And, even though the sides had been scooped out, it was still difficult to get into. That was because a starting handle and a spare petrol can were lying on the floor where her feet were supposed to go. Tony moved the starting handle and the petrol can. But there was nothing that he could do about the hand-brake and the gear lever. Marcia had to gather her dress round her knees so that he could even drive.

"Better look out," Tony reminded her. "This car's filthy."

Because of the cold and the rush of air on her face, Marcia did not attempt to speak. When Tony asked if she would like to eat something straight away, she merely nodded. She supposed that he'd understood. But she couldn't imagine where he was proposing to take her. He had been doubling through the smaller back streets of Soho. And now he was making for somewhere on the other side of Seven Dials. The Ivy, possibly? Or Boulestin's? Or Rule's? Or was it another quick way through to the Savoy?

He glanced towards her for a moment.

"Pub be all right for a sandwich?" he asked. "Get a proper meal afterwards.

This time Marcia did not even nod. She was too frozen. She simply sat beside him, shivering inside the mink, wondering what on earth her hair was going to look like when they got there.

On the whole, of all the parts of London that she knew, she felt that Covent Garden was the one she hated most. The surrounding buildings were either wired up and empty. Or shuttered like a row of catacombs. And up the narrow side streets barrows had been turned over on their sides and left roughly lashed to piles of empty baskets. The whole place had the air of having been evacuated after an unsuccessful spell of street-fighting.

It was not until they were actually inside the Opera House that Marcia began to feel better. The staircase was distinctly promising. And the chandeliers had just that note of elegance that had been so conspicuously lacking outside. Scarcely like a theatre at all, in fact. More like a private mansion. The sort that can be hired for charities and things. Marcia began to feel at home.

And as she went through into the auditorium she understood why Tony should have wanted to come. In a restrained cathedral-like way it was certainly impressive. It was the size that did it. And the emptiness. As though a giant oval gasometer had been cleaned up and furnished entirely on the inside. The one thing that was puzzling was why ballet of all things should have to be conducted on Cup Final scale.

The orchestra was just arriving. The players came trooping in, whole hordes of them, through the two doors leading from somewhere underneath the stage. It was the numbers that Marcia found astonishing. The whole thing was music-making as Cecil B. de Mille might have arranged it.

But from that distance, it was all unreal somehow. It might have been a marionette band that was being assembled. Then the puppet conductor himself was brought on. And all the real people near at hand began clapping. The house lights went down. And the conductor, very expertly manipulated, gave two peremptory taps with his toy baton. Immediately, the whole puppet orchestra —ingeniously hinged violinists, woodwind players, brass and percussion—straightened up as though the concealed strings had suddenly been pulled tight. The overture had begun.

" I wonder what time it all finishes," Marcia found herself wondering. " I forgot to ask."

But all that really mattered was that she was beginning to get warm again. And the music was pleasant rather than otherwise. Even though she couldn't truthfully say that she enjoyed it, it was nice being able to watch it all happening. And it was heaven, sheer heaven, having Tony there beside her. She glanced across at him. His hand was up to his cheek. His eyes were half-closed. And on his face was an expression of sheer inward happiness. It was wonderful, seeing him as happy as all that. But, in a sense, he was too happy. Too abstracted. He seemed to have forgotten about her entirely.

The dancing itself, Marcia had to admit, was just a teeny-weeny bit tedious. And—oh, so embarrassing. Really, those young men in sausage-skin tights. How they could do it. There must be *someone* who could have told them. One of the girls perhaps. They certainly looked serious enough. Not so much as a smile anywhere. Come to that, only about five out of ten for looks. And less for deportment. They all had a curious duck-like movement with their feet turned too far outwards. Marcia longed to go down on to the stage to show them just once how to walk properly. But why worry? Nobody else seemed to have noticed how much was wrong. And if you just sat there, not concentrating on anything, an agreeably anæsthetic sensation came over you. It was like taking a long hot bath without the nuisance of having to dry yourself afterwards. The only difficulty lay in being absolutely sure that you could keep awake.

" Like a drink? " Tony asked when the interval came round.

Marcia rose obediently. It was gratifying that he had even remembered that she was there. And he was actually looking at her now. That was better still. Because she could tell that he was admiring her. It was lovely to be standing there with him, and feel his admiration run all over her.

" Enjoying it? "

" Dreamy," she answered. " Absolutely dreamy."

But the drink, all the same, was a mistake. Because it wasn't really a drink that these people wanted. It was talk. And such talk, too. It wasn't enough apparently that they had just been watching all that dancing. They had to keep on about it. Go over it. Again. And again. And again.

Tony seemed to know so many people, too. Marcia found herself being introduced on all sides. To pale, untidy young men. And tall intense young women. And not very satisfactory introductions, either. Because immediately they met, they started talking. But not to Marcia. After one or two attempts, they were forced to give that up. Then they talked round her. Across her. Behind her. And all that Marcia could do was to stand there. Listening. Smiling. Looking beautiful.

" It's worse than a point-to-point if you don't like racing," she found herself thinking.

And, at the thought, it all came back to her. The big cold house.

265

The week-end parties. The bad weather. Her first husband. The endless talk about horses. . . .

The bell in the foyer started ringing. Tony took her arm.

" Not bored? " he asked.

By the time they got outside, the rain had started. Real steady stuff. The kind that always falls round Covent Garden. Marcia recognised straight away that it was hopeless. Nobody ever went out in rain like that.

Tony inspected things for a moment.

" Better bring the car right round," he said. " You wait there."

It was years—God knows how many years—since anyone had treated her like this. Not since the early thirties. But here she hurriedly checked herself. She mustn't go on having thoughts like that. It was terribly morbid remembering dates. And it really did break her heart seeing Tony dashing off into the downpour for her sake. That pleased her. It showed that, unlike so many other girls, she really had been getting steadily nicer all the time.

And even sitting there in the car with that ghastly mackintosh contraption pulled over her, she still forgave him. Didn't even mind the cold. Or the drips. Or anything. Because she had suddenly realised that this was the sort of girl she really was. Informal. Unselfish. Full of the simple joy of living. And so young, oh, so truly young, at heart.

Supper, too, was bliss. Absolute bliss. It was The Chalice that Tony chose. It might have been awkward, of course, if Mr. Bulping had dropped in on the off chance of finding her. But there was no sign of Mr. Bulping. He was up somewhere in the Midlands, arranging contracts and things. And, in any case, this wouldn't have been the kind of evening that Mr. Bulping understood. To-night everything was different. Ethereal. Out of this world. Pure.

The only thing against it was the sadness. No matter what she did, it kept breaking over her. Not just waves either. Long devastating rollers. Even out on the dance floor, actually in his arms, she was ready to weep. And all because Tony looked younger than ever this evening.

" Oh, God, make him love me," she kept imploring. " Make him feel that he can't do without me. Let me take care of him. Let me be the one who sees that he doesn't come to harm. I don't

266

mind how he behaves. Let him trample over me. Only don't let him ever go away."

It was nearly two o'clock when they got back to Marcia's block of flats. By then, the streets were quite empty. And there were no lights showing in any of the windows. Everyone else in London was asleep.

Marcia was shivering again.

" T ... t ... thanks s ... so much for a w ... w ... wonderful evening," she began, her teeth chattering.

But Tony did not seem in the least ready to go.

" Don't I even get a drink? " he asked.

As they stood there by the horrible little car, it seemed to Marcia that they were quite alone. Not just alone in London. It might have been a desert island, or the moon, it was so silent. And ever since she had been a girl, the thought of desert islands and the moon had always affected her strangely.

" It's t ... t ... terribly late," she started to say and then stopped herself. " D ... d ... don't ring. I've g ... g ... got a key," she added.

CHAPTER XXXII

IT SEEMED to Mr. Privett as though life had unaccountably flattened out somehow.

There had been those exciting few days down in the vestibule while Mr. Bloot was on honeymoon. But Mr. Bloot had been married for nearly three months now. Married. And missing. For all that Mr. Privett saw of him, it might have been Ultima Thule and not merely Finsbury Park where Mr. Bloot was now living. He never came near Fewkes Road at week-ends. Never suggested a meeting at the Highgate Ponds. Even seemed reticent and withdrawn at elevenses. In short, he had become a stranger.

And having no Mr. Bloot and no model yacht to sail, Mr. Privett was left with no definite purpose in life. Nor, the way things were going, did there seem much prospect of ever having one again. Mr. Hamster's letters had eased off of late. There had only been two in the last month. The Court Case on which everything depended still seemed as far away as ever.

For Mrs. Privett it was not so bad. She had at least rediscovered Nancy. And they had been seeing each other again. First rather guiltily on neutral ground in the tea-room at Victoria Station. Then in Nancy's own little flat in West Kensington. And finally in Fewkes Road itself. Secretly, of course. They both agreed that, in no circumstances, should it be mentioned to Mrs. Rammell. Nancy even added cryptically that it could only lead to further unpleasantness.

But secrecy is one thing. Reticence is quite another. And Nancy had been keeping everything bottled up for years. Mrs. Privett listened in amazement. She learnt how shamelessly henpecked Mr. Rammell was. How the only thing that Mrs. Rammell really cared about was a title, so that it could be as Lady Rammell that her name appeared in connection with all those concerts and recitals. How extremely Mrs. Rammell disliked Sir Harry. How cordially the dislike was reciprocated. And how worried they all were about young Tony who didn't seem to want to settle down to anything.

"You don't know how lucky you've been. About Tony and

Irene, I mean," Nancy confided. " He isn't like anyone on our side. Father was always so steady until the crash came. There's a streak of recklessness in Tony that's pure Rammell. Not his father, of course. That's why they don't get on. More like Sir Harry."

" So you think I did the right thing in stopping it? " Mrs. Privett asked.

" You'd have regretted it for the rest of your life if you hadn't. And Irene after you," Nancy replied. " I can tell you . . ."

It was the third time already that Mrs. Privett and Nancy had enjoyed this particular conversation. Neither had added anything new. But as a subject it still seemed as fresh and promising as ever. It was because both women wanted to go on with it that they arranged to meet again. Early next month. Over in Nancy's flat next time.

Mrs. Privett had not attempted to conceal these meetings from her husband. She did not repeat Nancy's general indiscretions. That would somehow have savoured too much of treachery. But the bit about Irene was obviously intended for him. And Mr. Privett knew it pretty well by heart. By now he was able to repeat Nancy's exact words before Mrs. Privett came to them.

Not that he was by any means convinced. He still admired young Mr. Tony. Envied Mr. Rammell having a son like him. But it was really of Irene that he was thinking. He knew how any girl must feel after her first love-affair has been suddenly broken up. That was why he admired her, too. If she hadn't been the sensible sort she might have done something really terrible. Not just run away from home and come back again. And, ever since, she had been so quiet and controlled about it all. Not letting on to a soul about how she must really be feeling.

He mentioned this aspect of the tragedy to Mrs. Privett. But Mrs. Privett would have none of it.

" She'll get over it," she said. " She has already. It never was anything."

" Then why . . .? " Mr. Privett began.

" Because it might have," Mrs. Privett told him.

" I still think . . ." Mr. Privett began again.

But again Mrs. Privett interrupted him.

" Well, I don't," she said. " I know."

That was why it was such a victory for Mrs. Privett when Irene began stopping in town in the evenings so that she could have dinner at the Hostel. Mrs. Privett had always guessed that it would work out that way. For some time now, Irene had been seeing less and less of her old friends from the Eleanor Atkinson. And it was only natural that she should be getting into a new circle, a Rammell circle, by now. It was the girl from Classical Records with whom she had become friendly—the one who had the brother in Travel.

"Why not ask her over for tea one Sunday?" Mrs. Privett finally suggested.

"I may do," Irene answered. "Thanks, Mum."

It was next Sunday that Irene chose. That showed how right Mrs. Privett had been in proposing it. And it showed, too, that Classical Records must be every bit as keen. Between them, Irene and Classical Records were taking the whole thing for granted.

"Do you mind if she brings Ted along with her?" Irene asked.

"Who's Ted?" Mrs. Privett replied. "Is she engaged to him or something?"

"Ted's her brother," Irene told her. "You know. You met him at the dance."

"What's she want to bring him for?"

"Well, why not?" Irene demanded. "He's only living in digs. You can't expect him to spend every Sunday at the Hostel."

"Haven't they got a home?"

"I don't know," Irene answered. "I've never asked them."

Mrs. Privett looked hard at her daughter. Indifference on that scale, she knew, could mean only one thing.

It was Mr. Privett, not Mrs. Privett, who objected. Not openly, of course. Just sulkily. He liked Irene to have her girl-friends to the house. They helped to keep the place cheerful. But a young man in the house was different. Young men smoked such a lot. And sat down heavily in chairs. And expected to be offered drinks. It wouldn't seem like home at all if there were a young man about the place.

And particularly not if he were someone from Rammell's. There are certain privacies that any father of a family demands. If he wants to keep his slippers in the alcove beside the fireplace there is nothing in law against it. But that doesn't mean that he would necessarily like other people to know about it. Least of all other people in the same firm. Somehow he didn't fancy having to walk through Travel and Theatre Tickets with the knowledge that the pair of wolf eyes on the other side of the counter shared even the smaller of his domestic secrets.

Not that the young man proved to be nearly so aggressively male as Mr. Privett had feared. He smoked only one cigarette. Proved to be good, even eager, about opening doors and passing things. And refused a drink when it was offered to him.

The only thing that marred the whole afternoon was the fact that when he did light a cigarette, Irene lit one, too.

Mr. Privett felt merely a sudden affectionate pang at the thought that Irene should have grown up so fast. But Mrs. Privett was more outspoken.

" And when did you start smoking, I'd like to know? " she said.

There was a pause for a moment after she had spoken. Irene looked across at her friend—the one from Classical Records—and they both raised their eyebrows. Ted himself continued to look downwards at his feet.

" Oh, years ago, Mum," Irene replied. " I've forgotten."

" We'll talk about it afterwards," Mrs. Privett told her.

But Irene recognised her strength. With Classical Records and Ted both beside her, it was her moment more than Mrs. Privett's.

" No, we won't, Mum," she said. " There's nothing to talk about."

2

Mr. Privett dreaded Monday morning. He recognised the signs. From the way Mrs. Privett was taking Irene's rudeness, this was the sort of thing that might drag on right through the week.

But by the following morning it was completely forgotten. A letter from Mr. Hamster put the thought of everything else clean out of their minds. The date for the County Court case had at last been fixed. In consequence, Mr. Hamster wanted to see Mr. Privett as soon as possible.

Mr. Privett arranged the appointment by telephone. Not that there was any difficulty about it. Things were rather slack with Mr. Hamster at the moment. Any hour of the day would have been convenient. He would have stayed on until midnight if necessary. And Mr. Privett was only asking for six-thirty.

As soon as he got there, Mr. Hamster started. It was practically a dress rehearsal. Sitting back in his little swivel chair and with his thumbs tucked up into his waistcoat, Mr. Hamster gave his client a complete lesson in County Court procedure.

". . . and remember, we've got nothing to conceal," he said slowly and deliberately. "Just go into the box, and tell the truth. The plain simple truth. No hesitation. No pauses." Mr. Hamster paused momentarily. "Don't rush it, of course. Give yourself time to think what you're saying. Don't give the impression of being too pat." Mr. Hamster paused again. "And speak up when you say it. No mumbling." There was another pause. "Mind you, that doesn't mean shout at 'em. They can hear you. And shoulders back so that you look as if you meant it." This time the pause was longer. Mr. Hamster was a thorough man and weighed every word carefully. "Don't try to look defiant or cocky, of course. No overdoing it. Be natural. That's the whole secret. Be natural." This pause was the longest of them all, and it was obvious that Mr. Hamster was leading up to something really important. "Above all," he said, "don't get rattled. If you're rattled, you're sunk. Keep calm. Calm and steady." Mr. Hamster's voice was now rising with excitement. "This case means a lot to you. Remember that. Very serious if it went the wrong way." He glanced out of the window for a second. "You're going to win. And you know it. But be prepared. That's the great thing. Be prepared. If they turn nasty, show some spirit. No rudeness, of course. Nothing funny. Just stick to facts. And keep cool. Cool and confident. That's the way. Be yourself. Be yourself, and you'll be all right."

Mr. Hamster rose. He thrust out his hand.

"I'll . . . I'll try," Mr. Privett said.

But Mr. Hamster had not quite finished with him. He had just remembered one other point.

"Ten o'clock on the 15th," he said. "County Court. Brecknock Road. Don't be late. If you are, they'll hear the case without you. Remember that. But don't get there too early. They'll think you're nervous. Just give yourself nice comfortable time. There's nothing to worry about. Get your mind clear. Then forget all about it. Don't lie awake thinking. And try to remember what I've said to you. It's for your protection. It's up to you now."

The rest of that evening Mr. Privett was moody and pre-occupied. He started drawing diagrams on the backs of envelopes, with X showing the motor coach and a poor demolished little Y that was himself right up in the corner practically under the stamp. But diagrams of moving objects are difficult to draw. They require dotted lines and arrows. And that is where the tricky part comes in. In some of the diagrams X and Y missed each other altogether. In others the dotted lines kept crossing as though he and the motor-coach had been playing dodge'ems up the whole length of the Kentish Town Road. . . .

And it was worse, not better, when he finally got off to sleep. Then the whole of Mr. Hamster's advice rose up and overwhelmed him. He was in the dock already. And things were going pretty badly for him. He had created quite the wrong impression. That was because he'd forgotten his trousers. And the false nose that he was wearing had definitely counted against him. The judge had ordered him to remove it, but he had another one just like it under-neath. And, even in the dream state, his own behaviour astonished him. There were some questions that he refused to answer at all. Others that he capped merrily with a quick joke or a snatch of song. He bawled. He whispered. He denied everything. He confessed and begged for clemency. He turned his back on the judge. He sat on the floor. He produced a banana and ate it. He blew soap bubbles. . . .

In the end, things got so bad that he started talking in his sleep and Mrs. Privett had to wake him up.

CHAPTER XXXIII

ON THE morning of the running-down case, Mr. Hamster woke an entirely happy man. And no wonder. Under his care and guidance, this case that might easily have been dismissed in a few minutes— might even never have come into Court at all—had branched and blossomed into an affair of unimaginable complexity. There were now claims, counter-claims, watching briefs springing up everywhere.

Mr. Privett, however, was already feeling the strain. He had not slept at all well. And he had a strange guilty feeling about turning right for the Brecknock County Court instead of bearing left as usual and popping into the Underground for Bond Street. Even though he had got special leave, it still felt like playing truant.

It was five minutes to ten when he reached the Court. The walk had helped to quieten his nerves. He felt righteous and confident. Then he met Mr. Hamster.

"Remember what I told you," Mr. Hamster began. "Think before you answer. But don't hesitate. Be natural. Don't let them get you rattled. You'll be all right. But look out for catches. And keep calm. Above all, keep calm. . . ."

It was not until nearly three-fifty when Mr. Privett was eventually called. It was the last case the Judge heard that day. And, in the interval, Mr. Privett's morale had gone completely. If he had been asked to play a violin solo instead of merely giving evidence he could not have been more agitated.

He took the oath loudly and defiantly, as though he had been taking oaths and breaking them all his life. And then, having taken it, he simply stood there looking sulkily down at his feet, cutting everybody. The Judge even had to speak to him about it. He asked Mr. Privett to have the goodness to look in his direction when he was addressing him. Thereafter, Mr. Privett stared. It was a baleful, unflickering stare like a basilisk's. And it would have been downright rude if it had gone on a second longer.

It was broken, in fact, only by the solicitor for the motor-coach company. He coughed twice rather loudly and then asked if Mr. Privett would mind sparing him a little of his attention, too. Mr. Privett thereupon turned his hypnotist's gaze full on him. But he forgot about the voice. Twice the Judge had to ask Mr. Privett to speak up because neither he nor the opposing solicitor could hear a word that he was saying. And Mr. Privett promptly began using a high-pitched strident kind of voice as though he were arguing with them.

They were now hard at it, the motor-coach solicitor and Mr. Privett. It was real diamond-cut-diamond stuff.

" How fast were you going when you reached the Kentish Town Road? "

There was a pause.

" I haven't got a speedometer."

The solicitor frowned. He seemed a pressing sort of chap, Mr. Privett thought. His air of gentle patience only made him that bit more dangerous.

" I didn't ask you whether you had a speedometer or not. I asked you how fast you were going."

Mr. Privett began looking down at this boots again.

" I wasn't going fast at all."

There was a quick intake of breath by the solicitor, a sudden snake-like hissing.

" But I take it that you were moving? "

Mr. Privett thought for a moment. Then he gave a quick furtive glance in Mr. Hamster's direction. Mr. Hamster was half off his chair with excitement and anxiety.

" Yes, sir," he replied quietly.

" Speak up, please. I still can't hear you. Were you moving? "

" YES I WAS! "

The solicitor pushed his glasses up on to his forehead and regarded Mr. Privett. Somehow the witness hadn't looked the kind of man who was likely to give trouble of this sort.

" Thank you," he said. " Well, was it, shall we say, five miles an hour? "

Mr. Privett looked again towards Mr. Hamster. But the strain had been too much for him. He was now crouching back with his face covered by his hands. Mr. Privett was utterly alone.

" I never timed it," he said.

The solicitor leant forward. He was doing his best to be quiet, persuasive, reassuring.

" Oh, come now. I don't want a stop-watch reading. I merely want your own estimate of your speed. Was it faster, say, than if you had been walking? "

Mr. Privett paused. Was it this that Mr. Hamster had warned him against? "

" Will you kindly answer my question? "

" Yes."

" Well, may I have the answer? "

" Yes. It's ' Yes! ' "

The solicitor sighed. At this rate he would be trapped in the stifling atmosphere of Brecknock Road Court until next morning.

" Now perhaps we are getting somewhere," he said. " Was it faster than anybody running? "

There was a longer pause this time.

" There wasn't anybody running."

" Well, then as fast as a horse and cart perhaps? "

Mr. Privett drew his tongue across his lips.

" I've never driven in a horse and cart."

This was too much for the solicitor. He flung the batch of papers that he was holding down on to the desk in front of him.

" I put it to you that you have no idea how fast you were going. That you were scorching along with your head down and didn't see a thing. That you haven't the slightest idea what happened."

There was no pause this time. It was obvious that if Mr. Privett had been holding anything in his hands he would have flung that down, too.

" YES I HAVE," he replied. He was fairly roaring by now. " I WAS RUN INTO. RUN INTO FROM BEHIND."

Mr. Hamster was waiting for Mr. Privett when he climbed down out of the box. And his eyes were moist.

" Magnificent," he whispered. " Absolutely magnificent. Just like I told you."

And it was now Mr. Hamster's turn. He had always rather fancied himself as a cross-examiner, a sort of Marshall Hall of the County Courts. He had cultivated a way of holding his head to one side while regarding witnesses, as though he were trying to make up his mind whether he had ever seen them before. It cast a vague but valuable aura of suspicion.

" Did you see my client's bicycle and trailer? "

" I did."

The motor-coach driver was a large red-faced man who might have been a butcher. His expression was one of simple, beefish confidence. But that soon wore off as Mr. Hamster pursed up his lips and peered at him through one eye.

" Did you think you could avoid it? "

" I did."

" But you couldn't, could you."

" No."

" Why not? "

" It cut across me."

" So you expected the other vehicle to avoid *you*? "

" I did."

" Do you always expect the other vehicle to do the avoiding? "

" No."

" But in your view nothing you could have done on this occasion could have prevented a collision? "

" No."

Mr. Hamster's one weakness as a cross-examiner was that he never had the slightest idea of where his questions were leading. He just went on putting them. Everything had been going so smoothly, too. Right up to this point he could hardly have done better. But now, he realised, he had practically cleared the coach driver. He recovered himself hurriedly.

" Was that because you were going too fast? " he asked.

" No."

" Then how did you come to demolish my client's trailer? "

" I told you, he cut across me."

" Were your brakes faulty? "

" No."

" And you were not going fast? "

" No."

" Just fast enough to cause this collision, eh? "

Mr. Hamster was purring to himself when he resumed his seat. That last remark had been brilliant. Really brilliant. A real scale-turner.

And there was still Mr. Hamster's own cross-examination of

Mr. Privett. By then Mr. Hamster was absolutely on the top of his form.

". . . and upon entering a main road from a side-turning do you always look right and left and then right again as laid down in the Highway Code?"

" I do."

" Did you do so on this occasion? "

" I did."

" And did you see the motor-coach approaching? "

" No."

" You are quite sure you looked? "

" Quite sure."

" Then it can't have been there, can it? "

Mr. Hamster passed his hand across his forehead. The line of reasoning was eluding him again. He reached out desperately.

" If it had been there you would have seen it? "

" Yes."

" But you didn't see it? "

" No."

" So it can't have run into you? "

" No. I mean, yes. It did run into me. From behind."

By now there was a red film across Mr. Hamster's eyes. His palms were sweating. He could hear his own life blood beating against his eardrums. He was in the Brecknock County Court. He knew that much. Otherwise his mind was a clean and total blank. This worried him. Because it had happened to him before. Always in Court. And always in the winning moment of an important case. . . .

After Mr. Hamster had sat down there was a prolonged silence. Even the Judge seemed a little dazed. The solicitor for the motor-coach company began rubbing his hands together. And then, afraid that any premature show of jubilation on his part might prejudice his clients' chances, he started to blow upon his finger-nails as if he were cold.

Mr. Privett sat, with head bowed, beside the still trembling Mr. Hamster and waited for the verdict. At any moment he expected the Judge to begin reaching out for the black cap.

That was why he nearly broke into tears of sheer happiness when the Judge did finally speak. And it was why the solicitor for the motor-coach company suddenly thrust his papers away from him as though they were contaminated. Because the verdict allowed of no possible misunderstanding. Fifty pounds' worth of damage had been done, the Judge said; neither less nor more. And the division of responsibility for the fact that there had been an accident at all lay as four-fifths on the shoulders of the motor-coach company and one-fifth upon Mr. Privett's own.

Mr. Hamster, however, was too much overcome to speak. It was the first case that he had won for months. The first since May, in fact. And, now that it was over, he realised how fortunate he had been. Because, when he had sat down after his blackout he had been under the impression that it was the motor-coach company whom he was representing.

2

But Mr. Privett with forty pounds of somebody else's money as good as in his pocket was a transformed man. He could begin living again.

Camden Town was where he was bound for. Lumley's in the Chalk Farm Road, to be precise. Just under the bridge and opposite the first lamp-post. But everybody knows Lumley's. The window is full of models of all kinds—Bermuda rigs, remotely-controlled gunboats, steam-driven cabin-cruisers, hydroplanes. Daisy II had originally come from Lumley's. On a one-to-twenty scale of things Lumley's has about the same kind of standing as John Brown's or Vickers'.

And then an extraordinary thing happened. Mr. Privett had just got off his bus and was cutting through the open entrance hall of the Underground station when all the sparkle and exhilaration went from him. At one moment he was rushing along like an intoxicated schoolboy, and at the next he had stopped dead. That was because another sensation, at least as powerful, had suddenly taken possession of him. He was now filled with a strange savage joy that the saints know. The joy of renunciation. Within the last ten seconds he had decided to buy something for Mrs. Privett instead.

But it was not easy to be so generous. It was nearly five-fifteen already. And at five-thirty everything in Camden Town closes down. Mr. Privett therefore had precisely quarter of an hour in which to

279

ransack the place. In consequence, he rushed. He tore from jeweller to jeweller. He examined diamond engagement rings, christening mugs, an infant's spoon and pusher, a cut-glass toilet set. He was almost frantic with frustration as he darted backwards and forwards. And then staring him coldly in the face from the Co-op's plate-glass windows, he saw the very thing that he wanted. It was a new and very shiny, treadle sewing-machine. There was a whole box of accessories that went with it. And, folded suitably, the instrument miraculously transformed itself into a kind of bedside-table. The contraption cost twenty-six pounds ten.

Mr. Privett went straight in and bought it. But here he ran into a difficulty. He had only fourteen and six on him. There was nothing for it therefore but to arrange for the instrument to be sent round C.O.D. in the morning.

Mr. Privett was still feeling happy and excited as he stepped out of the now empty shop on to the pavement. And then suddenly his mood changed again. An overwhelming sense of defeat came over him. Despite the immense rush, the urgency, he had achieved nothing—nothing at all that he could show for it. He might, he realised, just as well have waited until the morning and then ordered the machine through the Staff Association in the ordinary way.

Flowers were thus the obvious solution. Considering that they were all paid for by the motor-coach company he could afford to be reckless. But trying to buy flowers at Camden Town at twenty to six on a Thursday evening is impossible. The only shop that was still open was a greengrocer's. And even there the shutters were already going up. But Mr. Privett was desperate. Determined at all costs not to go home empty handed, he pounced. In the absence of flowers, he bought everything that he could see. The green-grocer served him in stolid but mounting astonishment. It seemed like the preparations for some kind of vast vegetarian orgy. Brown paper bag after brown paper bag was filled. And still Mr. Privett was not satisfied. When he finally left the shop, he had become the owner of two pounds of Cox's, two pounds of pale unhealthy-looking apples called Grannie's Sweetheart, a pineapple, a pound of assorted nuts, a stick of celery, two pounds of tomatoes, a box of dates and half a dozen oranges.

It was nearly six-forty-five when Mr. Privett at last reached Fewkes Road. And Mrs. Privett gave a little scream at the sight of him. She had been worrying all the time about the court case. When six, six-fifteen, six-thirty passed she became convinced that the worst, the very worst, must have happened. Even if he weren't actually in the cells already, he was probably tramping the streets afraid to come home and break the news that he had a new motor-coach to pay for.

That was why the sight of him with all those paper bags came as such a shock. If he had made himself up as a Red Indian she could not have been more amazed. As he stepped into the narrow hall, the odour of fresh fruit was overpowering. Mrs. Privett became seriously alarmed. Perhaps, under the strain, his poor overloaded mind . . .

" What's . . . what's happened? " she asked.

Mr. Privett was so excited that he was rather inclined to rush. " It's coming in the morning," he told her. " C.O.D. And it's not a table really. It does all sorts of things. Buttonholes and . . ."

He was unloading paper bags all the while he was talking. The one with the nuts in it gave him particular trouble because the paper had burst open. They scattered. Mrs. Privett gave one glance and went back into the kitchen. She now suspected drink.

" It's all right, Ireen," she said. " It's only your father. You stay where you are. I'll attend to this."

CHAPTER XXXIV

MARCIA had made her big decision. She had decided to break with Mr. Bulping.

In the circumstances, it was the only thing that a nice girl could do. Because during the past month she had been seeing far more of Tony than of Mr. Bulping. Almost every night, in fact. And now that she had really got to know Tony she had discovered the most astonishing thing. For all his marvellous opportunities, the sweet darling boy was every bit as lonely and unattached as she was. That was why he had been so grateful, so pathetically grateful, for her company. And so appreciative in his own peculiar fashion. He had a way of running his hand over her hair and then turning her face towards him so that he could kiss it that she found quite irresistible. No one else had ever said: "Darling, do you know, corpse-like or not, you're quite beautiful?"

And the attraction was not merely physical. That was what made it all so much worth while. It was a mingling of minds as well. They talked about so many things together. Marcia had discovered a three-and-sixpenny book entitled *The A.B.C. of Ballet*. And she had practically memorised it. If ever he invited her to Covent Garden again she would know exactly what to look out for. Because apparently it was all quite deliberate and intentional—even that funny duck-walk with the toes turned out too far. And so rehearsed, too. Marcia could see now that, in its own way, ballet dancing was every bit as exacting as modelling.

Nor was ballet the end of it. There was music, as well. Tony, bless him, was absolutely swoony about music. But no matter how utterly Marcia adored music too—and she could tell as soon as she tried it how musical she really was—it was definitely harder than ballet. There weren't even any simple books on it. There was nothing for it but to listen. And that took simply ages. It had been just darling of Tony to lend her his own record-player, because her little portable only took 78's. And he couldn't have been sweeter trusting her with all those glorious L.P. records of his. One day, any day now, she intended to stay away from Bond Street altogether and play them all right through. Really get the hang of them. In the meantime, she had to do the next best thing. Leave one of them—a different one each time, of course—permanently on the turntable so that she could switch it on the moment she heard Tony's ring on the door-bell.

Not that they spent all that much time in the flat. Most evenings they went out dancing together. And it was Tony's dancing that really astonished her. It was not merely bad. It was appalling. As though it meant nothing to him. He held her so limply that, if she hadn't known how much he cared, she could never even have guessed. Indeed, if it had not been for those rather special moments when he leant forward so that his cheek could rest against hers she would still have found herself doubting.

But really it was wonderful. Too wonderful, having him there when he brought her home afterwards. And there was nothing with which she could possibly reproach herself. She simply couldn't have behaved better. Practically every time he came she said the same thing.

" Silly boy," it ran. " I do believe you're beginning to get fond of me. But you mustn't, you know. It would be all wrong. You've got to go home now and forget all about me."

To-night, for example, was being perfect. It was one of the dreamiest of evenings. They had only just got back. Marcia had automatically flicked the knob of the record-player and the cosy little flat was filled with the muted horns of L.P. (New Series) 736/7X.

Marcia herself had just gone through to change into something looser. When she came back she was wearing a long padded house-coat. She had kicked off her shoes, too. And oh, the relief! In the little flat mules that she now had on she could really begin to live again.

Tony himself was lying almost full-length on the hearth-rug. Only *almost* full-length. Because that end of the room wasn't really quite long enough. His head was propped up against the wall. But that didn't matter. The extraordinary boy hardly ever sat on chairs like other people. He preferred floors. Window-sills. Corners of fenders. He had poured out a drink for both of them. And, gathering the long house-coat around her, Marcia sat herself down on the hearth-rug beside him.

Rather to her disappointment, Tony leant over and switched off the record-player. For one awful moment Marcia feared that it must have been an L.P. that she had played before. But it seemed to be all right. Apparently, Tony just wanted to talk. And before he spoke Marcia wanted to get in her little piece.

"You can't say, darling," she began, "that I haven't warned you. You mustn't start letting yourself get fond of me. I'm not worth it. Really, I'm not. It's only you I'm thinking of. I don't matter. You ought to find yourself some big strong hockey-playing girl. . . ."

Her voice drifted off to nothingness because he was stroking her leg again. And here again she realised how different he was, how precious. Because it was with the back of his hand that he was stroking it. And so gently, too. It was like being caressed by a feather. But so exciting somehow. Out of all the men she had ever met Tony was the only one who seemed to have appreciated how desperately fragile she really was. And now—still ever so gently— he was pulling her down so that her head could rest against his shoulder.

That was how they were lying when Mr. Bulping came in. Marcia realised at once how silly she had been ever to let him have that spare latch key of hers. It was only because he had been so insistent that she had consented. But what else could a girl do? That was where it was so downright hellish being poor. And, after all, Mr. Bulping had been generosity itself about things like telephone bills. And electric light. And all the other accounts that keep popping up unexpectedly.

Mr. Bulping stood in the doorway regarding them. And compared with Tony he looked really quite horrible. So male. And so aggressive. Not that he was violent. Or anything like it. On the contrary, he seemed positively to be enjoying himself. With his hat pushed on to the back of his head—Marcia had never been able to break him of that habit of coming into the flat with his hat on—he was wearing a broad grin right across his face.

" 'Ullo, 'ullo, 'ullo, 'ullo," was all he said.

Naturally Marcia had got up as soon as he came in. But Tony continued to lie where he was.

"Am I in the way?" he asked.

Marcia could have wept because of the sheer humiliation that Tony must be feeling. And for being so restrained, so civilised, about it all. If only Mr. Bulping could have been the same. But the sheer absence of niceness in his nature had been one of the things that had always worried her.

" Don't nobody move," he said. " I'm just going to pick up my pyjamas and my toothbrush and then I'm clearing out."

It was as he said it that Marcia decided to give up Mr. Bulping. For good. And for ever. Renounce him entirely. Cut him clean out of her life. It was madness, sheer madness, to have imagined that they could ever really mean anything to each other. At least, on her part it was.

And when he telephoned to her next day, her mind was already made up. All the apologies in the world weren't going to move her. Only it wasn't to apologise that he had telephoned. It was simply to be abusive. Straight vulgar abuse came pouring out at her. Which just showed how right she was to have nothing more to do with him.

2

Not that any real harm had been done. Not so far. It was simply that it had been horrid for Marcia to have to sit there— she was alone in the flat at the time—being scolded in that uncouth vulgar voice from Wolverhampton.

And her reading of Mr. Bulping was being proved the correct one. In short, he was not a gentleman. If he had been, he would have kept quiet about it. Not gone round repeating it. In Rammell's of all places, too.

It was the chief buyer, Mr. Galbraith, whom he told. And on the very next day. Lunch was the time Mr. Bulping chose for it. But not until the end of the meal when he had got his man properly receptive and conditioned.

" I don't say Rammell's isn't a valuable account," he led into it quietly. " But there are others, you know. There are others."

" Meaning what ? " Mr. Galbraith asked, expecting some objection to the present discount.

He was an elderly man. Practically on the edge of retirement. And he was no longer up to these enormous business lunches. Every Monday he came into the office swearing that he would never eat another meal that he hadn't paid for himself. And every week he was hard at it again, gnawing his way through great slices of smoked salmon and slabs of steak at the expense of Woollens, Worsteds, Knitwear, Rayons, Textiles, Model Gowns, Swimsuits and all the rest of them.

"Meaning that we all have our own standards," Mr. Bulping replied. "I'm prepared to go so far and no further. Last night..."

Mr. Galbraith drew in his breath sharply.

"You're sure Marcia is that kind of girl?" he asked at last. "I mean there's always a lot of talk about models."

"I should know," Mr. Bulping told him.

"And Mr. Tony? It's easy to make mistakes. And in those sort of circumstances..."

"I don't make mistakes," Mr. Bulping interrupted him. "I tell you I was introduced to the boy. At that blasted staff dance she dragged me to."

"D'you think other people know?" Mr. Galbraith inquired cautiously.

"Talk of London," Mr. Bulping replied. "Can't keep that sort of thing quiet. Not that way those two are behaving."

Mr. Galbraith sat staring glumly at the cigar that he was holding. It was something else he hadn't really wanted.

"I wonder what we ought to do," he said at last.

"That's your affair," Mr. Bulping assured him. "It's no business of mine. I couldn't care less about Rammell's reputation. It's mine I'm thinking of. Have another brandy?"

Mr. Galbraith was not the sort of man to be rushed into anything. Nor was he a trouble-maker. He had got where he was by a combination of known Tory principles, caution and, in his younger days, an astonishing capacity for going on drinking at the expense of other people. His first instinct was to do absolutely nothing.

But a new topic of conversation is always tempting. And more for something to say than for any other reason he mentioned it casually to Mr. Birt, the Chief Cashier.

Mr. Birt was no more than at the mid-point of his career. He constantly saw it stretching out ahead of him—Secretary, General Manager, Director. Even Managing Director if only the right sort of vacuum occurred. And he was constitutionally incapable of doing nothing. Up to that moment he had been thinking about a new system of slotted cards for the mail-order side. But this was every bit as interesting. He had to discuss it with someone.

The person he chose was Mr. Rappelly (Foreign Exchange). He brought the matter up while they were waiting for some bank statements to be brought down. They had been in the R.A.F. together, and this was by no means the first confidence that they had shared. Nor was it the first confidence that Mr. Rappelly had shared with Mr. Cousins of General Accounts.

Mr. Cousins in turn lived out at Esher and travelled home most days with a Mr. Sandalwood who was one of Mr. Galbraith's own buyers—on the Boot, Shoe and Leather side. Secretly, Mr. Cousins was a little bored by Mr. Sandalwood's company. He was glad to have something fresh to talk about. And Mr. Sandalwood, for his part, was a man always ready to talk to anybody. The first person he told was Mr. Galbraith.

That was what resolved Mr. Galbraith. Up to that moment he had decided that the sensible thing was to ignore Mr. Bulping's warning. Why, he asked himself, should he get himself mixed up with any unpleasantness during his last six months. But if there really were rumours around the place, then it was clearly his duty to tell someone. And the person whom he told was Mr. Preece.

In consequence, Mr. Preece spent an entirely sleepless night. It was always in the matter of personal relations that Mr. Preece was at his weakest. And, once he had made his mind up, he did the entirely wrong thing. He questioned people. Starting with Mr. Rawle of Shirtings where Tony was still working he moved on steadily and relentlessly to Miss Bywater, the Salon Supervisor. And it was fatal. If he had called a Press Conference, complete with hand-out, he could not have started more people talking. Not until he had got the whole place fairly buzzing did he go along to Mr. Rammell.

". . . so I thought I'd just mention it," he said. " I'm sure there's nothing to it but I thought you ought to know."

Nothing to it! Mr. Rammell could not imagine how anyone could be quite so idiotic as Mr. Preece. Of course, there was something to it. Mr. Rammell didn't doubt that for a moment. And he was already determined that this was going to be something that he would deal with single-handed.

" Thank you, Preece. Thank you," was all he said.

But before he went home that night he did two things. The first was to see if Mr. Adler of New York was still in town. And the second was to ask his secretary to fix up for Marcia to see him to-morrow.

Mr. Rammell was lucky to catch Mr. Adler. Another couple of hours and Mr. Adler would have been in the hired limousine on the way out to the airport. But quarter of an hour was all that Mr. Rammell needed. And Mr. Adler needed no persuading. Seemed rather flattered, in fact. He was President of Adler's Inc. in Fifth Avenue. Adler's and Rammell's. There was no tie-up that he could possibly have liked better.

"Sure, sure," he said. "Suits me fine. I'll have the boy. Just you send me a cable. I'll be back there in the morning."

3

Marcia decided to wear black for the interview. Not mourning black. Just black black. With pearls. And a dress ornament of some kind—a flower possibly—right up by the shoulder.

It was not until half past five, in any case. That gave her all the time in the world. She could cut short the afternoon tea parade. Only once round instead of twice. Above all things, she wanted to appear at her best when she saw Mr. Rammell. There was a new British fashion drive in Latin-America just about to start. Marcia had set her heart on going. And she had to admit that—to herself anyway—she had been looking the weeniest bit tired just lately.

But not half so tired looking as Mr. Rammell. He could hardly have seemed worse. Grey. Puffy. Dull-eyed. It had been one of the very worst of his bad nights. And after a thoroughly bad evening, too. He and Mrs. Rammell were no longer even on simple speaking terms.

"So you want to snatch the boy right away from me, do you?" she had demanded.

"Only for a year," Mr. Rammell had replied patiently.

He had told her that six or seven times already. Had explained that it was not exile to which he was proposing to send Tony. Merely New York. To Adler's in Fifth Avenue. So that the boy could learn something of American methods. See a bit of the world.

Find his own feet, in fact. He had deliberately avoided all mention of Marcia.

"But why? Why?" Mrs. Rammell had gone on. "There's no *need* for it. He's had his lesson. If you hadn't driven him into the shop in the first place none of this would ever have happened. Can't you see that Tony's whole future . . ."

It had been nearly one o'clock when they finally broke up. And sometime after four when Mr. Rammell had at last dropped off to sleep. In consequence, he had been intolerably sleepy all day. After lunch, particularly. The clock now showed five-twenty. It was one of his really strictest rules not to drink before six o'clock. But to-day he felt he needed it. He went over to the big cabinet in Rammell-Chippendale and poured himself out a large whisky and soda. And he timed it perfectly. He had even finished the charcoal tablet as well by the time Marcia was announced.

Mr. Rammell was at his absolute best at these difficult personal interviews. He had, in the first place, developed a technique. It consisted in meeting the visitor right over by the door. This was a very important stroke. It helped to establish the fiction that Mr. Rammell had been hanging about all the afternoon simply waiting for his visitor to arrive. And the second master stroke was to occupy one of the two arm-chairs that stood in front of the desk. Not carry on the conversation across the no-man's-land of the ink wells and blotter.

"Miss Tutty," Miss Winters announced.

Marcia squirmed. It was only up in Management where the staff records were kept that anyone ever used the name nowadays.

But Mr. Rammell put it right immediately.

"Come in, Marcia," he said. "Come in."

He regarded her closely for a moment. And really it was impossible not to admire her. Here she was at one of the most awkward moments of her life. For all she knew she was going to be out of a job by to-morrow. And she was unperturbed. Absolutely unperturbed. She was, if anything, taking things even more placidly than usual. Scarcely even walking. Drifting, rather.

"Cigarette?" Mr. Rammell asked as soon as they had sat down.

Marcia shook her head.

"No thank you," she said slowly.

289

She had been reading lately about what cigarettes did to you. Years and years off your life apparently. Even a month or two ago that wouldn't have mattered. But now it was different. She had so much to live for.

"Well, well," Mr. Rammell went on. "I expect you know why you're here."

The pause was rather longer than he had expected. And then he remembered. Marcia always did take rather a long time before actually saying anything.

"How long would it be for?" she asked.

"How long?" Mr. Rammell repeated.

Another pause.

"Before I get back, I mean?"

Mr. Rammell got up and began to walk about. Without actually realising that he had done so, he sat himself down behind his desk before he answered.

"What are you talking about?" he asked bluntly.

"About going away," Marcia told him.

"Where to?"

The pause was even longer than usual this time. That was because Marcia wasn't quite sure where Latin-America really was.

"Mexico," she said at last.

"Mexico?"

"The tour," Marcia explained. "The fashion tour."

Mr. Rammell let out a deep sigh. Not of relief. Of sheer irritation.

"I'm not talking about any kind of tour," he said.

Marcia did not raise her eyes. Mr. Rammell sat there regarding her. She really was quite strikingly beautiful. He had to admit that. The way she was sitting now, with her eyelashes brushing her cheek, he could understand everything. . . . He pulled himself together abruptly. Remembered his technique. Got up and came round to the chair on her side of the desk.

"What I want to talk to you about is Tony," he went on.

Another pause. But still no sign of any agitation. Not even emotion. Marcia hadn't yet raised her eyes.

"Tony," she repeated softly.

It was then that Mr. Rammell realised that he would have to be quite brutal if they were going to get anywhere.

"Yes, and it's got to stop," he told her.

This time it was more promising. He could tell that Marcia was getting ready to say something.

" But Tony and I . . ." she began.

Mr. Rammell got up and began to walk about. He was determined, absolutely determined, that he wasn't going to lose his temper.

" I don't care what you and Tony have been plotting together," he said. " My mind's made up. If this goes any further, out you go. Both of you. For good."

He was studying Marcia closely while he was speaking. And he could see that he had finally made an impression. Very slowly she uncrossed her feet and folded them again the other way.

" Oh, but I agree with you," Marcia said. " It's . . . it's what I've always been telling him. But he wouldn't listen. Really he wouldn't. I couldn't make him see it. I tried so hard, too."

Mr. Rammell came over and stood facing her.

" You mean you've had enough of him? "

" Oh, no," Marcia's reply was almost immediate this time. " I could never have enough of Tony. It's just that he's . . . so young."

" You're old enough to be his mother," Mr. Rammell reminded her.

For a moment Marcia raised one hand to her cheek as though for protection.

" That's what I tell him," she answered, even more softly this time. " But he doesn't realise. He'll . . . he'll need all your help."

Mr. Rammell took out his handkerchief and began running it across his forehead. He was aware that at last Marcia was actually looking at him. And not merely looking. She was staring. Those remarkable violet eyes of hers were fixed full on him. She was devouring and consuming him. Mr. Rammell looked hurriedly away.

But still Marcia's gaze did not waver. It had absorbed him completely by now.

" The poor darling thing," she was thinking. " How awful! He's embarrassed! So strong and powerful, too, if he only knew. But so unsure of himself. So painfully unsure. And so ill looking. So haggard. And all because of me. Oh, why can't I do something. How can I ever make him understand? "

Mr. Rammell had pulled out his cigar-case and was carefully removing a cigar. He fingered it gently. Lovingly. When he applied the cutter, he was delicate. Precise. It might have been surgery, not mere smoking, in which he was engaged.

Marcia's whole heart went out to him.

" Now he's just playing for time," she reflected. " He doesn't know what to say. That's because he doesn't really trust me."

Mr. Rammell lit the cigar and blew out a cloud of blue smoke.

" I think you're taking the whole thing very sensibly," he said. " Very."

" I'm . . . I'm glad you do."

" Must mean quite a wrench," he went on. " I see that."

Marcia raised her right hand again for an instant. But this time it was merely to run the back of her fingers across her lashes. She gave the tiniest of little sniffs.

" Oh, God," thought Mr. Rammell. " I hope she isn't going to start crying."

He decided that he had better say something. And say it quickly.

" I can tell you one thing," he said briskly. " I shan't forget about this. You can rely on me."

Marcia looked up again. Her eyes seemed even darker violet now.

" Don't," she said. " Please, please, don't."

Because it was so late, the adjoining offices were all in darkness. Only Miss Winters's light was still burning. The corridor ahead of them looked empty and deserted. Marcia experienced that strange mountains-of-the-moon sensation again. It seemed that she and Mr. Rammell were the only two people left alive. Survivors, as it were. In a world that had died around them while they had still been talking.

" Better use this lift," she dimly heard Mr. Rammell say to her. " Staff entrance'll be closed by now."

And again in the lift she had it. This extraordinary feeling of twoness. Of twoness that was somehow oneness. It was as though she and Mr. Rammell had been on terms of intimate confidences all their lives. When the lift reached the ground floor Mr. Rammell had to nudge her before she even noticed.

Outside the Downe Street entrance, however, Marcia drew back.

It was raining. Real heavy stuff. As though Covent Garden had moved up on Bond Street.

Marcia looked hard at the big Rolls-Royce parked opposite the doorway.

" Do . . . do you think someone could possibly get me a taxi ? " she asked helplessly.

Mr. Rammell did not attempt any resistance. He did the simple, manly thing.

" Get in," he said. " I'll drop you."

They drove round the Park in silence. Marcia was sitting back, the rug drawn round her and her eyes half-closed. Her hand, her long pale hand with the blue veins faintly showing, lay on the broad arm-rest between them.

" I . . . I feel terribly guilty," she said, " dragging you out of your way like this. Do . . . do let me offer you a drink when we get there."

But this time Mr. Rammell was prepared.

" No, thank you," he said. " I'm late already. Must be getting along."

The car had already reached Knightsbridge before Marcia spoke again. There was barely two minutes to go.

" It's . . . it's funny it should be New York you're sending him to," she said.

" Why, what's funny about it ? " Mr. Rammell asked.

" Because I've been asked to go, too."

Mr. Rammell started.

" You mean Tony's asked you ? "

" Oh, no."

Marcia gave a little laugh.

Her laugh was noticeably better than her speaking voice. When she laughed it was low and rather husky. " An agent. It's Adler's he wants me for. They . . . they like English models over there."

The car had stopped by now. And the chauffeur was standing out in the rain ready to open the door.

" What have you told him ? " Mr. Rammell demanded.

" I . . . I haven't really decided," Marcia replied. " It's . . . it's all so difficult now."

Mr. Rammell glanced across at the small gilt clock let into the walnut woodwork of the partition. It showed six forty-five. He was certain, absolutely certain, that he was late for something. But he couldn't let matters rest where they were.

" Just a minute," he said. " We ought to discuss this together. Why didn't you tell me before."

" I . . . I didn't think of it," Marcia answered truthfully.

" When have you got to let him know? "

" To . . . to-morrow," Marcia told him. "F . . . first thing." She paused. " Well, g . . . good night. And thank you ag . . . again."

But Mr. Rammell had laid his hand upon her arm.

" Not so fast," he said. " I'll come in for a moment. We've got to get this thing settled one way or the other."

CHAPTER XXXV

THE ASTONISHING thing had happened: Mr. Bloot was beginning to come round to Fewkes Road again.

And after so long, too. It was getting on for a year now since he had last dropped in alone. There had, of course, been the formal prearranged visits. Sunday evening suppers for Gus and Hetty at the Privetts'. And too much to drink, and a lot of gelatiney fancy stuff from the local *delicatessen* for the return visits to Artillery Mansions. But even these family reunions had lapsed.

Try as she might, Mrs. Privett could not help disliking Hetty. Disliking Hetty, and despising Mr. Bloot. Particularly when at Artillery Mansions. While the other three sat round, usually with a pack of cards stacked hopefully on the table in case Chick should drop in, it was impossible to be unaware of Mrs. Privett's disapproval. She remained silent and subdued in the corner, like a book-end. With her glass untouched and the ash-tray beside her empty, she loyally remembered poor Emmie.

But nowadays it was quite like old times. The unannounced ring on the door bell. The mumbled greeting. The insatiable thirst for tea.

And the difference in Mr. Privett was enormous. Having Mr. Bloot in the house again—and unaccompanied—had made a new man of him. He was like someone in the throes of a late love-affair.

Nor was Mr. Bloot's return the only reason for Mr. Privett's high spirits. He was about to become the owner of *Daisy III*. That was what really counted. Any day now he expected to receive the post-card from Lumley's saying that she was ready. Twenty-two pounds ten to pay, admittedly. But why worry? The money was there all ready in the Post Office to meet it. That was because Mrs. Privett had refused the new sewing-machine. And more than refused it. Rejected it point blank. Her old one was quite good enough for her, she had said. A pearl among machines, in fact. They didn't even make machines like it nowadays. She had been so emphatic, in fact, that there had been nothing for it but for Mr.

295

Privett to get off at Camden Town on his way in next morning and cancel everything. Not that he had any choice in the matter. It was bad enough, Mrs. Privett had said, to have all that fruit to get through. Let alone trying to fit a convertible sofa-table-sewing-machine into the drawing-room.

And it was just as well, as it turned out. Because Mr. Hamster lost no time in sending in his bill. He did not come of the school of solicitors which allow charges to go on mounting up month after month to a final reckoning at the end of the year. Why should he? Mr. Privett's was practically the only case on his books at the moment. He spent almost every evening gloating over it. In consequence, he knew to a halfpenny where the costs stood as he came out of the Brecknock County Court. And what he knew he slammed in immediately.

The bill came as a shock to Mr. Privett. A nasty shock. When he saw how large it was he felt frightened. And disgusted. The damages, or rather four-fifths of them, amounted to forty pounds and Mr. Hamster's bill was for thirty-two ten. Apparently being knocked off a bicycle, rolled in the gutter and having a famous model racing yacht demolished in front of his eyes was worth only about seven pounds ten in the eyes of blindfold Justice.

It was Mrs. Privett who underwrote Daisy III. Seven pounds ten was still seven pounds ten, as she put it. And fifteen pounds could perfectly well be found from her dressmaking account. If it would help to get Mr. Privett out of the house on Sunday mornings, eager to go and with a sense of purpose, she reckoned that the price was, on any showing, remarkably reasonable.

2

It was the absence of a telephone in Fewkes Road that made the newly-restored visits of Mr. Bloot so exciting. Telephones are remarkably convenient. Doctors and dentists, for instance, have come to rely on them. But they are the ruination of surprise visits. Take any home that is on the telephone, and unexpected callers hardly ever occur. Take any home that isn't, and the front door bell may still mean absolutely anything.

The bell on the Privetts' door was a good loud one. And simple in construction. It was screwed straight on to the back of the panel.

When you pressed the little china button outside, the whole thing sprang to life right under your finger-tip. It seemed to explode.

Not that Mr. Bloot need ever really have touched the thing at all. He had a naturally massive tread. Mr. Privett was usually aware of his approach as soon as he reached the metal drain-cover at the bottom of the front step.

It was like that this evening. A dull rumble outside like distant summer thunder, and Mr. Privett looked up from his paper.

" That'll be Gus," he said.

There was a pause. Then came the harsh *whirr-rurrk* as the bell mechanism unwound itself.

Mrs. Privett looked up, too.

" I'll put a kettle on," was all she said.

And it was needed. As soon as Mr. Privett saw his friend he could tell that there was something wrong. Mr. Bloot didn't look at all himself to-night. His collar had escaped altogether from the collar stud at the back. And below his right eye was a patch of angry redness as though he had bumped into something.

Mr. Privett stood there, staring.

" What's happened to your——? " he began.

But he got no further. Mr. Bloot raised his forefinger and placed it vertically across his lips.

" Ssssh! " he said. He glanced over his shoulder for a moment and added, almost in a whisper: " Later."

It was then that Mr. Privett became seriously alarmed. Large as Mr. Bloot was, he tried to put his arm right round him.

" Better come in here, Gus," he said. " Then we shan't be disturbed."

It was cold in the little sitting-room. Mr. Privett shivered as they went in. But Mr. Bloot did not seem to notice. He was breathing so hard that he might have run all the way there. He sat down heavily, collapsed almost, into the arm-chair by the fireplace.

" Ah'm all raht," he said. " Just shaken up a bit."

Mr. Privett took a small chair opposite. Then he leaned forward to pat his friend reassuringly on the knee. As he did so, he noticed to his surprise that Mr. Bloot was even more dishevelled than he had realised. On both feet, his bootlaces were undone nearly the whole way down.

" Sit back and take it quietly," Mr. Privett advised. " Eileen's making us some tea."

But, for once, Mr. Bloot did not respond. Not even to tea. He was too much consumed by his own secret thoughts.

" Take it quahtly," he repeated bitterly. " Take it quahtly. How d'you lakh——? "

It was Mrs. Privett who interrupted him. She opened the door and stood there in the doorway, not attempting to come in.

" Are you two trying to catch your deaths of cold? " she demanded. " It's like an ice-box in here."

She broke off because, now that she could see him properly, the sight of Mr. Bloot amazed her.

" What on earth have you been doing to yourself? " she asked.

Mr. Privett winced at the sheer callousness of the question. He had noticed many times before that Mrs. Privett seemed to have simply no idea how sensitive Mr. Bloot really was.

" Eileen! " Mr. Privett said sharply.

But he need not have bothered. Mr. Bloot had risen to his feet.

" Ah'm all raht. Ah'm all raht," he repeated.

He went across and stood in front of the small oval mirror that hung above the bamboo side-table. The light always had been bad there. Mr. Bloot had to crane right forward in order to see anything. And even he seemed to be surprised by what he saw. He refixed his collar. Flattened down his hair. Rubbed the back of his hand reflectively across the sore patch beneath his eye.

But that was not all. From where Mr. Privett was standing he could see that Mr. Bloot's lips were moving all the time. He seemed to be rehearsing something.

Then he turned round.

" Ah'm sorry if Ah upset you, Ahleen," he said. " Ah've 'ad er naccident. That's all it is. Just er naccident."

Mrs. Privett came forward. She was peering closely.

" You'd better have something on that cheek," she said. " When did it happen? "

The question obviously caught Mr. Bloot by surprise. The period of silent rehearsal started up again.

" On the bus," he said at last. " Coming dahn the stairs. Ah slipped." He paused and gave a not very convincing little laugh. " Maht have been really nahsty. Maht have been fatal." He paused

298

again and added, unnecessarily: " Yes, that's raht. On the bus. Coming dahn the stairs. Er 27 bus."

Mrs. Privett, however, was no longer listening. Either that, or not believing.

" You come in the other room where it's warm," she said. " And for goodness' sake do your shoes up or you'll be falling down again."

It was fortunate that they had some of the dark cherry fruit cake that Mr. Bloot liked. He ate two large slices. And ate them ravenously. As though he had been without food all day. But it was the tea that saved him. By the third cup, his naturally rather florid colour had returned. And a familiar light perspiration broke out across his forehead.

" Stoopid of me, wasn't it? " he kept saying at intervals. " Lakh er chahld. Falling dann stairs. At mah age."

As soon as Mr. Bloot had finished his tea, Mrs. Privett left them. The skin on Mr. Bloot's cheek was not actually broken. And she did not press the offer of first-aid. She could tell that the two men wanted to be alone together. And the sooner she went the sooner she would be able to get Mr. Privett's full report afterwards.

" Good night, Gus," she said.

" Good naht, Ahleen," he replied. " Thank you for everything."

It was getting on for eleven o'clock by now. Mr. Privett was leaning forward. Right on the edge of his chair, in fact.

" You mean this isn't the first time? " he asked. " She's actually hit you before? "

" Yurss," Mr. Bloot admitted. " Raht from the start. In the yotel. That was the first tahm. It wasn't mah fault, either. Ah didn't know how much she mahnded."

" Minded what? "

" Abaht mah shoes. Mah black ones. She prefers brahn on holidays."

" Was that all? "

" It was quaht enough," Mr. Bloot told him. " Lakh to-naht."

" What did happen to-night? " Mr. Privett asked.

" Nothing as you maht say. Absolutely nothing. She asked if Ah'd lakh to go to er cinema and Ah said ' no.' Then she asked if Ah'd lakh to play bezique with her and Ah said 'no' again. Ah was sitting there quahtly reading mah bird magazine when she flew at me. But Ah controlled myself. Ah didn't even answer. Ah put mah hat on and came round. Ah didn't even wait to do up mah boots."

Mr. Privett shook his head.

" Would you believe it," he said.

" She's lakh that," Mr. Bloot replied. " Sudden. And impeturous. A real woman. Not lakh mah Emmie." Mr. Bloot let out a deep sigh in which despair, nostalgia and the fading relics of admiration were all mingled. " Ah've been black and blue, Ah tell you. Only I haven't let on. Not to a soul. Not until nahw. It's been a matter of prahd."

" What are you going to do? " Mr. Privett asked.

Mr. Bloot sighed again.

" Injoor it, I suppose," he said. " Just injoor it."

There was silence between them for a moment. Mr. Privett sat back and stared gloomily downwards at his feet. His whole heart went out to Mr. Bloot in his misfortune. He wondered if he ought to offer to make him some more tea. Cut another slice of the dark cherry fruit cake. Then a faint sound made him glance up again. For a moment Mr. Privett could not believe it. But, when the sound was repeated, there could be no mistake. Mr. Bloot had broken down. He was in tears.

" Don't take on so," Mr. Privett said gently. " Things'll turn out all right. You see if they don't."

But Mr. Bloot was past comforting. He was crying quite openly by now. Handkerchief up to his eyes, and everything. His voice in consequence sounded sniffly and strangulated.

" It's not me Ah'm thinking of," he replied at last. " Ah can take care of mahself. It's Billy."

" Billy? "

" One of mah budgies. She 'ates 'im, Ah tell you. Yurss, ackshually 'ates 'im." Mr. Bloot paused long enough to wipe away a tear that was trickling slowly down his cheek. " Ah feel guilty leaving 'em. For fear of what might 'appen."

Mr. Privett was leaning forward again by now.

" Such as what? " he asked.

This time, however, Mr. Bloot could not answer immediately. He was struggling with emotions that were too deep for words. He blew his nose loudly before he could even attempt to speak.

300

"Said she'd give 'im to the cat," he blurted out suddenly. " Let the cat 'ave mah Billy if Ah didn't stop messin' abaht with 'im." There was another pause. Another paroxysm. " Mah Billy," he repeated. " Three Firsts and a mention. It'd be murder. That's what it'd be. It's drahving me raht aht of mah mahnd."

" She'd never do it," Mr. Privett assured him. " Never. She's only jealous."

" Ah know," Mr. Bloot replied. " Jealousy's a very terrible thing. She watches me. There's er crool streak in her somewhere. Er nard, crool streak." Mr. Bloot paused again, his shoulders heaving. " If anything 'appens to Billy," he went on, " Ah shall do something desprit. That's what Ah'm afraid of. Something desprit."

By now, Mr. Privett was rocking backwards and forwards in his chair in sheer misery. In the last quarter of an hour, he had grown to hate Hetty. Hate her bitterly. For being so horrible to Gus. For holding out threats to little Billy. Then, suddenly, he saw it all quite clearly. It was the voice of true friendship that was speaking.

" Why not have him here? " he said. " Bring him round cage and all. Just till it blows over."

As he said it, he wished that there were a spare bedroom in Fewkes Road. Then he could have invited Gus to come as well.

But Mr. Bloot was too much bowed down by the sheer misery of things even to remember to be polite.

" It isn't only the cage," he said. " It's the company. They're like little oomans. They fret if they're with strangers. Ah've 'ad Billy since the egg . . ."

He broke off for a moment and looked at his watch. It showed just after eleven-thirty. A flicker of apprehension, of fear almost, passed across the face of Mr. Bloot.

" Well, back to the fray," he said wearily. " Back to the fray. Ah'd better see what's 'appening."

It was after midnight by now. The lights were out in the front bedroom. But Mr. and Mrs. Privett were still talking.

" I told you so," Mrs. Privett had just said. " I knew the sort she was the first time I set eyes on her."

But Mr. Privett's thoughts had been racing on ahead of her.

" What about over by the dresser? " he asked. " In the corner. Out of the draught. Billy'd be all right there. He'd see Gus as soon as he came in."

3

The other person who was glad that Mr. Bloot had resumed his visits was Irene. It made things easier for her.

For some time now, the friend from Classical Records and her tall silent brother, Ted, had been coming round to Fewkes Road on Sundays. They were regulars. And, even when Classical Records herself couldn't make it, Ted came along without her. Mr. Privett raised no objections. He found Ted a most agreeable young man. Polite. Respectful. And obviously very much attached to Irene. Even Mrs. Privett was prepared to accept him. She liked the way he got up and opened doors for her. And it was useful having someone for Mr. Privett to talk to while she and Irene washed up together. But she did draw the line at leaving Ted and Irene alone together. She also disliked the idea of young people spending all their time in cinemas. In consequence, there had been a whole succession of Sunday evenings when Ted and Irene just sat.

It was Mr. Bloot who settled that. He filled up things so. With him in the one really comfortable arm-chair, there was no room for the young people. And no future, either. Mr. Bloot had only a limited number of topics of conversation. But he believed in going over them. There was some sort of trigger mechanism that meant that, in the same room and with the same company, he went over them all in the same order. On the third Sunday when they had heard Mr. Bloot's views on women in the police force (against), Socialism (against), young men with beards (against) and the smaller cage birds (in favour), Mrs. Privett recognised that she would have to let Irene escape from it. The only hold that she maintained was in telling Ted that he mustn't bring her back later than ten-thirty.

As a result, Sunday evenings were now perfectly heavenly. Her good work done, Classical Records had obligingly fallen out completely. It was just Ted and Irene. And they set off for the cinema together almost as soon as tea was over.

Not that they were alone when they got there. The local Odeon was full of other Teds and Irenes all sheltering from their own homes. It was warm. Discreetly dark. Deeply upholstered. No sharp corners anywhere. And it smelt nice. There were ash-trays for smokers within arm's reach. And, for the hungry and thirsty, there was popcorn, orangeade and ice-cream brought politely to the bedside. All life's needs had been provided for. Even the route to the lavatories was indicated by illuminated signs. And on the screen in front a film of some kind was showing.

Irene sank down into the deep arm-chair that Lord Rank had provided. Ted carefully rolled up his raincoat and thrust it under the companion-piece divan alongside hers. Then he reached out his hand. And hers was ready for him. They had been holding hands for the past three Sundays now.

At first, it had been no more than a loose, lingering contact. Like a handshake that wouldn't let go. Now it was the real thing. Fingers laced. And palms pressed closely together. It was hot. It was sticky. But it was what they were there for. And it was what they wanted.

It had come as an entire surprise to both of them to find how much they wanted it. For a start, it wasn't a bit like Ted. But a most distinct change had come over him lately. He was still keeping up his bookkeeping and accountancy classes in the evenings. And in a sense they seemed more than ever important now. But his mind was no longer really on them. It kept drifting towards life insurance. And impossible house mortgages. And domestic budgets worked out on the backs of envelopes.

Irene had changed, too. She was still an actress at heart. But somehow she never managed to get to the theatre. Hadn't been to one for months, in fact. That was because of Ted's evening classes. She didn't really enjoy going anywhere without Ted nowadays. But what was even stranger was that she didn't even read plays nowadays. Couldn't really settle down to them. When she tried, her mind kept straying off and wondering whether Ted got enough to eat on the evenings when he dashed off to the Institute. And how he would manage, supposing he felt ill. And who looked after his socks and things. . . . Fry and Rattigan and Priestley and Anouilh might simply have been living on pensions for all the support she was giving them.

Even on Saturdays they didn't go to theatres. It was only just lately—during the past month—that they had been seeing each other on both days during the week-ends. But after being cooped up in Rammell's all the week, Ted needed exercise. Lots and lots of it. Walking was the kind he principally fancied. And it was because it was hard to keep up with him otherwise that she had begun to take his arm.

There is something about arm-taking that is important. More important than cinema hand-holding. It is public. With hand-holding, usherettes don't see. But with arm-taking, everybody notices. Also, it is part of the training. There is nothing like arm-taking for reminding you that you can't just go on going your own way any longer.

Irene was used to it by now. Arm-in-arm, she and Ted had tramped over half London. There was one regular route that they took. It started off from Bond Street across Grosvenor Square into Hyde Park. Then over the bridge at the Serpentine. And it finished up at a small tearoom in South Kensington. By the end of it, Ted was beginning to feel nicely loosened up. All ready for the walk home again, in fact. And Irene was wondering what sort of shoes a girl could buy that would stand up to it. Something that would do for pavements. Gravel. Wet grass. Tea shops. Everything.

It was getting on for ten-forty-five when she and Ted came out of the Odeon. That in itself was promising. Mr. Bloot rarely stayed later than eleven. And it was important that Mr. Bloot shouldn't be there to-night. Ted and Irene had something that they both wanted to say to Mr. and Mrs. Privett.

But that was as far as agreement went. Left to herself, Irene would have done it the simple way. Just said: " Oh, by the way, Ted's asked me to marry him. And I've said ' yes.' So we're engaged. And we're going to get married."

But Ted was obstinate. Mulish. Adamant. He adopted a know-better, take-it-from-me kind of manner that she found maddening. He might have been going round getting engaged all his life he was so absolutely certain how the thing should be done.

" I'm only doing what's right," he told her. " After all, he is your father."

" Well, I think it's silly," Irene answered. " And there's no need for it. It isn't as if they didn't like you."

Ted shook his head.

"It isn't only just a matter of liking," he said. "This is different."

"Oh, well, have it your own way then," she replied. "Only don't blame me if anything goes wrong. My way it couldn't have."

She had removed her arm from his while they were talking. They were now walking along side by side like strangers.

"You . . . you don't think there will be any objections, do you?" Ted asked suddenly. "I mean about not having enough money, or anything."

But Irene was maddened with him. Really furious. She'd no idea he could be so stupid. That he cared so little for her feelings. She had planned everything. Got it all ready for him. And he had deliberately spoilt it.

She did not turn her head as she answered.

"That's your affair," she said. "Better ask him. Then you'll find out."

They had reached Fewkes Road by now. The light was still burning in the front room. And Ted followed her up the path without speaking. It was not until they were inside the house that she noticed how nervous he was. He stood there, with his back to the front door, pulling at his tie and going through a kind of dry, swallowing action in his throat. He looked grim. And awkward. For no reason that she could explain, she found herself loving him again.

She went up and kissed him.

"Don't worry," she said. "It'll be all right. I know it will."

His arms went round her so tightly that he left her breathless.

"It's got to be," he said.

They were still embracing when the door of the sitting-room opened. Mrs. Privett came out into the hall.

"That you, Ireen?" she asked.

Irene broke away hurriedly.

"We're back, Mum."

There came a gulp from close beside her.

"Good evening, Mrs. Privett."

"Good evening, Ted."

Irene went up and took Mrs. Privett by the arm.

"Come along, Mum," she said. "Ted's got something he wants to say to Dad."

"Then tell him to go in," Mrs. Privett said. "Dad's only got Gus with him."

". . . well, why didn't you say so before?" Mr. Privett was asking. "Then he'd have left us sooner. He's not the kind to stay if he isn't wanted."

He felt rather resentful as he said it. Up to that moment he'd always liked Ted. Even looked forward to seeing him. But this was rather overstepping it. He'd practically ordered Mr. Bloot out of the room just now.

"I had to see you alone," Ted explained. "It's private."

Mr. Privett stood in front of the fireplace regarding him. He'd never noticed before what an extraordinarily jumpy kind of young man Ted was. He was fiddling with a button with one hand. And tugging at the lapel of his coat with the other. And his feet weren't still either. He was shifting around all the time like a boxer.

"Well, what is it?" Mr. Privett asked.

There was a pause. Ted swallowed hard again.

"Irene and me want to get married."

"You want what?"

Mr. Privett had heard perfectly. But he had to play for time. He had guessed for some time how things were going. Known that sooner or later it might come to this. But he had always put the thought clean out of his mind. Never once really faced up to it.

"To get married," he heard Ted saying again.

There could be no further avoiding it. He couldn't pretend that he hadn't heard this time either. He would have to say something.

"Ireen's only eighteen remember," he said reproachfully.

More fiddling. More swallowing. So far as Mr. Privett was concerned this was another habit of Ted's that he had never noticed before. The boy gave a distinct, audible gulp every time he attempted to say anything.

"I know," Ted answered. "That's why we . . . we'd like to be engaged first."

Mr. Privett considered for a moment. There seemed to be a possible let out here.

"I see," he said. "You want to get engaged."

Ted gave another gulp.

"That's right, sir," he replied. "Get engaged."

306

He was glad that he'd remembered to say " sir." It was one of those things that were expected at such a moment. But it hadn't really helped. Instead, it seemed rather to have embarrassed Mr. Privett. To Ted's surprise, Mr. Privett seemed to be nervous, too. Rattled. He kept pulling at his watch chain. Moving from one foot to the other.

"How long have you known each other?" he asked at last.

"Nearly six months, sir. You remember.. At the last staff dance."

"The staff dance," Mr. Privett repeated dully. "Oh, yes. The staff dance. I suppose it must be about six months."

"Yes, sir. Nearly."

He paused.

"Does Ireen know you're asking me?"

"Yes, sir."

"Oh, she does."

"Yes, sir."

It wasn't getting any easier for either of them. Indeed, for Mr. Privett it was getting appreciably harder every moment. He couldn't go on asking questions for ever. Eventually he would have to say something. Be decisive. In the meantime, he wasn't going to be rushed by this nervous young man opposite.

"And does she want it?" he asked.

"Yes, sir."

Mr. Privett paused.

"Well . . ." he began.

But he got no further. The door opened. And Irene stood there. She was wearing the excited, eyes-shining expression that he remembered from the time when she had been quite a little girl. She looked younger than ever this evening. So young that it didn't seem possible that this tall, gulping, tie-pulling young man was seriously thinking of getting married to her.

"What did you tell him, Dad?" she asked.

Mr. Privett began pulling at his watch chain again.

"We hadn't quite got there yet," he admitted. "I was just . . . just asking him things."

Then Mr. Privett looked up. Over Irene's shoulder he could see Mrs. Privett. And beyond Mrs. Privett glowed the pink, moon-like face of Mr. Bloot.

307

" Maht Ah be the first . . ." he began.

Mr. Privett had just come back from the bathroom. Mrs. Privett was already in bed. She was sitting up rubbing some cream into her hands.

" Whatever were you two talking about all that time? " she demanded.

" I was asking him things," Mr. Privett told her. " About him. And Irene. About both of them."

" What sort of things? "

" About how long they'd known each other."

" And what else? "

" Whether Ireen wanted it."

Mrs. Privett put the cream jar down with a thump.

" Of course, she wants it. Otherwise he wouldn't have been asking you."

" I had to make sure," Mr. Privett replied. " It's very important."

" I know it's important. That's what I've been saying to you. What are his prospects? "

" You mean how much he earns? "

Mrs. Privett nodded.

" There wasn't time to ask," he told her. " I was only just getting round to it."

" Well, he gets eight-ten at the moment," Mrs. Privett continued. " And it'll be twelve if he gets the Counting House job. But that isn't certain. So they'll have to wait. About three years, I told her. Till she's twenty-one. And, of course, there's the commission. That's another thirty pounds."

" How d'you know about that? " Mr. Privett demanded.

" I asked Ireen."

" When? "

" While he was in there talking to you."

Mrs. Privett went over to the window and pulled the Venetian blind half-way up.

" It all came so sudden," he said. " I wasn't really prepared. I like him all right myself. But I didn't know how you'd take it if . . ."

But Mrs. Privett interrupted him.

" Do you think I'd have let him go on coming here if I hadn't thought he was suitable?" she asked. "It's been standing out a mile. She could have done better. But she hasn't. That's all there is to it."

"Ted's a nice boy," Mr. Privett said slowly.

"Well, I haven't said he wasn't, have I? All I said was our Ireen could have done better."

Mr. Privett went back across the room to put the light out. Instead of feeling pleased about Irene's engagement, he felt miserable. Utterly miserable. Miserable about everything. About how inadequate he'd been. And about how little Ted earned. And about how it might have been young Tony Rammell himself if only Mrs. Privett herself hadn't stopped it. And about the way Mrs. Privett kept on reminding him that Irene could have done better. She was exhibiting a kind of heartlessness that left him speechless and aghast.

When he reached the switch, however, Mrs. Privett stopped him.

"Don't put the light out," she said. "I'm just going through to Ireen. I never kissed her good night properly."

CHAPTER XXXVI

THE CHAIR in which Mr. Rammell was sitting was quite the wrong shape. Modern. Undeniably modern. And undeniably wrong.

Built of thin struts of some dark, sinister-looking wood, the seat was so close to the ground that Mr. Rammell could hardly see over his knees. The arms, too, were low. So low that Mr. Rammell wondered what to do with his own arms. Even the striped, zebra-ish cushions were hostile. Stuffed with a kind of rubber-sponge material they fought back again when pressed against.

The table alongside matched the chair. Same wood. Same height. The entire suite might have been made by pygmies for other pygmies. And the table itself was of an extraordinary near-oval shape that was scarcely a shape at all. Mr. Rammell had an uneasy feeling that it was still forming.

But the drink that stood on it was reassuringly normal. He had seen to that himself. The amount of soda was just exactly right. And even with the silly furniture, and the pictures that might have come out of the same factory as the chair and table, Mr. Rammell had to admit that he somehow felt relaxed. Relaxed. Rested. And refreshed.

It had been the same on the last two occasions when he had visited the flat. Each time a strange guilty sensation of complete freedom had come over him. Of holiday, almost. He had kept telling himself that it was an error of judgment on his part to have set foot in the place at all. It was that damn' rain that had been responsible. But for the rain he would never have had Marcia in the car with him. And if they hadn't shared a car he would certainly never have gone to her flat. Not even have considered it. But it hadn't proved all loss. Not by any means. It is always a ticklish business discussing intimate family affairs against an office background. And he was glad to have avoided it.

In the ordinary way, of course, he would simply have got Marcia to come round to Eaton Square. But that would have involved Mrs. Rammell. And keeping Mrs. Rammell out of it had always been his chief thought.

It was interesting, too, from his standpoint to see how a girl like Marcia really did live. On the whole, it was pretty much what he had expected. White paintwork. A trace of perfume and cigarette smoke in the air. Copies of *Vogue* and *Harper's Bazaar* left lying around. Drinks on a side table. And photographs of Marcia herself, heaven knows how many of them, stuck up everywhere. Dimly he wondered how she could afford it all. And then he remembered the Outside Activities clause in the Staff Agreement. That he reckoned must be bringing her in quite a packet. Probably doubling up, in fact. And perqs on the side, of course. That goddam-awful chair and table, for instance. Given to her by one of the agencies probably.

He glanced at his watch. If he had been at home at this moment, for instance, he would have been changing into a black tie ready to be dragged off to dinner with the Burnetts.

Avoiding the Burnetts was always its own reward. But there was another reason altogether why he was glad that he was not going. That was because he and Mrs. Rammell were not yet probably on speaking terms. They were out of the vulgar, recriminatory phase. Out of the silence phase, too. They were now in the third stage of the cycle, the ghastly politeness phase. Mr. Rammell held doors open for her. She thanked him. He passed her things. She thanked him. He asked if she had had a tiring day. She thanked him. He inquired after her neuritis, her slipped disc, her sinus. She said, "Better, thank you." As conversation goes, however, even a Trappist couldn't have pretended that it added up to very much.

But it wasn't simply to avoid the Burnetts that he had come. There was still some tidying up to be done on his own account. And he was not a man who liked leaving things half done.

" So we can take it that you've put New York right out of your mind, can we? " he asked.

Marcia was seated just opposite. Perched half on, half off, the zebra-striped divan that had evidently come out of the same herd as the cushions. She was listening intently.

" Oh, definitely," she said at last.

Mr. Rammell took another sip from his glass. Then he went on being business-like.

" You saw Mr. Preece, didn't you? " he asked. " The new arrangement quite satisfactory? "

Mr. Rammell was getting to understand Marcia by now. That was why he wasn't concerned when at first she made no reply at all.

He knew that if he waited long enough it would eventually come. "Yes, thank you," she said after an unusually long pause. "Thank you."

It had been specially difficult having to answer two questions at once. But, really, there had been more to it than that. It was blissy of course having a new contract. Just when she had begun to wonder whether the old one would ever be renewed at all. And Rammell's had been more than generous. Absolute sweeties, in fact. There was no denying that. But there were still all those horrid old debts of hers. The ones that she knew that Mr. Bulping would have taken care of if only she'd remembered to ask him in time. And God knows that no one could accuse her of being mercenary. She had never once even mentioned money to Tony. Theirs had remained a boy and girl friendship right the way through.

The memory of it brought a tightness to her throat. She would simply never have believed that he could be so callous. There had been that one completely dreamy, swoony evening when he had come to the flat to say good-bye. He had even remembered to bring a bottle of champagne with him. And there had been that last telephone-call actually from the airport itself. But, after that, nothing. Silence. Simply silence. Not even a post-card of the Manhattan skyline. She could see now how foolish she had been ever to squander so much love on him. He would never know, could not possibly imagine, how much she had really been prepared to give. It was as though they had been separated throughout by one of Rammell's own thick plate-glass windows.

And there was, she had to admit, something of the same strange remote quality in Mr. Rammell. As though he were an emotion short somewhere. Born without the complete set of feelings. He had behaved marvellously. Quite marvellously. She would have been the first to admit that. Wouldn't any father have been worried about a boy who was so obviously just drifting until Marcia had rescued him? And now that it was all over, now that she had explained everything, she could tell how relieved he was. How pathetically grateful. Like a dog that had just escaped punishment. But he was so cold. So terribly cold. Even now, after everything that had happened, if she were to go up to him and put her arms around him, explain that she knew everything that was in his mind, he would only misinterpret it.

And it only made it all the harder for her because she could tell how lonely and miserable at heart Mr. Rammell really was. Facts like that cannot be concealed from a woman. What Mr. Rammell needed more than any man whom she had ever met was someone to cherish him. Pet him. Make a fuss of him. Soothe him. Flatter him. It would have to be all one-way love, of course. She saw that. With his attitude towards life, Mr. Rammell himself could never be the lover. But did that matter? Hadn't there always been a place in this world for the kind of woman who was selfless? Dedicated? Giving?

She glanced upwards for a moment to make sure that Mr. Rammell was still there. But it was all right. He had just taken a cigar out of his case. And he was now engaged in clipping the end off. There was a degree of absorption in the job that she found deeply moving. He was so entirely self-centred. Like a child, she told herself. And gracious what an unattractive child he was. Even though he was quite important really, he looked seedy. Downright seedy. The only thing that could put him right was a holiday. Right away from Bond Street. Away from telephones. Away from everything. . . . She saw herself in some unknown spot completely off the map. Like Cornwall. Or Majorca. In quite a small sort of cottage, too. Just the two of them, with her nursing him. Literally waiting on him. Hand and foot. Fetching and carrying. Day and night. Slowly, wearily, thanklessly, building him up again. Restoring him. Making a new man out of him from the infinite reserves of her own devotion.

" Well, that's that," Mr. Rammell's voice said from a point located somewhere in space. " I just wanted to be sure that everything was all right. I've got to be going."

These moments of snap decisions were always difficult for Marcia. She knew that unless she spoke now, at once, she would lose him. Probably for ever. Then there would be no one, simply no one, coming to her little flat at all.

It was in a flash that the words came to her.

" Won't . . . won't you have another drink? " she asked.

In the matter of drinking, Mr. Rammell had frequently marvelled at himself. The weakness of his character was truly astonishing. Apparently, whether he wanted another drink or not, he simply couldn't refuse. Not that it was alcoholism. He rarely drank too much. It was merely that he automatically accepted.

Which was why he was still there. The time was now after eight-thirty. At this rate, he'd be there the whole evening. Either waiting for Marcia to say something, or wondering what to make of it when she had said it. Admittedly, it was restful. But it was also indescribably dull. "The moment I've finished this drink I must be on my way," he told himself.

The pile of long-playing records caught his eye.

" You musical? " he asked.

Marcia raised her eyes. Her deep violet eyes. They met his for a moment.

" Definitely," she answered.

She got up as she said it and moved slowly over to the machine. There was a record already on the turntable. She switched it on. Then she sat herself down again on the edge of the divan wearing her far-away expression. The one that Tony had always loved so much.

But this time she wasn't thinking of the tiny cottage where, for Mr. Rammell's sake, she would gladly, oh, so gladly have been wearing down her fingers to the bone. Instead she kept remembering the bleak, unhappy present. The last lot of photographs from *The Tatler*, for instance, that had come out all wrong because the studio had changed her make-up. The bill for the chair that Mr. Rammell was sitting in, and for the horrible little table beside it. What the dentist had said last time about having to crown it because ordinary stopping wouldn't work any longer. The fact that her mother's postal order was overdue again . . .

" Turn it off," Mr. Rammell's voice said quite distinctly.

Marcia moved just as slowly back to the machine. She turned the switch. The automatic arm lifted, swung clear and ingeniously stowed itself away. The room, to Mr. Rammell's relief, became entirely restful once more.

" Sure you don't mind? " he asked.

" Definitely not." Marcia assured him.

And then, as she turned, he saw that Marcia was crying. Not openly. Noisily. Nothing spectacular. It was simply that her eyes were moist. She was holding a handkerchief up to them.

" What's the matter? " Mr. Rammell demanded.

" Nothing," Marcia told him. " Really it's nothing. Nothing that I could explain."

314

Mr. Rammell, all knees and elbows, struggled up out of his chair and came across to her.

" I want you to know how much I appreciate the way you've been taking all this," he said slowly. " If there's anything else I can do . . ."

" Thank you," Marcia replied huskily.

" Well, is there? "

Marcia raised her face again. Her lower lip was trembling. How could she explain, how could she possibly explain, that she was crying only because she had just remembered that she had put that record on for Tony? Left it in the machine so that she could simply turn the switch the moment she heard him ring. That was weeks and weeks ago by now. And she hadn't had the heart to go near the damn' thing ever since.

" Well, is there? " She heard Mr. Rammell's words again.

" N . . . no, really. Please don't ask me. You wouldn't understand."

She was crying quite openly by now. A large tear formed itself in the corner of her eye and began to trickle down her cheek. Mr. Rammell looked at it fascinated. He had never watched a tear in live close-up before. Come to that he had never watched Marcia herself in live close-up before.

And now that he did so he was startled. The leading model look had disappeared completely. She seemed such a little girl. It was like having a limp, unhappy child standing there. Instinctively he put his arms out to her. And automatically she came into them.

Marcia could tell at once how pure the embrace was. And, really, she rather loved him for it. It was so obvious that he had never properly held any other woman before. He didn't know even the elementary things, like where to put his hands, and about not breathing down her neck. It was all as impersonal as if he had been comforting a sad aunt. Merely friendly. Nothing more. But even that was something. In her present deprived state it was wonderfully reassuring to have a shoulder again. Any shoulder. Just something to lean on. Something that smelt woollen. And cigarry. And male.

Because it seemed, even to Marcia, that her head had been there for a long time, and because nothing very much seemed to be

315

happening, she raised her face to his. Mr. Rammell kissed it just as she knew he would. It was a paternal, affectionate sort of kiss somewhere right up on the cheekbone. She started to move away from him.

" I . . . I'm sorry I was so . . . so silly," she began.

But Mr. Rammell checked her. He reached out and took hold of her hands. They were slim, delicate hands. The only thing that Mr. Rammell could feel was the large costume-jewellery ring that she was wearing. And it was the simple fact of Marcia's childlikeness and fragility that moved him. She seemed so completely defenceless. Unprotected. Without any armour against life at all. And at the very moment when he was telling himself that it was his duty—yes, his duty—to provide protection, to stand between her and the world, he pulled her roughly to him. She offered simply no resistance at all. But, by now, Mr. Rammell was conscious only of the fact that if there had been any resistance he would have overcome it. Holding Marcia in a close and suffocating bear hug he started to kiss her with a sense of conquest and possession that astonished him.

When he paused for a moment—and it was purely to catch his breath—Marcia spoke. This was one of the few moments in life when Marcia had never been at a loss for words. Suddenly, it all seemed so easy. So natural.

" Darling," she said. " Darling."

The effect of the words, however, were greater than she had anticipated. That was scarcely her fault, however. She was not to know that she was saying them to someone who had not heard them addressed to him personally for over quarter of a century. Mr. Rammell responded. And he responded violently. He began kissing her again.

It was wonderful, of course. Quite wonderful. To think that on their third meeting—because all the other fifteen years simply didn't count—he should have come to care so much. In the ordinary way she would have been ready to stand there in his arms for ever. But somehow it seemed so pointless. So silly, even. Because it was perfectly obvious that he didn't know what to do next. So long as he could come up for air every so often, he would probably still be kissing her by midnight.

She managed at last to break away from him. They stood there regarding each other. And she knew that this was just the moment for her smile. The slow, enigmatic one. But once again her instinct helped her through. She guessed that he would need more than a three-quarter turn away smile. Would need some definite re-assurance, in fact. Something positive so that he wouldn't start saying anything ghastly like, "You really must forgive me. I'm afraid I was just carried away."

Marcia had known what it was to have that said to her. And it was horrible. Short of being vulgar and clinging, she had never known how to be able to start things up again.

But this time, she was prepared. She raised her eyes to his and smiled straight into them.

"Darling," she said.

And then, remembering what had happened last time, she added hurriedly: "Just . . . just look what you've done to me. I . . . I must go and p . . . put my f . . . face back on again."

It was after eleven by now. Marcia had changed into her long house-coat—the one that Mr. Bulping had given her. And she was wearing a pair of plaited-straw mules that poor darling Tony had discovered somewhere and had insisted on lavishing. The perfume, just a trace too sophisticated for purely informal occasions, had come out of Rammell's sample stores.

"You know, Marcia, you're a strange girl," Mr. Rammell said.

He uttered the words slowly and reflectively as if they meant something.

And to Marcia, they did. This was just the kind of conversation in which she could keep level. Even lead if it came to it.

"Am I?" she said slowly.

"Yes," Mr. Rammell went on. "I can't make you out at all."

This was harder. Definitely harder. For a moment nothing whatever occurred to her. Then it came back to her in a flash.

"You . . . you could try," she said.

But it was no use. She had taken Mr. Rammell out of his depths by now. He was floundering, too. But there was more to it than that. He was ill. Downright ill. If he had been at home he would have mixed himself one of his patent emergency draughts—six drops of chlorodyne in half a medicine glass of warm angostura and water. And no wonder he needed it. It had been madness, sheer madness, ever to have eaten that omelette that Marcia had insisted on making for him. Eggs were the one thing that the specialist had warned him against. And now he was paying for it.

317

Because of the twinges, the pangs, he forgot all about trying to understand Marcia. He was intent on trying to understand the furniture instead.

" Why on earth did you get this bloody awful chair and table? " he asked at last.

Marcia hesitated for a moment. Really meant to hesitate this time.

" You . . . you won't like it if I tell you," she said.

" Why not? "

He was getting sick of the whole thing by now. Wished that he hadn't asked. Apparently even the simplest thing he said got itself trapped into some kind of complicated reply.

" Because . . . because it was Tony who made me."

Mr. Rammell shifted his weight in sheer irritation. The chair in reply bounced back again.

" I thought it probably was," he said.

Marcia paused. Was this the moment? Possibly not. But it had to be said some time.

" I . . . I haven't paid for them yet," she said softly.

Mr. Rammell's reply was immediate. And abrupt.

" Well, don't," he told her.

But this was Marcia's other good subject. The one where she could keep things going for hours. The one where she really came into her own.

" That record-player over there," she said. " That's really Tony's."

Mr. Rammell thought for a moment.

" I'll have it collected," he said. " Don't worry. I'll send you another one."

Marcia raised her hands to her face. It was a quick, birdlike little gesture. Quite different from her usual slow-motion movements. And wonderfully effective if only she remembered not to use it twice in the same evening.

" Oh, but you mustn't," she said. " Really you mustn't. They cost the earth."

" I'll send you one," Mr. Rammell repeated.

Marcia drew in a long, deep breath. This was obviously it. A chance like it might not present itself again for weeks. Never perhaps.

" If . . . if you would like to give me something," she said;

318

" but . . . but only if you really mean it, I mean you don't have to because . . . because why should you? Then I wish you'd . . . but I *can't* ask you, I just *can't*—it all sounds too awful . . . but . . . but you see, if you really did send me another record-player I . . . I'd only have to . . . to sell it because I'm so . . . so overdrawn or whatever it's called at the moment. And it . . . it feels so horrible. I . . . I lie awake thinking about it."

Mr. Rammell sucked in his lips.

" Which bank? " he asked.

Marcia paused. Really paused this time. It seemed such an extraordinary question. She was still wondering what to answer when Mr. Rammell repeated it.

" Oh, Lloyd's," she replied at last. " Definitely."

But, as she said it, she realised how unfair she had been. How disloyal. Besides, she couldn't possibly afford to say anything that might upset Lloyd's Bank.

" It . . . it isn't the Manager's fault," she added hurriedly. " Really, it isn't. He's . . . he's an absolute sweetie. He doesn't mind a bit. He'd be ready to wait for ever. It's . . . it's something to do with the rules. It's . . . head office, I think he said."

Mr. Rammell clapped his hands down firmly on his knees and started the long struggle to get up.

" Tell him not to worry," he said. " Tell him I'll guarantee it."

" Guarantee it? "

" That's what I said. How much? "

This was really worst of all. Marcia had never been quick at figures. Certainly not in her head. All that she knew was that the horrible little statement from the bank simply kept on coming out in red. And the bank kept writing her letters that she couldn't bear to open. Carried them about in her handbag for days, in fact. And there were all the other things that would have made the statement so much redder if she had ever dared to write out the cheques.

" Would . . . would a hundred be all right? " she asked, adding quickly before Mr. Rammell could reply. " It's just . . . just too wonderful."

" I'll see to it in the morning," he told her.

It was obvious that Mr. Rammell wanted to get away. He seemed suddenly to have grown distant somehow. That was one of the things that Marcia hated about money. It had such a way of coming between friends.

" It's terribly sweet of you," she said vaguely. " Really, it is.
I . . ."

But it was obvious that so far as Mr. Rammell was concerned,
the evening was now over. He did not appear even to be listening.
And, when Marcia raised her face to his, it was hardly a kiss at all
that he gave her. Merely a pressure.

" Time you were in bed," he said heartlessly.

But Marcia did not go through to the bedroom at once. She
sat there, gazing romantically into the twin elements of the electric
fire. Her life past, present and future flowed through her mind in
chance, uneasy instalments. For no reason at all she remembered
the time when she had been just a little girl and had been watching
some pigeons. . . . Then her American husband came back to her.
Of all the men whom she had ever known, he was the one who used
by far the nicest kind of after-shaving lotion. . . . Next it was old
Mrs. Tutty who suddenly became so real that she might have been
in the room there with her. And Marcia knew exactly what her
mother was thinking. She was wondering when the next postal
order would be arriving. Soon. To-morrow perhaps? Next week?
The week after? Never? . . . But, like the pigeons and the American,
Mrs. Tutty did not stay for long. She faded. And in her place it
was young Tony who was there with her. . . . This was worse. Much
worse. It wasn't merely that Marcia could see him. She could *feel*
him, too. If she arched her neck ever so little, there were the backs
of his fingers passing gently backwards and forwards across her
hair. Even though she despised herself for it, she began crying. . . .
Then Tony, too, returned where he belonged, somewhere three
thousand miles away right over on the other side of the Atlantic
Ocean. And Marcia was left by herself in that top service flat off
Sloane Square with the unpaid-for furnishings. She shivered. Not
from cold, but from sheer downright loneliness.

" Oh, God," she began thinking, " I might as well be dead.
I hope Mr. Rammell doesn't forget. I could . . ."—there was a
slight stammer, an impediment, even in her thoughts—" could
mean so much to him. Even if he doesn't know it, he still needs
me. It stands out a mile. I'm what he's been waiting for. There's
so much I could do, if only he'd let me. . . ."

She didn't feel tearful about Mr. Rammell, however. Merely
miserable. It was nice about the hundred pounds, of course. But,

after that, what was there? Something lasting and permanent—
and, if she could have her way, beautiful too, perhaps? Or nothing.
Just more loneliness. And more debts. And more birthdays.
Where would it all lead to? A nervous breakdown? In a Home
somewhere? Suicide . . .

Marcia got up and began patting the cushions back into their
right shape, straightening the covers. She was humming. That
was because she had just remembered that the agent had told her
that her new picture was going to be released to-morrow. It was of
Marcia in a sun-suit. She would be on the back of all the buses.
In the Underground. On hoardings. In the newspapers. Everywhere. It would be like waking up to a new life knowing that the
sun-suit photographs would be appearing.

For the moment she had forgotten even Mr. Rammell.

CHAPTER XXXVII

THE NEWS of Irene's engagement had come as a great relief to Mrs. Rammell.

She heard of it first from Nancy. Breathlessly and eagerly imparted. And, as she listened, she felt her whole mind lightening. Not that she approved of her sister's newly-revived friendship with Mrs. Privett. On the contrary, the mere thought of it made her shudder. She winced every time she remembered. Because it only went to show what Mrs. Rammell had all those years kept on trying so hard to make herself forget—how common at heart poor Nancy really was. Common and insensitive. Any woman with real feelings would have recognised that there was only one thing that could have been done after that unfortunate chance encounter in Mrs. Rammell's own drawing-room. And that was to drop Mrs. Privett again as soon as she had rediscovered her.

But it was not of Nancy that she was thinking. It was of Tony.

She knew nothing of the Marcia affair. And with Irene out of the way, it meant that her poor, darling Tony could come home again. His exile among all those dreadful New Yorkers was no longer necessary. He could return at once to Eaton Square. And Mrs. Rammell would see to it that he could pick up again the suddenly sundered strands of his young life . . . interior decoration, ballet production, print-collecting, or whatever it was for which his starved lonely soul was craving. This time Mrs. Rammell was determined. She was ready, if necessary, to carry the issue to a straight fight with her own husband.

She was, in point of fact, particularly critical of Mr. Rammell at the moment. And more than critical. She openly despised him. Hitherto, she had felt a mild sense of obligation. Of gratitude, even. That was because—even though he had absolutely no charm, no feelings—he had at least always been generous. Whenever she had been forced to speak first at Charity Committee meetings saying that she would take a dozen seats at five guineas, or a full-page in the programme, or throw her house open for the reception afterwards, he had supported her. Financed everything. Without even asking what it was all about. Anything so long as he didn't actually have to attend it himself. It was this freedom of action on her part that had made her so dynamic, so much sought-after. It was what had brought her to the very pinnacle of patronage. And, only this morning, she had toppled. Just when the Opera Guild and the Ballet Group and the Friends of Chamber Music were all beginning to turn the corner she had suddenly been demoted. Snubbed in the only way that really matters to any lifelong Charity patroness.

The insult had appeared in all the daily papers. In the second column of the Honours' List. Just where everyone would read it. And really she had scarcely been able to believe her eyes. Because the husband of her own Appeals Secretary, the insignificant little Mrs. Tom Davey, who always attended meetings carrying a small limp notebook like a typist's, had actually been knighted. For political services, too. It was unbearable. Even though Mr., so soon to be Sir Tom, Davey was a shoe manufacturer in quite a large way of business, wholesale as well as retail, Mrs. Rammell could not stand for it. It showed how hopelessly, irretrievably, her own husband had failed her. If she had said it once, she had said it ten thousand times that he ought to have asked more politicians to the house. Not only Ministers. Junior Ministers as well. Parliamentary Private Secretaries, too. The whole run of them. And what had he done? Nothing. All that he had ever thought about was Bond Street, Bond Street, Bond Street. . . . She realised now that she didn't only despise him. She hated him.

And she saw so little of him. That was another thing. Mrs. Rammell always took her breakfast in bed. Mr. Rammell, on the other hand, ate his downstairs. Naturally, he was out all day. The small luncheon parties that Mrs. Rammell gave to visiting singers, artists, dancers, choreographers, took place entirely without him. And nowadays he was scarcely ever in even during the evening. He arrived back in Eaton Square towards midnight, gave himself a final whisky and soda followed by a draught of two Alka-Seltzer tablets and slipped up silently to bed.

Just like to-night. It was after eleven already. Mrs. Rammell had long ago changed into a loose house-coat. And with her books and brochures, her magazines and folders, her Glyndebourne prospectus and her Festival Hall calendar spread around her, she was killing time waiting up for him.

She was at her most masterful, too. Felt the little electric thrills of nervous energy tingling through her. To-night she intended to get *everything* cleared up. As soon as she had arranged about Tony's return passage—and that immediately—she wanted to draw his attention to silly little Mrs. Davey's husband's absurdly undeserved title. Put things to rights for the future, as it were.

Even though he wasn't actually there beside her, Mr. Rammell himself wasn't far away. Only just off Sloane Square, in fact.

He was sitting as far back as he could manage—which wasn't far enough—in one of those ridiculous chairs that he disapproved of, quietly reflecting on the fact that Marcia had the most beautiful shoulders that he had ever seen on any woman. Smooth. And white. And rippling. Like a schoolgirl's. Only without any puppy-fat, of course. Just the firm, delicate bone structure showing underneath. Mr. Rammell had a particularly good view of them because Marcia had seated herself on a cushion at his feet.

He wondered dimly what thoughts, if any, were passing through that lovely smooth head of hers. As he wondered, he stroked. Gently, as one strokes a cat. And, like a cat, Marcia responded. Mr. Rammell could feel a faint, answering quiver coming back through his finger-tips.

" That's what she needs," he told himself. " Affection. Starved for it. Absolutely starved. Just love and be loved. That's her formula. Does something to her. Like rain and sunshine. Brings her out."

And as he sat there, still indolently stroking, it occurred to him that affection was what he had been in need of, too. The thought had never struck him before. But he saw it clearly enough now. Not that he would call his marriage a bad one. Or a particularly good one. Scarcely a marriage at all, in fact. No common interests. No topics of conversation. No friends in common, even. No sense of relief and relaxation when he got home.

And really it was incredibly restful just being here. Restful in an unpassionate, middle-aged fashion that completely lulled him. There were moments, of course, when it was otherwise. But were they, he had sometimes asked himself afterwards, entirely spontaneous? Or were they because the other partner had felt somehow that it might be expected? Whatever the cause they were not frequent. Not overwhelming. For the most part it was

like having a darling daughter, grown up and still entirely dedicated
to him.

The last three months with Marcia—and it was only during the
last three months that he had really come to know her at all—had
made him strangely introspective. He was now aware of emotions
that he had not previously known that he possessed. Complicated,
unfamiliar ones. Like compassion. And apprehension. And
solicitude. He woke nowadays wondering whether Marcia was
safe. Happy. Contented.

And even though she was there beside him—leaning right up
against his knees in fact—he still had to ask her.

" Everything all right, dear? " he inquired idiotically. " No
worries? "

It was another of those terrible double questions that Marcia
dreaded. But this time it was easy. There was no need even to
attempt to answer. Instead of replying, she snuggled closer to him
and pressed her left cheek lingeringly against his knee-cap.

" Anything you'd like? " he went on, snatching at the last few
crumbs of reassurance before it was time for him to go.

Marcia did not reply immediately. She turned and placed her
other cheek up against his knee. Now she was facing him.

" Only to . . . to go away somewhere," she said.

" Go away," Mr. Rammell repeated. " Where? "

" Anywhere," she replied. " Anywhere that's . . . that's right
away from here."

" How long for? " Mr. Rammell asked.

" Months and months," she told him. " For ever."

He had stopped stroking by now and was looking at her in
amazement.

" You mean you want to move? " he asked.

" I want to go away," she said again.

Mr. Rammell paused. He recognised that it would be no use
trying to rush her. This was one of those moments when she needed
to be helped along. Prompted.

" You mean somewhere like Brighton? " he asked her.

Marcia shook her head.

" Farther," she said. " Right away."

Her clear, deep eyes were staring up into his as she spoke. They
were profound, beautiful eyes. Mr. Rammell felt sure that there
was a meaning behind them somewhere.

" South of France," he suggested. " Get some sun."

But again Marcia shook her head.

" Farther," she said. " Everyone goes there."

For a moment Mr. Rammell became suspicious. He wondered whether Marcia was slowly, tortuously trying to tell him that she wanted to go to New York. To Tony. But her next remark reassured him.

" An island," was what she said. And, to explain her meaning, she added: " An island in the sea somewhere."

" You name one," he told her.

Naturally, she hesitated for a moment. She didn't want to say the wrong thing. And she had never been good at names. But it was all right this time. She had seen it written right across the beach-wear advertisements in big capital letters that were easy to read.

" Bermuda," she said.

" What would you do there? " he asked.

" I'd have you," she answered.

" You mean you want me to come along too? " he asked.

Her eyes were fixed on his more deeply than ever now.

" Of . . . of course."

Mr. Rammell took a deep breath.

" I'll see," he said.

" You . . . you promise? "

" I've told you I'll see," he said cautiously.

This was difficult again. Dreadfully difficult to put into words. But she struggled on.

" I mean you'll promise you'll see?"

" I promise."

" Then you will? "

" I'll see."

When Mr. Rammell left Marcia it was nearly midnight. He had to walk back to Eaton Square. That was because he had sent the car away long ago. There are moments when a car can be an embarrassment. The sense of freedom, of cutting loose, somehow gets whittled right down to nothing in the knowledge that the chauffeur is sitting outside timing things.

And, in any case, the walk was just what Mr. Rammell needed. It helped to clear his head. He hadn't the slightest intention of going off with Marcia to Bermuda. Or anywhere else for that matter. Indeed, as a lover he recognised that he was only somewhere in the second class. He wasn't the kind of man to do anything dramatic of that sort. Not that the idea wasn't attractive. The thought of endless sunshine and coral reefs and palm trees and . . . and Marcia of course—he had very nearly forgotten Marcia—made him feel restless and dissatisfied. Also uneasy. Because that last remark of Marcia's was just one more symptom of what he had been noticing for some time now. Marcia herself was changing. She no longer accepted things as they were. In a vague dreamy fashion she was becoming too loving. Too possessive. And that frightened him.

When he got back he went straight through to his study and poured himself a final whisky. He had just reached the pleasant moment of putting off any kind of decision until to-morrow when Mrs. Rammell came in. She looked austere, majestical, in her long house-coat. And Mr. Rammell's heart sank at the sight of her. He knew that there must be something very much on her mind if she was wandering about the house at that time.

And she began immediately. Before she had even closed the door. All in a rush. Speaking in the way in which only a distraught, agitated woman is capable.

" It's about Tony," she said. " I've got to talk to you. Now. To-night. Because I never really see you. Not to talk to properly. It's all right. He can come home again. That girl he was so fond of has got engaged to someone else. The danger's all over. He can come back straight away. I want you to cable him. Better still, speak to him. Time's quite different in New York. It's always earlier. Or later. Or something. He's sure to be up. Speak to him now. Tell him to get on to the first plane. Bring him back where he belongs. Let him *feel* we need him. . . ."

There was more of it. Much more. All in the same vein. Urgent. Impetuous. Slightly hysterical. Not that Mrs. Rammell could be blamed. She'd had it bottled up inside her all the evening. She had to say it. But it was no use. Mr. Rammell had stopped listening. Simply refused to go on hearing. He knew that it was no use trying to pacify her. Not yet, at least. That would have to come later. And when it did come, what the devil could he say?

Even if she had been quiet, reasonable, restrained, it would have been difficult to explain precisely why Tony's presence would have been quite so peculiarly awkward just at this very moment.

"The boy's all right where he is," he began quietly. "It's a wonderful chance for him. The experience . . ."

"Experience!" Mrs. Rammell's voice rose to a shrill scream as she repeated the contemptible word.

And then the worst happened. Remember Mr. Rammell was tired already. He had quite as much on his mind as Mrs. Rammell had on hers. And that last drink had been too much for him. He could feel it burning up his inside. In the result, he lost his temper. Quite suddenly he heard himself saying all the things that he had meant not to say.

"Oh, for God's sake be quiet," he shouted. "Go back to bed and leave me alone. I don't interfere with your blasted music. And don't you interfere with Tony. I don't want to see him turn into one of your long-haired kind. He's in New York. And that's where he's staying."

2

There are some people who are naturally prone to intruding. They are not usually the brash, pressing kind. Simply unfortunates who find themselves projected by Fate into situations that are better left unpenetrated.

Poor Nancy was one of these. Her re-meeting with Mrs. Privett was typical. Five minutes later and she could have saved her sister all that embarrassment. As it was, she inevitably became involved. Without any conscious effort on her part, she was now helplessly and inextricably tangled up in Mrs. Rammell's own most intimate affairs.

And Mrs. Rammell's private life was, at the moment, complicated and delicate. As a result of the last row, there was now a breach—a real breach—between herself and Mr. Rammell. If she had been seeing comparatively little of him before, she saw absolutely nothing now. They lived a parallel rather than converging existence. Mr. Rammell's business kept him out later in the evenings. At week-ends he left the house early, accompanied by golf clubs. And, in consequence, Mrs. Rammell lived her own life harder. More musicians. More sculptors. More painters. More choreographers. But still no Tony. That was where the bitterness lay. And that was why Mrs. Rammell was so implacable. So savage. She was ready to do anything. No longer cared how much it might hurt Mr. Rammell. Damage him. Ruin him. Kill him, even. He was now not a husband at all. Simply an enemy. And it was Nancy—stupid, unthinking, well-meaning Nancy—who handed her the murder weapon. Ready sharpened. Removed from the scabbard. Point outwards.

It was inevitable. Mr. Rammell had been seeing even more of Marcia. Practically every evening, in fact. And on Saturdays and Sundays, too. But he had kept her off the dangerous subject of islands. Had simply not referred to it. Whenever he had seen that fatal, far-away-from-it-all expression coming into her eyes, he had started hurriedly to talk of something else. Mink wraps, for instance. It was one mink wrap, in particular, a pale, electric blue one, that had been the cause of all the trouble. Marcia had worn it—heavily insured, of course—at a Charity Ball the previous evening and had forgotten to take it back into Bond Street the next day. She was wearing it, absent-mindedly draped round her shoulders, when Mr. Rammell arrived on the following night. And she looked marvellous, Mr. Rammell reflected. Simply marvellous. The blue of the mink, the dark violet blue of her eyes, the smooth sheen of her hair, the blackness of her dress that made her arms seem somehow whiter, more slender, all affected Mr. Rammell deeply. " My God," he thought, " that's how I'd like to have her portrait painted. Just . . . just to show people. Show 'em how beautiful she really is." But because he had never been brought up to pay compliments, didn't really know how to set about them, all that he said was, " You're looking very nice to-night, Marcia." And Marcia, knowing her line by heart, replied: " I'm glad you think so."

As she said it, she removed the mink wrap slowly, reluctantly and folded it across the end of the couch.

" I . . . I . . . shouldn't really be wearing it," she admitted. " Not now. It's . . . it's out of stock, you know."

But Mr. Rammell would not hear of it.

" Put it on again," he told her. " I like it."

It was as the pale fur went round her shoulders again, stroking her, that Mr. Rammell noticed her expression changing. Like a cat, it occurred to him: like a cat when it's chin's being tickled. She looked soft, sensuous, purry. He wanted—and this was unusual with him—to get up there and then so that he could embrace her.

But Marcia saved him the trouble. She came across to him herself, walking with the upright, faintly swaying motion of the trained model, and knelt down beside his chair. She looked lovelier than ever now that she was near him. Her forehead was faintly puckered. And her eyebrows were arched even more steeply upwards. Mr. Rammell recognised the signs. Knew that there must be something on her mind. Guessed that she was going to say something probably.

" Have . . . have you thought any more about it? " she asked him.

A little shudder of apprehension ran through him.

" About what? " he asked cautiously.

But Marcia was playing for time now. Being discreet. And tactful. The very last thing that she wanted was to appear to be rushing him.

" About seeing," she said. " You . . . you remember. You promised. Not really promised." She was pouting a little now. Looking schoolgirlish. As though ready to smile or break into tears according to the answer. " Just promised about seeing. You . . . you do remember, don't you? You did say you'd see if you could see."

Mr. Rammell paused.

" You mean about . . ." he began.

Marcia nodded. It was a smile after all. And one of her very sweetest smiles, too.

" I knew you wouldn't forget," she assured him. " I was quite sure you wouldn't. About . . . about seeing, I mean."

This was it. There was no escape from it now. Mr. Rammell braced himself.

" Well, I can't," he told her. " I have seen. And I can't. Can't get away from Bond Street. It's impossible. Absolutely impossible. Just can't be done. That's all there is to it."

He felt better when he had said it. More confident in himself. But he was totally unprepared for the effect that it had on Marcia. She covered her face with her hands as though he had hit her.

And when Mr. Rammell took her hands in his and looked down at her he saw that she was crying. Her eyes were big with tears. Real tears. The kind that go sliding down and make a mess of eye-black.

" You . . . you do mean now, don't you? " she asked brokenly. " Just now. Not . . . not never? "

"Of course not, dear," he lied to her. "It may be easier later on. But I can't at present. Not suddenly, I mean. You understand, don't you? I'll see again later."

"How . . . how much later?"

Now he was really cornered. He could feel himself sweating quietly inside his collar band.

"In the spring," he told her, adding unromantically: "After the Sales. When everything settles down again."

But this came as no comfort to Marcia. It wasn't definite enough. She was crying openly by now. Her make-up had started to run already. And her shoulders were heaving.

"It's . . . it's no use," she said. "We shan't go for ages and ages. I know we won't. And then I shall be too . . . too old."

Now she was really past consolation. The forbidden word had slipped out. And, in consequence, every little bit of her was miserable. She ached with sheer wretchedness. Putting her head down on her forearm, she wept and wept.

It was, in point of fact, the very last kind of manifestation that Mr. Rammell felt in need of. He had come, precisely as he had come on so many other nights. Not for passion. Not for sentiment. Not even for the sake of any immediately recognisable form of emotion. Simply for rest. For quiet. For relaxation. And here he was being practically blackmailed into booking a double passage to Bermuda.

He reached down and took Marcia's wrists in his. Again, as he did so, their smallness, their fragility, troubled him again

"Don't cry, darling," he said gently. "Please don't. It only upsets me, too. You know it does."

This was, as it happened, a little better than Marcia had expected. Right up to the last moment she hadn't intended to carry things so far this evening. Hadn't really meant to do more than remind him. And all the time she had been crying she had been afraid that he would be angry. Even be horrid. Possibly lose his temper, too. But the way he had taken it all was quite different. It showed that he minded. That he cared. That, even though he still didn't show it properly, her life had become part of his by now.

"I . . . I'll try not to," she promised. "It was silly of me. It's . . . it's only because I . . . I mind so much about . . . about us."

Because she was shivering a little now that the outburst, the *crisis*, was over, Mr. Rammell got up and fetched the wrap. He folded it round her shoulders rather as a parent covers up a child. And as he did so, he noticed how she gathered it around her. Snuggled down into it. Burrowed, almost. Soon only her eyes were left showing. And even these had begun to smile again.

A thought came to him.

" D'you like that wrap? " he asked.

" It's a heavenly wrap," Marcia answered.

" Care to keep it? " Mr. Rammell asked, trying to keep his voice as casual-sounding as possible. " For your own I mean."

The reply, even after making all allowances for something appreciable in the way of a time lag, did not come as soon as Mr. Rammell had expected. That was because this time Marcia was wondering what to say. Not merely how to say it. Because right up to the moment when Mr. Rammell had spoken she had still been thinking about Bermuda. And not about the mink wrap at all. Hadn't so much as hinted. Let alone asked. The idea of actually owning the mink wrap—or one just like it—had not crossed her mind since she had put it on before Mr. Rammell had arrived.

" It's a *heavenly* wrap," she repeated.

" But would you like it," Mr. Rammell demanded. " That's what I want to know. Would you like it? "

As he said it the second time, Marcia felt almost like crying again. Or laughing. Because it was all so odd and mixed up. Really, she had done nothing for it. Nothing special, that is. Except be a nuisance. She hadn't led into it. Not been extra loving. Or thoughtful. Or endearing. It had just come.

And at the realisation of what it meant—that this was love— she reached out her arms towards Mr. Rammell. Her eyes, still swimmy from the recent tears, were gazing full into his. The words she spoke were the plain, simple truth. Truth as Marcia herself saw it.

" I . . . I don't deserve it," she said.

Mr. Rammell was a business-like man. As soon as he left Marcia, he took out his little Morocco-leather notebook and made the single entry " mink-wrap." Then, relieved rather than otherwise that this was how the evening had ended, he made his way back to the Square.

But he was reckoning without Miss Winters. She was behaving in a more intense fashion than ever just lately. And she had taken to a new style of hairdressing. Instead of wearing her fringe cut square across the forehead like a neat Venetian blind, she now wore it ragged and serrated. It might have been a limp black comb. In the result, she looked distraught as well as intense.

And she was obtuse, too, when Mr. Rammell spoke to her. She stood there, obviously wondering, her large frightened eyes staring out from under the saw edge of what had been her hair.

" Note to the Fur buyer, copy to Accounts," Mr. Rammell told her. " I shall personally be buying the mink wrap worn by Marcia at the Charity Ball last Tuesday. Kindly arrange for it to be charged to my account at the bought-in price."

Mr. Rammell paused. In the ordinary way, he would have inquired the price. Even called the buyer down to see whether between them they could have discovered a flaw, a poor skin, a pulled seam—anything that might justify knocking a hundred or two off. All Mrs. Rammell's furs had been subjected precisely to that kind of scrutiny. But this was different. The one thing that Mr. Rammell wanted was to be done with it.

He looked up. Miss Winters was still standing there. Still staring.

" That's all," he said.

" Where do you want it sent? " she asked.

" Don't bother about that," he told her. " I'll attend to it."

" Will Mrs. Rammell be collecting it personally? "

" I'll let you know."

" Do you want any special arrangements about storage? "

" No," Mr. Rammell replied briefly. And to show that he had already had quite enough both of the mink wrap and of Miss Winters he repeated: " That's all."

She was back again within ten minutes, however. An efficient girl with a strongly developed sense of doom, she had run down to the Fur buyer before actually typing out the memo. Just to make sure, as she put it. And thank goodness, she had! Because the wrap wasn't anywhere in the building. Marcia should have returned it yesterday and the buyer simply hadn't done a darn thing about it.

" About that wrap," Miss Winters began, her voice taking on all the deeper voice tones of the true drama student.

" Yes, what is it? "

" It isn't there," Miss Winters told him. " But they're getting it."

333

Mr. Rammell started forward.

" What do you mean? "

" From Marcia." Miss Winters went on. " She didn't return it. But the buyer was sure it'd be all right. So she didn't do anything. She's on to it now. She's asked for it back. They're sending round to Marcia's flat for it."

" Then stop them," Mr. Rammell shouted. " Stop them at once."

Mr. Rammell paused.

" And ask Marcia to come up and see me," he said. " Now."

Marcia was charming about it. Absolutely charming. She was sure all the time that there must have been some horrible mistake, she said. But naturally when they had asked her for it, she couldn't refuse, could she? And what should she do now? Because unless Mr. Rammell did something it would go straight into storage. She wouldn't be allowed even to look at it. And she did love it so. Positively adored it. But above all things—and Mr. Rammell knew that, didn't he?—she didn't want to be a nuisance. Not the least little tiny bit. If Mr. Rammell himself hadn't suggested giving her the wrap the thought of it would never even have crossed her mind. . . .

Even with Marcia so reasonable, it still took up time. And to prevent anything else going wrong, Mr. Rammell told Miss Winters to have the wrap sent up to his own room. He would deliver it himself, he said. When all that was over, he mixed himself a glass of bismuth and water. Took one of the small, unpleasant charcoal tablets that usually seemed to do the trick. Washed his hands which somehow had become strangely sticky for so early in the morning. And got down to the routine business of the day.

On the whole, it was a rather quiet, ordinary sort of day. Sir Harry rang up twice. Once to say that he had come to the conclusion that they were wasting their time with Soft Furnishings and ought to shut the department down completely. And the second time to say that he had a scheme for enlarging it, making it something that would knock the rest of the trade for six. . . . There was the usual batch of letters to dictate. The quarterly accounts to go through. A long session with Mr. Preece about overtime and special pay. A telephone conversation with the auditors about stock write-off. Two or three callers. A twenty-five year bonus to present. An interview with the architect about the new dispatch bay in

Hurst Place. And then, after lunch, more letters. A deputation from the Staff Association about a separate rest room for the Juniors. Another session with Mr. Preece. A telephone call from Sir Harry warning Mr. Rammell that they were missing all the main chances and ought to begin opening new branches at once in places like Cheltenham, Buenos Aires, Johannesburg. . . . A long meeting with the buyers about special discounts. Preliminary discussions with a firm of business efficiency experts about electronic computors for the counting house. An emergency call from Mr. Preece about possible Union trouble on the transport side. A message—quite a brief one this time—from Sir Harry reminding him that it was no use trying to build up an overseas business unless it was all properly researched, planned, provided for . . . and what was wrong with Canada? Hadn't Mr. Rammell ever heard of Toronto? Or Melbourne for that matter? And would he please do a paper for the Board next Tuesday? . . . And then finally the day's letters to sign, fresh from Miss Winters's electric typewriter all looking very black and white and impersonal as though Mr. Rammell had bought the whole batch ready-made from a printer's

Just a normal, routine day, in fact. And now at last it was over. But not quite. Miss Winters came in. She was carrying one of Rammell's big white boxes.

" The wrap," she said. " It's been sent up. Like you told me."

Mr. Rammell felt more relaxed again by now.

" Thank you," he said. " Get it sent down to the car, would you? "

Then a sudden thought crossed his mind.

" Just a moment," he said. " Bring it here, would you? "

It was as he feared. The label on the box was addressed to Mrs. Rammell.

But already Miss Winters was speaking again. Beneath the windswept, urchin fringe, her eyes seemed wilder, more frantic than before. But it was obvious that she was doing her best to end the day on a cheerful note.

" I posted the insurance note to Mrs. Rammell," she said. " That was right, wasn't it? "

CHAPTER XXXVIII

IT WAS only Irene's second day in the Fur Salon. She had been transferred there, temporarily, because the junior assistant, Miss Anstey, had fallen sick. And suddenly at that. Pains. Shocking ones, too. Midnight call for the doctor. Appendicitis diagnosed. Ambulance at three a.m. On the operating table by nine. Off the danger-list by lunch-time. No further cause for anxiety. Nothing at all for the family to worry about. But still an awkward gap in Furs. And when a customer has screwed her courage up to the thousand-pound mark, it simply doesn't make sense to keep her hanging around until she may have cooled off.

Miss Anstey herself was tall, ash blonde, willowy. Irene, on the other hand, was small, dark, springy. There was nothing that they had in common. Except good looks. And undoubtedly of the highest order, too. Because there is no higher tribute that can be paid to an assistant in any big store than to be transferred to Furs.

Irene loved it there. It was scarcely like being in a shop at all. More like being seconded to Buckingham Palace. Holiday relief for one of the ladies-in-waiting, as it were. Thick, mossy carpet. Walnut chairs. Little, elegant tables with just the least fleck of gilt on the corners. Flowers, gladioluses mostly, in white vases on thin pedestal affairs. Mirrors that might have been doors. Discreet private rooms with still more mirrors. And silence. A plushy, expensive silence hung over everything. Even staff messages were passed on in whispers. Asking for a tape measure sounded like something out of a Shakespearian balcony scene. Only reverent, rather than romantic. All in all, the Rammell Salon might have been the inner-vestry of some well-endowed, go-ahead American cathedral.

And amid this calm, this quietness, burst the mink-wrap bomb. Fired off regardless of the consequences by Mr. Rammell, the barrage was taken up by Mr. Preece. Under the double fire, Mrs. Westlake, the buyer—fifty-five, perfectly groomed, blue hair, poised, soignée—went entirely to pieces. Called first to Mr. Rammell's room in the morning to be asked who had told her to make out an insurance note to anyone, and then whisked off to Mr. Preece's office to explain why she allowed thousand-guinea wraps to drift about London, unchecked and apparently unremembered, she became hysterical. First tears. Then laughter. And meaningless, contradictory explanations. Too many of them. Too garbled. In the end, there was nothing for it but to send Mrs. Westlake—still breathing, but by now hair all anyhow, tottery, pink-eyed—off to Welfare Supervisor, and then on to Earl's Court in a taxi.

And then, with the assistant buyer, Miss Hanson—plump, fortyish and unrufflable—in command, the astonishing sequel occurred. Marcia herself came into the Salon. Not in a rush. Dreamier than ever, in fact. Practically sleep-walking. Ever so slowly, as though along some imaginary line. At her most ethereal looking, too. A pale, inner radiance seemed to be escaping from her. She shone. And over her arm, hanging in the soft, ocean-like folds of which only the best mink is capable, was the wrap. . . .

It was something to do with the collar, she explained. Heavenly, quite heavenly as it was, it still didn't seem quite right. Not . . . not absolutely. She didn't know what was wrong. Just *felt* it. So would Miss Hanson look at it, please. Tell her whether there *was* anything. Even though looking wouldn't help, really. You had to wear it to know.

Even though Miss Hanson couldn't be ruffled, she could still stare. Marcia felt that she had never had such enormous, unbeautiful eyes fixed so intently upon her before. Or, for some reason, such unfriendly eyes. She couldn't understand it. Hostile, almost. Suspicious anyhow. Indeed, the whole atmosphere of the Salon seemed to have changed somehow.

Almost as though something had gone wrong, Marcia reflected. As though somewhere amidst the plush and the gilt and the silence someone had recently been unhappy about something.

2

It was Irene's early night. She was back at Fewkes Road at six-thirty. That was because, every Tuesday, Ted went along to his cricket practice. Love and romance, the engaged state and new responsibilities had made no difference to him. Wet or fine—even that didn't matter because the nets were under cover, anyhow—

he went along to bowl, bowl, bowl against men who knew his leg-breaks quite as well as he did and to bat, bat, bat against bowling that changed only when someone was away sick or something. But it helped to keep your eye in, he contended. And it kept the fellows together. And it kept you fit. And it wasn't expensive. And it had been on B.B.C. television. All in all, in fact, chaps who didn't belong to the Rammell Cricket Club were certainly missing something.

Irene resented the Club. Nowadays, she was living in that desperate half-life condition when to be parted from Ted even for a single evening meant misery. Wretchedness. Despair. But to-night was different. She had too much on her mind. News. And hot news at that. She wanted to tell Mrs. Privett all about it.

". . . and she went absolutely as white as a sheet, when she heard that Mr. Rammell *and* Mr. Preece both wanted to see her." She finished up breathlessly. " And then all the fuss about getting Miss Hanson to take over. But when Marcia came in actually *wearing* it. You could have knocked us all down with a feather. You never saw anything like it. Miss Hanson just stood there, staring. I thought she was going to faint, or something."

Mrs. Privett did not reply immediately.

" Does your father know? " she asked.

" I don't know," Irene answered. " I suppose so. Everybody else seemed to. You can just imagine."

" Well, until you know for certain I shouldn't say anything," Mrs. Privett told her. " It's not right. Not from someone in your position. There are some things best forgotten."

" Oh, this one won't be, I can tell you," Irene answered. " It's all over Bond Street. It is reely."

" We'll see," was all that Mrs. Privett said. " You leave this to me."

It was, in point of fact, by way of a victory for Irene that Mr. Privett no longer hung about the Staff Entrance waiting for her. But it was really Ted's doing. He was always there himself for certain. A couple of escorts would have been too many. And on Tuesday when net-practice night came round and Ted had to go off in the opposite direction, Mr. Privett had somehow got out of the habit of it.

They had to wait until nearly seven o'clock for Mr. Privett to arrive home. Irene had gone upstairs by then. And Mrs. Privett tackled him immediately. Not that she need have troubled. It was on the tip of his tongue, too. And it was worse than she had feared. Much worse. Apparently there had been goings-on for some time past.

". . . and he's out with her every night," Mr. Privett said despondently. " Dancing, you know, and all that sort of thing."

" How d'you know? " Mrs. Privett demanded.

" Gus told me," Mr. Privett replied, as though that were all the proof that could possibly be needed.

" Has Gus ever seen him? " Mrs. Privett persisted.

The question was a troublesome one. Mr. Privett didn't want to say " No." Because that would be like letting down a friend. On the other hand, he couldn't possibly say " Yes." Because, so far as he knew, Gus never went anywhere except back to Finsbury Park.

" He hears things," he said loyally. " Keeps his ear pretty close to the ground. Doesn't miss much."

" And you say he's paying for it himself? On his own personal account, I mean? "

Mr. Privett nodded.

" That's what Gus says. Got it straight from the Counting House. That's why there was such a row when they sent off the insurance note to Mrs. Rammell. And the label. You see . . ."

" I know," Mrs. Privett interrupted him. " You told me."

But Mr. Privett was still mooning over the tragedy of it.

" I do hope nothing comes of it," he said. " Nothing serious, I mean. Like a divorce. Or a scandal. Something that might get into the papers. There's never been anything like that at Rammell's. And that's really all Gus cares about. Avoiding a scandal."

" He'll be lucky," Mrs. Privett replied tartly. Then she paused. It was obvious that she was working up to something. " I still think it's wrong talking about it," she said. " It only makes it seem worse. And there may be a perfectly innocent explanation. You and Gus are as bad as the rest of them. You two ought to set an example. And you don't. When Irene comes down you go on just as though nothing had happened.

" But she was there," Mr. Privett objected.

" I don't care where she was," Mrs. Privett told him. " So far as you're concerned it's never happened. And perhaps it never will."

Mrs. Privett was in no doubt that she had done the right thing. It was with her a point of pride that she had never indulged in gossip. In her own shop days she had learnt, taught herself indeed, to ignore the ceaseless scum of rumour, tittle-tattle and invention that goes drifting round the surface of all staff cloakroom conversation.

And she had another reason at the moment for preserving silence. It was because of Nancy. She and Nancy saw quite a bit of each other nowadays. Every other week or so. Not that it was always easy to get hold of her. During her long wilderness years, while her sister in her own separate world had soared steadily upwards, Nancy herself had developed a kind of timid furtiveness, a self-protective and unnatural caution. She spoke nowadays as though she were running the gauntlet of invisible posses.

" I'll see if I can slip up again. Not next week. The week after," she would say each time at the moment of departure. " But don't count on it. Only if I can get away. I shall have to see how things are. I know what I'll do: if I can I'll send you a post-card. If it's inconvenient you just let me know. . . ." And with these words of politeness, hesitation and indecision Nancy would go back to her little back bed-sitter, where every day was the same and there was no one to miss her no matter how often she went out or how long she stayed away.

But the post-card always came. And Mrs. Privett always replied, again by post-card and by return of post. Nancy's card had come yesterday. That meant that Nancy herself would be arriving to-day. Mrs. Privett had been preparing for it. She had baked a small seed cake and made some scones. The massive block of cut cake that Mr. Privett was accustomed to feed, slowly and lovingly, slice by slice to Mr. Bloot was something that Mrs. Privett would never have considered serving to a friend. Not, for that matter, that Mrs. Privett had many friends. None at all, in fact, now that poor Emmie had gone. In the ordinary way, she saw no one from the moment her family left in the morning until they came back again at night. That was why it was so exciting having Nancy. Why, having found her, she had pounced.

And Nancy, just as friendless, cherished these meetings quite as

340

ardently. She opened up astonishingly. If it had been neat gin and not tea that Mrs. Privett had poured out for her, she could not have been less discreet. Less reticent. Never really at ease with her own sister, she confided in Mrs. Privett. The fears, doubts, misgivings, and foolish hopes of a whole lifetime came gushing forth. With Mrs. Rammell, she was always afraid that she was being pitied, despised, laughed at, disapproved of. Here in Fewkes Road she was at her ease. Blissful and unguarded. And all because, as she kept reminding both herself and Mrs. Privett, she knew that whatever she said wouldn't go any further. Mrs. Privett's front sitting-room with the sewing machine under the window and the seed cakes and scones at her elbow, had, in fact, become Nancy Parkinson's confessional.

And to-day she was more open and incautious than ever. Pushing back a stray wisp of hair from her forehead and dabbing at a corner of her lips where the butter from her scone kept running, she discussed Mrs. Rammell. Her woe-begone state. Her estrangement from Mr. Rammell. The whited sepulchre that their marriage had become. . . . Nancy knew all the right phrases.

". . . and she'd never have let on, not to me at least she wouldn't, not if things weren't serious," Nancy rambled on. " I'm the last person she'd tell. It's Tony, really. That's where the trouble lies. And Mr. Rammell "—even in her own mind Nancy had never got on to first name terms with her own brother-in-law—" won't discuss it. Simply won't let her mention it. She told me so herself. Not that she ever sees him. He might be dead for all she knows." She paused for a moment and began dabbing with her handkerchief again. " Or cares," she added as a frank afterthought.

" It's shocking," Mrs. Privett agreed with her. " That's what it is. It's shocking."

Nancy was silent for a moment. Not that she was too unhappy to speak. Overcome by her own sister's misery. Nothing like that. To be honest, she found it all strangely stimulating. Finding Mrs. Rammell's private affairs in such a mess had somehow promoted her. Made her superior. Now even her own dependent state, her near-poverty, her loneliness, her spinsterhood seemed suddenly to hold unforeseen compensations. It was with real relief that she realised that she herself was un-letdownable.

" And mark my words," she added, " there's more in this than meets the eye. There's something going on somewhere. I don't

know what. But I can feel it. There's something fishy somewhere."
Mrs. Privett forced the words out.

" You mean another woman? " she asked.

Nancy shook her head.

" Not that," she said confidently. " He isn't that sort. Hasn't
got it in him. It's debts. Or gambling. Or some big deal he's on to.
He's got something on his mind. That's what it is."

It was not easy for Mrs. Privett. Up to that moment it had not
even occurred to her to mention the silly little slander about the
mink wrap. That was something that she had promised herself she
would keep locked away for ever. But, faced by stupidity on such
a colossal scale as Nancy's, she wavered. And more than wavered.
She succumbed. She wanted to hit the woman. Thump her.
Anything to wake her up.

" That's what you think," she said. " Some of us may know
different."

The words alone would have been enough to startle. But it was
the tone of voice in which they were uttered that really overcame
Nancy. Spoken quite quietly, whispered through tight lips that
were scarcely parted, the remark sounded venomous and alarming.
Nancy's big silly heart gave a bump and she sat there staring.

" What . . . what do you know? " she asked.

After that, it was no use pretending. Mrs. Privett did not tell
her at once, of course. That would have been wrong. Downright
wicked, in fact. She denied having said it. Claimed that she didn't
mean it anyhow. Affirmed that wild horses wouldn't drag it from
her. Swore Nancy to secrecy. And told her everything.

The effect was disastrous. Nothing less. After remaining silent
for a moment, she began sniffing. Then little sobs came. Then
tears. Soon she was weeping quite openly. The wisp of grey hair
came down again across her forehead and she didn't notice. Didn't
care. She was just a collapsed, unhappy woman—no longer young,
no longer strong enough to bear it—contemplating the ruin of the
one thing in her life that had always seemed secure.

And the shame of it! Divorce was something that she held in
peculiar horror. Like blackmail. Or bankruptcy. Or being sent to
prison. The mere thought of it gave her the shudders. Her own
sister, too. It was easily the most dreadful thing that had happened
to the Parkinsons since poor father's business failure. Even though
she didn't pretend to understand about such things, she supposed

342

that divorce was inevitable now. And immediate. For all she knew it might be in the papers to-morrow. Displayed there, blatantly, for all the staff to read. She remembered those shockingly frank little paragraphs that were usually made worse still by the portrait-photographs: ". . . misconduct was admitted . . . intimacy took place . . . the Judge exercised his discretion in respect of the petitioner's own misconduct . . ." Nancy's heart gave another great bump. But no! That at least was unthinkable. Her own sister would never do a thing like that. Even without it, however, it was still quite bad enough. She had never been able to understand how, once the details had appeared in all the papers, either party ever dared appear in public again.

" Mind you, not a word of this to anyone," she heard Mrs. Privett's voice saying from somewhere quite remote, quite unconnected with her own thoughts. " I'd rather have had my own tongue cut out if I thought you were going to repeat it."

Nancy nodded her head. It was the best that she could manage. When at last she did contrive to speak, the words were little better than a moan.

" As if I would " she said reproachfully. " As if I would."

3

There are some people, women especially, who are born without the usual sense of self-preservation. They are the sort that cut themselves on kitchen knives. Shut finger-tips in cupboard drawers. Drop heavy objects on their feet. Catch their heels in gratings. Their nightdresses catch fire. They drink medicines out of wrong bottles. They spill acids over themselves. They engage in missions.

With Nancy, it was a mission that was the trouble. She left Fewkes Road a dedicated woman. Someone who was determined to save her own sister's marriage. All the way home by bus and Underground she thought of nothing else. And all night, too. By breakfast-time next morning she was exhausted, hollow-eyed, headachy. And more determined, more fanatically purposeful, than ever.

The only thing that escaped her was the method. Between two and three a.m. it had all seemed simple and straightforward. Demand a private interview with Mr. Rammell. Go in and denounce him to his face. Shame him, threaten him if necessary, into reasonableness. But somehow in the full light of day the scheme did not seem so attractive. She couldn't, now that she was back on the job, even think of any good threats. And she didn't know whether he had a sense of shame. But there were still other means left open to her. Subtle, feminine means. She could go behind his back. Undermine him. Appeal to Marcia's sense of fair play. Her pity. Arouse a guilt feeling. Then she would have to give him up. Have to renounce him. But again, as nine a.m. came round, she foresaw the same disadvantages, the same awkwardness. If Mr. Rammell had no sense of shame how was she to know whether Marcia would have any sense of fair play? And if she hadn't, Nancy would simply be wasting her time. And worse. Because of them the enemy would be alerted. On their guard. Ready to pop off any Good Angels that so much as showed their heads.

But there were still other ways. Nancy had thought of them all. Anonymous post-cards sent to Mr. Rammell's office. " WHO IS THE ATTRACTIVE MODEL WITH WHOM YOUR NAME IS BEING LINKED? " or " BEWARE. OTHER EYES ARE WATCHING YOU. LOOK OUT." That kind of thing. Indeed, as Nancy turned her mind in that direction, she was surprised to find how good she was at it. The texts came rolling out by the dozen. And this surprised her. Because she had never before realised that she was a born anonymous letter writer, a natural. But post-cards, she remembered, can be traced. Even when a typewriter is used, the typescript reveals its own secrets. And ordinary pen and nibs are nothing less than self-accusatory. Something to do with the thick strokes and the hair-lines, she recalled. On the other hand, there were always telephone kiosks. A few pennies in the slot. Button A. The poison message. Hang up. And away again, mysterious and undetected. Provided the pennies held out, she could conduct her wandering-voice purity campaign for years that way.

It was all terrible. Nightmarish. Nerve-wracking. She sat there, clasping and unclasping her hands. Indecision was no answer. She had *got* to do something. And, if she was not strong enough to do it alone, she would have to find a partner. Have to tell *someone*.

CHAPTER XXXIX

IT WAS Mrs. Privett who insisted. Lumley's of Camden Town had at last written to say that they had done up the yacht for which Mr. Privett had been waiting—practically the replica of *Daisy II*—and they were keeping her for him. The price was a stiff one. Over twenty pounds. On the other hand, she had cost nearly forty when new, Mr. Lumley said. And she had just been completely rerigged under Mr. Lumley's personal supervision. " This class racing craft " was how the letter described her.

Mr. Privett's heart gave a great bump simply at the thought. To be back amongst the brethren! An owner once more. But the price. It was a real shocker. Not the sort of thing that a man with the expenses of a grown-up daughter could even contemplate.

That was why he was so surprised when Mrs. Privett didn't even hesitate. He had waited long enough, she told him. And if he didn't do something about it now he might as well put it out of his mind for ever. He'd be too old for it, she added brutally.

What Mr. Privett did not know was that Mrs. Privett had been working things out in her mind for months past. She was living in a state of morbid trepidation for the future. With Mr. Bloot married and Irene getting ready for it, what was to become of Mr. Privett, she had kept asking herself. The thought of him left behind, with nothing except his own wife to cherish, nothing to occupy his mind, filled her with misery and foreboding. She became disconsolate for his sake. And if Mr. Lumley could provide happiness and a new purpose in life all for twenty-two pounds ten she felt that the offer should be snapped up.

Not that it was easy. There were still difficulties. Practical difficulties. Like how to get the thing, once Mr. Privett had made the purchase, up to the Highgate Ponds so that he could begin playing with it. And here Mrs. Privett was adamant. No cycling, she said. Either push it. Or nothing. And, she added, she didn't want some great ungainly perambulator-carrier blocking up her front hall. If Mr. Privett cared anything for her feelings he'd keep it right out at the back where Ted wouldn't see it. . . .

It was on Thursday when Mr. Lumley's letter came. And on Friday morning first thing Mr. Privett got off at Camden Town and dropped in a note saying that he would be back the same evening if Mr. Lumley would keep open for him. In consequence, it was a restless, preoccupied day for Mr. Privett. He could not keep his attention from straying. When an angry, important-looking woman demanded to be directed to the Complaints Department he sent her absentmindedly up to Toddlers and Nursery Furniture. And it was only around teatime that he realised that he had not once been down to the Fur Salon to see how Irene was getting on. In the ordinary way, these fleeting little visits, scarcely more than a peep, were something to which he really looked forward. Something, in fact, from which he got quite a kick.

But he didn't forget about Lumley's. And Mr. Lumley didn't forget about him. Even though it was getting on for seven, Mr. Lumley was there. And waiting. Nor did Mr. Privett need any further persuading. There was only one sailing yacht of the size, amid all those other miscellaneous steam and electrical contraptions. And Mr. Privett went straight up to her. She was called the *Dianthe*. As soon as he saw her, Mr. Privett knew that he would have to have her. For a moment, even, he was unfaithful to the memory of *Daisy II*. The hull of *Daisy II* had been simply a dark, business-like brown. *Dianthe* on the other hand was pale duck-egg blue. She was easily the most beautiful thing, after Irene, that had ever come into Mr. Privett's life.

And Mr. Lumley was helpful and understanding. He saw Mrs. Privett's point about bicycle trailers. He had known of nasty accidents with them before, he said. For an additional thirty bob he offered, therefore, to throw in a two-wheel carrier that he had picked up with an earlier lot. In the result, Mr. Privett was not only able to buy *Dianthe* but actually take her home with him the same night. Pushing the carrier in front of him, he marched proudly up the Kentish Town Road. Like a grandparent allowed for the first time to take the pram out. And this time he was so cautious—so extra cautious—about traffic that a policeman who was holding up a bus and two private cars specially for him had to call out, " Come on, Dad," before he could get Mr. Privett to venture off the pavement and come over.

It was nearly midnight when Mr. Privett finally went to bed. Not that he was doing very much. There are limits to what can

346

be done with sailing yachts in a back kitchen. The sheets tend to get entangled. And the sails flap idly. He nearly got butter on one of them. From eleven-thirty or thereabouts, he just sat there, staring. Gloating. Humble. And adoring. Remembering all the time that to-morrow was Saturday.

And there was another piece of happiness in store for him. Pure rapture. Because when he told Mr. Bloot about *Dianthe*, Mr. Bloot offered straight away to come up and watch her sail. Actually offered. No prompting. He added, not on Saturday afternoon, of course. But Mr. Privett understood that. Saturday afternoons had always been reserved by Mr. Bloot for his budgies. Sunday morning was a different matter entirely. And it was to be just the two of them. The way it had been before *Daisy II* had been reduced to matchwood and Mr. Bloot himself had taken on a wife.

" Ah reckon it would do me good," Mr. Bloot observed vacantly, staring down into his cup almost as though speaking to himself. " Get me aht of the flat for a bit. That's what Ah need. Er noutlet." He paused as though conscious that he had been allowing his thoughts to run away with him. " Mahnd you," he added, " if Ah should be requahred, you go ahead without me. Ah'm speaking without Mrs. B. If she's got plans, that does it."

2

There is no place in the world quite like the Highgate Ponds. Especially early on a Sunday morning. There may be other places that are more central. And more fashionable. Like the Round Pond in Kensington Gardens, for instance. But fashion never had any connection with serious yachting. And centralness is exactly what isn't wanted. There is no real feeling of escape, of being away from it all, with just the wind in your face and the splash and ripple of water coming up at you, if you can hear the sound of motor horns from all quarters and see the red sides of the buses as they go trundling along Knightsbridge.

Up at Highgate, there is nothing but green Nature. Great park-land trees. And rolling meadows. And the placid, duck-bearing surface of the lake. Standing on the little wooden jetty there is not a house to be seen. Not one. Not even in the misty distance. Just reed-beds and osiers. And willow-herb. And the massive forest skyline of Ken Wood where the whole dangling necklace of ponds begins in a dark, ferny grotto. Admittedly, by turning round you can see the top stages of the L.C.C. diving-board over in the bathing-pool across the path. That belongs to a lower order of things altogether. And on a fine day it can become quite unpleasantly crowded. But you can't expect everything. Even the farthest of the ponds, the fenced-in one, with its coot and moor-hens, its dragon-flies and its water-rats, is only five miles from the City. And at any time up to about nine-thirty you've got the whole thing entirely to yourself. It's like being a great landowner. But without the threat of death duties, of course.

Mr. Privett was the first person up there. At least he thought he was until a tall, sad-looking man with a large, damp dog passed him disconsolately homeward bound already. Anyhow, the pond was all his. It was like a one-man regatta. And it nearly had its incident. The first racing fatality of the season. Because the *Dianthe* was longer than Mr. Privett had realised. And heavier. A good fourteen ounces more of her than there had been of *Daisy II*. Also, the keel was entirely different. It was a scooped-out, backward-facing C-shaped affair like modern sculpture. The bit that Mr. Privett tried to get hold of wasn't there. When he grabbed, he missed. And, when he missed, he went forward with his left leg in the water right up to his thigh. The little lozenge with the word " Dunlop," on the top of his wader was completely covered.

But he clambered back on to the jetty all right. Heaved himself up with the thick bamboo rod with the rubber ferrule on the end. And after that he was extra careful. For a model yachtsman to fall in is to risk being made a laughing stock. He had seen it happen. And he knew. It wasn't easy to be careful, however. He was too excited. Trembling all over, as he finally lowered the *Dianthe* into her own native element. And not only excited. Slow as well. He had to keep on stepping back to admire. First, stepping back. Then leaning forward to stroke. Fondle. Caress. He might have been a bridegroom.

But science, cold and analytical, has a way of cutting across life's rapture. When Mr. Privett did finally push the *Dianthe* off from the jetty—and it was the merest nudge, a request rather than an order—he saw at once that she wasn't sailing properly. Instead of sliding artfully, cheek-by-cheek alongside the wind, she turned into it, fighting. She shuddered. Her sails flapped madly. She

348

shipped water. For a moment the *Dianthe* had ceased to be beautiful.

It was nothing serious, however. No basic fault on the drawing-board. Nothing that Mr. Privett himself couldn't put right in a jiffy. And, in a way, he loved the *Dianthe* all the more because of it. It showed that she had her secrets. Temperament. A streak of overcomable obstinacy somewhere. And he alone understood her. Give her to any other man, no matter how experienced, and she would make the same lamentable exhibition of herself.

By ten o'clock, the *Dianthe* had made her measure of the pond. Running with the wind. And against it. She was big. Unbelievably big. A good head taller than Mr. Privett himself. She towered. And, now that she was tamed, disciplined, she was unbelievably beautiful again. She became one with the water. Temporarily dividing, rather than cutting through it. As Mr. Privett hurried along the bank to her, she might have been a huge, white bird, a swan straight out of legend, that he was standing there so romantically to meet.

But romantic or not, he was sweating. After all, he had run three times round the pond already. Before he left home Mrs. Privett had reminded him about his thick undervest. The woollen one. And he had not disobeyed. In consequence, he might have been on fire underneath his flannel shirt, his reefer-jacket and his raincoat. He could feel ants crawling all over him. There was nothing for it but to take a breather. After he had swabbed the *Dianthe* out, even using his handkerchief to get up the last tiny droplets, he sat there on the jetty, his collar undone and the *Dianthe* in dry dock beside him, an entirely happy man. He basked.

By eleven o'clock there was still no sign of Mr. Bloot. But the jetty had become populated by now. The members of the N.L.M.Y.R.A. were there in force. All five of them. And all wearing the little flag and anchor badge that matched Mr. Privett's own. As a reunion it could not have been more cordial. There were wet handshakes all round. The North London Model Yacht Racing Association was a body of nice steady men. They were genuinely pleased to see Mr. Privett. Most sailing yacht owners are somewhere on the other side of middle age. Distinctly elderly some of them. And prolonged absence from the jetty may mean anything. Even the worst.

Also, they were openly eager to see the *Dianthe*. They crouched round her on their haunches, gum boots creaking, like a group of elderly, heavily-breathing infants. At one point Mr. Privett got elbowed completely out of it. But he didn't care. There is nothing in life more profoundly satisfying than to be envied for one's possessions.

And it was only natural that the *Dianthe* should cause a bit of a stir. She was a stranger to these parts. A complete stranger. It was from somewhere up north by Bridlington that Mr. Lumley had bought her. All her previous sailing had been under steely grey skies, with the threat of sudden squalls and a hint of ice in the rigging. This morning's was her first voyage in the balmy, southern lagoons of Highgate. Blue sky. A gentle breeze. Barometer high. Temperature in the upper sixties. It might have been angel-fish and coral gardens rather than sheer London clay over which she was sailing.

Not that the water was without its dangers. Every five minutes or so a new menace arrived. And not merely the litter of small craft that children with parents kept bringing. There were unpleasant, mechanical-looking men with bottles of methylated spirit and petrol, bent over motor boats. Miniature two-stroke engines that roared and crackled like machine-guns and then spat themselves out in fury somewhere in the mid-channel. Hydroplanes with whirling aeroplane propellers that went bouncing along the surface like demented tea trays. Scale models of gunboats with bows like an ice-breaker's, churning up the surface, ready and waiting to ram anything with sails.

But just when the N.L.M.Y.R.A. had decided that there was nothing for it but to sit back and wait for the lunchtime lull, Mr. Bloot arrived. And that took Mr. Privett's mind off everything. Because Mr. Bloot was looking particularly imposing this morning. Like glossy and prosperous autumn. He was wearing a brown topcoat with a black velvet collar. And a brown Trilby with a bound brim. It was a costume, including the brown shoes, that Hetty had personally selected for him. Originally inclined towards tweeds, she had finally compromised on gaberdine. Provided it was brown. Anything, she had said, rather than his Sunday black which was too much like a mute's and gave her the creeps any way.

The others, too, were pleased to see Mr. Bloot. He had been away just as long as Mr. Privett. With his friend absent, there had been simply nothing to come up for. And it gave a certain undefinable note of class to the Club simply having him standing there. The sleek brownness of the coat, the bound brim, the broad stock and the gold-banded umbrella suggested the Chairman of the line rather than merely an interested spectator.

And, at twelve-thirty when Mr. Bloot announced that he would have to be getting back, Mr. Privett left with him. He would have liked to stay longer—one more run against the wind at least—but he felt that he couldn't let a friend down like that. And, for the first time since the wedding, Mr. Privett felt grateful to Hetty. Because this time Mr. Bloot himself suggested a drink at the Woodman on the way back.

They didn't walk quite side by side on the way there. Mr. Bloot tended to step out a little. And Mr. Privett followed up a few paces behind with the carrier. But that was only natural. The pavement down from the ponds is a narrow one. And, in any case, Mr. Bloot wasn't dressed right to be shoulder-to-shoulder with anyone pushing anything.

But in the saloon bar it was different. Crowded. Elbow-jogging. Convivial. Mr. Bloot and Mr. Privett forced their way into the window so that they could talk unimpeded, and Mr. Privett could keep his eyes on the *Dianthe* up on her two bicycle wheels outside.

Mr. Bloot, moreover, was at his most confiding.

" Er nawkward journey," he said. " Ah've been travelling for er nouranerarf. Three changes. Ah ought to 'ave trahd a one-one-six. Then Ah could have walked dahn the hill."

Mr. Privett felt quite ashamed of himself. " I should have thought of that," he said. " I could have suggested it."

But Mr. Bloot was bland. Indifferent.

" No matter," he said. " Ah'm not pressed. Not this morning. 'Etty's got a few friends in."

" But oughtn't you to be there? " Mr. Privett asked.

Mr. Bloot shook his head.

" 'Er friends," he said briefly. " Not mine."

He paused for a moment as though undecided whether to continue.

" Ah reckon Ah've learnt something," he went on at last. " Abaht marriage, Ah mean. Live and let live, I say. Works out quahter that way."

" D'you mean you don't like her friends? " Mr. Privett asked.

Mr. Bloot blew his cheeks out.

351

"Just not mah kahnd," he said. "That's all there is to it."

He was silent again for a moment. And when he spoke it was in that intimate undertone that sets the seal on all old friendships.

"Funny thing," he said. "Ah never 'ad any of this trouble with Emmie. No trouble, at all. But then you see she didn't 'ave any friends."

"There was me and Eileen," Mr. Privett corrected him.

Mr. Bloot acknowledged the rebuke. He raised his glass in Mr. Privett's direction.

"Present company," he said, "excepted."

Then he stretched his legs out in front of him and sat looking at his brown shoes.

"Ah've enjoyed this morning, Ah have," he went on. "Lakh old tahms. Away-from-it-all as you maht say."

CHAPTER XL

Mr. Tattan (Garden Furniture) suggested it. Mr. Cuffley (Export) thought it was a good idea. Mr. Maple (Household Appliances) disliked rushing things. Mr. Langdale Senior (Restaurant and Catering) considered that the claims of Mr. Langdale Junior (Television and Radio) were somehow being overlooked. Mr. Privett naturally was delighted. Mr. Bloot said that he would drop a word in the raht quartah. And Mr. Finlay (Sports Goods) was completely opposed. Offended, even.

But that is always the way it is with staff changes. There is nothing that upsets people like promotions. They have a disturbing effect all round. People who are left entirely unaffected still resent them. And no one could pretend that Mr. Finlay wasn't affected. After all, it was *his* Sports Department. He had built it up from a few golf clubs and a cricket bat or two into something that stretched right across the fourth floor, with a Wimbledon at one end, Gleneagles over on the Downe Street side, Lords over in the corner and even a canoe and sailing dinghy section—practically a small Hayling—over by the lift.

It was obvious, however, that something had to be done. Mr. Finlay was now sixty-four. Coming up to sixty-five in July. You couldn't have a he-ancient in charge of a Sports Department. Mr. Finlay saw that all right. But, he kept telling himself, it wasn't necessary to make things over to a mere youngster. And Ted Waters, at twenty-eight, was less than half his age. Surely somewhere in Rammell's, he kept telling himself, there was someone in the middle fifties, respected, reliable, hard-driving.

But who? Mr. Preece had asked himself the question a hundred times. The list, the short list, was lying there on the desk in front of him. Mr. Bennett (Cycles and Touring)? No initiative. Mr. Gibbs (China and Glassware)? Too specialised. Mr. Langdale Junior (Television and Radio)? Not the right type at all for Sports Goods. Too glossy: he looked like a ladies' hairdresser. Mr. Waters

(Travel and Theatre Tickets)? A bit on the young side, admittedly. But did that matter? Mr. Preece liked to think of himself as a discoverer of new talent, a seer. And Mr. Waters certainly *looked* right. Tall. Clean-shaven. The open-air type. Women customers would undoubtedly respond. And he was a member of the Sports Club: Mr. Preece had established that. Subject to Mr. Rammell's approval, Mr. Preece was prepared to appoint him.

It was not Mr. Rammell, but Sir Harry who opposed it. Not for any personal reason. Simply because he was feeling unusually skittish and alert at the Board Meeting. Why not a well-known sportsman? he asked. Get in someone from outside. A County cricketer. Like . . . like Tyldesley. Dead, they told him. Or a leading jockey? But Rammell's did not sell saddlery, Mr. Preece pointed out. Or a Davis Cup player? He would lose his amateur status, Mr. Rammell snapped back. Or a woman golfer? Or a track athlete. Or a table-tennis champion? Or a rugger Blue? Or a cross-Channel swimmer? Or a . . . But, unusually fertile though his mind was this morning, here Sir Harry paused for a moment. He had only just realised that there was more than management that was wrong with the sports department. It needed livening up, enlarging, re-thinking. Why not a swimming-pool? he started off again. Or a putting green with real turf? Or a rifle range? Or a ski-jump packed solid with artificial ice? Or . . . It was while Sir Harry was replanning the whole department, that Mr. Preece was able to slip Mr. Waters's name quietly forward again. Perhaps only an acting appointment, he suggested tactfully. But that was his blunder. Why only acting? Sir Harry demanded. Hadn't Mr. Preece got the guts to back his own hunches? What was going to happen to morale when the staff discovered that the management didn't trust them? Planned promotion was the most important thing in any large firm, he went on. If boards of directors had to begin looking round for strangers to come in and run the business for them they might as well put the shutters up. . . .

Over the directors' lunch afterwards, Sir Harry was unusually silent. He merely toyed with his lamb cutlets. Left the pear flan untouched. It wasn't that he was exhausted by his performance in the board room. Simply saddened. Depressed by the sheer lack of energy and ability all round him. It didn't matter so long as he was there to step in and take charge. But he couldn't last for ever.

Wasn't immortal, he reminded himself. And, after he had gone, what then? Who would there be to make decisions? How would anything ever get done? Where would the drive come from? Just waffle-waffle-waffle round the board table while the whole place went to pot downstairs. . . .

2

Mr. Preece lost no time. The board lunch—at which he was no more than a regular, resentful guest—was over at two-thirty. And at two forty-five he had sent for Ted Waters. Had him there standing a little awkwardly in front of him at this very moment.

" Take a seat, Mr. Waters," he said. " Take a seat." He paused for a moment and pushed the box of office cigarettes forward.

" Would you like to smoke? " he asked even though he was known to be a non-smoker himself. " Do by all means if you want to."

This was one of the moments in life that Mr. Preece really enjoyed. There was the subtle delicious savour of power. Reprimands and dismissals produced something of the same sensation inside him. They made him wriggle, too. But he did not really enjoy them. Because his one defect as manager was that he liked being liked. Promotions therefore were perfect. At the mere thought of them he could feel himself becoming bland, majestic, godlike. With his pale, hairless hands clasped together beneath his chin as though he were praying, he fairly basked in himself.

" Now, Mr. Waters," he resumed. " I wonder if you know why I've asked you to come and see me? "

He was observing his visitor very closely while he was speaking. Trying to find out whether managerial secrets really did leak out as he had always suspected.

But it was obvious that Mr. Ted Waters knew nothing. His whole expression was one of honest bewilderment.

" No, I'm afraid I don't, sir," he said, hope and untruth mingled.

" Ah! " Mr. Preece separated his finger-tips for a moment and then brought them together again. " The board has authorised me . . ." he began. That was at two-fifty. At three o'clock precisely Mr. Preece had reached his winding-up.

355

"Very well then," he concluded. "You can start in next Monday morning. With Mr. Finlay, of course. He'll show you everything. You'll have one month's overlap with him. And then you're off on your own. Don't hesitate to come back to me at any time you want to. That's what I'm here for. And remember the future is up to you."

As he spoke the last words, Mr. Preece got up from his chair. He came round to the other side of his desk with his hand stretched out all ready for the formal handshake, the accolade.

"And let me offer my own congratulations," he said. "I'm sure you're not going to disappoint us."

What is more, he really meant it. There was one infallible sign. The box of cigarettes had been open at Mr. Waters's elbow all the time. And Mr. Waters had not so much as reached his hand out towards it.

As soon as Ted had left Mr. Preece's office he went straight along to the staff lavatory on the second floor. Now that the interview was over he felt shaky and slightly sick. He needed support. The tiles round the walls were too cold to lean against. And he chose the cleaners' cabinet over in the corner instead. Then, taking out a packet of ten Players, he lit a cigarette.

He didn't attempt to finish it, however. After a few puffs, he went over to the washbasin and pushed the unsmoked end out of sight down the little grating. Finally, he passed his pocket comb a couple of times through his hair and pulled the knot of his tie smartly back into position. When all that was done, he felt calm enough to tell Irene the news. She was temporarily in Gowns.

But this was not easy. Irene was in the middle of trying to serve a somnambulist. A large, middle-aged woman, she was clearly deep in the dream state. Whenever Irene brought her anything she merely smiled and shook her head sadly to show that she didn't like it. And as soon as Irene had left her, she would go across herself to the racks and run her fingers thoughtfully along the dresses as though counting them might help.

"Had you anything *particular* in mind, madam?" Ted heard Irene ask at last. She was wearing her most attentive expression, Ted noticed. Half sales assistant, half sick nurse. It might have been a thermometer and not a pencil that was tucked under the flap of her sales book.

356

But the direct question had somehow got through.

" Oh, just something different," the woman explained. " Something new, you know. Like the little black one. Only different."

This time when Irene went back towards the stock room, Ted caught up with her. He was breaking all the Rammell rules by being in the dress department at all. But somehow for the moment ordinary staff regulations didn't seem of any real importance.

" It's all right, Irene," he said. " I've got it. I start in next Monday."

It was then that Irene risked losing her job, too. Because, instead of concentrating on something different for the large sleep-walker, she gave Ted a kiss. Not a real kiss, admittedly. But it was enough to have got her the sack. And it was enough for Ted, too. It showed that getting married meant as much to Irene as it did to Ted himself.

" I'm going up now to tell your father," he said.

But here Irene stopped him.

" No, don't do that," she said. " Better leave that part to me."

At five forty-five when they all met in the Staff Entrance the news of Ted's promotion came as no surprise to Mr. Bloot. But it was obviously immensely gratifying to him. Of late he had been looking thoroughly run down. Out of sorts. Peaky. Mr. Rammell had been worried about him. And this piece of good fortune in the family seemed exactly what he needed to revive him. He blew his lips out almost as if he were drinking tea.

" What did Ah tell you? " he said exultantly. " Ah told you Ah would and Ah did."

" Did what? " Mr. Privett asked.

And then he learned, even though he knew it so well already, what a friend it was whom he had in Mr. Bloot.

" Ah dropped er nint or two," he said slowly, as though Mr. Privett should have known all along that without this intervention nothing would ever have happened. " Er nint or two in the raht quartah. Ah'm normally a bit on the aloof sahd. So when Ah do come dahn it means something."

Mr. Privett was so grateful that he could have hugged Mr. Bloot. He felt fonder than ever of him at this moment.

" I suppose there wouldn't be any chance of getting you round

357

this evening, would there? " he asked hopefully. " Just for a cuppa and chat, you know."

And again it seemed as though this was exactly what Mr. Bloot was needing most.

" Ah maht," he said, not even attempting to conceal the eagerness that was in his voice. " Yurss, Ah think Ah maht. Does you good to get aht a bit in the evenings."

3

" Well, if Gus's coming round here I'm going up to bed," Mrs. Privett said firmly.

As she spoke she began gathering up the socks that she had been darning. Rolling them up into a small, tight cocoon, she thrust them abruptly down into the bottom of her work bag as though burying something.

" Won't you just stay down long enough to say good evening? " Mr. Privett inquired.

" Not to-night," Mrs. Privett told him. " I'm tired."

Mr. Privett gave a little sigh. He had noticed before that Mrs. Privett somehow did not share his enthusiasm for Mr. Bloot. Not fully, that is. But manners were manners. And it would have been nicer if she could have been there to pour out the first cup of tea. Even ask after Hetty, perhaps.

" Gus only wants to congratulate us on Ted," Mr. Privett started to explain.

But it was no use. Mrs. Privett's mind was made up.

" I've had quite enough about Ted for one evening," she said. " Just when we'd got everything arranged, too."

Mr. Privett looked at her in amazement.

" What's the matter, Mother? " he asked gently.

Mrs. Privett did not reply for a moment. When she did, the words came in a sudden rush.

" Ireen's still only a child," she said. " That's what's the matter. If things had gone on as they were, we'd have had her here for another couple of years. As it is, they'll think they can get married to-morrow. And if Gus wants to talk about that, I don't."

She gave a little sniff as she finished speaking and began to move off towards the door.

" We . . . we don't know about that, Mother," he said. " Not for certain. Not till we ask them."

" And where are they now? " Mrs. Privett demanded, her hand already on the door knob. " Out somewhere. Planning. If Ireen hadn't been concealing something she'd have come straight home and told me."

Mrs. Privett paused for a moment. Then she spoke again.

" You can take it from me," she said. " We've as good as lost her already. I only wish Ted had been turned down. I do really."

The room seemed suddenly to have grown very quiet. Quiet and cheerless. Mr. Privett went round tidying up for Mr. Bloot's arrival, pulling the chair covers straight and folding up the evening paper into its original creases. This, in itself, was an indication of Mrs. Privett's distress. Usually she insisted in doing the tidying up herself. Regarded men as incapable of the necessary thoroughness.

As soon as the room was to rights again, Mr. Privett went through into the scullery and put on the kettle. Then he arranged the tea tray with the cups and saucers. And, going over to the cupboard he took out the large circular cake tin with the portrait of Queen Mary on the lid. It was the remains of a chocolate cake that was inside. Thick chocolate on top. Then broad veins of brown sponge with white cream running thickly across it. It looked rich and geologic. Mr. Privett cut two generous slices and put them on a plate beside the empty teapot. Even so he was sorry that it was chocolate. Fruit cake, he knew, was what Mr. Bloot preferred. Cut from the solid block. The dark kind with preserved cherries in it. Marzipan icing on the top if you like. Even shredded coconut. But definitely fruit. And preferably cherry.

By nine-fifteen everything was ready. And by nine-thirty Mr. Privett had turned off the gas and refilled the kettle. Nine forty-five. Ten o'clock. Ten-fifteen. And still no Mr. Bloot. Mr. Privett began to wonder if he was coming. There was something queer about his non-appearance. Unaccountable. Because when Mr. Privett had invited him Mr. Bloot had seemed so eager. Had fairly jumped at it, in fact. Mr. Privett could not help being vaguely anxious.

And then a strange feeling came over him. It was as though Mr. Bloot were already beside him. If not actually in the room, at least in the passageway just outside. And needing him. Urgently.

Requiring help and assistance. Bodily and spiritual. Desperately crying out for it. The feeling was so strong, so suddenly overwhelming, that Mr. Privett got up and reached out instinctively for his jacket.

"Perhaps I ought to go round to him," he told himself. "Perhaps something's happened. Perhaps he's ill, or something."

It was only when he was actually standing up that he realised how foolish it was. Mr. Bloot had behaved this way before. It wasn't the first time that Mr. Privett had arranged the cake, the tea things, the extra jug for the hot water—only to have to put them all away again. And at ten-thirty it was obviously too late to expect him now.

The sensible thing, of course, would have been for Mr. Privett to make himself a cup of tea. Just sit there, quietly sipping it on the off chance that Mr. Bloot might after all pop in if only to say good night. In the ordinary way a cup of tea would have been just what Mr. Privett would have liked. But he was too dispirited to go to the trouble of making it. Even if it had been there ready on the table in front of him, he doubted if he could have brought himself to drink it. That funny feeling about Mr. Bloot being there when he wasn't, had upset him. Left him feeling faintly sick. Twingey. Out of sorts.

He started nervously when he heard a sound outside. And at the front door, too. But it was only Irene. She had her own key. And compared with Mr. Bloot's movements this was nothing. Just a light tap of a heel on the top step. The thin slither of the key sliding into the lock. The door closing almost silently behind her. It was only since her engagement had become official that Mrs. Privett had allowed her to stay out like this. And Irene had responded wonderfully. Her old schoolgirl banginess had disappeared overnight. She was now so quiet that Mrs. Privett had to leave her bedroom door open to make sure of hearing her.

Irene did not come through to him. She ran straight upstairs. Down below in the kitchen, Mr. Privett caught the sound of voices, Irene's and Mrs. Privett's. Then there was the faint noise of Irene's door shutting. And, after that, silence. Mr. Privett himself had not called out. This was strange because in the ordinary way he always looked forward to kissing Irene good night. The day did not seem complete somehow without. But to-night he was too much preoccupied by thoughts of Mr. Bloot. He didn't feel like kissing anybody.

By ten-forty everything was put away again. Mr. Privett switched out the light and went along to the front door to lock up. It was the same every evening. He opened the front door. Took a deep breath or two of the fresh air that blew straight in down the Kentish Town Road from the north. Peered out to make sure that the ornamental iron gate was closed properly. Then shut and bolted the front door top and bottom as though border raiders might have been expected. Put the chain up as an extra precaution. Kicked the mat straight. And went up to bed.

But to-night when he opened the front door he let out a little cry of sheer surprise. That was because Mr. Bloot was standing there. Simply standing. Entirely stationary. Half-way between the gate and the front door. Massive and motionless, he was staring up at the Privetts' bedroom window.

At the sight of Mr. Privett he started. It was the first time that Mr. Privett had ever seen his friend give a little nervous jump like that. And it showed how much on edge poor Gus's nerves must be. But what was more remarkable still was the fact that he made no attempt to come forward. Instead of moving, he was standing there. Beckoning.

Mr. Privett went along the little path to greet him.

"Ah hoped Ah'd see you," Mr. Bloot said in a hoarse, half-whisper. "Ah was afraid you'd gone to bed."

"Where've you been?" Mr. Privett demanded.

"Aht here," Mr. Bloot told him. "Aht here. Waiting. Ah was just going to ring when Ahreen and Ted came along. So Ah moved off. They've been saying good naht to each other. Ah thought they'd never stop. Ah'm cold."

Mr. Bloot shivered a little as he said it and pulled at his fawn overcoat with the brown velvet collar.

"Well, come on in," Mr. Privett replied. "I'll make you a . . ."

But Mr. Bloot stopped him. He laid his large, soft hand on Mr. Privett's arm.

"Ah couldn't," he said. "Not to-naht. Ah'm too upset. That's why Ah couldn't face Ahreen."

Mr. Bloot turned slightly, and the light of the street lamp fell on his face. Mr. Privett could see then that his friend had been

361

crying. Either that, or drinking. But his words sounded distinct enough. And between sentences he kept giving little telltale sniffs. They were tears all right, Mr. Privett decided. Big, wet ones. They meant that something really dreadful must have happened. And whatever it was had knocked Mr. Bloot out completely. He had the appearance of a man who has been drained. Usually, slightly flushed, rather mulberryish in complexion, his face in the lamplight showed up chalk-white and sunken.

" Not come in? " Mr. Privett asked incredulously.

Mr. Bloot shook his head.

" Not to-naht," he repeated. " Ah'm not stopping. Ah couldn't face it. It's just that Ah had to tell someone. Had to get it off mah chest."

" Is . . . it Hetty? " Mr. Privett inquired.

Mr. Bloot nodded.

" Has she left you? "

The reply was slow in coming. Mr. Bloot was on the verge of tears again. And he could speak only with difficulty.

" It's worse," he said at last. " Much worse."

" Then what is it? "

" She's let mah budgies aht," he said. " Deliberate. Cold and deliberate. Opened the cages. Let 'em flah away."

But the reminder of his loss had been too painful for him. He had reached for his handkerchief while he was still speaking and was now mopping damply at his face.

Mr. Privett felt ashamed at himself for feeling so relieved. In the face of bird-love such as this, he was no better than an outsider.

" They'll come back," he told him. " You're always reading about it in the papers. They'll come back. You see if they don't."

But Mr. Bloot was beyond comforting.

" Not with her there," he said, still from behind his handkerchief. " And not with Billy's chest. Think of him. Aht there "— Mr. Bloot raised his face for a moment and gazed upwards into the empty sky—" aht there on a naht lakh this."

" Then what are you going to do? " Mr. Privett asked him. " You've got to do something."

" Do? " Mr. Bloot repeated. " Ah'm going to leave her. Ah've had enough. If Ah lay mah ahs on her again Ah may do something desprit."

" You mean you're not going back there?"

362

" Only to pick up mah possessions. What's left of them. Then Ah'm orf. Scarpering. Done with it."

" Would . . . would you like to come here? " Mr. Privett inquired. " Just till it blows over? "

" It won't blow over," Mr. Bloot answered. " Not this tahm. And not with me in charge."

" We could put you up, you know," Mr. Privett persisted.

But Mr. Bloot was too much preoccupied with his own misery even to say thank you.

" Not with friends," he said. " Not any longer. Ah've got to face this aht alone."

He turned as he said it and began to walk towards the front gate.

" Ah'm glad Ah told you," he said over his shoulder. " Nahw you understand what Ah've been through."

Mr. Privett went after him. He couldn't bear to see his friend go away from him like that.

" Would you like me to come round with you? " he asked.

But again Mr. Bloot only shook his head.

" Better not," he said. " If she's still awake things may get ugly. Ah'd rather keep it prahvit."

He closed the gate behind him, and paused for a moment.

" Juhst think of it," he said. " Billy. And Tiddleywinks. Ah was going to exhibit him. And nahw . . ." Mr. Bloot spread his arms out in a little gesture that indicated Fate and the unknown.

BOOK FOUR

Case of the Missing Budgies

CHAPTER XLI

THERE WAS no sign of Mr. Bloot at Rammell's next morning. No sign. No letter. Not even a telephone call. By ten o'clock Mr. Privett had already slipped down twice to see if his friend had arrived. And he might just as well have saved himself the trouble. Because, at five minutes past ten, Mr. Preece sent for him. Would he take over please in the front hall, he said, and hang around there until Mr. Bloot got in touch with them?

What was particularly alarming was Mr. Preece's final remark. They had been phoning Artillery Mansions, he said, but could get no reply. In Mr. Preece's view, this confirmed that Mr. Bloot must be somewhere on his way to Bond Street. Held up in the Underground, possibly. Or delayed at Oxford Circus, the temporary victim of roadworks and traffic jams.

No one took Mr. Bloot's absence very seriously. No one, that is, with the exception of Mr. Privett. And he wouldn't have said anything. It would have savoured too much of disloyalty. How could he start talking about mysterious conversations in the lamplight? And the danger of things turning ugly? And the temptation to do something desperate? And scarpering? And little fugitive budgerigars perishing on the London roof tops in the crisp October air?

It was the second time that morning that he had said nothing. The first time had been at breakfast. Mrs. Privett had still wanted to know why Gus had kept her husband hanging about in the cold instead of coming indoors like a reasonable human being. And Mr. Privett had not told her. Simply could not bring himself to divulge so much intimate misery. Instead, he had lied. Told her that the evening had grown suddenly warmer. Even close. That Gus had already had a cup of tea before coming round. That they hadn't wanted to disturb the household by sitting about indoors, gossiping at that hour.

But already the strain was beginning to tell on Mr. Privett. He had not been able to sleep for thinking about it. And now as he

367

stood there, with the long carpeted aisle of the store behind him and the black, shiny cars drawing up outside, it all came back to him. He'd heard enough about Hetty's ungovernable temper to know the risks which Mr. Bloot had been running. Suppose under the influence of rage, drink and jealousy she had turned on him? With her nail-scissors. Or the breadknife. Or with one of Mr. Bloot's own cut-throat razors. . . . The fears were so real and terrible that Mr. Privett could think of nothing else. He was nightmare-ridden. As a floor-walker he was entirely useless.

And worse than useless. Off-putting. With head thrust forward, leaving the gap between his neck and his collar more pronounced than ever, and his mouth drawn down at the corners, he scowled at people. In consequence, no one approached. The whole crowded business of Rammell's, casuals as well as regulars, simply flowed past avoiding him.

2

But it wasn't only Mr. Bloot's disappearance that was causing anxiety in Rammell's that morning. The private affairs of top management were in disorder, too. The affair between Marcia and Mr. Rammell was brought suddenly to a head. And by Nancy Parkinson. Nor could there be any turning back. Because in the end, it was to Mrs. Rammell personally that Nancy spoke. It had to be *someone*. And, from the moment Nancy chose Mrs. Rammell, she felt a great weight being lifted from her mind. It was all so simple that way. So straightforward. So transparently honest. If Mrs. Rammell had to be told somehow—and to leave her unwarned would in Nancy's view be nothing less than treachery—how better than by her own sister?

Nancy therefore did not hesitate. She plunged in like an exhibition diver. At the deep end. And with a flourish. She kept nothing back. Told everything. Described the general alarm that Mr. Rammell's sudden infatuation was creating. Outlined her own alternative schemes for rescue and retrievement. Emphasised a score of times that it was no affair of hers. That she didn't want to intrude. That for her part she would rather have kept out of it altogether. That it was only her concern for Mrs. Rammell's happiness that had made her speak at all.

And it was fatal. Mrs. Rammell resented everything about it. The approach itself. The manner of it. Nancy's own ill-concealed excitement in being the chief instrument. The very fact that Nancy knew. And, above all things, the source of her information. Mrs. Rammell shuddered—felt goose pimples of sheer shame running up her spine—as she reflected that her real informants were the wife of one of Mr. Rammell's own floor-walkers and a teen-age assistant, a junior.

In consequence, she was simply horrid to poor Nancy. Peremptory. Offensively casual. Dismissive. When Nancy appealingly put her face up for a farewell kiss Mrs. Rammell deliberately avoided it.

"Now, you run along, dear," she said. "And don't bother your head any more about it. It's all too ridiculous."

That was while Nancy was still there. While there was an audience. She was a brave woman, Mrs. Rammell. But not so brave as all that. As soon as Nancy had left she went to pieces. First she flung herself back down on the couch where she had been sitting. Then she rushed over to her desk to see what the insurance cover-note really said. And Nancy had been perfectly right. The note did say "blue." And Mrs. Rammell's own mink was "natural." She felt tears of rage coming into her eyes as she looked at it. To think that she could have been so stupid. To have had such evidence in her possession all the time and not have known it.

She got up from her desk and began walking to and fro. Over to the window. Then back to her desk again. Across to the fireplace. Over to the window, stopping on the way to pull meaninglessly at the flowers in the tall vase on the centre table. Back once more to the desk. Across to the fireplace again. Anything, so long as she was moving about. She reached for her handkerchief. At some point since Nancy's disastrous intervention, Mrs. Rammell must have hurt her finger. The skin around the nail was all torn and frayed. It was bleeding.

It was while she was standing there, her handkerchief wrapped like a cocoon around her finger-top, that she made her decision. The most fateful one that any woman can make. She was going to divorce Mr. Rammell. Now that he had betrayed her, she wasn't going to allow her present state of wifely reticence to continue for another single day. She would have to tell someone. And at once. But whom? Obviously her solicitor was the man. He would be the person to arrange everything. Have Mr. Rammell watched. Shadowed. Spied on. It was up to the solicitor to prepare the evidence. Institute proceedings. Take him into Court. Make a free, unhumiliated woman of her once more.

The only trouble was that her solicitor was not only hers. He was Mr. Rammell's as well. And the other solicitors she used— Mr. Pitmoss for the Opera Guild and Mr. Larrymore for the Ballet Lovers' Association—were so obviously not the right sort. She couldn't imagine either of them getting to grips with a divorce case. Nor, for that matter, could she imagine herself asking them. Mr. Larrymore least of all. He was deaf. Distinctly deaf. And though he was a help sometimes at board meetings, she refused even to consider bawling her most intimate private secrets into a hearing-aid. Besides, he might refuse. Tell her bluntly that he didn't handle that kind of case.

At the sudden realisation of how helpless women are, even in the twentieth century, of the extent to which this is still a male world organised exclusively for the convenience of man, Mrs. Rammell burst into tears again. With no warning. At one moment she was calculating. Self-controlled. Vindictive. At the next, she was desolate. Unsupported. Despairing.

"If only there were *someone*," she kept repeating. "*Someone* I could talk to. *Someone* who would understand."

Mrs. Rammell was still so much preoccupied by her own misery that she did not hear her own butler when he entered. She was aware merely of a disturbance somewhere in the room behind her. Nor could she very well turn round. Her handkerchief was by now screwed up into a tight, sodden ball. And she knew that her eyes must be looking terrible. Completely give-away. All bloodshot. And with red rims, probably.

But, even if she could not see the butler, she could still hear him. And what he was saying was unthinkable. Utterly unthinkable. Bad enough at any time. At the present moment it was beyond contemplation.

"Sir Harry to see you, madam," were the words that he had just said.

What made it even worse was that she could not trust herself to speak. All that she could do was to shake her head. When, however, he did not go away, she realised that she would have to make the effort.

"Dot id," she said in a strange, catarrhal voice not in the least like her real one. "Dot dow. Say I'b out."

But it was no use. She had been reckoning without Sir Harry's natural brashness. His exuberance. Instead of waiting quietly in the small green-and-gold morning-room where the butler had tried to put him, he had insisted on following the man upstairs. He was edging his way into the room already. Talking hard as he came. And what he was saying set her teeth on edge.

"Don't you bother yourself," she heard. "If her Majesty's here she'll see me all right."

Her Majesty! It was precisely that kind of practically senile skittishness on the part of her father-in-law that always set her teeth on edge. There was something so indescribably common about being facetious in front of servants.

But it was obvious that he was unstoppable. There was, in fact, a note of even more than usual excitement in his voice. That was because he had just had a new idea. An idea that would affect Mrs. Rammell vitally. And he had rushed round to tell her about it. There was something in music, he had just realised. Remembering that Tuesday was always their slackest day, why not a series of Tuesday Concerts in the Palm Court? Chamber Music and Recitals. Big stuff. Top names. Barbirolli at the piano. Beecham with his violin. Boult, too. Like a Festival Hall. Only better. Do it at lunch-time. Serve light refreshments. Finish up with a dress parade. . . . And he'd get Mrs. Rammell herself to fix up everything on the musical side. Give her a real break. Full fees all round. Nothing off for the publicity. She could even alternate with a bit of ballet if that was the way she fancied it.

"Ah, there you are," he said deliberately, as he finally got round the butler. "I've got something for you. Right up your alley. Put you on the map in one go."

When Mrs. Rammell did not reply, Sir Harry came nearer. He could see that there was something wrong, something odd about the way she was standing. Shoulders all humped up. Hands pressed against her face. Then, when she turned, he understood. Understood immediately.

"Hallo," he said. "Hay fever. Ought to go and see my man. Got his number on me somewhere."

371

It was while Sir Harry was thumbing through his little notebook that Mrs. Rammell spoke. Her voice was clearer by now. Clearer and stronger.

"Go away," she said. "I don't want to see you. I don't ever want to see anybody again. I've had it."

I've had it! The vulgarity of the phrase astonished her. Astonished and appalled. But it was not the Mrs. Rammell whom she knew who was speaking. It was a different woman altogether. A hurt, angry, hysterical woman whose words came tumbling out all anyhow.

She went towards the door as she was speaking, but Sir Harry blocked the way.

"Upset about something?" he asked.

Mrs. Rammell laughed. It was a shrill, horselike whinny. Scarcely a laugh at all, in fact.

"You may ask," she said, using another of the strange, hideous expressions that she had always imagined were foreign to her.

She paused.

"I'm on my way to see a solicitor," she added. "*Now.*"

The word "solicitor" had slipped out. Entirely unintentionally. And disastrously. She had shown her hand before she'd had time to play it.

Not that Sir Harry seemed unduly concerned.

"That's the ticket," he said. "Pick a good-lookin' one."

Mrs. Rammell did not flinch. That perpetual cocky cheerfulness of Sir Harry's kept him completely insulated from any kind of real emotion. Shallow psychologically, was how she had long since diagnosed him. But she was not going to be put off. It would be enough if once, just once, she could puncture that complacency.

"You may care to know," she went on, "that I'm divorcing Eric."

"Thought you must be," Sir Harry replied. "Have you told him?"

"I've told him nothing," Mrs. Rammell answered. "I don't have to."

But again this was not what she had intended. Of all people, to be confiding in Sir Harry! It was the first time in the whole twenty-three years of her marriage that she had done so. And on such a subject. She turned hurriedly away.

" It's not the slightest use trying to dissuade me," she went on. " My mind's absolutely made up."

" Well, that's that then."

Sir Harry removed his fancy-patterned cigar-cutter from his pocket and began playing with it. He was not actually cutting anything. Just going *snip-snip, snip-snip*.

" Whatcher goin' to live on? " he asked.

He put the question casually as though the answer either way meant nothing to him.

But the answer was not in the least casual. It came snapping back at him almost before he had finished speaking.

" Alimony," she said.

And then the other voice, the one that she did not recognise as her own, continued for her.

" And I'm going to get all I can out of him," she added.

Sir Harry went *snip-snip* again.

" You're entitled," he said. " He gets plenty."

For a moment, the vision of Marcia—pale, beautiful, dream-like—rose before Mrs. Rammell's eyes. It was in a long, white brocaded dress, one of Rammell's own model creations, that she saw her. With a wreath of artificial orange blossom in her hair like a bride. It was horrible.

" To think of it," she exclaimed. " One of his own shop-girls! "

Snip!

Sir Harry's patent cutter froze stationary in mid air.

" One of what? " he asked.

" One of the girls out of the store," she said. " Someone on his own payroll. It's disgusting."

" What's her name? "

Sir Harry's voice had suddenly lost its earlier cheerfulness.

" It's one of the models," she told him. " The tall stupid one. The one who calls herself Marcia."

Sir Harry looked grim.

" That old tart," he said.

She winced. It was the choice of words that was so offensive. Offensive to her as well as to Marcia. Once more it showed how fatally wrong, how stupid, it was even to attempt to discuss anything with Sir Harry. And in face of such behaviour Mrs. Rammell was rapidly becoming herself again.

"Thank you," she said; "but I'd rather not discuss that aspect of it."

"Just as you say," he replied. "All I want to know is what 'appened."

He was leaning forward as he spoke. Leaning forward, and breathing heavily. The dropped " h " was symptomatic. Mrs. Rammell had noticed long ago that whenever Sir Harry became really intense about anything he reverted to that dreadful social limbo that had been his substitute for polite childhood.

" I'm not discussing it," she said firmly.

" Oh, yes, you are," Sir Harry told her. " It's Eric's business what he does with women. And good luck to him. But if 'e brings the firm into it that's different."

" Not to me, it isn't," Mrs. Rammell replied. " Not in the slightest."

Sir Harry had got up by now. He was standing with his back to the fireplace. Staring at her. And Mrs. Rammell was staring back at him. She could not help noticing what extraordinary vitality there was in the old man. In the face of this unprecedented family crisis he seemed suddenly to have become younger. He was rocking backwards and forwards on his heels as he stood there. Positively enjoying himself.

" If a line of this ever gets into the papers," he said, " out 'e goes." Sir Harry gave a broad sweeping gesture with his right hand. " Like that. On his ear."

" Oh, it's outrageous! "

The words had slipped out involuntarily. And, as soon as she had spoken, Mrs. Rammell saw how foolish it was. She could hardly go down on her knees and ask Sir Harry to overlook the incident. Beg him to make everything all right for her own husband and that dreadful model woman. On the other hand, to cut off Eric's career just at the moment when he was about to step into the inheritance, to have an unemployed enemy instead of merely a divorced husband on her hands—it was disastrous.

And already Sir Harry was speaking again.

" Cash settlement," he said. " That's all it'll be. No income, no alimony. Stands to reason. Out they go. Both of 'em. Him as well. I'm not going to have anyone fouling his own nest in Rammell's."

Even though it was his own name that he mentioned, he spoke

374

reverently. It might have been a religion and not a retail store to which he was referring.

" I tell you I'm going to keep this out of the papers if it's the last thing I ever do," he finished up.

Mrs. Rammell felt a little spasm of irritation run right through her.

" Is that all you care about? " she asked.

" That's all," Sir Harry replied briefly.

" Oh! "

Sir Harry sauntered up to her quite slowly.

" Of course," he said. " There are other ways. Suppose I handled this, for instance."

Mrs. Rammell stiffened.

" He'd never listen to you."

The hint of a grin passed across Sir Harry's face.

" 'E mightn't be the one I spoke to," he explained.

" You mean you'll make her give him up? Never see him again? " Mrs. Rammell asked suddenly. " You think you can do it? "

" Could try," he said. " D'you still love him? "

Mrs. Rammell let out that same unlaughlike laugh.

" Love him? I haven't loved him for years. I loathe him."

" Don't wonder," Sir Harry answered. " You're not his sort."

He had moved away from the fireplace and was walking about the room again.

" Better try my way," he said. " Better for the boy. It's quieter."

For once Mrs. Rammell heard her son mentioned without her whole heart turning over.

" And if she refuses? " was all she said.

This time the grin was more pronounced.

" There's always Eric," he said. " You leave 'im to me."

At the door, he paused.

" Can't remember what it is," he said. " But there *was* something else. On Tuesdays, I think it was. With light refreshments. And a dress show. Never mind. Leave it all to me. I'll look after it. And don't worry. I'll give you a ring when it comes back to me."

CHAPTER XLII

NOT THAT Mr. Rammell knew anything of what was happening. So far as he was concerned, the whole of the Marcia affair had been kept discreet. Concealed. Unobtrusive. And the other piece of trouble, the extraordinary non-appearance of Mr. Bloot, his first unexplained absence in nearly twenty-seven years of unblemished service, had not yet even been reported to him. It seemed at the time altogether too insignificant to be brought to the ears of the managing director.

In any case, Mr. Rammell was busy. He had discovered a new kind of dyspepsia tablet that had to be dissolved in half a glassful of warm water. It was pale pink in colour. Like drinking crushed geraniums. And Mr. Rammell was watching one of the little tablets dissolve at this moment.

He certainly hoped to God that it would do the trick. He needed something. Marcia had been on again about that desert island of hers. And the strain had been too much for him. As usual, it had been his digestion that had suffered. If he had been living on a diet of Worcester sauce and toasted feathers he could not have felt more uncomfortable inside.

When Miss Winters, paler than usual and keyed-up like a watch spring, came in to say that Sir Harry was on the phone, Mr. Rammell merely shook his head. " Not in," he said. " Say that we'll ring back later." How much later was for the little pink tablet to decide. Mr. Rammell was not his own master this morning.

Sir Harry, on the other hand, had never felt better. From the moment he had left Mrs. Rammell's, a source of new life had been flowing through him. He adored delicate negotiation. Handling people. Intrigue. It was right up his street. And he wasn't afraid, if necessary, to show his strength. That was where the secret of his mastery lay. It was, in fact, why he had just telephoned to his son. It had occurred to him at breakfast that after all the best course would be to get him round to lunch. Just the two of them. Talk it over, man to man. Have it out with him. Knock some sense into his head. Show him where he got off. Give him a real thick ear, if necessary. But nicely, of course. With all the gentle understanding of which only the truly loving father is capable.

But, of course, if his own son did not want to talk to him that was different. And if he thought that he could prolong his love nest activities just by not answering the telephone he was making a big mistake. Shilly-shallying was something that Sir Harry had never been prepared to stand for. Action was his motto. Strike while the iron was hot. If there was a bud, nip it. . . . At the mere thought that he was being played about with, given the brush off, Sir Harry felt his blood mounting. He'd show them. He'd get his spoke in first. Reaching out for the receiver, he dialled Bond 7000.

But it was not to speak to Mr. Rammell this time. It was the Staff Supervisor he asked for. He wanted to get hold of Marcia, he explained. Now. At once. Before she went in to Bond Street. She was to come round to his suite at the hotel. Straight away. Take a taxi. Expect her within half an hour. Suite 314. Just ask at the desk. Centre lift. Come straight up. Third floor, and turn left when you got out. . . .

It was nearly ten-thirty when Sir Harry phoned. And nearly midday when they found Marcia. That was because she had just been trying out a new beauty treatment. Radio-active moss. It was an American woman beautician of over sixty—either miraculously well preserved by her own imported lichens or merely lying inversely about her age—who had introduced it to London. And she had been writing and telephoning to Marcia ever since she had got here. Inevitably, there is something flattering about personal invitation. Especially when it is repeated. And Marcia was particularly susceptible to anything that was free. Always had been. Ever since childhood. Had been forced, in fact, to *train* herself to refuse. But she saw now how wrong she had been to refuse this one. Already a well-known Viscountess had given an interview to the Press saying how much better she felt after wallowing about in the stuff, and two TV lady panellists were next on the list. Marcia had felt that she could wait no longer. And, in the result, she was at that moment in a clinically redecorated Knightsbridge basement, lying in a kind of bath, with a load of faintly evil-smelling undergrowth on top of her and the smooth pink-and-white face of the proprietress smiling down like an expensive moon.

Even when the Staff Supervisor's message reached her, there was nothing that Marcia could do. She was only about half-way through the treatment. And the stuff all had to be scraped off again. It was getting on for twelve-thirty before she re-emerged into the daylight. Hot and rather prickly feeling, as though it might have been measles and not merely moss that she had contacted, she called a taxi and set out for the hotel.

Sir Harry had a brandy and soda in his hand when she got there. And he was smoking one of the lighter sort of cigars that he preferred before lunchtime. Marcia refused the glass of sherry that he offered her. Declined even a cigarette out of the big, silver box with the two kinds in it. Just sat there, pale despite the prickly heat that was still running all over her, her hands in her lap and her legs half-crossed as the deportment school had taught her. On the whole, Sir Harry was rather pleased with her. Seen at close quarters, she was less hard and brassy than he had expected. And Marcia felt herself every moment warming more and more towards him. For a start, he was so much younger than she had realised. Not in years, exactly. But in manner. And appearance. As long as she could remember she had always adored men in fancy waist-coats. And Sir Harry's was certainly one of the fanciest. Tapestry damask of some kind, she supposed it was. She would rather have liked an evening-dress in the same material. But it wasn't only his waistcoat. It was his shoes, as well. Obviously handmade and rather pointed, they were pin-pricked all over the toecaps with that kind of lacework design that comes from only the most expensive kind of shoemakers. It was all strangely warming and reassuring. Like the room they were sitting in. Wherever she looked, she saw comfort. Luxury. Affluence. And naturally she relaxed.

She was so much relaxed, in fact, that she did not hear Sir Harry when he spoke to her. As it happened, she was thinking about his shoes again. Wondering whether they all had designs like that on them. Even the slippers. She was therefore surprised when he seemed to be speaking to her so loudly. Almost as though he hadn't been able to make himself heard. And the words, now that they reached her, sounded strangely familiar. It seemed the way in which all Rammells began their conversations.

"Well," he said. "I expect you know why you're here."

Even so, she paused for a moment before answering.

" No," she said, at last slowly and distinctly.

" Then d'you want me to tell you? "

Marcia paused again.

" Yes," she said. And because just " yes " seemed so brief, so perfunctory, so rude almost, she added " please."

The " please " was said in a lower tone than the " yes." It was slightly husky. And strangely pleading. Sir Harry lowered his cigar for a moment and looked at her.

" You're a cool one," he said.

She raised her eyes for a moment to his. This, she knew, was the moment for the slight stammer, the almost imperceptible one.

" Am . . . am I? " she asked.

It was then that Sir Harry experienced for the first time the basic difficulty of all conversations with Marcia. There was no progress in it. Nothing coming back. No assistance. Purely a one-way traffic.

He started up again.

" I'll say you are," he told her.

He leant forward as he said it, thrusting his head out towards her. It was a gesture that would have been recognised immediately by his colleagues as definitely threatening. Something unpleasant was obviously bound to come. And it came.

" What's more," he added. " I've had my eye on you for some time."

But Marcia misunderstood it. Mistook the whole gist of it. It seemed so terribly sudden, that was all. Before she had scarcely sat down. It took her completely unawares. She knew that under all that flat pancake make-up blushing was impossible. It would have been no use even attempting it. But it was funny that she should so much as have been thinking about it. The thought was something that simply hadn't occurred to her for years.

" Have . . . have you? " she said.

" Yes, I have. And let me tell you . . ."

There was a knock, and the door opened. It was the floor-waiter, with Sir Harry's lunch all laid out neatly on a trolley. Sir Harry waved the man away. It had been a long-standing rule of Sir Harry's that if there were something unpleasant to be done it was better to get it over. And he hadn't even begun yet with Marcia. On the other hand, it was ten past one already. He was hungry. Never had liked being kept hanging about for his food. And it occurred to him that at this rate he'd be missing his tea as well He called the waiter back again.

"Bring the menu," he said. "There'll be two of us."

He was naturally a good host. Always had enjoyed entertaining people. And it was years, literally years—getting on for quarter of a century in fact—since he had entertained a lady. The Edwardian in him took possession. He chose oysters. Nine of 'em apiece. And half a Chablis. And two small Tournedos. With a bottle of his favourite Barton. And some fresh pineapple.

He looked across at Marcia when he had finished ordering. But she hadn't moved. If it had been a photographer's sitting, she could not have remained more motionless. And he could tell at once what it was that Mr. Rammell had seen in her. Something to do with the way her head joined on to her neck. A sort of graceful droop. And her eyelashes. Half-way down her cheeks when her gaze was downwards. And, as he looked, he wondered what on earth his son could ever have seen in Mrs. Rammell.

But Sir Harry did not allow himself to be distracted. He had not forgotten the purpose of Marcia's visit. And he smiled a little to himself as he reflected on the sheer devilish smoothness of it all. The quiet, elegant lunch. The good wine. The coffee and liqueurs afterwards. The feeling of safety and security as he led the conversation along pleasant, conventional lines. . . . Then, *Bingo!* Let her have it when she was least expecting anything. The whole works. Cancelled contract. Detectives round at her flat to see if she had been hiding any of Rammell's property. Threat of an enticement suit from Mrs. Rammell. . . . Unless, of course, she decided to do the sensible thing, and let go. He was quite ready to make things easy for her. And, once he had really shown his strength, she'd be cracked wide open. Ready to agree to anything.

The waiter brought in the Chablis in a little silver bucket, and Sir Harry looked at it appreciatively.

"That's the ticket," he told himself. "If she's not used to it, so much the better. She'll never know what hit her."

But Marcia refused the Chablis, too. Refused it, firmly and adamantly. She had been weighed in that mossy Knightsbridge cavern. And the result had appalled her. She had put on nearly five ounces. If Sir Harry had invited her to eat a block of milk chocolate she could not have been more determined. Or explicit.

380

" No, thank you," she said. " No. No wine. No, thank you."

And it was the same with the claret. That meant that Sir Harry had to finish the bottle of Barton, too. While Marcia pecked and toyed with her Tournedos, Sir Harry filled and refilled his glass and kept the conversation going.

He was, in point of fact, surprised to find how easy Marcia was to talk to provided that no answer was required. Easier than any other woman he had ever met. That was because she was so good at not interrupting. And how he talked. About race meetings of long ago. About important deals he had pulled off in the smoking-room of the old Grosvenor. About days at Brighton with friends no longer living. About wasp-waists and picture hats. And about photography. Mostly about photography. With Marcia's deep, intense eyes fixed full on him he described stops, exposure meters, Pan F, trick effects, coated lenses. And, as he talked, he felt himself warming towards her. She was the first person with whom he had ever really shared his hobby. He felt as though he had known her for years.

Over the liqueurs, when they had moved back into the pair of easy-chairs by the fireplace, he brought out his collection of colour stereoscopes. They were the real pride of his collection. Shove the slides into the black vulcanite box, press the little red button at the side and there, miraculously, the three-dimensional world, glowing in the hues of God's creation, was held imprisoned in the human hand. Together they went through the whole boxful, the failures as well as the successes. Laughing like children—at least Sir Harry was laughing—over the one of the strangely inclining lamp-post. Soberly admiring the stark magnificence of the red bus passing Marble Arch. . . .

It was while he was bending over her, showing her how to hold the black box properly, that he was aware of the strange perfume that she was using. It was faintly briny. Like dried seaweed. Or moss that had been gathered and left neglected. It didn't seem worthy of her. And suddenly he felt sorry for her. Just because, any moment now, he was going to be so truly horrible there seemed no reason why he shouldn't be kind as well. Even indulgent. If his son hadn't got the sense to buy her any decent scent he'd buy it for her himself.

" D'you like *Je reviens*? " he asked her suddenly.

It was the only real French that Marcia knew. That was because *Je reviens* was the scent that she always used.

Even in Sir Harry's accent she still recognised it.

" I . . . I adore it," she said.

" Like a bottle? A big one? " he asked.

" Definitely."

" It's yours," he told her.

And, as he said it, he cleared his throat for the unpleasant part that was coming. But it was not easy. He had left it too late. Marcia had gathered up her gloves and bag and was on the point of leaving.

" Thank you so much," she was saying. " Thank you for a lovely lunch. And thank you for showing me your snaps. Thank you."

It took Sir Harry some time to get her seated again. And, saying what he had to say, proved harder than he had anticipated. He was missing his afternoon sleep. In consequence, his mind no longer seemed as clear as it had been. It was inclined to wander. He told Marcia that she was making a big mistake. He said that the one thing that counted with a woman was her reputation, adding that he was sorry that he hadn't met her when they were both younger. He warned her against lying tongues. He asked whether she'd prefer a lump sum or so much monthly. He offered her a stereoscopic camera of her own if she'd promise to learn to use it properly. He said that no good ever came of trying to snatch at life. He advised her to go easy, and let the youngsters have their fling. He told her that she had the longest eyelashes he'd ever seen on a woman with the exception of an actress whose name began with the letter " L " which was all he could remember of it. He asked for a point-blank answer " yes " or " no," was she prepared to do as he said, or wasn't she?

It would have been a difficult argument, even for eminent counsel to follow. For Marcia it was frankly impossible. The fact that he had entirely omitted to mention Mr. Rammell's name only made it harder. All the time he had been speaking, Marcia had simply been sitting there admiring him. Never in her life she realised had she been in the presence of a man so wonderfully vital, so dynamic. What he had been saying had been way above her head, she had to admit. But that was always the way of fearfully clever men. It was why she hadn't dared to interrupt him. Why, even

382

now that he had apparently stopped, she couldn't think of anything to say except " thank you."

But apparently it had been the right answer. Because Sir Harry seemed so pleased, even delighted, with her. He had poured himself out another drink and was sitting there beaming.

" Then what about me setting you up on your own somewhere?"

" Oh . . . on my own? " The words sounded familiar and full of a vague foreboding.

" Little hat shop somewhere," Sir Harry went on. " Or a beauty parlour. Choose your own site."

" I . . . I don't understand," she said finally.

Not that Sir Harry was in the least put off by that.

" Don't you bother your head about the details," he said. " Just leave all that to me."

He was cutting himself another cigar as he was speaking. One of his big ones this time. He had a large cabinet, practically a chest-of-drawers, just beside him. And the cigar was certainly one of the very largest that Marcia had ever seen. As she looked, she realised that, in the sheer art of living, all the other men she had ever known were no better than amateurs. Whereas Sir Harry was a professional. From those beautiful, skin-tight shoes of his, right up to the neatly-cut white wings of hair on either side of the bald part, he exuded the authentic aura of well-preserved expensive maleness. Whatever it was that he wanted her to do, Marcia supposed that the sensible thing would be to do it.

" Of course, you'll need some pocket-money," he said suddenly. " No fun being without it. Better leave that side to me, too."

" Thank you," Marcia answered.

" And you'd better not go back there," Sir Harry went on. " Only cause a scene. Just lie low for a bit. Till it all calms down."

There was a pause.

" Till all what——? " Marcia began.

But Sir Harry was not listening. He had jumped up and gone over to pick up *The Times*. He went rapidly through the paper and then found what he wanted.

" That's it," he said. " Solves everything. Why not have a breakdown? "

The fears, the forebodings, began to return to Marcia's mind. She allowed herself the nearest thing to a frown that would not cause permanent wrinkles on her forehead.

" A breakdown ? " she asked.

Sir Harry gave a little laugh.

" Not a bad one," he said. " You'll get over it. An ocean cruise is what you want. Something to put you on your feet again. What about three weeks in Bermuda ? "

Marcia was so much behind him by now that she did not even attempt to catch up.

" It . . . it sounds divine," was all she said.

" O.K., then," Sir Harry told. " That's settled. I'll send the tickets round to you. And the hotel. Fix you up in a good one. Everything paid for. And a bit over," he added, with a wink. " Quite a nice little bit. More than you're expecting."

" Thank you," Marcia said, dropping her eyes from his while she was speaking.

" In the meantime," he went on, " just keep away from Bond Street. Don't answer the phone. Be out if anyone calls. And return any presents. Make a clean break. And you won't regret it."

" Shan't I ? " Marcia asked helplessly.

She was confused. Really confused by now. But what a wonderful man. So rich in experience of the world. And in the other way, too. Really rich, rich. It had been like living in another world just being with him. So different from his son. She could see how silly it was ever to have imagined that she was in love with Mr. Rammell. It hadn't been love at all. It had been pity. The pity of a truly loving woman who recognises when a man is in need of someone. But nothing permanent could ever have been built on such a foundation. It was fatal. The kind of love that all too easily turns into contempt. With Sir Harry, on the other hand, it was sheer admiration that she felt. She admitted quite frankly that he was her superior. Would be ready to worship openly at his feet for ever. . . .

Sir Harry was already on the phone to Mrs. Rammell.

" Just as I told you," he was saying. " That's the end of that. Took it very well after I'd explained everything. Saw how hopeless it was. You can go on now just as though nothing'd happened. She'll be out of the country before he knows about it. Just the way I wanted it. Purely private. No scandal. Nothing in the papers."

384

CHAPTER XLIII

By FIVE-THIRTY there was still no Mr. Bloot. No reply from
Artillery Mansions. And no reply from Hetty's little shop. That
was what decided Mr. Privett to go round to Finsbury Park and
find out for himself.

And it was Chick who opened the door to Mr. Privett when he
got there. At least, half-opened, that is. He stood there, as no more
than a thin strip of a man with his horseshoe braces showing, and
peered suspiciously out into the narrow hallway.

" She's not in," he said.

But Mr. Privett had no intention of being simply brushed off
like that.

" It's not Hetty I want," he said firmly. " It's Gus."

Chick kept his shoulder up against the door. Even closed it
ever so slightly.

" Not in either," he told him.

" Has . . . has he been in? " Mr. Privett asked.

" Not to my knowledge."

" You . . . you mean you haven't seen him? "

" That's what I said, isn't it? "

Mr. Privett paused.

" Did he come back here last night? "

But Chick did not seem inclined to prolong the conversation.

" How should I know? " he replied. " I don't live here, do I? "

It was this that made Mr. Privett put the direct question that
he had been trying to avoid.

" Then what are you doing here now? " he asked.

" Comforting Hetty," Chick told him.

And that was all. Before Mr. Privett could answer, he had shut
the door in his face.

For a moment, Mr. Privett stood where he was. His hand went
out towards the door. And then he checked himself. He had no
wish to cause a scene. No more ringing. Or kicking at the panels
of the door. Nothing like that. But he was already determined on

his course of action. That was why he left so hurriedly. And, as soon as he reached the corner of Tregunter Road, he saw what he was looking for. A policeman. He went straight up to him, his voice trembling a little as he put his question.

" Could you tell me the way to the Police Station, please? " he asked. " I want to report a missing person."

The policeman wasn't exactly the one that Mr. Privett would have chosen if there had been time to look around properly. Too young. And inexperienced. He knew where the station was. But he was doubtful about the procedure for missing persons. Seemed to think that forty-eight hours had to elapse before the police would do anything. And, even after forty-eight hours, he did not seem to know exactly what.

But Mr. Privett was all ready to see to that. When they heard his story they'd do something all right. And then Chick would *have* to open the door.

It was the thought of what the police would find when Chick opened it, that terrified Mr. Privett. He had read of murders in Finsbury Park before. Mr. Bloot wasn't by any means the fighting kind. Too much of a gentleman. Wouldn't raise a hand to defend himself even if Hetty suddenly attacked him. And with Chick there, too! Mr. Privett knew that violence was in Chick's line. Two against one, and Mr. Bloot wouldn't even have stood a chance. . . .

That was why Mr. Privett was so surprised when he reached the station to see Hetty herself coming out. And she made no attempt to avoid him. Nor did she have the air of a woman who has just been grilled. Questioned. Put through it. On the contrary, she was open. Forthcoming. And defiant.

" Well," she demanded, " what have you done with him? "

" I . . . I came round . . ." Mr. Privett began.

But Hetty was away again. Practically accusing him.

" If you think you can hide him from me, you're wrong," she said. " I'll find him all right, don't you worry. And he's going to get a piece of my mind when I see him. Going off like that all because of nothing."

" D'you call his budgies nothing? " Mr. Privett asked.

Immediately Hetty rounded on him again.

" So he told you, did he? " Hetty asked. " That means you *have* seen him."

" Not since last night," Mr. Privett told her.

" What time? "

" About half past ten. He said he was on his way round to you."

" Oh, was he indeed? " Hetty replied. " That was nice of him." She paused for a moment, pondering on the significance of what she had just heard. And when she did speak it was obvious that the piece of information had deeply upset her.

" And next time you see him you can tell him to stay away, so far as I'm concerned," she said. " Running round the corner to tell somebody I'd let his blasted budgies out. I might have known it'd be you."

" He was very upset," Mr. Privett told her.

But Hetty was not prepared to listen.

" He'll be even more upset when he finds out what's coming to him," she went on. " Biggest mistake I ever made was marrying him. You can tell him that, too. He's just a big lazy sponger, that's all he is. I can get on better without him."

" Then why did you come round to the police station, if you don't want to find him? " Mr. Privett asked.

" Because I want to put myself in the right," she answered. " If he's lost his memory or something, that's his affair. He'd better find it again. I don't want my name in the papers just because of him."

Mr. Privett took a deep breath. Then he braced himself and faced up to her.

" I think you're being very cruel," he said. " For all you know, he . . . he might be dead."

" Well, he can't be dead enough to suit me," Hetty replied. " You can tell him that, too, when you see him. *And* with my compliments."

It struck Mr. Privett after he had left her that he had never met any other woman whom he hated so much. It wasn't that she was bad looking. Just not his type. Too full. Too big-boned. But he was ready to concede that she was handsome. And even in her present distress she had not let herself go. She was wearing her big fur wrap. And a new hat that Mr. Privett hadn't seen before. No, it was nothing to do with appearances. It was what she had said about Mr. Bloot. Even if she hadn't killed him yet, he certainly wouldn't put it past her now. She was a hard and horrifying human being. . . .

Or just common, as Mrs. Privett contended.

" How he could ever have thought of marrying her, I don't know," she said when Mr. Privett described the conversation. " I knew the first time I met her. Saw it at a glance. Common as dirt, that's what she is. He must have been out of his senses. Good riddance, I say."

" If he's still alive," Mr. Privett reminded her.

But Mrs. Privett was not inclined towards the gloomy view.

" Can you imagine Gus——? " she began, and then stopped herself. It wasn't so much that she was callous about it herself. Nothing like that. But she did know Mr. Bloot pretty well. Had shouldered his troubles before this. And she had never known him to be exactly the impetuous kind.

But what had really stopped her was the time. That little jaunt to Finsbury Park had made Mr. Privett more than an hour late already. And, if they were planning to eat anything at all that evening, they might as well have it now before it was completely ruined.

The suspense, the awful feeling of not knowing what had happened, was too much for Mr. Privett. He refused to go to bed. Said that he would rather sit up all night just in case Mr. Bloot turned up suddenly and needed him. Then, Mrs. Privett pointed out that they'd heard him at the front door every other time he'd come, hadn't they? And Mr. Privett went reluctantly upstairs. But not to sleep. He lay first on his back with his hands folded under his head. Then he tried his right side. Then his left. Next he sat up, pulling all the bedclothes off Mrs. Privett. Then he tried lying on his back again. And finally he went downstairs to make himself some tea. That really woke him up. It was nearly three in the morning before he finally dozed off. And then only to dream of stabbings and suicide, bodies flung into wayside ditches or dropped overboard and left drifting pathetically out to sea. . . .

He was in poor shape next morning. And the ride by Underground was poignant in the extreme. Everything all round him seemed so heartlessly normal. He didn't know what he had expected. But not this. He felt somehow that because of Mr. Bloot's disappearance the whole of London Transport should have been sombre and subdued. Either that, or talking of nothing else.

It was not, indeed, until he had actually reached Rammell's

that there was any sign of awareness of what had happened. Then it all came on him in a rush. The doorkeeper was on the look out when he got there. Actually standing at the foot of the stairs waiting.

" Mr. Preece has been asking for you," he said. " Straight away."

Mr. Privett's heart gave a bump. This was it. They'd found the corpse. Either that, or Rammell's wanted him to take over the main foyer again.

And when he reached Mr. Preece's room he could tell that it was more than the front hall that was bothering him. Mr. Preece looked so pale and bloodless. And anxious. He was sitting there, tight-lipped, with his hands clasped on the blotter in front of him. In the easy-chairs on the other side of the desk two large, calm men were sitting.

Mr. Privett knew them at once for police officers. He had never seen police officers before, when not in uniform. At least, not to recognise them. But he supposed that it *was* uniform of a kind that they were wearing. The senior one, who had iron-grey hair cut rather short and parted low at the side, was wearing a blue suit and a blue overcoat. And the younger one, whose hair was inclined to be wavy, had on a sports coat and flannels and a grey, belted raincoat with one of those extra storm flaps to it. Mr. Privett felt his sick feeling come over him again. It was because the thought suddenly came to him that all over London there were other men, in pairs—one in blue cheviot, the other in grey gaberdine—out hunting Gus down at this very moment.

Mr. Preece got up as he entered.

" Ah, Mr. Privett," he said thankfully. " So you've got here. You know about Mr. Bloot, of course. Being missing, I mean."

" Oh, yes, sir. I know about that. I wondered if you'd heard anything."

He paused, aware that two other lots of eyes were looking at him.

Mr. Preece squeezed the fingers of his two hands more closely together.

" I'm afraid not," he said. " But these two gentlemen are here to help us find him. They're police officers."

Mr. Privett turned and faced them.

" Good morning," he said politely.

The grey-haired one leant forward.

" Good morning, Mr. Privett," he began, and stopped again almost immediately. " It is Mr. Privett, isn't it ? "

Mr. Privett swallowed hard for a moment.

" That's right," he said. " Alfred Privett, 26 Fewkes Road, North-West . . ."

But the policeman didn't seem interested in all that. At least not for the moment.

" Do sit down, won't you ? " he asked. " I only want to ask a few questions to see if you can be of any help to us."

" Be of assistance you mean ? " Mr. Privett repeated dully.

The awful fear suddenly crossed his mind that perhaps they suspected him. Indeed, now that he had thought of it he didn't see how they could avoid it. They were bound to suspect everyone who had ever known poor Mr. Bloot. He could tell that they were sizing him up as he stood there. Seeing if he were the kind of man who would know about disposing of bodies and that kind of thing.

The inspector pushed a chair forward.

" When did you last see Mr. Bloot ? " he asked.

Mr. Privett hesitated. He realised the dangers of giving false information. But he realised also how it might appear if he were the last person to have seen Mr. Bloot alive. He could practically feel the chill of the handcuffs closing round his wrists.

" The night before last," he replied without looking up.

" And where would that be ? " the inspector continued.

He had a quiet, naturally friendly-sounding voice. It was ideal for prompting.

" At home," Mr. Privett told him.

" At Artillery Mansions, you mean ? "

" No, sir. At my home. Number 26. Mrs. Privett'll remember. She heard him."

The inspector held out a large silver case with an inscription of some kind inside the lid.

" Cigarette ? " he asked.

Mr. Privett shook his head.

" I don't smoke, thank you, sir."

The inspector snapped his case shut again. He realised that he would have to reassure this nervous little man in some other way.

" Don't you worry about what other people heard," he said.
" We can do all the checking up afterwards. Just you take things
easy and tell us everything you can remember. What time was it? "

" About . . . about ten-thirty."

" What did he come round for? "

" Just for a cup of tea. Same as usual."

" And did you give him one? "

Mr. Privett shook his head. This was where it was beginning
to get difficult. He had already lied to Mrs. Privett, and now he
had to make sure that it was the same lie that he was telling to the
inspector.

" No, sir. He'd just had one."

" So he just dropped in to say good night? "

" Yes, sir. That's all it was."

" And how did he seem? "

" He was all right."

" Not upset about anything? "

Mr. Privett was finding it physically difficult to speak.

" Yes, he was," he said at last. "Very. It was on account of his
budgies. You see, she'd let 'em out. That is, Mrs. Bloot had.
On purpose. He told me."

" Was that all? "

" Well, it was enough, wasn't it? He was very much attached
to those budgies. They were like . . . like children to him."

" And she let them fly away? It was deliberate, you say? "

" That's what he told me."

" Now why would she do a thing like that? "

" I just can't imagine," Mr. Privett replied. " Really I can't.
Not unless she wanted to hurt him."

" Why would she want to do that? "

Mr. Privett shrugged his shoulders.

" I'm not married to her," he said.

" You and Mr. Bloot are old friends, aren't you? " the inspector
went on.

" He's my oldest friend," Mr. Privett said proudly.

" And would you call his second marriage a happy one? "

Mr. Privett ran his tongue round inside his mouth."

" At first," he said. " You . . . you see she was younger than he
was."

" And had he got any other young lady friends? " the inspector asked quietly. " The kind that might understand him in time of trouble, I mean."

Mr. Privett shook his head.

" He wasn't that kind of man," he said firmly. " Mr. Bloot was good."

The inspector was silent for a moment.

" I suppose you've no idea where he might be now? " he asked. This time there was no hesitation. No swallowing.

" If I knew, I'd go to him," he replied.

2

It was, from Mr. Rammell's point of view, the worst of all possible mornings for anything like this to have happened. Why Mr. Bloot of all people should suddenly start behaving like a runaway schoolgirl entirely passed his comprehension. As soon as Mr. Preece told him, he felt angry. Angry at the one moment of his life when all that he wanted was a little peace and quiet.

But there was more than Mr. Bloot on his mind now. There was himself. It was ten o'clock. And he was on his way round to Harley Street. To see his stomach man. For one of his periodical check-ups. The way he was feeling nowadays, he simply dare not miss it. As it was, he'd been living on nothing stronger than boiled fish and Melba toast ever since Tuesday.

Harley Street, except for the specialists themselves, is scarcely one of the more joyous thoroughfares of London. The houses, for the most part, are rather good. There is a restrained magnificence about the whole terrace style. They must have been quite something. Once. But hardly now. That is because every one of them is so terribly sublet. It is the Gorbals all over again. Only with a separate brass plate for every tenant. Rented out in single rooms most of them. Nothing less. And, once you come to that, any neighbourhood has got the skids under it.

Because of the overcrowding, parking wasn't easy. Mr. Rammell's chauffeur had to stop right in the middle of the roadway. And Mr. Rammell knew what it would be like when he came out. Rollses and Bentleys everywhere. Patients trying to get in to see the specialists. Specialists trying to get away to see other patients.

The ceaseless busy throb of a commerce where it is always boom time.

Even inside the houses, the unmistakable note of multiple tenantry was still apparent. The shared living-room, for instance. Mr. Rammell knew his community settlement waiting-cell absolutely by heart. The mock Chippendale chairs. The pictures of wild geese. The horse bronzes. The old copies of *The Tatler* and *Country Life*. The brass ash-trays.

The woman who showed him into this little snuggery was as familiar to him as the room. Practically on his own staff, as it were. He saw her about every three months. Had done for years. And the same thought occurred to him every time. Despite the white, surgical-looking overall and the low-heeled nurse's shoes, she looked more like a patient than one of the profession. Perhaps it was the air of suffering that she so resolutely bore. Or her pallor. Not that Mr. Rammell was in the least surprised by either. He wondered how his secretaries would look if he stuck them out in the hall, tucked into the scooped-out part under the staircase, with only a telephone and an appointments-pad for company, and the visitors' lavatory right there alongside the filing-cabinet.

It was while he was sitting in that awful waiting-room that he wished that somehow he could get to a telephone himself. A private one. He had been on to Mr. Preece twice already this morning. And the third time he had tried, he had just missed him. In the result, he had failed to deliver his most important instruction. Whatever had happened to Mr. Bloot, he wanted the name of Rammell's kept out of the papers. And, no mention of Bond Street, either. The disappearance of a six-foot shopwalker was the very last thing that he wanted to see publicised.

Then the nurse-patient returned and spoke his name. Mr. Rammell felt himself tightening up all over. It was the same on every occasion. This strangely nervous feeling. As though he were guilty of something and was about to be rebuked for it. If it had been a magistrate and not a specialist in the other room, Mr. Rammell could not have felt more apprehensive.

Or more in need of him. As he settled himself in the period-reproduction chair—walnut, this time—he could hear his own heart beating. Right up somewhere behind his ears. And his breathing was in bad shape. From the way his chest was rising and falling he might have been running right up to the top of the house instead of simply coming in quietly from the next room.

"Well. And how are we feeling to-day?"

The same idiotic question that Mr. Rammell had heard a score of times before. It maddened him anew every time he heard it. As though any man in his senses would be there if he were feeling well. And the same infuriating plural. Not royal. Not editorial. Simply the old witch-doctor convention that they were both in it together, holding hands in a jinn-infested world, hoping that their squibs and rattles would keep the worst of the evil spirits from settling.

Not that anyone need have worried about Mr. Huntley Cary. He carried his own offensive aura of good health about with him. A large man, he had played rugger as a medical student. And he looked as though, between operations, he had somehow secretly contrived to keep it up. If not rugger, at least golf. Even squash, possibly. As soon as Mr. Huntley Cary came into the room there was a strong suggestion of cold showers and rough Turkish towelling. Mr. Rammell could hardly bring himself to look at him. Not that he was really any worse than the other sort. The thin, pale ones. Like gentlemen undertakers. With cold, spatulate hands. And gold-rimmed spectacles. And a tendency to grow roses. Or the mad kind. Shaggy and intense, who didn't care so much for symptoms but wanted to know all about Mr. Rammell's secret fears, his night thoughts, his love-life. Or the Continental-émigré variety. Smooth-looking. Soft-fingered. Smilingly confident. Serene. With memories, cherished ones, of cases so much worse back in old Vienna. Mr. Rammell had tried them all. And he had come gradually to understand why his own G.P. in Belgravia, quite undistinguished looking and abysmally normal, had never been able to make the specialist grade.

Mr. Rammell was undressed by now, and Mr. Huntley Cary's strong, almost nailless fingers were prodding into him, pressing, squeezing, probing. Considering his size, he was astonishingly gentle. Mr. Rammell had to concede him that much. But it was only assumed, Mr. Rammell knew. Deep in that healthy, athletic, schoolboy soul of his, Mr. Huntley Cary was aching to get the wrappings off. See the wheels go round. Dismantle him.

"Nothing there," he said at last, only partially managing to conceal the natural disappointment in his voice. "Not a sign."

He stood over Mr. Rammell, wiping his hands on a small towel while he was speaking.

" Why don't you take things a bit easier? " he asked. " What about a sea voyage? Try a banana boat. West Indies. Go somewhere hot. So you won't want to work. Just sit around and relax. Teach yourself to be lazy."

Mr. Rammell smiled grimly. He had heard it all before.

" Can't," he said. " Not just at present. Too much on hand."

" Well, that's all it is," Mr. Huntley Cary assured him. " Nothing there that six weeks at sea wouldn't put right. Think it over. See if you can get away. And, in the meantime, leave it to other people. Sit back a bit. Above all, stop worrying."

Stop worrying! Mr. Rammell was dumbfounded, absolutely dumbfounded, by the sheer imbecility of the remark. Because it wasn't as if he were the worrying sort at all. Never had been. It was simply that he was concerned about his health. Not for any foolish reason. Just because he wanted to be able to get on properly with his job. And how could he if he didn't know whether it was anything serious? For that matter, didn't even know how long he had to live. Wouldn't Mr. Huntley Cary do a bit of worrying himself if he felt a pain like a harpoon shoot through him every time he tried to eat a square meal?

It was as he was re-knotting his tie that he put it frankly. Point blank. Told Mr. Huntley Cary exactly where he got off.

" If I told a dissatisfied customer not to worry what d'you think he'd say to me? " he asked.

Mr. Huntley Cary looked up from his big desk where he was writing something. He smiled. There was an open-air, holiday kind of freshness about the smile.

" Oh, I didn't mean worrying about your tummy," he said. " That's nothing. I meant worrying about your business. Let it run itself for a bit. Don't let it run you."

Because he was still in a bad temper when he got back to Bond Street, his tour of the store was more thorough and military than ever. He visited everyone. Shot questions. Drew attention to slacknesses. Pointed out that the sales-point advertising for electric timepieces completely blocked out the cuckoo-clock exhibit next to it. Complained about the state of the floor. Spoke sharply to an assistant who was checking her sales sheet while a customer was being kept waiting. Asked why no one had reported an elevator sign that wasn't working properly. Said that Kitchen Utensils was a shambles and that he would expect to see it looking entirely different to-morrow, or else. Inquired politely after Mr. Gibbs's father who had been ill. Took his usual stroll along the pavement just to make sure that the windows were dressed properly.

On the way out he passed Mr. Privett. The look of the man annoyed him. He simply wasn't large enough. It was a big entrance hall. And it needed someone of the guardsman size to fill it. But there wasn't time to do anything about that now. The one thing was to carry on as though nothing had happened.

He caught Mr. Privett's eye.

" Everything in order? " he asked. " No problems? "

Mr. Privett looked straight back at him.

" No, sir," he said. " No problems. Except that we haven't heard, sir. About Mr. Bloot, I mean."

By lunchtime Mr. Rammell had begun to come round to Mr. Huntley Cary's way of thinking. Why did he drive himself so hard? Why didn't he let the shop run itself for a bit? But it was no use. He remembered now what it was that had put him in a bad temper even before he had gone round to Harley Street. The letter had been in the post that morning. Simply because he had not handled the matter personally, they had lost a valuable account with a cherished overseas customer. The plain truth was that he ought to be doing more. Not less. That was why it was important that he should get his health back.

It was while he was mixing himself a bismuth and soda that he remembered that he had not phoned Sir Harry.

Not that he need have bothered. Sir Harry seemed to have gone off somewhere. Incoming telephone calls dropped off to normal. And there was no answer from Sir Harry's suite. Mr. Rammell got down to the serious job of running a big business. Maddening as Mr. Huntley Cary had been, he supposed that there was something reassuring in what the fellow had said. Nothing physical. That was certainly a relief. He could go on working with the real anxiety removed.

By the time Mr. Rammell had got through the rest of his papers it was nearly seven. He walked across to the side cabinet. This time it was a whisky and soda that he mixed himself. That made him feel better, too. And he decided that there had been enough of work for one day. He would follow Mr. Huntley Cary's advice. Take the whole evening off. Go round and pick up Marcia. Dine quietly somewhere. Go in to a film, possibly. And then back to her flat, afterwards. At the thought he did not merely feel better. He felt younger, too.

Indeed, he felt so much younger that he began wondering whether Marcia's island idea really was so damn' silly after all. Suppose that he did decide to take a few weeks off. Then he could take the sea trip that he had always been promising himself. He could easily arrange a separate booking for Marcia. If it was one of the smaller boats it was improbable there would be anyone on board whom he knew. And in any case ships were different from hotels in that respect. If they weren't, the whole cruising industry would simply be finished. Not that he had definitely decided. Didn't want to go rushing into anything. But he'd think it over. Have a look at his diary. Try to keep a fortnight or so entirely free. Might even drop a hint to Marcia when he saw her.

The car had reached the block of flats off Sloane Street by now, and Mr. Rammell got out.

" Wait here," he said. " I shall only be a few minutes."

And it was in less than five that he came out again. He had gone straight up to Marcia's flat. And, when he could get no answer, he had rung for the porter. The porter had come almost immediately. He was a sensible, steady sort of fellow. And he seemed surprised that Mr. Rammell, as a regular visitor, should not know what he was telling him.

" But she's left, sir," was what he said. " I got a taxi for the lady. About four-thirty it must have been. Had a gentleman with her, sir, to see her off. An elderly gentleman. Going abroad, sir, I understood. Bermuda I think it was. Said she was giving up the flat altogether, sir. Said that she wouldn't be requiring it."

CHAPTER XLIV

THAT EVENING, around nine o'clock, the police inspector and his wavy-haired assistant called round at Fewkes Road. It was Mrs. Privett who opened the door to them. And she took them straight through into the back room where Mr. Privett was sitting.

Not that it was any interruption. Not really. Mr. and Mrs. Privett had been talking all the evening of nothing but Mr. Bloot's mysterious disappearance. And they had got nowhere. Worse than nowhere, in fact. Because every time Mr. Privett repeated his worst fears, Mrs. Privett merely drew the corners of her mouth down still farther, and said nothing.

Mr. Privett had been sitting in his shirt sleeves when the two policemen got there. And even though the inspector begged him not to bother—said that he would probably be taking his own off in a moment, if they'd let him—Mr. Privett insisted on putting his jacket back on again. It seemed more respectful somehow.

It was mostly about Mr. Bloot's habits and general way of life that the police wanted to find out. A subject on which, so they said, they felt sure that Mr. Privett could help them more than anyone else. And it was a sad story as it unfolded itself. Simply heartbreak leading on to heartbreak.

" No relatives at all that you know of? "

" He was an orphan," Mr. Privett replied.

" No brothers or sisters? "

" No one. Just him."

" Any friends? "

" Only me."

" No lady friends? "

" Only Hetty."

Mrs. Privett brought in the tea and they all had a cup. But it wasn't a very cheerful sit-down. Even though they deliberately tried to keep the conversation light and purely social while they were drinking, there were hidden undertones to everything. And the inspector kept coming back to the purpose of his visit.

" I wonder if you could refresh my memory about what he'd be wearing? " he asked.

Mr. Privett told him. Told him all about the long overcoat with the distinctive velvet collar. And about the cravat. And the brown Trilby with the bound brim. And the way he never went anywhere without his umbrella. And the natural dignity of his appearance.

" You couldn't miss him." he finished up. " Not if he was there. He looks so . . . so sort of important somehow. Handsome's the word."

" And what would you say were his favourite haunts? " the inspector went on. " If he took a day off where would he go? "

Mr. Privett thought for a moment.

" He didn't never take a day off."

" Well, Bank Holidays then. That kind of thing."

Mr. Privett thought again.

" He stayed at home mostly."

It did not sound a tremendously exciting or eventful sort of life as Mr. Privett put it. And the inspector wasn't getting the lead that he was needing.

" Didn't he even go for walks? "

" Only up to the Ponds and back," Mr. Privett said. " Just to watch me sail."

" The Ponds," the inspector repeated. " The Ponds." He was tapping his lower front teeth with his thumb nail while he was speaking. This was certainly a new line. But it was also a very tedious one. Dragging large ponds was something to exhaust the patience of any police force. He dismissed the thought.

" And before he lived at Artillery Mansions? " the inspector was asking. " It was Tufnell Park, you say? "

" Tetsbury Road," Mr. Privett told him. " Number seventeen."

" And before that? "

" Other side," Mr. Privett told him. " Number twelve. He was born there."

2

But it was not only Mr. Privett who was having a bad evening. Also around nine o'clock a big Daimler ambulance was drawing up at the London clinic. Mr. Rammell was inside. He had a nurse

399

with him. And within the clinic his own doctor and Mr. Huntley Cary were already waiting.

" Just as I told him," Mr. Huntley Cary said, rubbing his hands together while he was speaking. " Warned him. Gave him my advice. But he didn't take it. It's always the same. Look at him now."

Mr. Rammell's own doctor did not reply immediately. He was staring out of the window at the tops of the cars in Devonshire Place. When he turned, he was frowning.

" Curious," he said, " that it should have come on so suddenly."

Mr. Huntley Cary looked at him in surprise. There was nothing curious about it so far as he could see. From his point of view, it was all perfectly plain. Straightforward. Even obvious. Up to now it had just been so much guesswork. X-ray plates. That sort of stuff. No substitute for the real thing. Nothing like opening up and having a proper look see.

" Well, there it is," he said. " If the pain's continuous we've got to do something. Can't have anything like that hanging over us. Been boiling up to this for a long time."

He broke off and began flexing his left forearm. It had been a day full of consultations. And he now felt the need for exercise. Physical exercise. A ball of some kind was needed. But, as he hadn't got one, he had to do the best he could without. Selecting a knot in the parquet flooring for a tee, he half-turned his back on the doctor and began addressing it. Imaginary tee. Imaginary ball. Imaginary club. Imaginary everything. But completely real the feeling of satisfaction that he derived from it.

" And keep him quiet," he said. " No visitors. Not till we know what it is."

" I expect Mrs. Rammell will want . . ." Dr. Webber began.

But Mr. Huntley Cary stopped him. He was no psychologist himself. Didn't believe in 'em. Created more anxieties, in his opinion, than they ever managed to allay. And procrastinated. Never recognised when it was the knife and not simply more good advice that was needed. Like now. But, over the years, he had formed one or two conclusions of his own.

" No, you don't," he said. " Not now. Or, at least, I wouldn't. He's come in here to get away from them. All of them. That's what pain's really for. Gives you an excuse. Cut loose, and no questions asked."

He glanced for a moment at his watch.

"Lucky you caught me," he said. "I was just going off to the country. Can't stop very long as it is."

The matron came in. Calm. Quiet. Efficient. She seemed a member of a more highly developed species. There was an imperturbability about her that mankind does not produce. And a stainless cleanliness. She was clinically sterile. And smiling. A visitor from outer space.

"Mr. Rammell's all ready for you," she said. "I'll take you along there now."

She walked smoothly and silently. And swiftly. Not quite touching the floor probably.

In the corridor she turned her head ever so slightly.

"Mrs. Rammell's downstairs," she said. "And Sir Harry has been telephoning. He'd like you to ring him back."

From about ten-thirty onwards, it was Sir Harry's evening. And, all in all, he had never had a better one. He enjoyed every moment of it. The rushing about. The telephoning. The late hours. It was perfect.

By midnight, he had brought Mr. Preece to the phone on four separate occasions. Twice to say what he had just said. And once to contradict what he had said the other time. He'd been on to the police. The clinic. Mr. Rammell's doctor. Mr. Huntley Cary. The night watchman in Bond Street (twice). Mrs. Rammell (incessantly). And New York. The whole of the Manhattan Telephone Service was now out hunting for young Tony.

Not that there was anything to worry about, Sir Harry had just assured his daughter-in-law. Mr. Rammell would be as right as rain in the morning. He was confident of that. But, of course, with stomach cases you could never be sure. Safer not to take chances. Be ready for surprises. The surgeons themselves never knew what to expect until they had actually got their man on to the table. And then . . . Sir Harry humped up his shoulders to indicate the absolute unpredictability of life and left the rest of the sentence expressively unfinished.

He was seated in Mrs. Rammell's own drawing-room by now. That was because he felt too much cut off over in his own suite at the hotel. There was the clear need to concentrate. Make one command headquarters. Be on the spot in case of emergency. Direct things.

As soon as he got there, he put another call through to Scotland Yard to ask whether they were keeping a watch on the Continental boat-trains in case Mr. Bloot should try to slip the country. Then he turned to Mrs. Rammell. What was the point of leaving young Tony over there all this time? he demanded. Hasn't she heard about the dangers of New York? Gangsters. Drugs. Call-girls. It would be a miracle if the boy was still all right when they got him back again. And if Mr. Rammell was to be away for any length of time, they would need him. Not that he necessarily anticipated a long convalescence. A week or two, probably. Or a month, at the outside. Anyhow, they'd know soon enough. And be prepared for the worst: that was his motto. If it turned out to be anything really serious the sooner they looked round for someone else to take his place the better. Either way, it was a marvellous chance for young Tony. Not the sort of thing a lad of his age could afford to miss. Sir Harry was going to feel a good deal better once he knew Tony was on that plane. Not that he could expect to step into the top job at once, of course. What he needed was experience. Send him somewhere first. Overseas preferably. . . .

Sir Harry paused and poured himself out a whisky and soda. He needed it. Been taking too much out of himself all day. Killing pace, too. Absolutely killing. Always a strain thinking of everything that everyone else had forgotten. But it brought its own rewards. You had to admit that. The satisfaction of knowing that everything was under control. That no grass had been allowed to grow anywhere.

He turned to Mrs. Rammell.

" Seems a long while ago that trouble with the model woman, eh? " he remarked. " Told you there was nothing to worry about. Hardly put up any fight. Knew when she was beaten. Cost a bit, of course. But cheap at the price. Nice girl. Intelligent, too, for a model. Got a most unusual interest in photography. Talked of next to nothing else."

" Really," Mrs. Rammell said.

She raised her hand to shield her eyes as she said it. She had an absolutely raging headache. It was getting worse with every minute Sir Harry went on talking. But she had to be nice to him. He was trying so hard to be helpful.

" Yes, really keen," Sir Harry assured her. " Not just *click* "—
Sir Harry raised his two hands to eye-level as he said it—" and take
it round to the chemists'. Nothing like that. Natural sense of
composition. And colour. Bit of the artist in her somewhere, I
shouldn't wonder." He paused. " Well, she's gone out of our lives,
thank goodness. No more to worry about there. And no scandal.
Thank goodness for that."

He turned and placed his hand affectionately on Mrs. Rammell's
knee. It was of all gestures the one that she detested most.

" Expect you're glad now you took my advice, aren't you? "
he asked. " Just think how you'd be feeling if you'd gone ahead
and anything happened to him. Didn't come out of the operation,
for instance. Or only had a few months to go. You'd be kicking
yourself, wouldn't you? As it is, everything's taken care of."

It was nearly one o'clock when Sir Harry left. That was because
he suddenly remembered what he had come round about the other
time. Musical Tuesdays in the Fur Salon. Now if only Mrs.
Rammell would really put her mind to that. . .

CHAPTER XLV

IT WAS the fourth day of Mr. Bloot's disappearance. And, with
every hour that passed, it was becoming more dire. More absolute.
And the worst had happened, too. It had got into the papers. One
of the agencies had put it out. And little paragraphs, headed
MISSING SHOPWALKER, began appearing all over the place. Rammell's
wasn't actually mentioned. Not by name, that is. But the phrase
" a well-known Bond Street store " pin-pointed it just the same.
And that started all the assistants, even those on other floors,
gossiping about it again.

Twice that day Mr. Privett had heard Mr. Bloot's name
mentioned. Not that he needed any reminding about it. Mr.
Bloot was in his thoughts constantly. At night as well as by day.
Even though he was absent, he still lived with him. And it was not
just so much idle pining. There was action, too. Twice without
telling Mrs. Privett where he was going, he had set off for Artillery
Mansions on the off chance of encountering his friend. It was only
an outside chance, of course. But it still seemed worth it. On both
occasions, he had imagined just how it would be. The familiar
figure. The joy at greeting. The warm handshake. The muttered,
half-inarticulate explanations. The brief visit to the police station
just to set their minds at rest. The triumphant return to Fewkes
Road. And tea. And fruit cake. And peace of mind. . . . And on
both occasions it had been the same. Just the empty streets. The
blank windows of 23b. The loneliness. The evening desolation.

It was perhaps just as well that Mr. Privett had said nothing of
those two entirely useless pilgrimages. Mrs. Privett would not have
understood.

In the ordinary way, Mr. Privett looked forward to the week-
ends. But not to this one. On other week-ends, there had always
been the chance that Gus might drop round. Mr. Privett had
wasted weeks, months even, of his life just sitting there waiting for

that to happen. But this time it was different. It would be like waiting for someone from the dead.

And because it was Saturday, Mr. Privett was home for lunch by one forty-five. Ted and Irene were out somewhere—looking at flats, Mrs. Privett suspected. And it was a quiet, rather sombre meal that the Privetts sat down to. Outside, there was a fresh breeze with a hint of something more behind it—ideal sailing weather for anything in the *Dianthe* class—but when Mrs. Privett suggested that he should go up to the Highgate Ponds, Mr. Privett merely shook his head. It's a funny thing, sailing. For small worries, it is perfect. There is something in a good race that puts them entirely out of your mind. But for a real major anxiety, it is useless. Entirely useless. Worse than useless. That is because there is so much standing about to be done. And there is nothing like just standing for reviving past miseries.

" Not this afternoon, Mother," he told her. " I couldn't face it. Not up there. I'd . . . I'd keep on expecting to see Gus. Really, I would."

Mrs. Privett did not press the point. She only hoped that the mood would pass quickly. If Mr. Bloot took very much longer to find, it was going to be a terrible waste of money all that outlay that had gone on the new boat.

And the mention of Gus's name had set Mr. Privett's thoughts off again.

" Terrible, isn't it," he said, " about Gus's budgies. In weather like this, I mean. It would have been different, if'd been summer. They'd have stood a chance."

" No they wouldn't," Mrs. Privett pointed out. " The sparrows would have mobbed them." She paused. " How many had he got, anyway? " she asked.

She was not particularly interested in the answer. Was talking, rather, simply to keep the conversation going. Trying to make everything seem reasonable and matter-of-fact.

" Three, pairs" Mr. Privett told her. " Joey. And Billy. And . . ." He stopped. And his jaw dropped. Then he jumped up. " You've hit it, Mother," he said. " There was Tiddleywinks. I'd forgotten all about Tiddleywinks."

" Well, what about him? "

" Gus was going to exhibit him," he said. " He told me."

" What difference does that make? "

" Don't you see? " Mr. Privett asked her. " I mean this is what we've been waiting for."

Mr. Privett was so sure that he was right that he insisted on going straight round to the police station. And he created quite a sensation when he got there. It was the form of his introduction that startled the station staff.

" It's about a missing person," he said. " I've come to make a statement."

The sergeant on duty asked him to wait a moment. But only for a moment. And then he took him straight in to see the superintendent. Mr. Privett was rather pleased about this. And a little flattered. It showed that they were taking him seriously. And the superintendent was a thoroughly nice kind of man, Mr. Privett discovered. Friendly. Considerate. And not a bit searching or suspicious.

" It's very good of you," he said after Mr. Privett had told him his name. " We need all the help the public can give us. It's the only way."

That put Mr. Privett entirely at his ease. Before that, he'd been feeling a bit nervous. He didn't like the way the sergeant on duty had looked at him. But with the superintendent, Mr. Privett got along swimmingly.

". . . so if you can find out where the Bird Show is," Mr. Privett finished up confidently, " you'll be able to find Gus. . . . Mr. Bloot, I mean . . . too. He's bound to be there."

The superintendent, however, had a distinctly slow side to his nature. He didn't press buttons, or pick up the telephone, or do any of the things that Mr. Privett had expected.

" We've had a lot of our men out looking for him," he said. " All divisions. And we've issued a full description. He must be lying low, or we'd have found him."

" I know," Mr. Privett replied. " That's why I came round."

" But you say that all his birds have flown away. She let them out or something."

" That's right."

" Well, why should he want to go along to the Bird Show then? "

" He'd want to see what the competition was like, wouldn't he? " Mr. Privett replied. " I mean he . . . takes budgies seriously."

The superintendent thanked Mr. Privett again. And he got up as he did so. They'd make some inquiries, he said. And if they found out anything they'd let Mr. Privett know. If every member of the public came forward as Mr. Privett had done, their work would be a great deal easier, he added.

But Mr. Privett was not going to be put off like that. He was going to stay where he was, he declared, until they'd found out about that Bird Show. Because it seemed easier to humour him, the superintendent allowed Mr. Privett to remain. Not in his office, of course. There were too many other things going on. But he was quite comfortable on one of the shiny benches in the reception hall. There was the case of sports cups and the life-saving shields to look at. And a long Roll of Honour of other policemen who had given up their lives in the cause of duty.

Mr. Privett began to feel sleepy. The last few nights had not been good ones for him. Too much waking up with a start and remembering everything. He felt the need to make up for it now. His chin fell forward on his waistcoat. He dozed.

Saturday afternoon is never a good time for finding out about anything. Too many places closed. Too many people away. Not that Scotland Yard is like that. No Saturday afternoons there. Or Sundays for that matter. But even a full staff can't do very much if people at the other end don't answer the telephone. It was getting on to four o'clock in fact before they managed to find the Editor of *Fur and Feather*. Then it was easy. He knew everything. Carried it all in his head. There was one at Ipswich, he said. Starting next Monday. The big one, the Northern Counties, was the following week at Bradford. And the Southern Area Show was just closing. Brighton, that was. Marine Pavilion.

Mr. Privett was still asleep when they went up to him. But he woke very quickly.

" Then Brighton it is," he said. " Let's go there."

But that wasn't so easy apparently. The police force just wasn't run that way. Superintendents don't go rushing about all over the country whenever they feel like it. And, moreover, there are strongly entrenched preserves. Chiefs of Police keenly resent poaching. Once someone has entered their territory they don't like policemen from other parts even to talk to him.

The superintendent had a solution, however.

" Why don't you go down by yourself? " he asked. " Cause less

commotion that way. And it's a nice afternoon. Do you good."
He paused. "And when you find him," he said, "give us a ring.
You can reverse the charges."

Mr. Privett tried to persuade Mrs. Privett to go down to
Brighton with him. But he failed. It was, in her opinion, a proper
wild-goose chase. And she told him so. Said that of all the
ridiculous ideas that she had ever heard . . .

In consequence, Mr. Privett went alone. First by Underground
to Victoria. Then by electric train, at five-fifteen, to Brighton. And
it was cold when he got there. Very cold. He realised that he should
have wrapped up for it. But that's the way it is with Sussex.
Practically a London suburb on one side, and just wild nature on
the other. And it was getting on for night already. The lights were
shining all along the front. Practically to Worthing in one direction.
Out towards Rottingdean in the other. And over the sea just
primeval blackness. The wind, moreover, was getting up. Small
violent gusts that had become detached somehow—mere isolated
centres of turbulence—caught him slap in the face as he stood there.
And splashes of something that could have been rain but might
have been spray kept sluicing down from nowhere. Mr. Privett
shivered.

He had some difficulty in finding the Marine Pavilion. For
some reason or other he had imagined that it would be on the Pier.
But the Pier was all closed down for the night. And the kiosks
had a melancholy out-of-season appearance. He had to ask
someone. And, as always happens, he chose a stranger, a thin
melancholy man who had never been to Brighton before.

But he reached the Marine Pavilion at last. And, after the
blackness and bluster of the night ouside, it was suddenly all warmth
and brilliance. And uproar. As soon as he got inside there was the
authentic treble clamour of a Bird Show. A shrill, screaming chatter
that came from nearly three hundred little cages. And it was
interspersed with other noises. Sounds like cat-calls and wolf-
whistles. And the scrape of small, horny feet on metal bars. And
the peck of hard beaks on porcelain. And the tinny rattle of glass
against wiring. And miniature swings creaking. It was like the
endless tuning-up of a toy orchestra, with all the bass missing.

The whole show was due to close down by nine o'clock. And,
because it was getting late, it was not crowded. Mr. Privett was

able to walk round unimpeded. Not that it was any use. There was no sign of Mr. Bloot anywhere. At least, there was no sign beyond a sad, passing mention. In the catalogue there was the single line: *No.* 237 " *Tiddleywinks* " *shown by Augustus Bloot, Esq.*

Mr. Privett found the secretary at last and asked if he had seen Mr. Bloot. But the secretary did not happen to know Mr. Bloot. Also, he was busy. When Mr. Privett described his friend—the overcoat with a velvet collar, the Trilby with a bound brim, the cravat, the umbrella—the secretary merely shook his head. If there had been anyone like that, he assured Mr. Privett, he would have been certain to notice him. But, he added, he hadn't been on duty all the time, of course.

After the blank that he had drawn, Mr. Privett tried the cafés on the front. But he could tell at once that he was simply wasting his time there. With their king-size sticks of Brighton Rock and their 7-Up advertisements they weren't in Mr. Bloot's class at all. Something quieter, less *hoi polloi*, would be more in his line.

The sensible thing, of course, would have been to call it a day. Simply go straight back home. But having come so far it seemed a pity not to have one last look round. And Mr. Privett tried one of the side turnings leading off the front. Then he really got lost. He'd only been to Brighton a couple of times before. And then only straight down to the Aquarium. This was a different city. Mr. Privett not only felt lost, he was lost. He was in a labyrinth. Scarcely wider than upstairs corridors, the lanes branched off at angles. Turned back upon themselves. Stopped abruptly. And the shops on either side showed such an astonishing variety of articles. He kept noticing paper-weights, lampshades, coins, Georgian silver, soup tureens, dumb-waiters, commodes, sofa tables, spinning-wheels, work-boxes, every so often, something really odd like a trayful of ostrich eggs or a stuffed bear. If he had been on a tour of a mad museum he could not have felt more bewildered.

Mr. Privett knew when he was beaten.

" I'm giving up," he told himself. " It's no use. Mother'll only be worrying."

CHAPTER XLVI

JUST AS Mr. Privett was turning back, Mrs. Rammell's Rolls-Royce was drawing up outside the clinic.

A distinguished-looking woman at all times, she was at this moment wearing an expression of relief mingled with anxiety. It suited her. The relief softened the lines of her face that tended to be hard ones. And the anxiety gave her a keenness that would have been impossible to assume. It was the second visit that she had paid to the clinic that day.

And everything was going to be all right. That was something that she kept telling herself. Over and over again. She had her doctor's word for it. And Mr. Huntley Cary's. And the matron's. And the day sister's. But it was not enough. Even though they couldn't have been kinder at the clinic—and everything so spotless and efficient, too—she demanded more from them than that. Something positive. A definite statement. Not just a vague assurance.

Her own doctor was the most adept at consoling her. He had a habit of not letting go of her hand while he was talking. And, at moments like this, it was strangely comforting. It amounted to an unspoken declaration that, come what may, they would see this thing through together. She had never been more grateful for a hand-clasp.

Mr. Huntley Cary, on the other hand, was frankly discordant. She had begun by merely not liking him. Now she recognised that it was actual dislike that she felt. He was so insensitive. So impersonal. If it had been a piece of broken down farm machinery and not her own husband that he was discussing he could hardly have shown less emotion.

And, as soon as she got out of the lift, she saw him. There he was, talking in the corridor to Dr. Webber. Looking so well, too. The sight of all that brawn and muscle in such a smartly-cut grey suit jarred on her. And there was nothing there in the face, bronzed and weathered as it was by sun and rain, to reveal what he must have been through that morning. The ordeal, the sense of awe, at having a human life in his sole keeping. Evidently he had felt nothing. No emotion at all. Just a craftsman's superior pleasure at the job in hand.

Mr. Huntley Cary saw Mrs Rammell at the same moment. He came forward. His step was the springy, confident one of someone who has successfully finished a difficult job and now expects to be thanked for it. And he could not understand why Mrs. Rammell drew back from him a little.

" Well, Mrs. Rammell," he said. " This must be a great relief to you. You'll find him quite comfortable."

Mrs. Rammell braced herself.

" Thank you," she said. " I'm sure I will."

" Stood up to the anaesthetic very well," Mr. Huntley Cary added. He spoke as though the anaesthetic were the only really dangerous part of any operation. " Not quite out of it yet. So don't expect too much. But nothing to worry about. Going along very nicely."

Dr. Webber had come sidling round behind him. Compared with Mr. Huntley Cary he looked half-dead from the strain. Almost as though he'd been the one on whom they had been operating. He reached out his hand to Mrs. Rammell and another of those long manual embraces began.

" You're not to worry," he said. " He's come through splendidly. His heart's in fine condition." He paused. " Of course it was quite a big operation," he added. " So don't be upset when you see him. It's only the after-effects. He'll look very different to-morrow."

" But . . . but what was it ? " Mrs. Rammell could not restrain herself from asking. " Why did it happen like that ? Nobody's told me anything."

Dr. Webber looked across at Mr. Huntley Cary.

" It's nothing serious," he said. " I think we can set Mrs. Rammell's heart at rest about that, can't we ? "

Mr. Huntley Cary seemed almost surprised by the question.

" Oh, no. Nothing like that. Nothing to worry about. Just one of those things. Lucky we operated when we did, though. Got in just in time."

" But . . . but what was it ? " Mrs. Rammell persisted.

It was difficult to talk in the corridor. Too many people passing. And the Clinic isn't like other nursing homes. It is half hospital,

411

half hotel. The trolley that a nurse was pushing past them might have been on its way up to Sir Harry's suite in Mayfair. From underneath the folds of a white linen napkin the narrow top of a Hock bottle was just showing.

Mr. Huntley Cary drew them into a small waiting-room on one side.

Mrs. Rammell repeated her question. And Mr. Huntley Cary, balancing his weight on the radiator and thrusting his long legs out in front of him, answered her.

" That's what we're finding out now," he said. " But don't you worry. He's in good hands. The danger's all over. There's no cause for anxiety. You can just relax."

Relax! Idiotic word. How could she possibly relax when she still didn't know? And wasn't there something sinister, something furtive, about the way they wouldn't tell her? Dislike Mr. Huntley Cary or not, she had to throw herself on his mercy.

" Then it's not . . . not . . ." she began.

But when it came to it, she could not utter the word. Even saying it made it seem somehow more possible. So Mr. Huntley Cary said it for her. Not that he actually used the same word that she had been afraid of. In his profession he had encountered just this situation so many times before.

" Carcinoma? " he said blandly. " Why should it be? Your husband's a very fit man. None of the usual signs. We made a very thorough examination, remember. If there had been anything like that we'd have found it. No suggestion of anything malign. Nothing like that." He came forward and gave Mrs. Rammell a handshake that she felt was brutally strong. Brutally strong and ominously firm. " Now just you go in as though nothing had happened," he said. " It's all over now. No more worries."

He broke off and looked at his watch.

" Well, I must be off," he said. " I'll look in again in the morning. And don't worry, Mrs. Rammell. Don't worry."

2

There was a small cul de sac on the right-hand side. And Mr. Privett decided to have one last, farewell look along it. The other little shops were all shut. But, at the far end, there was a window with a light still glowing. On an ornamental bracket outside hung the sign Peggoty's Pantry.

" Might as well make sure," Mr. Privett told himself. Then he made his way towards the little café.

The light in the interior did not look so bright as it had done from the far end of the alley. And the blind was half-down. Mr. Privett's heart sank, moreover, when he saw that the table in the window had two wicker chairs piled on top of it. Either Peggoty's Pantry was shut already, or it was just shutting.

But Mr. Privett had come too far to turn back now. And, when he pushed the door, it opened all right. A chime-mechanism set high up under the rather fancy fanlight went *ding-dong*, and Mr. Privett was inside among the empty cake trays, the piled-up chairs, the dimness.

There was only one light on. And that was burning in a small alcove at the far end. Mothlike, Mr. Privett made his way towards it. He was already half-way there when a tired-looking woman in a gaily flowered overall came round from behind the service screen.

" Oh, A'ime afreed we're clewsed," she said in the polite accents of all serving gentlewomen.

But Mr. Privett was not listening. He scarcely saw her. All that he could see was a pair of feet. They were facing towards him, stuck out through the flimsy legs of the small wicker table with its orange tablecloth. Nothing else was visible. Because on the table stood a tall vase of Michaelmas daisies. And leaning against the flowers was a spread out copy of *Fur and Feather*.

Mr. Privett ignored the serving gentlewoman and went forward. At the sound of approaching footsteps, the *Fur and Feather* trembled. There were movements behind it. A moment later, a large, rather puffy hand reached out. It folded down one corner of the paper. And there, over the top of it, Mr. Privett's eye met Gus's.

It was a difficult reunion. The serving gentlewoman kept interrupting them to say that she reahly merst ersk them to leave because she should have clewsed herf-en-ewer ago. Mr. Bloot kept lifting the empty teapot and putting it disconsolately down again. And Mr. Privett was too near to tears to be able to say anything very much.

What chiefly upset him was Mr. Bloot's appearance. Instead of the florid, slightly purplish complexion, Mr. Bloot's skin was a kind

413

of dull, elephant grey. It sagged. There were pouches under his eyes that Mr. Privett had never noticed before. And the folds of his cheeks had grown looser as though he had been fasting for days. He no longer looked a large man. Only a large-boned one.

And Mr. Privett could see at once why the Brighton police had failed to pick him up. The description that he had unwittingly given was so entirely false. Mr. Bloot was in disguise. He was wearing a check overcoat on top of a red Harris tweed jacket. And in place of the usual cravat he had a yellow tie with a design of stars and anchors. The tie clashed violently with the pink sports shirt. Mr. Privett could not take his eyes off it.

Mr. Bloot saw him looking.

" Ah don't wonder," he said. " Ah feel ashamed mahself." He paused. " She wouldn't let me have mah others," he went on. " Not after Ah'd told her Ah was leaving her. Ah'd undressed by then. Ah thought she was sorry. But Ah was wrong. Quaht wrong." He paused again as though reluctant to relive those moments of his sad past life. " These were all there were," he added. " In mah suitcase in the hall. Mah honeymoon togs. It was 'etty who chose 'em."

The serving gentlewoman came up and went away again. Mr. Privett tried to bring the conversation round to the difficult bit.

" Why didn't you let us know where you were? " he asked.

Mr. Bloot shrugged his shoulders. " Too much on mah mahnd," he replied. " Ah've had er sorter blackaht, I suppose. Because of mah budgies. You understand. The shock. Losing all of them. And Hetty. Just lahk that."

He snapped his fingers feebly in the air as he said it.

" Poor old Gus," Mr. Privett said feelingly.

" You're raht. It's been er nahtmare," Mr. Bloot confessed. " Er nabsoloot nahtmare. Ah don't rahly know how Ah've survived it. Ah haven't eaten a thing just for thinking abaht it. Four days withaht a proper meal. Just hanging arahnd waiting."

" What for? "

" To make mah mahnd up," Mr. Bloot told him. " Decahd what to do."

" Where . . . where have you been sleeping? " Mr. Privett asked.

As he put the question, he regretted it. He feared that the answer was going to be too heart-rending. He suddenly saw his

414

friend on the pebbles under the Pier, beside the hull of some up-turned boat, sitting up all night in a steel-and-glass Corporation shelter.

" Ah fahnd er notel," Mr. Bloot told him. " Very comfortable. Rather nahce, in fact. In nappier circumstances, that is. No complaints on that score."

" You know the police are looking for you," Mr. Privett told him. " You've been reported officially as missing."

Mr. Bloot passed his hand across his forehead.

" Ah maht have known it," he said. " That's what Ah was afraid of."

" It's a wonder they didn't spot your name. In the hotel register, I mean."

But there Mr. Bloot only shook his head.

" Ah didn't use it," he said. " Ah used 'Etty's. It was all Ah could think of. Ah didn't want to be fahnd. Ah needed tahm to sort things aht. Tahm to think."

" And have you decided? " Mr. Privett asked.

Mr. Bloot shook his head.

" No," he admitted. " Ah'm still thinking."

" Don't . . . don't you wonder how I found you? " Mr. Privett asked.

He was a little hurt that Mr. Bloot had not been more openly astonished. Frankly incredulous.

Mr. Bloot did not reply immediately.

" It must have been Fate," he said at last. " Bringing you here lahk that. Ah was just leaving when . . ."

But he was allowed to get no further. The serving gentlewoman had reappeared. She had her hat and coat on this time. And she was carrying her handbag.

" Ay ebsolutely merst ersk you to leave new," she said. " A'm definitely clewsing. It's fer too leet already."

She moved towards the electric light switch as she said it. Mr. Bloot folded up his paper and got rather unsteadily on to his feet.

" Ah quaht understand," he said. " Ah'm afraid me and mah friend have been detaining you. We're much oblahged."

Once outside in the alleyway, Mr. Privett made a fresh attempt.

" Well, you can't stay in Brighton for ever, can you? " he said.

" Ah've got nothing to go back for," Mr. Bloot replied. " Not nahw."

415

" There's Rammell's," Mr. Privett reminded him.

But Mr. Bloot did not seem so sure.

" Ah've blotted mah copy book," he said. " That's what Ah've done. Ah've blotted it."

" Well, what about coming back home with me? " Mr. Privett asked. " To Fewkes Road? Until it blows over."

" This won't never blow over," Mr. Bloot told him. "This is it."

" But you will come? "

Mr. Bloot inclined his head courteously.

" If you insist," he said. " After Ah've paid mah bill, of course. And got mah bag."

They walked on in silence for a moment. Then Mr. Privett reverted to the secret of their miraculous meeting.

" It was all because of the Bird Show . . ." he began.

But Mr. Bloot stopped him.

" If Tiddleywinks had been there," he said, " it would have been er walk-over. Er bloomin' walk-over. That's what Ah can't forgive."

3

Mr. Huntley Cary had been right. And so had Dr. Webber. Mrs. Rammell had never seen anyone look so utterly ill as her own husband. He was asleep when she went in to him. And more than asleep. Drugged and unconscious. Simply lying there, existing.

So small looking, too. Mrs. Rammell felt a pang pass through her as she realised what a *little* man he was. Scarcely larger than a child. And no longer young. Definitely ageing, in fact. Without his teeth, his lips were limp and sucked inwards. They revealed new lines, new hollows, in his cheeks. It was more than ageing. He looked ancient. And the nurse, in combing his hair, had chosen quite the wrong parting. She had revealed all the pure silvery white parts underneath. Whereas the way Mr. Rammell did it, there was never anything to suggest more than here and there a sober flecking of respectable middle-aged grey. It was pathetic the way, now that he was defenceless, all the secrets about him were suddenly being exposed.

And about her, too, she supposed. She was only eighteen months younger than Mr. Rammell. If he was breaking up at that rate, showing all the signs of time, so must she be underneath it all. It was only that she always took such care. Studied herself. Never allowed things to go too far. And she had been more than ever careful since the episode of that dreadful Marcia woman. She had deliberately remade herself. Spent hours in the hands of a masseuse, the hairdresser, the chiropodist. Literally hours. That was the dreadful part of it. Soon it would be very nearly a full-time job just going on being Mrs. Rammell.

The sudden rediscovery of their joint ages brought a lump into her throat. She felt closer to him than she had done for years. She saw how silly all their bickering had been. How totally unimportant Marcia really was: a mere outsider who had tried, desperately no doubt, to invade this marriage that had outlasted her. How unimportant, too—yes, that was the only word for it—her music was compared with her own husband's health and happiness. She was a woman of quick decisions. But also of immense resolution. As she came out of that drowsy, ether-laden air her mind was made up. Her one duty was to get Mr. Rammell well again. That and nothing else. She was ready to give up everything for it.

The last, long handshake with Dr. Webber was now over. But it had been *too* long this time. She had glanced at her watch during the course of it. Because it was not only her husband who was in her mind by now. It was her son. Her Tony. She had the flight number, the E.T.A., scribbled on a piece of paper in her bag. And her secretary had telephoned the Terminal before she had left.

In an hour—and she wanted to allow a full hour to make sure that she was there ready at the barrier when he arrived—she would have him in her arms again. It would set the seal on everything that she had decided about herself and Mr. Rammell.

There is a distinct flavour of wartime and prison camps about the Trans-Atlantic side of London Airport. Something to do with the huts and the wire, no doubt. And only the very simple living could be overwhelmed by the magnificence within. The basket-weave chairs, the pedestal ash-trays, the strip-lighting brackets clipped on to the ceiling struts are no more than the foundations of the jet age. Not the fullness of the age itself.

417

But it's a sacred meeting place, all the same. The air is thick with expectation. Little pools of hope everywhere. And it's curious the way the barrier divides emotions as well as people. There's the stupid helplessness of waiting on one side. The eager joy of coming forward on the other. Vaccination certificates and airport coffee are both forgotten as the two sides come together. Then it is Re-union United and Arrivals Unlimited. A continuous twenty-four hourly festival. The everlasting celebration party of all the travel agencies.

Mrs. Rammell sat there alone, eyes closed. She was too tired. Too utterly exhausted. She had a headache. Her hands were trembling. And she felt slightly sick. It would have been more sensible, she realised, if she had managed to fit dinner in somehow. Or at least a sandwich. And a drink. But she had forgotten all about food. Hadn't eaten properly, in fact, ever since Mr. Rammell had been rushed off. Now she was beginning to pay the price. She had just caught sight of herself in one of the B.O.A.C. mirrors. And she had been shocked by what she saw. She was pale and haggard-looking. That was what she had been most anxious to avoid. It would only alarm young Tony if he found her looking an absolute wreck, a spectre. Make him think that it was a death-bed to which he had been so suddenly called back.

And everything was going to be all right, she kept on telling herself. It was nothing serious. If it had been, they would have found out. But would they have told her? That was the point. Were they keeping something back? Mr. Huntley Cary might have been. But not nice, kind Dr. Webber. He was a friend. He couldn't be so cruel as to deceive her. It was unthinkable. She was just worrying, agonising herself, unnecessarily. They had told her that the best thing she could do was to relax. And they were right. It would only make things worse for Tony if he found her all nervy and on edge. She *must* relax.

She was a woman of strong character. Quietly, deliberately she sat back in the basket-weave chair with the Speedbird emblem on the wall behind her, and willed herself to relax. She made her limbs go limp. She drew deep breaths. She stopped herself thinking. Her mind became a dim, empty blank. And into it, from nowhere, came the image of Mr. Rammell, so pathetically small and still, lying there in that ether-laden bedroom in Devonshire Place.

Instantly she felt her fingers begin to tighten. Her legs went rigid. The waves of sickness came back again.

The plane was on time. That was something. But the waiting was intolerable. Passports, currency exchange, Customs. How could they be so heartless? Mrs. Rammell wondered. She had been up to the policeman at the barrier three times already. And heaven knows it would have been simple enough to allow Tony through first. Just this once. It wasn't favouritism that she was asking. Only ordinary decent feeling. She wouldn't have asked at all if it hadn't been urgent.

That was what made it all the stranger that, when she did see him, she did not recognise him. His back was towards her as he stood at the Customs counter. All that she could see was one of those long, sacklike American sports coats with a camera strap slung over it and a pair of blue, non-U trousers.

It wasn't until he turned that she saw that it really was Tony. And even then she could scarcely believe it. Because his hair was so entirely different. The long lock that fell across his forehead was the last thing that she remembered about him. She had fondly pushed it back when she had kissed him good-bye. Had told him to remember to get his hair cut when he got there. But not like that. The result was appalling. Conscript stuff. He looked like some kind of awful college sportsman as he came towards her.

But it was still wonderful to have him in her arms again. It was the same Tony underneath. But was it? He seemed to have put on weight. Grown thicker all over. More muscular. She was still aching from the embrace that he had just given her.

". . . and how is he?" she heard him asking.

This was the moment on which everything depended. She must be reassuring. Must be strong.

"Thank God, it's nothing serious," she said, not believing a word that she was telling him. "But it's been a big operation. He's terribly weak. We must get him to go away somewhere. Just as soon as he can be moved. He mustn't think of going back to Bond Street."

She watched his face closely while she was speaking. It was her duty. She had to be quite sure that he really did believe her. That she had convinced him. It would have been criminal to leave him brooding, anxious, fearing the worst. His reply, however, surprised her.

" Pity it had to be an English surgeon," was what he said.

" Oh, but Mr. Huntley Cary . . ." she began, astonished to find herself actually defending the man.

" I'm afraid they've got us licked over there," Tony told her. " All the way along the line. If a second opinion's needed we'd better get one over. No point in taking chances."

The suggestion that they hadn't done everything was so hurtful —even though she knew that it was quite, quite unintentional— that she winced. And more than winced. She nearly wept. She had to keep on biting down hard on her lip so that Tony should never know that she was actually crying.

But already the dear boy was trying to make amends. Clumsily seeking to prove how much he really loved her.

" You poor old dear," he said. " You certainly have had a packet."

There had been something in Tony's voice that she had always loved. It was not in the least like either hers or Mr. Rammell's. And being called a " poor old dear " moved her strangely. Just when she had thought that she would really be able to stop crying, she found herself wanting to start all over again.

By the time they had got out of London Airport and the lamp-posts and the little villas of the Great West Road went sliding past them, Mrs. Rammell felt better. So much better that she felt that she could tackle him.

" Tony, darling," she said. " What *have* you done with your hair? "

He grinned. Rather self-consciously, she thought.

" Oh, that," he said. " That's because of squash. I've been playing rather a lot of squash. Harvard Club mostly."

Mrs. Rammell felt herself groping.

" But . . . but you don't like games," she reminded him.

" Had to do something," he replied. " And I've come on quite a lot." He paused. " Better keep it up, I suppose. If I don't, I'll go off again."

Mrs. Rammell glanced out of the car windows. More lamp-posts. More little villas. More Great West Road. But she did not want to say anything for a moment. This was not the son she knew who had just been speaking.

" What music did you hear? " she asked at last. " How was the Opera? "

This at least was something that they could share together. It had always been one of the strongest bonds between them, their deep love of music.

" Didn't get there," he told her. " Hadn't really got the time."

" No time? "

" That's right," Tony answered.

Mrs. Rammell turned and faced him.

" But what ever were you doing? " she asked bewilderedly.

" Oh, this and that, you know," he replied. " Seeing people mostly, I suppose."

" And have you made a lot of new friends? " she asked encouragingly. " You must keep in touch with them. Write to them as often as you can."

" Or telephone," Tony said briefly.

Mrs. Rammell looked away again. Same lamp-posts. Same villas. Same Great West Road. Same stranger sitting on the seat beside her. If it had been the moon and not merely Manhattan from which he had just returned he could not have seemed more foreign.

This time it was Tony who spoke.

" How's the Old Man? " he asked.

" Grandfather, you mean? "

Mrs. Rammell tried to speak easily, casually. Only by being quiet and civilised could she hope to break down this dreadful, artificial brashness that Tony had picked up on the other side.

" He's just the same," she went on. " Really wonderful. Quite wonderful. He was coming out to the airport to-night. But he changed his mind."

" Thank God for that."

Mrs. Rammell tapped Tony's hand.

" Now you're not to be naughty about him," she said. " You're not to be rude. You know he's very fond of you. And he only stayed behind because he had some business to do. He's seeing Mr. Preece."

" Whatever for? "

Mrs. Rammell paused. Inside her black suède gloves she drew her fingers together and pressed hard. Above all things, she and

Tony mustn't quarrel. There mustn't be even the smallest hint how desperately vexed she was becoming.

" There must have been something he wanted to discuss with him," she replied. " Because . . . because your father's away, of course."

" Preece is all right in his own way," Tony said. " He's useful. But not big enough."

" Big enough for what? "

" To take over from father."

Mrs. Rammell jumped as he said it.

" Take over? " she repeated. " Whatever do you mean? There's no question of that. Nobody's suggesting it. Mr. Preece of all people! Besides, your father'll be back in a few weeks. If anybody takes over, it ought to be . . ."

Tony, however, had finished the sentence for her.

" Me, I suppose," he said.

Mrs. Rammell started forward to deny it. Contradict him. Put his anxious, schoolboy mind at rest. But she was too late.

" That's what I was coming to," he said. " Somebody's got to do something. It's not good enough the way it is. We don't know it, but we're slipping."

It was as much as anything else the use of the word " we " that frightened her. She had never heard Tony use it in that way before. And she had to be certain that she had understood him.

" You . . . you mean the business? " she asked.

Tony nodded.

" Uhu," he said, using one of those maddening Americanisations that he had acquired since he had gone away. " We're behind the times. Archaic. We used not to be. The Old Man had all the right ideas. Before he went ga-ga, that is. Dad never really got to grips with it. They shouldn't have put him there. It isn't really his life."

There was a pause. An angry, hostile pause.

" I don't know what you're saying," Mrs. Rammell heard her own voice declaring. " I don't really. Your father's nearly killed himself "—her voice almost broke for a moment as she said the words—" working, working, working all the time. He's never spared himself for a single moment."

" But no new ideas," Tony told her. " Not one. They all come from the Old Man. They're barmy most of them. But he's right, you know. What a business like ours needs is some fresh thinking."

422

It was no use. Mrs. Rammell was crying quite openly by now. Not so that Tony could see, of course. She had turned her head away again. The lamp-posts remained. But the little villas had disappeared. And the Great West Road had gone on. They had reached the factories. Big ones. Fancy ones. Factories that looked as though they had been turned out of ice-cream moulds. Industrial Neapolitan specialities. With chrome and neon decorations. They were swimming past her, looking bigger through the tears.

"What do you intend to do?" she said at last.

She spoke slowly, carefully, separating the words to make sure that she would be able to say them.

"Talk to 'em about it, of course," he said. "Make 'em see sense. Get Dad to go to America. Brighten them up a bit. Think big."

It was the second time already he had used that vulgar word. And it made her forgive him everything. As she glanced down at him she could see how ridiculously young he really was. Of course, a clever, impressionable boy was bound to have been affected by America. She had heard that the influence of New York on otherwise quite mature and steady people was really quite remarkable. It was one of the reasons why she hadn't wanted him to go there in the first place.

And they were holding hands by now. He had reached out and found hers. That showed how much of a grown man he was. It showed that he still needed her. Felt the want of security that she alone could give. She clasped her fingers on his and sat there saying nothing.

As they drew up at the house, Mrs. Rammell felt quite different. Like herself again. It was wonderful. After the anxiety, the waiting, of the last twenty-four hours, she really could relax. Nothing was going to happen to Mr. Rammell. She felt sure of that now. And Tony really belonged to her again. She hadn't lost him as she had begun to fear she had.

"Now you go straight up and get into bed," she told him. "I've said you're not to be called. I want you to have your sleep out."

But Tony wouldn't hear of it.

"Not till I've been round to the nursing home," he said. "He may be wanting something. You know what those places are."

Mr. Privett's homecoming was a bit of an anti-climax. It seemed so normal, so ordinary, to be walking up Fewkes Road with Mr. Bloot there beside him. But Mrs. Privett seemed to think that the whole thing was a put-up job between the two of them.

" Good evening, Gus," she said coldly. " So he found you, did he? "

Mrs. Privett was so offhand, in fact, that Mr. Privett had to take her to one side and explain matters.

". . . and because of the shock, he's had a sort of breakdown," he said carefully. " He . . . he needs nursing and looking after."

" And you expect me to do it, I suppose."

" There's no one else," Mr. Privett told her. " Not now. Only me. I'll help, of course."

Mrs. Privett drew her mouth down.

" I never heard anything so ridiculous," she said. " All because of a few budgies." She paused. " Oh, well, I suppose I'd better put a kettle on. You'll both be needing something."

" Thank you, Mother . . ." Mr. Privett began.

But Mrs. Privett turned on him.

" And now you both go round to the Police Station," she said. " He's caused quite enough trouble already. It's not fair letting them go on looking for him when he's just sitting here. They've got more important things to do."

By the time they got back from the Police Station, Mrs. Privett had got a meal ready. And Mr. Bloot brightened up at the sight of it. Considering his ordeal, his appetite seemed remarkably healthy. He even recovered sufficiently to take an interest in other than his own affairs. Mr. Rammell's illness in particular distressed him.

" Mah mah," he said. " To think of it. Him and me. Both away together. Ah can't believe it."

The gravity of Rammell's predicament continued to impress him.

" If only Ah'd known," he kept saying, " Ah could have trahd to oblahje." He paused. " Ah wonder how they managed."

" *He* looked after it," Mrs. Privett told him pointedly.

" Ah know, Ah know," Mr. Bloot replied. " Ah'm sure they all did their best. But Ah'm all raht again now. Ah'll be able to take over on Monday." There was a pause. Then he resumed. " Ah can just see Mr. Preece's face when Ah walk in. The look of relief on it."

Mr. Bloot asked Mrs. Privett's permission, and poured himself another cup of tea.

" Of course," he said. " There's more to it than Mr. Preece. There's 'Etty. That's going to be unpleasant. 'Er begging me to go back, Ah mean."

Mr. Privett started to say something and then stopped himself. Mr. Bloot, however, was ready to speak again.

" Mahnd you," he said. " Ah don't regret it. Marrying 'Etty, Ah mean. She had something. Ah was very prahd of 'Etty when we went aht anywhere. Before she cooled off, that is."

But Mr. Bloot was tired by now. Tired, and obviously relaxed. He gave a long, luxurious sigh.

" Quaht lahk old tahms," he said to nobody in particular. " Rahnd the fah. Just the three of us."

BOOK FIVE

Bond Street in Retrospect

NOWADAYS THEY never even mention Mr. Bloot. Not any longer.
Too many other things have been happening. Too much going on
in all departments. After all, three years is quite a time. There are
some assistants in Rammell's, with their probation period and two
annual increments both behind them, who have never so much as
heard of Mr. Bloot. Simply do not know that he ever existed.
Sounds incredible. But it's true.

You see, the management didn't feel that they could have Mr.
Bloot back. Not after those newspaper paragraphs. His unexplained absence, his scarpering, was too unsatisfactory. When Mr.
Bloot did turn up in Bond Street on the next day, Mr. Preece
sent him away again. Told him to take extended sick leave. Said
that he would be hearing from them.

Mr. Bloot heard all right. The letter said that the firm had
decided to retire him. And, in recognition of his long service, they
were going to pay him a pension of three pounds a week. It was
Mr. Bloot's day of gloom when he received the letter. And
the gloom came a good forty-eight hours too late. He had
failed to notify the Staff Supervisor that he was staying with the
Privetts. And Hetty in her present mood wasn't forwarding
anything.

Naturally, Mr. Privett wanted Mr. Bloot to go on living with
them. Make Fewkes Road his headquarters. Look on it as home.
But here some latent instinct of reserve asserted itself. He refused.
And he was adamant. Less than six weeks after he had moved in,
he moved out again.

Just in time, too, for his presence to be remembered as a tender
incident. And not as a major imposition. Another fortnight—
another week, even another twenty-four hours—and so far as Mrs.
Privett was concerned, the charm of Mr. Bloot's presence might
easily have evaporated. Sorry as she was for him and deliberately
making herself remember poor Emmie, she still didn't see why she
should be expected to spend the rest of her life boiling kettles, cutting

cake, spreading bread and butter, making pastry, peeling things, washing up so that their visitor would feel strong enough to take a little stroll with Mr. Privett in the evenings.

The only surprise came with Mr. Bloot's choice of residence. Not that it was really surprising when you came to remember the long quiet history of his domestic background before Hetty came into the picture. He was not a man with an army of friends posted strategically all over London. Not someone given to dropping in and being dropped in on. There was, in fact, only one address that he knew. And, when he finally decided that he needed a place of his own so that any budgies he might have could get indoor exercise, he went to the only address that he knew. Back to Tetsbury Road. To the Gurneys.

And they simply couldn't have been nicer. The sight of Mr. Bloot, fresh and pink from the effort of walking, standing there in her own porchway was enough for Mrs. Gurney. She took it as a vast, unspoken apology. Forgave him instantly. Asked him in. Reunited him with Mr. Gurney. Gave him tea.

Of course, it required a bit of arranging to fit him in again. It wasn't his old rooms that he got back. That would have been too much to hope for. But Mr. Bloot was philosophical about it. He recognised that life is all change. Transformation. Metamorphosis. That nothing on earth remains the same for ever. And that it is a brave man who is ready to accept the unknown. So when the Gurneys offered him the first floor back instead of the second floor front, Mr. Bloot accepted.

What's more, it was a turning point. With good luck waiting round the corner. He got his old dining-table back—the big one with the casters—and the small bamboo piece on which he had always put his watch at night. But that wasn't all. Discarded by Rammell's, he suddenly found himself sought after elsewhere. There was a new bird food—TWEETIE, BUDGIES LOVE IT—that had just come on to the market. And the manufacturers asked Mr. Bloot if he would like to represent it. Asked him very tactfully, too. Explained that they needed someone of his standing, his professional record, to introduce the product. Otherwise, of course, Mr. Bloot wouldn't have considered it. Not common, commercial traveller stuff. Not bag work.

As it is, he is doing very nicely. A good five pounds' commission most weeks. And there is a big future in it. More hungry little budgies being hatched out every day. More packets of TWEETIE disappearing from the shelves.

The firm is so pleased, in fact, that they've offered Mr. Bloot the South of England. The whole of it. And a car. A Hillman. But only on condition that he can drive. And that looks like being a stumbling block. He's been taking lessons at a driving school. But the instructor isn't hopeful. Mr. Bloot isn't by any means a natural. It's the gears mostly. And the starting. And backing into places. And hand signals. And remembering about traffic lights. And other cars. And stopping. He's dented one wing of the driving school car quite badly. The Privetts don't see very much of Mr. Bloot nowadays. Except at week-ends, of course. Not with TWEETIE by day. And driving lessons in the evenings.

And Fewkes Road tends to be a bit quiet and lifeless now that Irene is married. Mrs. Privett had the idea at one time of having Nancy Parkinson over to live with them. Nancy's nerves had been bad lately. And it seemed the sensible thing to do.

When it was suggested, Nancy jumped at it. Fairly jumped. It seemed everything that she could want. Company. Friendship. Love. That warm feeling of being among people who really cared. She was ready to move in on the Saturday. Then she remembered about Mrs. Rammell. And she realised at once that Mrs. Rammell wouldn't like it. Not having her own sister in digs with one of the staff. She might think that Nancy was getting at her. So nothing came of it. And Nancy remained where she was. She still sent Mrs. Privett post-cards.

Not that the Privetts needed the money. Not since Mr. Privett had got his promotion. He is permanently in Mr. Bloot's shoes now. Main vestibule. New frock-coat. Cut to measure. Dress allowance to cover things like shirts and ties. And another two pounds a week. For the first few weeks Mr. Privett felt too guilty to enjoy it. As though, by accepting, he had somehow been disloyal to Gus. But he's got over the feeling now. Too many other things on his mind. Too much responsibility. And the sense of supreme command certainly leaves its mark on a man. Mr. Privett has taken to wearing a buttonhole. And he can afford to. He no longer has to queue up with the rest of them on Fridays for his pay envelope. He's monthly salaried now. He's senior.

And successful. The *Dianthe* has proved a real winner now that she's been back to Mr. Lumley to have half an inch *and* half an ounce taken off her keel. Obviously, a desperate measure. But there *was* something wrong with the *Dianthe*, even though Mr. Privett wouldn't admit it. As it is, she's perfect. Almost too good. She is now the most heavily handicapped yacht up at Highgate.

Mr. Bloot turns up regularly to see her sail. And he's looking more imposing than ever. New hat. New overcoat. New shoes. So imposing, in fact, that the rumour has got about that Mr. Bloot is the real owner of the *Dianthe*, and simply allows Mr. Privett to do the sailing. Not that Mr. Privett minds. He's happy enough just seeing Mr. Bloot and the *Dianthe* both up there.

But even though Mr. Privett's Sundays may seem full again, there is still something missing. Irene. That is because she and Ted chose Wembley of all places to live in when they got married. Why? Neither Mr. nor Mrs. Privett could possibly imagine. Nor, for that matter, could Ted and Irene. They didn't know anyone at Wembley. Had no friends there. Weren't particularly enthusiastic about being so near to the Stadium with all the noise and commotion of the football crowds. Had never dreamed of living in Metroland at all. It was simply that they went there one Saturday afternoon merely for the bus ride—and the nesting instinct caught them unawares. Nice little flat, though. With telephone. And constant hot water. And a very good-sounding address. The Buckingham Court bit fully makes up for its being N.W.9.

Irene isn't in Rammell's any longer. Not properly, that is. You can't look after a baby and be a career girl, too. Not at the same time. And, when it came to it, Irene put the baby first. He's over eight months old already. Coming up for nine. There was some trouble about his feeding at first. No appetite. Wouldn't suck properly. But, thank goodness, that's all over. He's simply enormous by now. Going to be an engineer. Or a scientist. Or something. You can tell that by the way he's interested in anything moving. Especially in things that go round. And it's a full-time job just coping with him.

Even so Irene hasn't cut adrift from Rammell's completely. She's been at the annual staff dances. The last one wasn't so bad. But the time before was terrible. She was expecting junior practically at any moment. And, of course, she goes along to the Sports Club.

Because Ted is secretary now. There is his position to be kept up. Fortunately, the sports ground isn't far away. Neasden is one of the few places that Wembley is really near to. And quite a lot of Rammell wives live out somewhere in that direction. And on fine Saturdays there are almost as many prams as players.

Of course, Irene is missing Bond Street. No good pretending she isn't. Even though she knows she's doing the right thing staying by Junior she feels out of it somehow. She's stood over by the sink in the little kitchenette washing up bottles and things after Ted has left in the morning, with the flat suddenly silent and empty-feeling behind her, and envied the other girls, complete strangers, that she can see in the road outside all going in the direction of the station.

And it is worst of all in the evening when Ted begins talking about Rammell's. Mere minor gossip. Like who's ill. Or about a row over a sale's slip with the date left off. Or the surprise love-affair between Office Stationery and Children's Hairdressing—just when everyone thought that Office Stationery was interested only in Electric Mixers, and Children's Hairdressing seemed all set for Travel Goods. Then she really feels an outsider. As though she'd been expelled, or something.

That's why she looks forward so much to Christmas. She's on Rammell's temporary list, of course. One of the permanent temporaries, so to speak. Good assistants aren't three a penny. And she can go back whenever she wants to. Last Christmas, for example, was heavenly. The same rush in the morning. Standing up in the train. Worked off her feet as soon as she got there. Only half an hour for lunch because there were all the things to put straight again. Ten minutes for tea. A splitting headache by five-thirty. And the glorious sense of being in the swim again.

It was during one of the Christmas periods that she saw Tony. Irene was back in Gowns and young Tony—Mr. Rammell by now to the staff—came through the department. Their eyes met. And he came over and talked to her. Asked about the baby. And about where she was living. And how she liked life in general. Stayed there beside her for a good two or three minutes. And it didn't mean a thing to either of them. Funny when you come to think of it. At one time he couldn't get that gleaming, dark head of Irene's out of his mind. And she had felt strangely disturbed, as though all her bones had turned to jelly, if she even caught sight of him. And

433

now there was just nothing there. No flame at all. Not even a flicker.

On Tony's part it wasn't simply that he'd known rather a lot of other girls since Irene. Not counting Marcia, that is. There'd been Mary-Lou and Brenda and, ultimately, Desta over in New York. And there'd been Pamela and Imogen over here since he'd come back. All—with the exception of Marcia—small, dark ones. With distinctly upturned noses. Evidently his biologic type. His fate. But he was too busy for any of them now. Was living a practically girl-less existence. Coming into Rammell's before nine and not getting away again much before seven. It's because of the long hours that he's moved into Albany. Only two rooms. And a bath. And distinctly dark in winter. But the best address in London. And so close to Bond Street.

Some of Tony's American ideas have caught on. Not all. But some. Particularly on the accounting side. There's been nothing less than a revolution up there. Calculators, microfilm records, photostat machines, electronic computors. The whole works. There was an article on Rammell's in " Business Efficiency " only the other month. And all Tony's doing. Not that he has become managing director in the meantime. Nothing like that. You can't expect to spend a few months in the States enjoying yourself and then shoot up like a rocket the moment you return. He's on the board all right. But that's as far as it goes.

It is Mr. Preece who is managing director. But he has only just moved into Mr. Rammell's old room. Still feels a bit awkward about being there. Rather self-conscious amid so much solid splendour. Even looks wrong. He's paler than ever. And thinner. So neatly dressed, too, that there seems to be nothing of him. Whenever he sits back for a moment it is obvious that he ought to get himself a smaller chair. But he's happy all right. Oh, so happy, He's got where he meant to be.

And, in consequence, Mrs. Preece is happy, too. They've just moved into a larger house. Farther from the station. Not because the old one wasn't big enough. Simply because they both felt that, with Mr. Preece's position, they ought to have something a bit more secluded. Gates and a drive, you know. Well, they've got it. And, as a result, Mrs. Preece is nearly dead with fatigue. She's having

434

servant trouble. And local labour won't come out so far. But it's worth it, seeing her husband go sweeping off in the morning in his new Sapphire.

As for Mr. Rammell himself, he's given up caring. After the operation he made a thoroughly good recovery. Even a lightning one. He was back on the job again inside six weeks. Six weeks too soon, as it turned out. Because all the old trouble started up again. More pains. More doctors. More nursing homes. For the next twelve months he was hanging over the office rather than actually a part of it. And, after the last bout, Mr. Huntley Cary advised him to throw his hand in for good. Cut clear and go off somewhere. Put Rammell's right behind him. Regard himself as having had it. Said that, otherwise, he wouldn't accept any further responsibility.

Pretty cool, when you come to think of it. After all those fees. And pooh-poohing everything. All the professional soft talk, in fact. But just like Mr. Huntley Cary. And very good advice all the same.

Because Mr. Rammell is much better now. He's put on weight. And cut down his smoking. And he's sleeping eight hours every night. With a cat-nap in the afternoons as well most days. But that's probably the sea air. He spends most of his time on cruises nowadays. He's been to all the places he ever wanted to visit. Romantic places, too. He's seen coral fish over the side. He's smelt the scent of cinnamon coming in on the shore breeze. He's seen palm trees apparently rising from the surface of the ocean. And frigate birds overhead. And flying-fish. And dolphins playing. Even a whale. Everything he could have imagined.

And one thing that he didn't ever imagine. Mrs. Rammell. Because she insisted on coming, too. At the first hint, she dropped everything. Resigned from her committees right, left and centre. Closed the house up. And moved into the double state room alongside her husband.

Just so that she could be there to look after him, she said. Not that it worked out quite that way. She was a terrible sailor. Even the gentlest of swells upset her. The stewardess alone could not cope. Mr. Rammell had to act as sick-nurse as well. It was a bit of a strain naturally, coming so soon on top of his own illness. But it certainly helped to keep his mind occupied.

They're off Cape Town at the moment. On their way to the Far East. And it is working out better on this trip. Mrs. Rammell has engaged her own companion. And Mr. Rammell has a separate cabin. He's comparatively undisturbed. Almost a bachelor. And, as he drops off to sleep at night, he's started playing an old, childhood game again. It's his ship. And they're sailing on a secret mission. There's danger in the air. Mutiny among the crew. The glass is falling. Fuel's low. And his wound is worse than he's admitted. It's going to be all right, of course. But not yet. Not till he's revealed his secret weapon. . . . Five or ten minutes of delightful, half-waking dream-drivel every evening. Real nursery stuff. Only better. Because now he can actually feel a ship under him. Hear the long creakings, as he dreams.

Mrs. Rammell's own night thoughts are not so restful. But then they never were. And there is one thing in particular that keeps coming back into her mind just when she thinks that she really is going off to sleep. She will never be Lady Rammell now. Doesn't see how she can be. Not now that poor dear Eric, bless him, of course, is so much of a back number.

There is another reason, too. But Mrs. Rammell has taught herself not to think of that one. Has closed her mind to it entirely. It's connected with Marcia, you see.

Marcia was too much dazed when she first arrived in Bermuda to do anything very much. Just sat about in the sun, reminding herself that this was where she had always wanted to be, and wondering vaguely about the future. Not worrying. Just wondering.

It was certainly a delightful hotel. She had noticed the names of two peers in the register when she signed in. And Sir Harry could not have been more generous. Everything paid for. And he'd opened an account for her just as he said he would. She'd never had more money in her life. More money. Or less to spend it on.

Naturally, she was grateful. That was why she sent him a postcard of the place. A colour postcard, addressed in that rather strange, backward-sloping handwriting of hers. But Sir Harry was not interested in the handwriting. Didn't even motice it. It was the colour that hit him. Fierce Prussian-blue sky. Indigo sea. Mustard-yellow sand. Veridian palm trees. He realised instantly that red omnibuses here in London were no substitute. And

B.O.A.C. did the rest. Forty-eight hours later he was out there beside her.

They're Sir Harry and Lady Rammell now. Special licence. Just like that. All on the spur of the moment. Entirely Sir Harry's idea. And, when he put it to her, she found it beyond herself to say " No." In the circumstances, it would have seemed so ungrateful. So unfeeling. She's learning Scrabble and Canasta. Or, rather, trying to. Scrabble is way beyond her, because of the spelling. And Canasta is almost as difficult. Naturally, it's simply heavenly being Lady Rammell. It's all she ever dreamed of. And so rich, too. Nor does the difference in their ages matter. Not in a place like Bermuda. The whole island is a love-nest for improbables. But she's finding it a strain. Make no mistake about that. She's out on her heels already. Can't keep up with him. The late hours. And so much loving attention. And the drink. And the photography. In all that sun she's stood up against balconies for hours, literally hours, while Sir Harry's been getting the stop right. Because he likes to have her in all the pictures. And she's only beginning to realise how much in the old days the professional in charge really helped. But life for Marcia nowadays is both so tranquil and, at the same time, such a rush that she never remembers the other men who once shared it. Not even Mr. Bulping.

And that's fair enough. Mr. Bulping doesn't remember her. There's a marvellous little hostess, a widow, at a country club outside Wolverhampton. She's taking up all Mr. Bulping's spare time. She's under thirty. And 34—21—34. He's crazy over her. Must be. He's just given her his Bentley. Lent it, rather. Anyhow, it's all hers. And he's got one of the new ones with a downswept tail. Still, if Mrs. B. will only do the decent thing and divorce him, he's reckoning on getting the old one back. He can take it. Wouldn't look at any house that hadn't got a double garage.

And that about accounts for all of them.

Except for Hetty, of course. But she was never really one of the Rammell family. Simply married into it. And, when she broke with Mr. Bloot, she broke with Rammell's, too. Mr. Bloot himself never so much as saw her again. He went round to Artillery Mansions the second night he was back. Made a regular evening pilgrimage. But either there was no answer at all or it was Chick

437

who opened the door and merely closed it again. And even when he wrote to her, she did not answer. Not that there were any charges or recriminations in the letter. Nothing emotional. Simply straightforward appeals for what were indubitably his. His other suit. His black boots. His umbrella. His linen. The empty bird-cages . . . in the end, still in the absence of any reply, it was Mr. Privett who had to go round to collect most of them.

When letters did begin to arrive, they were from her solicitor. All about desertion. And cruelty. And instituting divorce proceedings. They shook him up badly, those letters. Mr. Bloot had always strongly disapproved of divorce. It was, in his opinion, one of the signs that the country was going to the dogs. He didn't want to play any part in a divorce case. Least of all as the guilty party.

That was why, on Mr. Privett's advice, he went round and consulted Mr. Hamster. Naturally, Mr. Hamster was delighted. He saw the point immediately. As soon as he heard about Chick, he said that they would defend the case. And more than defend it. Petition themselves. He spoke of having the flat watched. Of tipping off the Queen's Proctor. Of getting Hetty turned out of the flat because it was being used for immoral purposes. Of having a quiet word with a policeman he knew, to see if they could get Chick run in for anything. Of suing for the return of the balance of his personal property.

All in all, the case—which might have been merely one of the undefended kind—is developing very interestingly. Mr. Hamster is pleased. He's putting his best into it. In some ways, it promises to be about the biggest divorce case he has ever handled.

Meanwhile Hetty and Chick were really getting along very well together. Rather too much to drink, perhaps. And thoroughly slack in their habits. Slopping around in dressing-gowns until midday on Sundays. Eating everything out of tins. Not tidying up the mess of ash-trays and glasses after the weekly card parties. But obviously made for each other. And it has to be admitted that the flat is a happier place since Gus left it. He did tend to spoil the fun rather whenever she had her friends in. " That old wet blanket " is how nowadays she generally refers to him.

But there's too much going on to waste our sympathy on anyone like Hetty.

Take to-day, for instance. Mrs. Privett didn't get to bed until nearly midnight. But she was up again at six-thirty. Up, and boiling things. The porridge was simmering in its double saucepan. The milk with an asbestos mat under it, stood ready to be brought over the flame as soon as it was needed. And there was an extra kettle on. Everything was ready in fact a good half-hour earlier than usual. The clock on the kitchen mantelshelf even now showed only two minutes past seven.

Mrs. Privett had laid the table the night before. And it was obvious that it was not by any means an ordinary Monday morning breakfast. Someone extra had been invited. Rather a special guest, too, from the look of things. One of the upright chairs, the one with arms, had been brought through from the drawing-room. And, as though that in itself were not enough, two of the best cushions, also from the drawing-room, had been wedged into it. If it had been a Pasha they were entertaining, things could not have taken on a more deeply-upholstered look.

Mrs. Privett herself seemed clearly keyed up. Her lips were drawn down more tightly than ever. And she was humming. Not any tune, in particular. Merely a faint, buzzing noise that indicated happiness, preoccupation and a sense of inner urgency. When she went over to the gas-stove and removed the larger of the two kettles, she gave one of those little signs that indicate that things are planning out the way they have been intended.

Then, kettle in hand, she went quickly upstairs to the bathroom. Filling the basin, she added just the right amount of cold water, spread out the clean towel, saw that all the odds and ends—tooth-brush, toothpaste, hairbrush, comb, skin ointment—were there ready in the little toilet bag, and went through on tiptoe into Irene's old room.

The door was already open. Had been open all night, in fact. Carefully wedged by a folded-up piece of newspaper. The curtains were drawn. But the sash-window behind them was down a good foot. And a screen had been placed in between the window and the bed so that a direct draught was impossible even with the open door. Still on tiptoe, Mrs. Privett pulled back the curtains, folded up the screen, closed the window and went over to the bed. Only then did she allow herself to come down on to her heels and set about waking up the occupant.

He was certainly asleep all right. Flat out. And blissful. A bit pallid perhaps after more than twelve hours without food. Even dissipated looking. With a tremendous sweep of eyelashes across the pale cheek. But still alive. And protected from everything. It seemed a sin to wake him up at all, she reflected. Better to let him go drifting along as he was until he woke up on his own account. But Irene had been emphatic on that point. Just because he was spending his first night away from home, she didn't want his regular habits, his routine, upset. She hadn't really wanted Mrs. Privett to have him at all. It was only because of Rammell's that she had even considered it. And it was all so sudden, too. Other Sale times Irene had got it all worked out. Ted's sister knew someone who could come over to be with Junior. But she required proper warning. Two or three weeks' notice at least. And this time she had let them down by going into hospital. Without her, it was impossible. So clearly impossible that Irene hadn't even bothered to fill up the Staff (Temporary) form that the Supervisor had sent her. Simply put it out of her mind. Told herself that Junior must come first. And tried hard to forget about the extra money.

Then, just when everything was settled, the Supervisor phoned up personally. It was nothing less than an emergency, it seemed. The 'flu epidemic had seen to that. Half the assistants away. And the Sales already started. Rammell's would take it as a special favour, she said, if Airene could possibly mennege it just to hailp them out for a day or two until their other gairls were beck with them again.

There's always something flattering about being rung up personally. It's nice to think that something enormous like Rammell's can't get along without you. Irene said at once that she didn't see how she could, but she'd try. And she knew perfectly well as she said it that she would.

Less than an hour after the Supervisor had telephoned, Irene was on her way by bus with Junior over to Mrs. Privett's to make all the arrangements. Not that she was ready to do the sensible thing and leave him then and there. She would bring him back later, she said, with all his things. He had possessions, it seemed, from which separation was unthinkable.

But it had all worked out perfectly. Even though she felt strangely callous and childless, as though she had just had Junior adopted and was never going to see him again, she was able to leave Wembley with Ted next morning, catching the eight-ten that he always took. And it was certainly like being home again to find herself in Rammell's. There was a warm, pleasant familiarity about everything. Same smell of the grey Wilton on the floor. Same dust-sheets to be whisked off and put away. Same murmur as the shop began to fill up and come to life. Same little treble *ting* as the elevator doors opened. Same rustle of packing paper. Same hum from the street outside. Same well-oiled whirring sound of the sliding doors to the stock cabinets. Same assistants, most of them. And so pleased to see her, too.

It was Gowns that she was sent up to. And just as well. There were two assistants away and the beginner, a Miss Hammans, was already complaining of a headache and a sore throat. In desperation, the Supervisor had even brought Miss Sulgrave over from Staff Stores. She was more motherly and affectionate than ever. Nearly wept when she saw Irene looking so young and pretty after the ordeal of motherhood. But Miss Sulgrave had always been a bit emotional and over-demonstrative with the youngsters. And Irene didn't consider herself a youngster any longer. Besides, all those years in Staff Stores had rubbed some of the gloss off Miss Sulgrave's technique. She wasn't really main-building class any longer. Still full of smiles and endlessly patient, she was nevertheless liable to lapses. Try as she would, " dear " kept slipping out, instead of " madam." And, even at Sale time, that was hardly a thing that could be overlooked.

In consequence, Irene might have been in charge of the place. It wasn't easy because she didn't know what stock they were carrying. But it wasn't really difficult because she was trained to it. And more than trained. It was something that was in the blood. She was in her element.

Not that Irene would even have considered it if it had been any other store that had asked her. She wasn't hireable. Not just like that. Loyalty came into it, too. And sentiment. And a bit of snobbery as well. After all, Rammell's was Rammell's. Though at Sale time you'd hardly know it. For a start, there was a different class of customer altogether. Different clothes. Different accents. Different manners. They weren't Bond Street regulars at all. Didn't come near the place in the ordinary way. They were invaders. Barbarian women from the hills around London. Female suburban Goths who swept in just for a day, intent on a little pillage in the plain.

Rammell's knew how to cope with them, however. Had been preparing for months, in fact. These Annual Sales were an institution. And there isn't much to choose when you get down to the morality of the market-place. There has to be a good deal of give and take on both sides. After all, it was the label as much as the dress that most of the huntresses were after. Anything to show that it had really come from Rammell's. And, in the circumstances, Rammell's was clearly to be excused for having done a little special buying so as to be ready for the rush. Simple little afternoon frocks, and even rather gorgeous evening-gowns, from workshops that were left entirely unpatronised during the rest of the year. Two-piece woollens and cocktail dresses, that you wouldn't find again on any of the hangers for another twelve months. Irene even felt rather ashamed of one or two models that had been brought in. Would have passed them by herself without giving them a second thought. Couldn't quite reconcile the way the seams had been turned in and the zip-fasteners sewn on with what Rammell's really stood for. But she had learnt her lesson when she first came there. In any big store, even the best of them, it is only the newcomer who ever questions the buyer about where all the fresh stock at Sales time has suddenly come from.

And there was no question of its not being wanted. By ten o'clock she had got thirty-four pounds' worth of business down on the check sheet in her book. But that's always the way it is at Sale time. There's a belief that only the dawn marauders get what they really come for. The others have to take the left-overs, the rubbish. It isn't true, of course. There's more coming up from the Stock Room practically all the time. But it's more than a mere fiction. It's part of the true faith about all Sales. It's what keeps up the spirit of the thing. Gets middle-aged housewives camping out on little stools with Thermos flasks beside them, just to be first at the counters in the morning.

It wasn't only the assistants who suffered. It was tough on Mr.

Privett, too. They took some handling, these customers. After all, he was the one who had to face them. He was the one who actually had to open the doors. And, having opened them, he was the one who had to step back smartly. Otherwise they would just have overwhelmed him. Because they weren't the kind to waste time by asking. They dashed. Straight through the departments as though they owned the place. By five past nine the sacking had begun. And Millinery was usually the worst. There were some hats that had been crammed on and snatched off again upwards of a dozen times before Mr. Privett had been able to take up his proper position again in the main foyer.

Because of the rush, Irene hadn't seen Ted since she had left him that morning outside the Staff Cloakrooms. Didn't even catch sight of him at eleven when she went up to the canteen for a cup of coffee. But it was quite understandable. He had his own world up there to look after. A world of catgut and rubber and stainless steel shafts and pale willow. All marked down. And all being pawed and swung and taken out of their stands by a separate race of male invaders. Only with a difference. There were more of the Rammell regulars among them. Steady, sensible chaps who had put off buying another dozen golf balls or a new tennis racket until they had seen what the Sale had to offer.

It was at lunch time when Irene went up to see him. And it gave her a real pang of sudden happiness to be reminded of how important he was. If you're in the trade, you can tell at a glance when something's a success. And there was achievement written large over the whole department. And that wasn't just the opinion of an over-loving wife. If things hadn't been pretty good, the management would never have knocked down the partition in the Downe Street corner to enlarge the floor space. As it was, Ted now had cycles and motor scooters too. It was garage as well as sports pavilion up there on the fifth floor.

Because it was the Sale, there was no time for the sort of lunch that husband and wife might have been expected to eat together. Nothing leisurely. No graceful living. Just a sandwich and a cup of coffee up in the canteen. No time even to get out of the place for a breath of air. Not that Irene minded. She was thinking of Junior. She was sure that he was all right, of course. Quite sure. With Mrs. Privett in charge nothing could possibly happen. It was only that Irene couldn't help imagining things. Like faulty

443

fire-guards. And loose stair rods. And cupboards crashing over. And traffic accidents when Mrs. Privett took Junior out for a walk. And dog bites. . . . Even while serving there in Bond Street, Irene in reality was far away.

By four o'clock, she had had it. Tired. Really tired. It was worse than housework. Worse than pram-pushing. Worse than anything in the whole world except being a shop assistant at Sales time. She hadn't sat down properly since she got there. Been on her feet since a quarter to nine. Had taken down more than a hundred dresses. Put eighty-six of them away again. Jammed her ball-point pencil because she had dropped it on the parquet flooring. Scraped her arm on one of the hangers because the dresses were jammed in so tight in the cabinets. Been rude to a large, hostile woman who had wasted her time by insisting on trying on a 38 when she could see that she needed a 42 at least. Made a mistake of ten shillings in her Cash Sheet. Had mistaken a regular for a casual, and had refused to change something because she thought it had been bought at the Sales. Had breathed other people's air for nearly seven hours. Had a headache. Felt swimmy when she reached up for things. And there was still another ninety minutes to go.

It was funny somehow to see Mr. Privett standing there waiting for her at the bottom of the stairs by the staff entrance. He was standing in exactly the place where he always used to stand. It seemed as though she had never got married at all. And there was the little smile on his face that was always there whenever he saw Irene.

" I've just seen Ted," he told her. " He won't be a moment."

This rather relieved Irene. Not because she was worried about Ted. But because Mr. Privett himself did not seem to be worried. There had been that awkward period while she and Ted had been engaged. Then Mr. Privett had always been at pains not to get in the way. Had moved off whenever he saw Ted coming. Seemed to feel that they were just waiting for him to go. Whereas, now that they were married, things were easier. The old jumpiness had disappeared. And Mr. Privett was himself again.

But she wasn't really thinking of her father any longer. Or even of Ted. It was Junior who still filled her mind. And all the way back in the Underground she realised that she could never be quite

444

the perfect assistant again. Not single-minded, that is. Anyhow, not until he was older. At school all day. And by then there might be another Junior. Someone who needed her even more than Rammell's did. She and Ted had always told themselves that they were going to have more than one. An only child can be such a problem. It isn't fair to them to be left entirely to themselves so much. And the gap should never be too long anyway. . . . In the meantime, all that she wanted was to get back to Fewkes Road and have Junior to herself at last.

But this was not so easy. It had been Nancy's day to go round there. And Mrs. Privett hadn't liked to put her off. Nor would Nancy have been willing to be put off. Childless herself, she found babies—toddlers, especially—irresistible. As it was, she had spent from four o'clock that afternoon practically flat on the hearth-rug, piling up bricks, pushing toy motor cars, giving her playmate things that he could bang, rolling balls at him, letting him pull her hair. Mrs. Privett had felt that she was rather overdoing it. And told her so. In consequence, Nancy had sulked. Mrs. Privett had been forced to do something about it. Give way gracefully. That was why she had allowed Nancy to help in the bathroom. Sprinkle the powder, while Mrs. Privett patted it in.

But it was not Nancy's presence that was the trouble. It was Mr. Bloot's. He was there as well. In this re-acquired bachelor state, he tended to come round to Fewkes Road rather a lot. Usually at meal-times. But not as a burden any longer. As a rather ostentatiously generous family friend. A bottle of port, or sherry, tucked under his arm. Or, in season, a pineapple. Even, on occasion, a small bunch of flowers for Mrs. Privett.

That was because TWEETIE was doing so nicely. Fairly booming. With budgerigars thriving on it. And Mr. Bloot's commission more than doubling. Mr. Bloot, with only himself to care for, was in the thousand-a-year class now. And he was enjoying himself.

But suddenly seeing Nancy and Irene again proved too much for him. He became reminiscent. About Nancy herself as a girl. And about Irene as a baby. About how Woodbines had been twopence a packet, and he and Emily had once been young. So young that from sheer happiness in living they had done silly, impulsive things, like hiring a boat on the Serpentine late one Saturday evening, and how the attendant, a rough-voiced man, had been forced to scull out to them in the gathering darkness to bring them in again. And about a hat of Emily's with white flowers on it that a horse had attempted to eat while they were waiting arm-in-arm to cross the Edgware Road. And about some shrimps that had nearly killed them both, bringing them up in a violent, mulberry coloured rash, after having been eaten on a sunny August afternoon at a small café with an outside awning at Westcliff-on-Sea. And about Emily's unreasoning fear of mice....

It was Emily, not Hetty, who figured in all these stories. But quite impersonally. As someone who had apparently existed only during those few distant months of courtship. A mere snapshot-collection of memories. Like the rowing-boat attendant. And the horse. And the outside awning. And the mice.

It was Rammell's that was continuous. Rammell's that was the full-scale documentary. How Sir Harry, as plain Mr. Rammell in those days, had once made everyone stay all night to prepare a new window display that had been the talk of London the next day. And how Mr. Preece had started at fifteen shillings a week in dispatch—and look at him now. And how Mr. Rammell, the present one, had always been a bit afraid of his father. And what a surprise it was that young Mr. Tony looked like settling down at last. And how Mr. Bloot, not so blind as some others he could mention, had always known that Marcia was no better than she should be. And how he didn't envy Sir Harry having to keep an eye on her out there with all those bathing-beaches and cocktail-bars and American playboys around.

Mr. Bloot was in a particularly frank and expansive mood this evening. Rammell's, in his opinion, was in the wrong hands at the moment. But would weather it. Retail commerce, he believed, had a big future. Bond Street had come to stay. There would always be a Rammell's. And it would take more than a little pip-squeak like Mr. Preece to bring it down.

But there was more than past bitterness in Mr. Bloot to-night. He moved irresistibly forward. Spanned generations. And it was on Junior that he fastened. There was a new life. And it was, he insisted, up to them to make sure that the best was made of it. No wrong moves. No false steps. Outside representation, on the road, was all right, he explained, for someone of his standing, his experience. But not for a young man. A beginner. Too many temptations. Like drinking. And women. Some of the things he'd seen since he'd left Rammell's . . . only the presence of the ladies prevented him from describing them. No, all in all—financial reward, included—he'd advise them to put Junior into Rammell's. Get him started there. And, even though he might not cut much ice himself with Mr. Preece at the moment he still had good friends in high places and when the tahm came would be ready to put in a word or two in the raht quahter.

When Nancy said at last that she really had to go or her landlady would be wondering whatever had become of her, Mr. Bloot said that he'd better go along, too. He had his own commitments. A new pair. Blue and white. Championship stock with a whole row of First and Seconds and Honourable Mentions on both sides. But for them he would have been ready to stay all night. As it was, he left with the name of Rammell's still on his lips. Nattering on about openings. And chances. And not minding too much about the pay. Not at first, that is.

Mr. Privett fell asleep as soon as he got to bed. To-day had been something of a strain. And to-morrow was sure to be as bad. Sales took it out of him. He had to admit that. But then he wasn't as young as he used to be. And being at the top naturally had its responsibilities. Everything depended on him nowadays. Mr. Privett, in fact, *was* Rammell's.